THE
WINTERSEA
The Godsfall Trilogy: Two

MICHAEL
MEYERHOFER

Unlocking New Worlds

The Wintersea
The Godsfall Trilogy:™ Book 2
Copyright © 2016 by Michael Meyerhofer All rights reserved.
First Print Edition: July 2017

Print ISBN-13: 978-1-940215-94-5
Print ISBN-10: 1-940215-94-3

Red Adept Publishing, LLC
104 Bugenfield Court
Garner, NC 27529
http://RedAdeptPublishing.com/

Cover and Formatting: Streetlight Graphics

PROLOGUE

S TANDING ON THE SUN-SCORCHED ROCKS of the Dead Shores, Miriam thought about the corpses she'd seen the day before, hoping the memory might distract her from her hunger pains. She and her brothers had found the bodies farther north, lying in the sand. Miriam had seen drowned people before, seen how they swelled up, but this was different. All the dead had been charred to a crisp, especially their faces.

"Did the sun do that?" Miriam remembered asking.

Jem and Will laughed at her. "Men did that," Jem said. "With torches. Or pyres, maybe."

Miriam was about to point out the absence of burnt wood near the dead. Nor could she imagine where men could have found wood for a fire in the first place, since few trees grew in these lands and even fewer people existed to cut them down. Then she noticed something her brothers took far longer to see: all those wide eyes flecked with purple, those ears rising to points like daggers. Jem said the dead must be Shel'ai, running from the Wytchforest. Will thought a mob must have caught them and killed them.

"That's what you do to wytches," he had said to Miriam. "But you ain't no wytch, so don't worry."

Miriam wondered if the memory of the burnt bodies really was better than being hungry. She decided to push the sight of the corpses from her mind. Finally, bored, she waded out into the water, thigh deep, scanning the western horizon for some sign of her brothers' little boat.

Her brothers had been out fishing since dawn, but Jem and Will never let her come along, insisting the rickety vessel was too small. Thus, she had been left alone for hours, wandering amidst rocks and sand too hot to lie down on. She had always been afraid of the water, too, but at least it was cooler than the shore. She scanned the horizon again, unable to understand why her brothers always went out so far to fish, but she suspected that had something to do with her. She could tell they did not want her around. However, they'd promised her parents they'd care for her, swearing oaths before the gods. Miriam remembered standing with them in the doorway of the old house, crying, far from their parents' bed so they wouldn't catch the same plague reducing their parents to living, reeking husks.

Miriam shook her head, trying to drive away the memories as though they were the mosquitos that used to follow her everywhere on the old farm. She thought instead about how good the fish would taste and how much kinder her brothers might be once they had full bellies. She looked back over her shoulder at the firewood she'd already gathered. Then she checked her rope belt to make sure her knife was still there. After all, they would expect her to clean and cook the fish while they sat around and sipped from that foul-tasting wine jug.

But Miriam did not mind. She'd left her old knife inside the farmhouse when her brothers burned it down, not realizing that until after Jem started the fire, and neither of her brothers would run in and get it. Luckily, though, she found a new knife in a cave along the Dead Shores—a funny knife made of black glass. It made her feel strange when she held it: sometimes a little sick, sometimes tired, as though she'd just been running from something. But it was much sharper than her old knife, and sometimes when she was scraping the scales off fish or cutting the guts out of an urusk, she felt as if the knife was using her hand rather than the other way around.

"It's just a knife," she told herself. Still, she pulled it out of her belt and held it up, using its thin black blade to cover the sun. She expected the sun to shine through, but somehow, it didn't. She turned the knife over and over then tucked it back into her belt.

Something brushed against her legs. She wondered if it was a fish. Her heart leapt at the thought of catching her own food, but then she told herself her brothers might be angry when they got back and discovered what she'd done. She did not think it would make sense for them to be angry, but recently, her brothers often did things that did not make sense. Then she looked up again and saw the boat.

Laughing with joy, she started to wave, then she stopped. The boat was much too big to be her brothers'. It even had sails, though they looked as though they'd been torn to shreds. Miriam tensed. She wondered if she should run and hide. Will had told her stories about pirates who lived on the islands off the coast, pirates who acted like Olgrym and did terrible things to women and girls. She touched her knife.

"They won't do that to *me*," she said, tossing back her head with defiance.

She decided to wait. The boat rocked and tipped on the water, moving listlessly over the waves. After what felt like an eternity, it drew close enough for her to study the deck. She saw wooden railings but no people. If it *had* been a pirate ship, maybe the crew had abandoned it for some reason.

"There might still be treasure on the ship," she said to herself. She imagined swimming out and climbing onto the ship, finding it filled with jewels, clothes, and food.

Then she bit her lip. Her brothers had also told her stories about diseases that bred on ships like rats. Perhaps the same thing that had killed her parents happened to the pirates, too. If so, the ship might be full of corpses.

Miriam took a step back then chided herself. What did it matter if the ship was full of dead bodies? The dead could not hurt her... and disease couldn't hurt you if you didn't get too close. If she held her breath and was careful, maybe she could climb on board and take a few things left behind.

As though encouraging her plan, the sea seemed to bear the boat toward the shore faster than before. Then Miriam's heart sank. She realized the boat was heading directly for a great outcropping of rock. She wondered if someone might be on the boat after all, someone she had not noticed yet, who was oblivious to the danger. She screamed a warning even though the boat was still too far away for anyone to hear. She even pressed her hands together and prayed to the gods. But a moment later, as she watched in horror, the boat slammed into the rock. Timbers splintered and shattered. The boat hung on the rocks for a moment then spun and tipped on its side.

Miriam cried out in despair. She imagined someone hiding within the boat—someone tired and hungry and all alone, like her. Before she knew what she was doing, she waded farther and farther from the shore. Cold water rose past her waist, to her chest, then her throat. Miriam shivered and considered turning back. She barely knew how to swim—certainly not well enough to save someone who needed her. But then the ground seemed to rise beneath her. She realized there was a rough hill just under the waves, leading all the way to the rock that had smashed the ship. She followed it, only waist deep in the waves. Though she was drenched and shivering, she kept her eyes fixed on the capsized boat.

The closer she got, the bigger the ship looked. By the time she reached the edge of the rock, so close she might have leapt and landed on the boat's tipped-over side, she realized the boat was huge. She guessed it had to be at least ten times the size of her brothers' little fishing boat. Ropes hung from everything, shimmering strangely. Barrels and trunks bobbed in the water. Her pulse quickened as she wondered if the trunks were treasure chests. Then she saw a boy.

He bobbed on the water, one arm tangled in a mass of ropes still clinging to a gigantic barrel. His head sagged. Golden hair covered his eyes. She guessed from what she could see of his face that he was about her age, though instead of tattered rags, he wore a rich man's clothes: tunic and britches of purple silk, trimmed in gold, with a big sword hanging from his waist and a medallion around his neck, the same color as his damp hair. Everything looked too big for him, though, as though he'd dressed in his father's clothes a moment before being knocked unconscious.

"That doesn't make any sense," Miriam said.

She wondered what to do. The boy was close, but she still did not think much of her chances of diving into the water, grabbing him, and swimming back to shore. She looked around. Nearby, she spotted a splintered shaft of wood and fished it out of the water. She cried out when a splinter slid into her palm, just below her thumb. Then her eyes moistened at the thought of how her father used to soothe her whenever he removed her splinters, how he would even yell at her brothers if they teased her for crying.

"I'm not going to cry," Miriam told herself. Holding the splintered shaft of wood, she moved to the very edge of the rock. She was still too far to reach the boy, but she managed to catch hold of the shimmering ropes floating in the water. Slowly, carefully, she guided the ropes back toward her until she could grab them with her hand.

She paused and stared down at the ropes. Though they felt rough, they looked slick, almost like metal. They were cold like metal, too. Shaking her head, Miriam started back toward the shore, slowly pulling the ropes after her. The barrel followed and the sleeping boy with it. Step by step, she neared the shore. Then the boy's arm came loose somehow, and his body sank below the water.

Miriam screamed. She let go of the ropes and dove. Water closed over her head. A little seawater slipped into her mouth, salty and terrible, before she remembered to purse her lips. She'd closed her eyes when she dove, but she forced herself to open them. She tried to find the sleeping boy, but the world blurred, hiding him from her. An awful burning seared her lungs. She thought she would have to give up and return to the surface, leaving him to drown. Then she spotted him—a swaying mass of purple just in front of her. She reached out, caught hold of a handful of cloth, and pulled.

Holding the boy with one hand and pushing against the water with the other, she turned and kicked and kicked, struggling back toward the shore. Her lungs ached. The urge to open her mouth became maddening. *This isn't going to work. I'm going to have to let him go, or I'll drown!* But then her feet touched solid ground.

Miriam tightened her grip on the boy and drove her body forward with all her strength. A fresh chill told her she was out of the water and the wind was pressing her sea-soaked hair against her forehead. After a few more steps, her mouth was above water. She took a breath, coughed, and breathed again. All the while, her legs kept working, stubbornly carrying her and the boy closer to the shore.

Some time later, Miriam opened her eyes and found herself lying on a patch of warm sand, staring at the setting sun. She could not remember having gone to sleep, and her lungs hurt. She remembered the boy. She turned and saw him lying next to her, facedown, on rocks instead of sand. His head was turned away. Miriam grasped him frantically and rolled him over.

The boy was deathly pale, with small scratches all over his face. She wondered if he was dead. Unsure what to do, she yelled at him to wake up. She struck his chest. To her surprise, his eyes fluttered open—pale blue eyes, the color of ice.

The boy blinked then frowned. "I can't... breathe..."

Miriam realized she had one knee on his chest. She moved off him and knelt in the sand instead. The boy tried to sit up and failed.

Miriam helped him up. "Are you hurt? It looks like your face is hurt a little, but I don't see blood anywhere else." She studied the boy's oversized clothing again and realized he was barefoot. She guessed he'd tried on his father's boots, as well as the rest of his clothes, but those had slipped off in the water. "Are you rich?"

The boy rubbed his eyes. "I don't... know what I am." He faced the sea. "Where is this place?"

"They call it the Dead Shores," Miriam said. "Not much grows here. Too much rock, not enough dirt. That's what my da used to say. But there're bugs and fish and some people, if you know where to look. And Olgrym, to the south, but it's good to stay away from them, even the nicer ones who can't talk."

The boy looked at her as though he had not understood a word she'd said. "Who are you?"

"Miriam," she said. "My brothers are Jem and Will. They're out fishing, but they should be back any minute." *What will my brothers do with the boy?* She didn't think they'd kill him, but they'd surely rob him. "Listen, do you have any other clothes? Around here, it's better if you look poor. If you have coins, you should hide those, too." She scanned his waist, noticing for the first time that he'd lost his gigantic sword in the sea. The golden medallion still hung from his neck, though. "Can I have that? I won't keep it. I promise. I just don't want my brothers to take it from you."

The boy blinked. For a moment, Miriam thought he still wasn't understanding.

He looked down and studied the medallion around his neck as though he had not even realized he was wearing it. "This is... important to me."

"That's fine," Miriam said. "I'll give it back. I promise. You can trust me. I saved you, didn't I?"

The boy hesitated then slipped the medallion over his head and handed it to her. "Miriam," he said softly, "who am I?"

Miriam frowned. "Are you sick or something?" She pulled back, afraid whatever disease he had might be catching. When the boy did not answer, she studied the medallion instead. It was bright and shiny, so beautiful that she almost felt bad touching it with her grubby hands, and carved with a strange symbol. "What is this, a dragon? It looks like it's wearing a crown." She traced it with her finger. "Pretty."

When the boy still did not say anything, she turned to look at him. To her surprise, he had recoiled as well, his eyes wide with terror. He looked as though he might crawl away, just to get away from her, if he had the strength.

"What's wrong? I told you, I'll give it back. I'm not a thief. I just didn't want…" She followed his stare and realized he was eyeing her knife. "Oh, this?" She pulled it out. He recoiled even farther. "Don't be afraid. I won't hurt you. I promise. What's your name?"

When the boy still did not answer, Miriam returned the knife to her belt. "Oh, that's right. You don't know. Well, what *do* you remember?"

The boy settled down a little but continued to eye her with mistrust. "Water. Pain. Others with me, but I can't see their faces." He rubbed his throat and faced the surf. "I'm thirsty."

"Well, don't drink the sea. The water's got too much salt in it. It'll make you sick. But I have fresh water hidden with our other stuff. If you promise not to steal, I'll show you." She felt silly saying it. Given the boy's rich attire, she doubted he would care to touch anything she had, let alone take it.

"I promise," the boy said.

Miriam stood up and held out her hand. The boy hesitated then took it. With surprising strength, he managed to pull himself to his feet, though Miriam still had to help him along. She led him farther up the shore, to where her brothers had buried their possessions in the sand behind a rock before going out in the fishing boat. There, she hesitated. She had no doubt what her brothers would do if they returned and found out their things had been stolen.

"Listen," she said, "I know you already promised, but don't steal anything, all right? You look nice, but my brothers can be mean, and they'll beat *me* if you steal something."

"I won't take anything," the boy answered, still rubbing his throat. He rasped as though he was in pain, and his eyes were wet.

Satisfied, Miriam pulled away the ratty cloak covering their possessions: a jug of bitter wine, a bronze knife, a cooking pan, a canteen, and a knapsack containing a few articles of clothing. The knapsack had spilled. Miriam blushed, snatching up one of the rags her brothers had recently started forcing her to wad up in her britches. The rag was flecked with blood, but the nameless boy did not seem to notice. Miriam handed him the canteen, and he drank deeply.

"Slow down," Miriam warned.

The boy did not listen, and moment later, he fell to the ground, retching. Miriam knelt beside him and rubbed his back. The boy wiped his mouth and drank again.

Miriam said, "I didn't see any other bodies floating in the water. I think you were alone on the boat. You said there were others. Maybe they forgot about you?"

"I... I don't think so." The boy handed her the emptied canteen and eyed her glass knife. "What is that?"

"I told you it's just a knife. I found it in a cave not far from here. We should wait for my brothers, but once they get here, we could go see the cave if you want. I'll show you where it is. There's nothing else inside there, though, except for some funny symbols carved into the walls." She gave the boy's medallion one last look, wondering why she was still holding onto it, then tucked it in her pocket.

"I don't think so." The boy turned as though to leave.

Miriam grabbed his arm. "Wait..." She reached into the knapsack. "Your pants are falling down. Here, take one of Jem's old belts. And these sandals. They're old and too big, probably, but at least they'll keep you from cutting your feet on rocks." She gave him the items then picked up the bronze knife and offered that to him as well. "And take this in case you get into trouble."

"I won't." The boy accepted the belt and sandals but gently pushed the bronze knife away. "Thank you." He stepped back.

Miriam stopped him again. "Where are you going?"

The boy looked confused, as though he had not even considered that. "I don't know. East, I think. Toward the sun. Then north. I… I feel like I'm supposed to go north, where it's cold."

"Why?" Miriam realized the boy could not answer and tried a different tactic. "Maybe you should stay with us. There are lots of bad people out there. My brothers can be mean, like I said, but there are a lot worse people you could run into. See, there's still fighting everywhere, especially up in Dhargoth. Da said wars make peaceful men mean. You should—"

"No," the boy snapped.

Miriam recoiled, touching her knife.

The boy's expression softened. "Listen, it's better if I go alone. I don't know why, but I know that it is."

"But…" Miriam blinked, unable to comprehend why she suddenly did not want this boy to leave. "I pulled you out of the water. I saved your life. You *owe* me!"

The boy smiled slightly. "Fine. Then keep the medallion. It looks prettier on you anyway." He took a step back and bowed, the way Knights always bowed to their finely dressed ladies in her father's stories. "Goodbye, Miriam." He turned and walked away. Already, he seemed even stronger than before, practically running.

Miriam blushed. She realized that somehow, in the space of a few seconds, she'd forgotten she still had the medallion in her pocket. She pulled it out and was about to insist that the boy take it back, but a ray of falling sunlight flashed red-gold off the crowned dragon, catching her eye. By the time she looked up, the boy was already far away. She looked from him back to the medallion then the sea.

For the first time, she saw a dark speck on the western horizon. However, instead of the joy she expected to feel at the sight of her brothers' fishing boat, she felt only dread. She realized that if they were coming back that late, they'd hardly caught a thing, probably. They would already be angry, even before they noticed some of their things missing. Miriam shuddered to think what they would do to her. She turned east, toward the boy, just in time to see him clambering up a rocky hill, farther and farther from the shore. He was moving so quickly that, in no time, he would be gone—completely out of her life.

Miriam wiped her eyes. Then she stuffed the medallion back in her pocket, turned her back on the distant fishing boat, and ran.

CHAPTER ONE

Prince Saanji rubbed the sleep from his eyes and stepped out of his war tent into the rain. He tried not to shudder as an evening chill soaked through his armor. He reminded himself of the necessity of appearing stern in front of his men, especially to counter the fact that, unlike the strong build of his battle-tested soldiers, he still had a bit of a gut, resulting in the affectionate nickname, the Tomato Prince. Thinking of the nickname, Saanji started to laugh, but the rain ran in his eyes, and he remembered how much he'd rather be sleeping. Concealing his bemusement over the foul weather behind an ornery scowl, he so quickened his pace that his bodyguards had to rush to keep up with him.

Armed men stepped aside to let him pass. Some of his men cheered when they saw him making his way through the camp. Others nodded or raised their cups. Saanji fought the impulse to nod back. He'd always been informal with his men, often to the point of joining in the laughter when they made fun of his flushed cheeks and round belly, but lately, he'd been trying a different approach.

Saanji reached the edge of the camp and faced what appeared to be the wall of a wooden fortress. Signaling for his bodyguards to remain behind, he ascended rough-hewn steps to the top of a wooden watchtower overlooking a high palisade. Two soldiers manning the watchtower straightened and saluted at his approach. One handed him a Soroccan spyglass. Saanji accepted the spyglass but looked up, noting the roof of the watchtower had so many holes in it that it hardly slowed the rain at all.

Saanji shivered then blinked away the rain and raised one gauntleted hand. Before he had a chance to look through the spyglass, the sound of rain plinking off metal confused him. Then he realized it was coming from his own metal glove, and he smothered a grin.

Gods, Royce! It's been years since my damn brother carved you up at Hesod, and I'm still not half the soldier you were. But at least my gut's a bit smaller than it used to be. He looked through the spyglass.

One of the watchmen pointed over the barrier, well beyond the dark field, toward the distant city of U'dan, aglow with the usual broad span of torchlight. "There, my prince."

At first, Saanji saw nothing. Then a shadowy motion caught his eye. He tried to hold the spyglass steady. A moment later, he realized a thick mass of horsemen was slowly making its way through the no-man's-land separating Saanji's camp from the besieged city.

"If that's supposed to be a sneak attack, they're in for a surprise," he said, thinking of the archers, pit traps, and siege weapons that perpetually guarded the walls of his well-fortified camp.

Saanji looked through the spyglass again. A moment later, he caught sight of a standard bearer moving just ahead of the horsemen. The soldier was having an impossible time keeping the rain-soaked flag unfurled, but through the spyglass, Saanji saw the look of terror on the young man's face.

Saanji whistled. "On second thought, I think we're about to have visitors."

The watchmen frowned.

"A parley?" one asked.

"No flag of truce, my prince," the other noted.

"Nor would there be." That time, Saanji's scowl was genuine.

He moved to the ladder and descended the watchtower to the muddy field below. Moving past his bodyguards, he motioned to a familiar officer in the distance—a tall, lean man with painted eyes and a long goatee. The man was handsome, save for a crooked nose.

"Laanti, some friends are coming out from the city to say hello. Make sure the archers know not to shoot them… until I say otherwise, that is."

"Emissaries?" The young officer stroked his braided goatee with one hand, unfazed by the rain.

"Not exactly." Saanji sighed. "They didn't come to attack, I'm sure, but I doubt they came to surrender, either." Before Laanti could ask for clarification, Saanji turned and strode toward a pair of tall, narrow gates leading through the wall surrounding his camp. He waved for the guards to open the gates and realized, as he did so, that his hands were shaking.

Saanji glanced up at the parapets again, eyeing the bristling row of archers. *It would be so easy. One command, and they'd fill the bastards full of arrows. The siege, this whole damn war, could end tonight!*

He thought of Arnil Royce again. *What would you do, my friend?* He suddenly had a vision of the late Lancer striding out of the camp, armored and alone, his kingsteel longsword in hand, to face whatever horrors were riding toward them. Saanji touched the hilt of his sword again—Royce's sword—and tried to stop his hands from shaking.

"All right," he said gruffly, "I'm going out to talk to them. The rest of you, stay behind. I'll look more confident if I face them without you."

His bodyguards nodded, though all looked uneasy. One stepped forward: a middle-aged man with one blue eye and one green, his pockmarked face crisscrossed with scars. Unlike the others, armed with only daggers and shortswords, he also carried a Queshi composite bow—though Saanji had never gotten up the courage to ask how he'd obtained it, since he doubted he would like the answer. The bodyguard said, "My prince, might I suggest—"

"No need, Vaari. I'm pretty sure I know what you'd advise."

Vaari scowled. "Well, if you won't kill them, might I at least suggest not getting *yourself* killed?"

Saanji smiled at the bodyguard's concern. "I'll try." He started forward alone then said, "Tag along if it'll make you feel better." He stared through the open gates, into the impenetrable darkness beyond. "Nothing personal, Vaari, but I wish Zeia were here instead of you."

"Just so long as you don't expect me to fulfill her bedroom duties, too." The bodyguard added a belated "m'lord."

Saanji chuckled. "I'm not sure how she'd feel about you calling them *her bedroom duties.*"

"I won't tell if you won't." Despite his easy tone, Vaari's eyes scanned

13

the darkness, even as one hand drew a wickedly barbed arrow from the quiver at his side and fit it to his bowstring. "Want to tell me what we're walking towards?"

"And spoil the surprise?" Saanji loosened his sword in its scabbard and eyed a sun-bleached ribcage lying in the mud at his feet. Then he turned and saw a skull staring up at him with hollow eye sockets, its jaw wide open. He nudged the jaw shut with his boot.

A sound made him jump, half drawing his sword, but it was only General Laanti. The officer ignored Vaari but saluted Saanji. "The guards know not to fire. But I'd feel better if you let me put you on a horse. Or better yet, we'll take their weapons—"

"I told you, it's not an emissary. More's the pity." Saanji answered the rest of the general's suggestions by turning his back on him and scanning the darkness again.

The general said, "Might I at least suggest a little more light, m'lord?"

Saanji nodded, and Laanti called stern orders back toward the camp. Moments later, servants raced out with torches, and Laanti took one. At the general's command, longer torches were thrust into the ground like blazing staffs. Though the flames of the torches were housed in tin braziers, they sputtered nonetheless.

Saanji trained his eyes on the remaining darkness before him. A moment later, he spied motion in the distance. Slowly, across a muddy field littered with bones, tattered bits of cloth, and rusted armor, a party of horsemen took shape. A dozen strong, all wore armor of dark scales decorated with tassels of black silk. Like many of Saanji's men, they had braided goatees and painted eyes. But there, the resemblance stopped, for those men also wore necklaces of dried ears around their necks— tokens of past battles. For all their efforts to appear fierce, though, the approaching horsemen looked pale and gaunt, as starved as their horses.

The horsemen slowed to a halt. One rode ahead of the rest. Unlike the others, he was an old man with a long white goatee and a necklace that contained so many pairs of ears arrayed in tiers that it completely covered his chest—a kind of grisly breastplate. Saanji also noted that, unlike the rest, the old man appeared healthy and well fed.

Resisting twin impulses—one to back away, the other to order Vaari

14

to put an arrow through the white-haired man's throat—Saanji stepped forward instead. He forced a smile. "Hello, Father."

The Red Emperor glared down from his saddle. "I do not acknowledge you as my son."

"Well, that's going to make your ceremonial surrender rather awkward."

The Red Emperor laughed. "You think I've come to surrender?"

Saanji turned his gaze from his father to his father's bodyguards. Despite their numbers, all trained nervous gazes on the dark walls of Saanji's camp, obviously eyeing the countless archers training arrows on them. "My mistake," Saanji said. "It's been a long war. Years, in fact. I must be tired. I should have realized you'd sooner ride out to your own execution."

"I haven't come to die, either," the Red Emperor snapped.

"Well, I wish you'd make up your mind. You don't have much of an army with you, and my scouts tell me you're damn near out of food." Saanji eyed his father's stomach, the way it pushed out his heavy necklace of ears. "Though it looks like you haven't been going hungry. So tell me, what did you have in mind? A tender embrace, perhaps?"

The Red Emperor said nothing for a while. Then he dismounted, tossing the reins to his nearest bodyguard. Before the emperor had taken two steps, Vaari and Laanti moved to block his path. While Laanti drew his shortsword, Vaari drew back his bowstring, unflinchingly aiming his arrow right at the face of his former emperor.

The Red Emperor regarded them for a moment then snickered. "Such loyalty... and to the Tomato Prince, of all people!"

Vaari turned his head and spat. "Call him that again, m'lord, and the only thing squishy will be your skull."

Saanji touched his bodyguard's arm. "I appreciate that, Vaari, but we really must work on your metaphors." He touched Laanti's arm as well, pushing both men back. "Come now, I doubt my father rode all the way out here in the middle of the night just to kill me."

"I didn't," the Red Emperor conceded, tapping the hilt of his sheathed sword, "as much as I'd like to."

"So you didn't come to surrender, you didn't come to die, and you didn't come to kill me. Why, then, are we having this pleasant conversation?"

The Red Emperor looked past Saanji. "Where's your wytch? The dark-haired bitch with sharp ears and no hands."

"What a lovely description." Saanji resisted the urge to answer his father's words by drawing his sword, reminding himself that his elderly father was probably still thrice the swordsman he was. "I'm afraid Zeia is elsewhere. Too bad. I know she's been anxious to meet you."

"And I, her." The emperor grunted. "They say she's personally killed, what, five of my best generals, not to mention the twenty or so assassins I sent to deal with you? She might be a woman, and a wytch besides, but at least *she* has the heart of a Dhargot."

"I'll be sure to pass on the compliment, dear Father. If you'd like to wait, I expect her back any day now. I'm sure she has some choice words for you as well."

The Red Emperor eyed the sword at Saanji's waist. "Is that the Ivairian's sword… the one my *true* son killed?" A derisive smirk tugged at the corners of his mouth.

Saanji drew the sword and held it, letting torchlight shine off the snowy swirls in its kingsteel blade. "Royce was the best swordsman I've ever seen. Karhaati got lucky."

"They say *you* killed Karhaati afterwards." The emperor eyed Saanji with disgust. "No amount of luck could have made that possible. So tell me, what was it?"

"Trickery," Saanji answered without pause. "I hid poisoned caltrops in the snow, then when Karhaati was already paralyzed and dying, I used Royce's sword to hack him to pieces. Afterwards, I slept better than I had in years." *A lie.* Saanji remembered the sickening feeling and the tears he'd shed later, in private.

"I expected as much," the Red Emperor scoffed. "You never did have any guts or honor, unlike your brothers. Tell me, what happened to Karhaati's sword?"

Saanji thought of the terrible broadsword, its steel surface etched with images of rape and murder. "I gave it to the Iron Sisters. The last I saw, it was hanging in Hesod as a trophy—along with my dear brother's ears."

For the first time, the Red Emperor winced. "Damn you. He deserved better than that."

"No, not really." Saanji cleared his throat. "Forgive me, Father, but it's late, and I am tired. For the past three years, you've refused all invitations to negotiate. Now, you tell me you haven't come to surrender. Seeing as how you don't have enough of an army left to raze a nunnery, I'm going to cut this short. Do you have anything else to say before I have you chained in disgrace and advance my army into your city?"

The Red Emperor snickered. "I don't think I'll be wearing chains tonight. But in answer, I do have two questions that I would like to ask before we proceed. Here is the first. Where is Rowen Locke?"

Saanji frowned. "What do you care?"

"They say he's a bold man. A hero. He killed that Dragonkin, Chorlga. He killed Fadarah and Algol and Crovis Ammerhel, too. Quite a man. I wonder if I'd like him."

"I doubt it. He has a rather different take on honor than you have."

"Where is he?" the Red Emperor asked again.

Saanji shrugged. "In Cadavash, probably... surrounded by Knights and Shel'ai. Not that you'll be alive long enough to send assassins—"

"And Knightswrath?"

"Is that your final question?"

The Red Emperor did not answer, but his cold smile broadened.

Despite all the archers watching from a distance, despite Saanji's bodyguards just a few yards away and the gaunt, terrified look on the faces of his father's men, Saanji felt a chill race through him. *There's something wrong here.* He turned long enough to glance at Vaari—who still had his bow drawn and aimed at the emperor's face—then gave Laanti a quick look.

The general caught his meaning, turned, and waved his hand. Saanji's bodyguards marched out, joined by a squad of horsemen. They encircled the Red Emperor's entourage, outnumbering them three to one. Weapons glinted in the torchlight.

Saanji relaxed a little. "Forgive me, Father. You asked about Knightswrath. Every question deserves an answer." He took a step forward, fixing a derisive smile to his lips to match his father's. "Knightswrath is locked up in Shigella's Tomb. The way I hear it, Ammerhel tried to bring down the Dragonward, but Rowen Locke used Knightswrath to stop him."

17

The Red Emperor nodded slowly. "Then Algol and Crovis Ammerhel succeeded. They killed the guardians. The Dragonward fell."

Saanji frowned. "No. I told you, Locke used Knightswrath to—"

"To take the guardians' place," the Red Emperor interrupted. "Still, for a moment, the Dragonward was down. The way into Ruun was wide open. The Dragonkin were free to return."

"Good for us that they didn't," Saanji said, "or else we'd be the least of each other's worries." He stepped back and turned to face Laanti. "General, if you would be so kind, please put my father in chains. Make sure they're tight and uncomfortable. Then wake the army. We will march into U'dan in full force. After that, I suppose a celebration—"

"You weren't listening," the Red Emperor called, his voice strangely shrill.

Saanji turned back to his father, noticing his father's bodyguards were drawing away from him even though that forced them to edge even closer to their soon-to-be captors. "What are you talking about?"

Unblinking, the Red Emperor said, "You told me what I'd already suspected. About Knightswrath. Still, I had to be sure. I could have tortured you, of course, or dragged the answers out of your brain, but subtlety has its rewards. And its amusements. Besides, I need you."

Saanji realized he was still holding his kingsteel longsword. Tightening his grip on the hilt, he stretched out his arm so that the tip pressed against his father's chest. The Red Emperor did not recoil. Saanji twisted the blade, and its edge—sharper than a razor—easily sliced through the necklace of ears, allowing his father's grim trophies to fall onto the dark ground. They formed a grisly pile, which Saanji then hooked on the tip of his sword, lifted away, and dumped on the ground behind him.

"I always knew you were mad, Father. But I'm afraid—"

"You weren't listening," the Red Emperor repeated. His voice took on a strange accent, such that Saanji wondered if he were being mocked. "I already told you, you're not my son. That means I am not your father."

Saanji noticed that his father's bodyguards had drawn away as far as they could, some actually colliding with Saanji's men. "Please," one said. Another faced a spear that had been aimed at his throat and, with just a moment's hesitation, impaled himself upon it.

Madness seemed to spread through the ranks. Some of the Red Emperor's bodyguards leapt from their horses and ran or fell to their knees, pleading. Others bolted and tried to ride away, only to be pursued and surrounded. Vaari shifted his aim from the Red Emperor's face to the fleeing men and brought down man after man with well-placed arrows until Saanji finally ordered him to stop.

Meanwhile, Laanti seized the reins of the horse of the man who had impaled himself on a spear. Hauling the dead man from the saddle, the general mounted. Then Laanti shouted up at the walls, ordering the archers not to fire—lest they strike Saanji by mistake—but calling for more men. Fresh soldiers streamed through the open gate, out of the camp, both on foot and on horseback. They formed an even denser circle around the Red Emperor and his dwindling bodyguards.

Throughout all that, Saanji kept his eyes on his father's expression. Though the Red Emperor's smile remained unchanged, his eyes had widened. Flickering torchlight reflected in the pupils—dark circles, wreathed in green. Then, the green became purple. The darkness turned white as bone.

Not my father...

Somehow, Saanji found the courage to attack. Gripping his sword with both hands, he swung. Though the motion was clumsy, he put all his strength behind it, hoping will alone might push the sword clean through the imposter's head.

Instead, something struck Saanji, driving him backward, clear off his feet. A sea of searing heat swept overhead, punctuated by wild laughter. Horses screamed. Men cried out in pain and panic. A fierce, purple glare blinded him. Then, for a moment, the glare faded.

As though peering through a break in a wall of fog, Saanji saw his father—only it was his father no longer. His armor flared white hot then dripped to the earth. Silk burned away. The imposter stood naked, grinning triumphantly, bathed in a fog of heat so intense that the air around him rippled. The imposter's body continued to change.

Saanji tried to crawl away, but he had hardly made his first motion when the purple eyes turned and locked onto him. The eyes narrowed then widened. Fresh laughter filled the night a moment before the Dragonkin raised his hands and unleashed a pent-up ocean of wytchfire.

Saanji shut his eyes to block out the sight of running men and agonized, flailing limbs, but the screaming filled his ears anyway.

Then, all at once, it stopped. For a moment, Saanji thought he had gone deaf. He opened his eyes and saw the same burning carnage roiling all around him. Still, he heard nothing. Then, the voice—half his father's, half something else—sliced into his mind, still speaking with the same strange accent as before.

"This is just a demonstration. I need you to know and believe what I am and what I'm capable of."

Saanji opened his eyes and spotted the Dragonkin standing nearby, surrounded by chaos, still looking at him. He forced himself to stand. "Don't waste your time. Whoever you are, whatever you are, I won't help you hunt down Rowen Locke. You might as well kill me."

The Dragonkin smiled. Then he waved his hand, and the chaos stopped. Wytchfire flickered out of existence. Men who had been writhing on the ground a moment before, certain they were burning to death, found themselves whole and unharmed. In their expressions, Saanji saw the same fear and disbelief that must have been evident on his own face.

The Dragonkin laughed then approached him. In an easy, almost friendly voice, he said, "My name is Krym. And I fear you've mistaken me. I have not come to hunt down Rowen Locke. I've come to help him."

CHAPTER TWO

ROWEN WATCHED THE SQUIRES SPARRING in the practice yard and wondered if he should intervene. The squires' instructor had been pushing them especially hard that day. An hour earlier, the instructor had organized the squires into two opposing rows so that each faced off against an opponent armed with an identical practice sword. The squires were told to utilize the same strikes and blocks they'd been learning for the past month—only this time, without the benefit of armor.

Though made of wood instead of kingsteel, the curved practice swords were basically still heavy clubs, and the squires' instructor was infamous for punishing those who appeared to hold back. As a result, all the squires had been bruised, and more than a few were bloody, in addition to the sweat streaming off their faces and soaking through their clothing. Two looked dizzy with bleeding foreheads that would almost certainly require magical healing once the practice ended.

However, their instructor, who appeared keen on proving the necessity of endurance, showed no signs of stopping. He paced the yard, fiercely eyeing each squire. Instead of a wooden sword, the instructor held a staff fixed with a bell. When he rang the bell, one row of squires shifted to the right, with the squire at the end forced to sprint around to the left so that each squire faced a new opponent. The instructor rang his bell a second time, and the fighting resumed. Wooden swords clacked together. One squire grunted and fell to his knees, a knot rising on the back of his shaved head. The instructor scowled and moved briskly toward him.

Before the instructor had time to berate the squire, though, the latter forced himself to rise and keep fighting.

He's pushing them hard, yes, but he's not doing it to be cruel. And they are getting better—one of them, in particular.

Most of the squires were young men from the Lotus Isles, with almond-shaped eyes and olive skin, plus a few from the various realms throughout the mainland. Two women trained alongside the men, as well—one from the Lotus Isles and a husky, dark-skinned woman from Sorocco. Most of the squires were comparable to each other in terms of skill, but one gigantic figure at the center of the line had earned a reputation for being the one squire absolutely no one wanted to fight.

Rowen eyed the mute Olg, whose name no one knew, whom Igrid had affectionately nicknamed Breaksteel after he snapped a sword with his bare hands, like a dry twig. The Olg stood over a foot taller than the next tallest squire, with long dark hair and gray arms that bulged with muscles larger than a grown man's thighs.

Rowen shook his head in quiet awe. He had known men in the past who exhibited great strength but very little endurance. The Olg was different, though. Somehow inexhaustible, he swung his wooden sword with such speed and power that it occasionally shattered. Unlike the other squires, the one unlucky enough to face Breaksteel was permitted to wear a dented kingsteel helmet, which was taken off and passed down the row every time the instructor signaled a change.

Something caught Rowen's eye, and he turned in time to see the afternoon sun cascading through Igrid's long red curls. In place of the form-fitting armor she usually wore out to the practice yard, the Iron Sister wore a simple tunic and britches despite the shortsword hanging from her waist. She slipped her arm through Rowen's.

"Is Jontin still pushing them?"

Rowen nodded. "I'm trying to decide if I should stop him."

"Maybe."

Igrid winced and squeezed Rowen's arm a bit harder when another squire went down, bleeding. That one was slower to rise, though rise he did.

"How's Breaksteel doing?" she asked.

"He's holding back," Rowen answered in a low voice. "Jontin's letting him. Good thing, too. He's almost cracked four skulls as it is."

"Looks like they certainly aren't going easy on *him*, though."

For the first time, Rowen directed his attention to something other than the Olg's massive strength or the damage he was inflicting and realized that Breaksteel's gigantic arms were covered in cuts and bruises. Like the other squires, he wore loose white fighting clothes, though his were splattered with more blood than the rest.

"He's got a broken rib or three," Igrid said.

Rowen wondered how she could know that since the Olg was holding his place in line and fought without hindrance, but then the wooden sword of Breaksteel's opponent slipped under his guard and rapped his chest, and the Olg shuddered.

Igrid's voice hardened. "The other one did that on purpose."

Rowen winced but said, "If I were fighting something that outweighed me by seven stone, I'd probably use a cheap trick, too." Nevertheless, Rowen caught Sir Jontin's eye and shook his head.

Sir Jontin nodded then rang his staff three times, signaling an end to the practice. While ritual required the squires to bow to their opponents, only three had the strength to do so: the two women and Breaksteel. The rest collapsed in exhaustion.

"Not something," Igrid whispered.

"What?"

"You called Breaksteel some*thing*. Not some*one*." Igrid flashed him a cockeyed smile but dug her nails into Rowen's arm until he pulled away.

Rowen rubbed his arm. "Gods, woman. You know I didn't mean—"

Igrid's smile thinned. "Jontin's harder on him. So are the other squires. You've said so yourself. And you let it happen."

Rowen glanced at the squires, who were trying to rise to their feet and retire to the barracks. Breaksteel, still standing, grabbed one under both arms and hoisted him to his feet. The squire pulled away without a word of thanks. Breaksteel turned and held out his hand to another squire, who rose without accepting his help.

"Not so loud," Rowen said. "If you want to berate me, do it by the chasm."

"Why, so I can push you in?" Igrid slipped her arm back through

Rowen's and accompanied him as he walked away from the practice yard. They made their way toward the dark chasm that led down into the pits of Cadavash, where at one time, dragonbones had been mined—both for profit and as objects of worship. Presently, though, the chasm was surrounded by a low wall and shrouded in quiet, mournful darkness.

"I told you, I can't interfere," Rowen said. "This is part of the training. When I was on the Isles, I had to—"

"Get beaten by the other squires like the red-headed orphan you are," Igrid finished. "I know. But you also said they were cruel just because you weren't from the Isles. You said you hated them, and you hated being there. Why—"

"They were cruel," Rowen conceded, "but they also did what they did for a reason. The last thing a Knight needs is a fellow Knight who can't control his emotions in the heat of battle. They sensed I had a temper. Their bullying pushed me to learn how to control it."

"Which you didn't," Igrid pointed out. "At least not until after you were expelled."

"You get my point. Breaksteel is an Olg. As far as we know, no Olg has ever been an Isle Knight. His kind..." He sighed again. "Look, I don't hear Breaksteel complaining."

"That's because he doesn't have a tongue."

"But he can read and write. He learned. And Keswen knows his hand-speech. If he wanted to tell us—"

"He's learning to read and write in Shao *and* in Common," Igrid pointed out. "Quite an accomplishment for a savage."

"I never called him a savage."

"No, just a *thing*."

"Well, maybe you don't know his kind the way I do, woman. I saw what they did at the Wytchforest, how they tore people in half—"

"Was Breaksteel there?"

Rowen blinked. "No."

"I didn't think so," Igrid said. "And when he suggested learning hand-speech might be a good idea for your Knights, in case they found themselves stuck in a place where it paid to keep quiet?"

"I agreed," Rowen conceded. "A good idea is a good idea. I'm just saying—"

"Also, I don't hear anyone blaming Isle Knights for what the Dhargots did. And why not? They're both Human, aren't they?"

Rowen frowned. "Funny to hear *you* talking this way. I seem to remember a time when you wanted to kill every Dhargot on the continent."

Igrid shrugged. "And I seem to remember you telling me I was wrong."

"I do that a lot. You just don't listen half the time."

Igrid's cockeyed smile returned. "Oh, a little more than half, I think."

Rowen held up his hands. "Fine, I get it. You're right. I'm sorry." He sighed. "Look, Breaksteel's still here. I admit it—he's doing better than I or anybody else thought he would. But he's only been here a month. If he lasts four years, I'll knight him myself."

Igrid scoffed. "You still think these squires need four whole years of training?"

"That's how long squires usually train on the Isles. I can only bend traditions so far before they break."

"Let them break," Igrid said lightly. "Maybe they'll grow back as something worth keeping."

Rowen was about to keep arguing with her when the sound of children's laughter echoed up from the depths of the chasm. He cursed. "I told Thessa not to go down there!"

"Oh, she knows, dunce. That's *why* she went down there!"

Rowen caught her meaning. "She's trying to impress the Shel'ai children."

Igrid nodded. "They're starting to respect her a little, now that she's learning how to fight, but they still don't think of her as their leader."

Rowen frowned. "Their leader? Why would they—"

"She's the daughter of the Sword Marshal of Cadavash… *Wytchfriend*, as they're starting to call you." Igrid laughed. "That's a big deal to a child. She can't just be another member of their gang. She either has to be their leader or their enemy." Her eyes narrowed. "Gods, I thought you grew up in the Dark Quarter! How do you not understand how this works?"

"I'll let you in on a little secret. I wasn't very good at being a child."

A second, nearer chorus of laughter echoed up from the chasm, followed by another child's voice attempting to shush them.

Rowen said, "Bad enough you're grooming her to be a godsdamned fighter. Now I have to pretend I don't mind that she's skulking around in

25

a place where dragon-worshippers used to abuse their young and leave their dead to rot!"

Igrid shook her head. "Don't pretend you don't mind. Yell at her the next time you see her. Let the Shel'ai children see you do it, so they'll think Thessa's brave for defying you. But wink at her when they're not looking."

"Fine. I guess they can't cause much harm, anyway. There's not much left down there except Namundvar's Well, and that's guarded." *Not that it works anymore, anyway.*

"Exactly," Igrid said. "I miss Sariel," she added abruptly, her voice tinged with embarrassment.

Rowen tensed, remembering how the Shel'ai toddler had scalded one of their servants and nearly burned the manse to the ground. In fact, Sariel had become so unruly lately that they'd agreed to send her to stay with Jalist and Maddoc for a time since the latter seemed to be the only one who could control her.

"I do, too," he confessed. "I still feel uneasy, sending her to Stillhammer, of all places. The Sons of Maelmohr—"

"Have been disbanded," Igrid reminded him. "Gaulgodd's still on the Lotus Isles, in chains. Stillhammer's not what it was."

Rowen knew she was right. The most recent visit from Jalist and Maddoc had been full of surprises. Despite having once been banished from his homeland, Jalist was made the new governor of Stillhammer. Though forced to resign as Captain of the Red Watch, he still managed to negotiate a trade agreement with Lyos, which gave him an excuse to keep a hundred men of the Red Watch nearby. Jalist's bodyguards included Maddoc, the powerful Shel'ai, who was apparently also serving as both Jalist's right hand and his lover.

"Sariel will be back in two weeks," Rowen said. "Hopefully, Maddoc will have taught her some manners by then."

"Either way, I'll keep a bucket of water on hand." Igrid traced one fingertip down his bicep. "In the meantime, between Sariel's absence and Thessa's rebellion, at least we have the manse to ourselves."

Rowen's pulse quickened. "Well, except for the servants."

"True," Igrid said, "but they won't hear anything they haven't heard a hundred times before." She winked then started back toward the manse, tugging Rowen after her.

Thessa ducked into an abandoned bone-shop to hide from a passing patrol of Jolym. They shambled by, soulless and hollow eyed, their hands ending in blood-drenched blades that had been fused directly to their metal bodies. She knelt, and a jagged shard of stone bit into her knee, but Thessa knew that if she screamed, she would alert the enemy to not only her own presence, but also that of her companions. She bit back a cry as warm blood ran down her calf.

When the patrol was gone, Voriel signaled them to rise. A few started forward, but Voriel waved for everyone to wait then stepped out alone into the hallway to scan for enemies herself. She turned one way then the other. The motion made her hood fall, revealing tapered ears and long hair the color of burnt gold. A moment later, Voriel nodded, satisfied, and signaled everyone to come out of hiding.

She's so brave. Thessa hoped someone would see the cut on her knee as she stepped into the hallway, which was dimly lit by torches left in brackets every hundred paces. She hoped, too, that the others would notice how easily she handled the pain.

Voriel addressed everyone, detailing a complex plan to fight their way through the Jolym and recapture Namundvar's Well. Then the Shel'ai child looked at Thessa and grimaced. "You're bleeding!" Instead of concerned or impressed, Voriel sounded annoyed.

Thessa looked down and feigned surprise. "I didn't even notice." She poked at the wound with her finger and shrugged. "It's nothing. Iron Sisters are trained to resist pain, you know. One time, I took an arrow in my leg, and I still—"

"You can't come with us." Voriel crossed her arms. "Jolym can smell blood. If you come with us, you'll get us all killed."

Thessa frowned. "Since when can Jolym smell blood?"

Voriel rolled her eyes. "Jolym are made from magic. Since when did Humans know more about magic than Shel'ai?" She uncrossed her arms and rested one hand on Thessa's shoulder. "I'm sorry, but this war is too important. We have to leave you behind. If the Jolym come back, you should kill yourself so they don't rape you."

Thessa pushed Voriel's hand off her shoulder. "That's stupid! Jolym don't rape people. They just kill them."

A Shel'ai boy frowned. "Says who?"

"Says everyone! How could a Jol rape somebody? They don't even have anything down there!"

Voriel said, "How would *you* know?"

The boy scoffed. "*You* know how she knows."

The children laughed, and Thessa felt her face go hot. She tightened her grip on the wooden sword she was holding and imagined how good it would feel to swing it at the boy's head.

"Enough," Voriel snapped. "We have a war to win." She turned and started to walk away.

"What if you healed her?" a quiet voice offered.

Everyone turned. The speaker was the only other Human in the group: a boy, younger than the rest, with torn clothes and a dirty face.

"You should heal her," the boy said, a little louder. "Then there won't be no blood. Besides, you'll need her sword if you want to stab those Jols through the eyes."

"Jol*ym*," Voriel corrected. "And we can't waste magic. We'll need it later." She turned and strode away. The other Shel'ai followed. Voriel pretended she'd stumbled into a guard and summoned a tongue of wytchfire to kill him before leading the others onward.

"Sorry," said the boy. "They should have fixed you."

Thessa faced the boy—one of a handful of children abandoned at Cadavash by dragon-worshippers—and wished he'd kept quiet. "No big deal. I wish I'd had my luminstone with me. Rowen gave me one. He got it in the Wytchforest. Even Voriel doesn't have one." She took a step, winced, then forced herself to walk without limping. "I need to get back to the practice yard anyway."

The boy's face brightened. "I'll go, too!"

Thessa struggled a moment to remember the boy's name. When she did, she forced herself to place one hand on his shoulder. "No, Galem. You have to stay here and warn the others if the Jolym try to attack them from behind. It's important."

"All right," Galem answered gravely, playing along. "I'll stay." He stooped, picked up a rock, and ducked around the corner. A moment later, he leapt out and bashed an imaginary foe with his rock. "Thessa, run! I'll hold 'em back! Save yourself!" He tackled his foe and bashed the floor with his rock, over and over again, skinning his knuckles in the process.

"Thanks," Thessa muttered and headed back toward the stairs.

Alone, she shuddered at all the dark windows and empty shops around her. She pretended that the depths of Cadavash were actually the ravaged city of Hesod, whose people she would have to avenge. After a moment, she thought she saw Dhargots smiling at her from the shadows.

Thessa swung her wooden sword at the darkness, this way and that. "There's nothing there," she told herself.

However, when she turned, another Dhargot was looming over her, his chest bare except for a necklace of Human ears. The Dhargot grinned and loosened his belt.

She shuddered then raced up and stabbed him through the chest. "You're not real!"

The Dhargot vanished, but the moment she turned, she saw him again, walking toward her with some of his friends. All of them were naked.

Thessa glared at them. "Not real," she repeated.

She turned and headed toward the stairs again, doing her best not to run, but when she heard footsteps behind her, she broke into a sprint. She ran and ran up the long, twisting stairwell, never slowing despite the pain in her knee. By the time she reached the surface, she was exhausted and crying.

She pushed through the wooden gate in the low fence surrounding the chasm then stopped and wiped her eyes and her nose on her sleeve. She realized she'd lost her wooden sword somehow, though she could not remember dropping it. She considered going back to look for it then turned toward the practice yard instead. A gray shadow blocked her.

Thessa stared up at Breaksteel. Her heart leapt in her throat at the sight of the Olg, but she fixed a defiant expression on her face. "Get out of my way."

The Olg stepped to one side, nodding his shaggy head. He made a motion with one arm and appeared to smile.

As Thessa passed him, she noticed the blood on his tunic. "Take a bath. You stink!"

The practice yard was empty except for Keswen, who was busy firing multiple arrows at a time at a line of straw dummies in the distance. Thessa sat down on a nearby stone bench to watch. She noticed that the more arrows Keswen fit to her bowstring, the less powerful and accurate they became. On the other hand, the huntress was so quick that she could draw, nock, and fire three arrows from her quiver at the same time.

"I bet you could kill a lot of Dhargots like that," Thessa said.

Keswen answered without turning her head. "I haven't killed a Dhargot in years." She unleashed a trio of arrows that tore into the chest and throat of a single target.

"But you did before, right? Like, when you escaped from that general's palace or whatever it was?"

That time, Keswen turned and gave Thessa so cold a look that the latter felt as though she was back down in Cadavash again. "Pardon me, little one, but that's not something I care to talk about." She turned back to the targets but began firing arrows one at a time. Her limbs blurred. The bowstring hummed. She placed arrow after arrow through the eyes of her distant targets.

Thessa shuddered. *She's still mad about her baby... the one they filled her with, who came out dead.* Thessa chided herself, half afraid Keswen might read her thoughts, but then she reminded herself that even though Keswen had tapered ears, she was a Sylv, not a Shel'ai.

"You're more like me than them," Thessa said.

Keswen frowned at her. "I'm what?"

Thessa blushed. "Sorry, I don't know why I said that..." She stood up. Despite the lump in her throat, she said, "Have you killed a lot of Olgrym?"

Keswen turned slightly. Her eyes followed Breaksteel as the squire shambled wearily towards the barracks. "A few," she said finally and reached for another arrow. "Why?"

"I haven't killed any," Thessa said. "I haven't killed anyone yet."

"Good for you." Keswen tilted her bow slightly and unleashed two arrows at once. One struck a dummy's chest. The other struck the chest of the dummy right next to it.

30

Thessa was about to compliment her, but she could not tell from Keswen's stony expression whether the huntress was pleased by or disappointed with the shot. "I think I'm going to kill a lot of people, eventually. Like Igrid and Rowen. And Jalist and Maddoc, too, I suppose." She paused. "I mean, I'm not going to kill *them*. I'm going to kill... *like* them."

"That's certainly one way to live." Keswen set down her longbow and went to retrieve her arrows then returned and began firing again.

Thessa wondered if the archer had forgotten she was there.

Then Keswen said, "You might want to try something else, though."

"Why?"

Thessa waited a long time for Keswen to answer. Finally, shrugging, she got up and started toward the manse. She'd only gone halfway when someone called out to her. She turned and saw Galem, sprinting in her direction.

"The others told me to leave." He smiled and held out Thessa's wooden sword. "You dropped this on the steps!"

Thessa snatched the wooden sword out of Galem's dirty hands. She suddenly felt childish holding it. She wished it were made of metal that she could wield in a real-life fight. She held up the wooden sword, which Jalist had carved for her, and resisted the impulse to throw it away. She gave it back to Galem.

"Keep it. It's just a dumb baby toy, anyway." She walked away.

CHAPTER THREE

ZEIA GAZED DOWN THE HILL, at the mounted figures riding by, and wondered if she had gone mad.

She'd been on the way back to Dhargoth after scouting in the south, eager to assist Prince Saanji in his final push into U'dan, when she spotted three riders heading in her direction. At first, despite her surprise, she was tempted to cry out with joy at the sight of Saanji's new standard: a black dragon squaring off against a ripe tomato, a joke adapted from the men's penchant for teasing Saanji because of his weight and red cheeks. She even saw the prince, riding at the head of the column. Something stopped her, though.

Concealing her horse in a copse of trees, she climbed the nearest hill and pressed herself flat against the ground. She had no spyglass, nor did she need one. Summoning her magic, she momentarily enhanced her vision so that Saanji might as well have been close enough to touch.

Something was wrong. Saanji was armed and armored, but he white-knuckled the reins. Next to him rode Vaari, his loyal but detestable bodyguard. The usually unflappable soldier appeared as uneasy as his charge and frequently cast wary glances at the third rider, who wore the same Dhargothi scale armor as Saanji and Vaari.

Zeia only needed to study the third rider for a moment to sense strong magic emanating from him. In fact, the air around him seemed to shimmer. Though young, he had stark-white hair gathered behind his tapered ears in a long ponytail. His smug grin reminded her of Chorlga.

Despite the sudden lump in her throat, Zeia had the presence of mind to clear her thoughts. Then, she imagined a thin veil stretching over her mind, followed by another then another. By the time she was finished, the combined thickness of the veils was equal to that of a stone wall. Even then, Zeia tried to keep her thoughts clear. After all, concealing oneself from a Dragonkin was not easy.

Zeia waited until the riders passed by, then she stood up. For one wild instant, she considered speaking telepathically with Saanji, reassuring him that she was close by. But the Dragonkin would almost certainly sense that.

They're heading southeast... away from the fighting. Saanji had been warring against his wicked father for years. Zeia doubted he would abandon the siege voluntarily, but the thought of another Dragonkin on Ruun seemed equally implausible. The Dragonward had collapsed, yes, but that was only for a moment—and that, more than a month before. Ships had scoured every shore. Surely, if any Dragonkin *had* managed to slip back into Ruun, they would have heard about it by now.

Unless they're playing the same game as Chorlga: hiding, biding their time. Zeia considered that and shook her head. Then a new thought chilled her blood. *What if that was Nekiel?* For a moment, an even greater fear gnawed at her—not just fear for what would happen to Ruun, but despair over the fact that she could not possibly rescue Saanji from such a being. Reminding herself of the need to clear her thoughts, she returned to her horse. The palfrey stirred at her approach, sensing her unease.

Zeia hesitated. Part of her wanted to ride the rest of the way back to Dhargoth to see what had become of the siege. She had not seen Laanti with the trio. If the general was still alive, he could help her. Additionally, Saanji was well loved by his troops. With luck, enough of his Earless remained to raise so vast an army that even a Dragonkin would have to take notice.

But that'll take time...

Zeia reached out. Arms that ended in scarred wrist-stumps moved toward the reins. Hands of violet fire unfurled from the stumps, gripping the reins as Zeia fit one foot into the stirrup and hoisted herself into the saddle. She noticed the reins smoldering in her magical hands and chided herself. Expending too much magic made the wytchfire burn too hot. Something told her that, before long, she would need all the strength she could muster.

She turned her horse after the others and set off. Already, she had a bad feeling that she knew where they were going.

Saanji tried to ignore the sick feeling in the pit of his stomach. He told himself that it was there just because he had not slept or eaten for a day and a half, but he suspected the reason had more to do with his new traveling companion. He glanced at the Dragonkin who called himself Krym, and wondered if that was even his real name. After first pretending to set aflame a good portion of Saanji's army, Krym had laughed and informed Saanji with chilling nonchalance that he'd already been in U'dan, that he'd finished Saanji's war for him, erasing any need for Saanji to venture into the ancient Dhargothi capital.

Saanji went anyway. A quick search had confirmed that the Dragonkin spoke the truth. Saanji shuddered at the memory: temples and city streets choked with charred corpses, hundreds strong. Krym had not just killed soldiers, either. Saanji saw dead women and children in the streets, though he supposed—*hoped*—they had died earlier and burned accidentally in the later fires.

In the throne room, Saanji had found his charred father fused to a chair of solid bronze. The heat that had melted the Red Emperor's armor had only seared the crown to his skull and caused molten gold to drip down his father's face before cooling into a kind of ghastly mask. His father's eyes were wide, his mouth twisted in agony. Though Saanji had no affection for the man, the sight of anyone killed in such a manner had left him speechless and had haunted his waking thoughts ever since.

"You Humans are a strange lot," Krym said. The Dragonkin's grin told Saanji that the former had been reading his thoughts. "In one night, I end a siege that had troubled you for years, cost you thousands of lives. And as an added gift, I slew a man of whom your every memory includes scorn, humiliation, and pain. And still, you do not trust me."

Saanji tried to speak and found he could not. He took a moment to steady his nerves, cleared his throat, and tried again. "I'm afraid I don't have much experience trusting Dragonkin. I'll try to do better."

Krym nodded slowly. "Then you never met my old friend, Chorlga?"

Saanji wondered if Chorlga really was Krym's friend or if that was just a figure of speech. "I'm afraid… I never had the honor."

"If you had, you wouldn't refer to it as an honor. Chorlga was a dog. Nekiel was wrong to trust him." Krym yawned. "But I am different. Surely I've proven that."

Saanji flashed back to the bizarre ruse Krym had played—pretending to be Saanji's father and also pretending to annihilate a good portion of Saanji's men—after truly annihilating nearly the entire besieged army at U'dan. "You've certainly made a strong impression in the course of one day, m'lord."

Krym eyed Saanji, unblinking, his expression intense but unreadable. Eventually, Saanji turned away.

Krym said, "You think I'm mad."

Vaari gave Saanji a warning glance, begging him to keep quiet, but something told Saanji that would be a mistake.

"You haven't exactly acted with humility and temperance," Saanji said, "and now, you say you want to help Rowen Locke… the same man who fought Chorlga, not to mention Nekiel's pet, Algol. Locke should be your *enemy*. And all that, in addition to about a thousand fairy tales of Dragonkin using everyone—even the Shel'ai—as slaves. Or food, of sorts. You'll forgive me if I'm a little slow to sing your praises."

Krym's eyes narrowed slightly. "You say many words when you are nervous."

Saanji swallowed hard. "Some men clam up. I babble. Not sure which is more likely to end in death. If you have some input to share, I'm listening."

For a long time, Krym stared at him as they rode, and Saanji wondered if he was about to be burned alive.

But then Krym smiled. "You have courage, too, I think. I was right to trust you. I considered allying myself with your father instead, you know. But I browsed his thoughts, his soul, and found him decidedly unworthy."

"I hope I'll prove otherwise."

"You already have." Krym bowed slightly. "I beg your forgiveness for all that's happened. I judged it to be necessary, and in truth, my ordeal, the manner in which I entered Ruun, may have left me more... unraveled than I'd care to admit. I will do better."

Another crazed Dragonkin... Just what we need! Saanji cursed himself for thinking such a thing, since Krym had been reading his mind only a moment before. "You met with my dear father just last night, you said. But the incident at Shigella's Tomb happened more than a month ago."

Krym nodded. "And you are wondering where I've been since then."

"That," Saanji said, "and how many other Dragonkin are currently unleashed in Ruun, doing whatever hellish nonsense they've spent ten-odd centuries dreaming about."

Though Vaari cast Saanji another warning look, Krym laughed. "A good question, and one I'll be happy to answer, but I prefer to wait until we join Sir Locke. It will be easier to explain everything at once. In the meantime, I have a task for you. We are being followed. Please tell your handless lover that I mean you no harm. In fact, I would be honored if she would join us."

Saanji's eyes widened. "Zeia..."

Krym turned in the saddle and nodded at the hills behind them. "I must say she's doing a fine job masking her thoughts. Much better than any Shel'ai I've ever known, save Algol. Still, her concern for you might as well be a trumpet."

Saanji scanned the hills. The thought of being reunited with Zeia brought a smile to his face even as part of him wanted to shout for her to run as far and as quickly as she could. Then, something else that Krym had said gave him pause.

"Did you meet a lot of Shel'ai while you were living in exile, m'lord?" Saanji asked.

Krym's smile vanished. "I dislike being followed almost as much as I dislike being probed and mocked. Invite your woman to join us. I give you my word, if she behaves, she won't be harmed."

Saanji felt a cold chill sweep through his body. He felt as though he'd been stabbed in the chest with a sword made of ice, after which tendrils of cold swept out, filling his veins. He choked. Then, all at once, the pain vanished. Saanji realized he'd half drawn his sword, and he let it go. The blade rasped as it slid back into its scabbard.

"Yes, m'lord." He turned his horse around.

Rowen watched Igrid in the practice yard. Her fighting skirt swirled teasingly high as she spun away from Thessa's hasty charge. Rather than thwack the girl on the rump with her practice sword, as she'd done the last time, Igrid pretended to stumble. Thessa's eyes widened at the opportunity, and the girl charged again, swinging fast and hard, but Igrid managed to roll clear, tapping Thessa's thigh in the process.

Still, Thessa grinned. "I almost had you that time!"

"Sunset got in my eyes," Igrid said, grumpily.

Rowen smiled and glanced at the audience. A handful of Knights and squires watched, probably more interested in Igrid—for which Rowen could hardly blame them. Keswen sat on a bench, inspecting a quiver of arrows. A grubby boy a few years younger than Thessa stood there, too, clutching a wooden sword and watching intently. Rowen recognized him as Galem, one of those orphaned some time before and taken in by Igrid's kindness. In the distance, a circle of Shel'ai children were playing a game, conjuring a fist-sized sphere of wytchfire and levitating it slowly from person to person. They spoke loudly, encouraging and chiding each other, and they seemed to be making a point of not looking at Thessa.

Gods, how does anybody survive childhood?

Thessa's squeal of delight caught Rowen's attention. He turned in time to see Igrid on one knee. He could not tell whether Thessa's attack had knocked her down or if Igrid was faking, but he strongly suspected the latter. Thessa was trying to press her advantage, hacking at Igrid's exposed thigh with her wooden sword, but Igrid deftly blocked each swing, rolled backward, and leapt back up. Thessa kept coming, unperturbed.

"Slow down," Igrid warned. "When an opening's gone, it's gone." To prove her point, she parried Thessa's sword then prodded the girl gently in the chest before she could recover.

However, Thessa charged, a wild grin on her face. That time, the girl swung high then dropped to her knees and cut at Igrid's ankles instead. At the last instant, Igrid jammed her wooden sword into the ground to intercept the blow then swung one leg high. Instead of kicking the girl in the face, she rested her boot on Thessa's shoulder.

"See? I told you—"

Thessa's grin vanished. She screamed and shoved Igrid's leg. She flung her sword and walked away. Rowen moved to intercept her, but Igrid caught his eye and shook her head. Meanwhile, Galem ran to fetch Thessa's sword, called out to Thessa, and started to run after her. Rowen caught him instead.

"Best leave her alone for a while," Rowen said, "but I see some robbers who just breached the walls and need to be stopped before they reached the nursery." He pointed at a distant shadow.

Galem's eyes widened. "Yes, sir." He sprinted in the direction Rowen had indicated, hacking wildly at the air with both swords.

Igrid joined Rowen a moment later. For the first time, Rowen noticed a bruise on her thigh.

"Did I do that?" he asked.

"No less than I gave you." Igrid winked. "Seriously, she's getting better. I've never seen anyone improve so fast. She just needs to control that temper."

Rowen noticed that the Shel'ai children had stopped their game and were speaking in conspiratorial whispers, glancing in the direction Thessa had gone. "That would help when Sariel gets back. Thessa's always shown more patience with her."

Igrid shook her head. "I don't think it's a matter of patience. Part of it's anger. The rest is age. She's already had her first moonblood, you know. And she's starting to grow a bosom, though she's doing her best to hide it."

Rowen's expression soured. "I hadn't noticed."

"The boys will."

"I've heard enough," Rowen said. "We'll just have to send her to a temple and make her a cleric."

"Not in my lifetime." Igrid sighed. "She has to learn to control herself. I'm no mother, but I know when I acted like that, I got the piss beaten out of me."

"And we both know how *you* turned out."

"Exactly."

Igrid flipped her wooden sword, caught it by the blade, and offered Rowen the hilt. He reached for it.

Igrid gently smacked it against his cheek. "Not that you're much better."

"Agreed." Rowen reached for the wooden sword, but Igrid pulled it away. "So we won't hang her by her toenails. What, then?"

"Reward her," Igrid said. "Give her a palace somewhere. Lots of servants. Pretty dresses."

Rowen tried to snatch the practice sword from her grasp. Igrid twisted clear and swatted his forearm.

Rowen winced but said, "Maybe Aeko will take her."

"And make her into an Isle Knight? No, thanks." Igrid backed up.

Rowen followed. When he stepped too close, Igrid swung. Rowen caught the blow on his wrist, grabbed the blade, and pulled it from Igrid's grasp.

"No fair," Igrid said. "You just cut your hand off."

"Pretend I'm wearing gauntlets." He moved to kiss her.

Igrid leaned in to receive him then twisted clear, kicked the back of his knee, and retrieved her sword before he could regain his balance.

Rowen cursed. "You realize half the garrison is watching, right?"

Igrid's eyes widened. "Forgive me, Sword Marshal! My cunt is at your disposal." She curtseyed then flung the sword at Rowen.

Stunned, he nevertheless managed to catch the whirling hilt before it struck his nose. "Gods, woman! What—"

"Wait." Igrid's expression turned serious as she nodded behind him.

Rowen turned. The gates of Cadavash had just opened. A scouting party—a young Isle Knight and two squires—was returning on horseback. The way they rode spoke of urgency. Rowen started toward them, tossing Igrid's practice sword to one of the onlookers. When the scouting party saw him, the Isle Knight removed a helmet with a fox-shaped facemask and rushed to meet him. The squires hung back, their faces flushed, hands folded.

"What is it, Issa?"

The Knight bowed. "Something strange, Marshal. Riders approaching. Four people on three horses. One appears to be Prince Saanji, with Lady Zeia riding behind him."

Rowen frowned. He glanced at Igrid, who had just come up beside him.

Igrid said, "Saanji and Zeia wouldn't leave the front like that. Is there an army behind them?"

Issa shook his head. "Just those four. They aren't riding hard, but I saw their faces through the spyglass, and they look none too happy. Nobody's talking. I don't recognize the other two riders, but they're armored like Earless." He hesitated. "One has purple eyes and pointed ears."

Igrid swore. Rowen saw by Issa's expression that the young Knight was thinking the same thing.

Rowen said, "I'll ride out to meet them. Close the gates behind me. And get some Shel'ai and archers on the walls, in case there's trouble."

As Issa turned to go, Igrid reached out, grabbed his sword by the hilt, and drew it. She gave it to Rowen. Then she strode forward and did the same to one of the squires, keeping his curved shortsword for herself.

Rowen said, "I take it you're coming with me, then."

Igrid answered by mounting one of the scouts' horses. Rowen took another. A moment later, they were outside the walls of Cadavash, the gates slamming shut behind them.

Saanji glanced at Krym. "I suggest you let me do the talking."

The Dragonkin nodded. "I had not intended otherwise."

Saanji urged his horse ahead of the rest. Zeia's flaming hands tightened around his waist. The faint tingling sensation that always accompanied her magical touch felt hotter than usual. He smelled singed fabric and glanced down to see his tabard smoldering.

"Try not to kill me before the fighting even starts," he whispered.

"Sorry." Zeia withdrew her hands, probably touching her sword hilts instead.

Saanji waved at the approaching riders then reined in and dismounted. He moved to offer Zeia his hand, but she leapt down on her own. Saanji shared a quick look of dread with her then turned to face the riders.

Rowen and Igrid had dismounted as well. Both held drawn swords in the crooks of their arms. Though Rowen smiled at them for a moment, his eyes scanned the hills beyond. "Good to see you, friends. But something tells me this isn't the kind of surprise visit that ends with hugs and too much wine."

"No," Saanji conceded.

He glanced over his shoulder and saw Krym watching them from a distance. A faint smile shone on the Dragonkin's face. Vaari was trying subtly to edge his horse as far away from Krym as possible.

Igrid said, "You've brought a friend."

"Sort of." Saanji swallowed hard, unsure how to continue.

Zeia took over. "Not a friend… and not a Shel'ai, either."

Both Rowen and Igrid answered with wide eyes and speechlessness.

"He says he just wants to talk," Saanji said. "His name is Krym. He says he's come to help. And—"

"And he's listening to every word we say," Zeia said.

"Indeed, I am."

The looks on the others' faces confirmed that Krym's voice had blasted through their minds, as well as Saanji's. Igrid started toward the Dragonkin, moving the sword from the crook of her arm. Rowen stopped her.

"He says he just wants to talk," Saanji repeated. "Listen to him. Besides, I'm not sure we have much choice."

"Life is full of choices," Krym said, a touch of mirth in his voice. He urged his horse forward. As he neared, he held up his empty hands and switched from telepathy to speaking aloud. "I am not your enemy. Perhaps not a friend yet, but with time, that will change." He reined in his horse so close to Igrid that the latter had to step back.

Rowen said, "If you've come for Knightswrath, it isn't here. If you've come for Namundvar's Well, it doesn't work anymore—something Chorlga did. It's closed from the other side. The Light—"

"I came for neither." Dismounting, Krym faced Rowen. "I've heard a lot about you, Sword Marshal. But most of what I've heard came from visions and pilfered memories, so time will tell how much proves true." His smile faded. "Nekiel has returned to Ruun. I have come to help you fight him. You may refuse my help without penalty, but the consequence would be the death of everyone you have fought so hard to protect."

For a moment, silence hung in their air. Finally, Saanji said, "That sounds like a penalty if ever I heard one."

Krym smiled. No one laughed.

After another moment, Krym said, "Perhaps we should find someplace to talk."

41

Rowen and Igrid exchanged looks. Saanji saw Rowen white-knuckling his sword and prayed the Knight would not attack.

"So be it," Rowen said finally. "But I warn you—"

"I'll do no harm to anyone, least of all the Shel'ai children," Krym interrupted. "Believe it or not, circumstance has declared that, for the first time, I must treat your kind as allies... even equals. The gods have a strange sense of humor, do they not?" Abandoning his horse, Krym strode past them, toward the gates of Cadavash. He did not look back to see if they were following.

CHAPTER FOUR

ROWEN WAITED UNTIL EVERYONE HAD dismounted then led the group through the gates of Cadavash, toward the temple in the distance. Saanji ordered Vaari to stay behind with the horses. The latter relaxed a little, scratching at his scarred face.

The temple often stood deserted since the Isle Knights preferred to meditate in a nearby grove and Shel'ai had little use for religion. That suited Rowen fine, since he wanted as few people around as possible. He was glad Thessa was still angry at them and keeping her distance. Sir Jontin frowned and started toward him, though.

Rowen shook his head in warning. "See that we're not disturbed," he called.

Whether or not the old Knight understood their true peril, he came no closer.

The temple doors were open and unguarded. Fortuitously, the temple itself was empty. Rowen stood aside while the others entered. He shuddered when Krym flashed a narrow smile and closed the gates behind them. *Gods, why does he keep smiling?* Rowen wondered if the gesture was intended to reassure them or fool them. Then he reminded himself that Krym might very well be reading his mind and forced his thoughts to clear.

Krym led the group forward as though he'd been to the temple before. He stopped to admire statues of Zet—depicted as half man, half dragon—and the other figures of the pantheon: the huge-breasted fertility goddess, Tier'Gothma; the coy hermaphrodite, Dyoni, raising a cup of wine; fierce Maelmohr, scowling with his armor and axe; and Armahg, smiling behind an open book.

The temple had been built ages before to honor Zet, the Dragongod. However, as Cadavash had really been nothing more than a bone pit, the temple was quickly overtaken by dragonpriests who plied their dark religion among fanatical, self-harming followers. Rowen had first entered the temple to do battle against Chorlga. He was so frightened at the time that he'd hardly noticed the ghastly statues and gruesome carvings. However, all that had been scoured away, and the temple was a simple place of worship, patterned after the minimalist shrines to the Light on the Lotus Isles.

Rowen wondered dimly what had become of the temple's old statues, a disproportionate number of which had featured Zet in various poses of triumph and agony or shown the other gods and goddesses with cold, cruel sneers. He hoped they'd been smashed. Following the others, he noted that Krym was leading the group down the aisle, past simple benches and braziers of lit candles, up a dais, toward the very spot where Rowen and Chorlga had fought. As Rowen recalled, Chorlga had placed an equally ghastly throne of dragonbones up there, though that was gone, too.

Coming to a halt, Krym turned and fixed his eyes on Rowen. For the first time, Rowen realized they were a deeper shade of purple than any he'd ever seen, almost bruise-colored.

Krym said, "Allow me to be blunt, Knight. Nekiel is here. He's somewhere on Ruun, and left unchecked, he will rebuild the same bloody empire that your people have probably spent centuries lamenting in fairy tales." Another faint, aggravating smile tugged at the corners of Krym's mouth. "However, you're in luck, for despite being a Dragonkin, I do not share my master's ambitions. I will help you hunt down and destroy Nekiel in exchange for"—his smile broadened—"something we can discuss later."

Rowen resisted the impulse to glance at the others and forced himself to keep his gaze fixed solely on Krym's eyes, which seemed suddenly like tiny disks of bone set in pools of violet fire. "I'd prefer we discuss it now."

"I'm sure you would. But you don't have Knightswrath, and I've just told you that an enemy far stronger than any you have ever faced is loose on your precious continent, preparing to strike. You're not in a position to argue."

He's right, Rowen realized. "I've read about you," he said instead. "In a scroll telling the story of the Shattering War, you are listed as one of Nekiel's lieutenants."

Krym snickered. "Is that all? I shall try not to be offended." He paused. "First things first. You need to understand *how* we got here. You have probably surmised that we passed through the Dragonward after the guardians were slain, in the moments before the barrier was restored. Actually, we did not. Algol moved more quickly than Nekiel anticipated. We were sailing toward Ruun, but when the Dragonward fell, we were still far away, too far even to teleport."

"Then how—"

"The Dragonward isn't as strong as it used to be. Instead of being continually fed and maintained by the bodies and energies of six Dragonkin, it's now fueled solely by Knightswrath."

And Silwren, Rowen wanted to say, remembering how she had given her soul to power the blade, sacrificing herself to undo the damage wrought by Algol and Crovis Ammerhel. "A bit more than that," he said instead.

Krym nodded. "Despite its power, the sword itself is not alive—at least, as you consider it—so I'd gather the spirit of Silwren is acting as a conduit. In short, all of that is barely enough to maintain the Dragonward at half strength, to keep out the rest of my kind. The barrier can still prove deadly, but a Dragonkin of sufficient skill and luck might teleport through… which is why I'm standing before you." Krym offered a slight, mocking bow.

Saanji took a step forward. "How many of you are there?"

Krym said, "I trust you mean how many of us attempted to reenter Ruun. Unless you mean how many Dragonkin remain alive after what you call the Shattering War, which has grown to a number beyond reckoning." He paused. "There were nine of us, originally. Nekiel and his strongest. Seven died, passing through the Dragonward. I saw their bodies on the Dead Shore. Nekiel was not among them. That means he survived. I tried to find him on my own, without success."

Saanji said, "Perhaps he changed his mind."

"I doubt it," Krym said, his smile vanishing. "Passing through the Dragonward was difficult enough for the rest of us, so much so that only I survived. For Nekiel, though, the method I used would have been impossible. The Dragonward was crafted to target him, in particular. Even with the barrier at half strength, he could not have done it."

Rowen asked, "Then how—"

"There is another way. After Chorlga failed to bring down the barrier from within, Nekiel searched for a way to tear it down himself. He could not find one. But he *did* come up with a way in which to fool it. Though a rather extreme tactic, it was his only option, even more dangerous than the road the rest of us faced."

Saanji said, "Seven of nine killed, and you're telling us Nekiel's way was even more extreme?"

Rowen tensed. *Is Saanji trying to goad him or test him?*

Krym answered without ire. "Perhaps after I explain, you will understand. You see, the Dragonward has a kind of consciousness. It must, in order to ascertain the true nature of whoever approaches it and decide whether to let them pass. But it can be fooled. If a Dragonkin were to bury his powers, bury them so deep that he forgot he even had them, then become something else entirely... some*one* else... he might pass through unharmed."

"Doesn't sound as dangerous as walking through fire," Saanji said.

Krym shook his head. "I cannot fault you for failing to understand. None of you are Dragonkin. Even the Shel'ai"—he glanced at Zeia— "cannot grasp the kind of power we wield and how terrifying it would be to surrender it—to bury it so deep that you genuinely risk losing it."

Rowen flashed back to how he had tricked Chorlga by filling his own mind with false memories, a moment before the Dragonkin probed his thoughts. It had been among the most difficult things he'd ever done. He shuddered to think of the force of will it would take to maintain such a deception for more than an instant. "So where is Nekiel now?"

Igrid added, "And why isn't he busy turning cities to cinders?"

Krym said, "You still do not understand. In order for such a deception to work, it must be perfect, flawless. Nekiel could not just *pretend* to become someone else. He had to literally do it. That means he had to forget who he was, what he had been, down to his very core."

46

Saanji said, "So there's a powerless Dragonkin wandering around with no memory. I suppose that's not as bad as it could be."

"He won't be powerless for long," Krym said. "I'll confess, I probably could not recover from such a thing. But Nekiel will. Of that, I have no doubt. Gradually, his memories and power will float back to the surface, as will his ambition. Obviously, it would be in our interest to find and kill him long before that happens."

Igrid frowned. "If he doesn't look like a Dragonkin anymore and doesn't even know what he is, how are we supposed to find him?"

"Because I know where he's going. As deeply as he buried his true self, Nekiel would not have erased that." Krym paused. "Passing through the Dragonward weakened me considerably. I confess it. But Nekiel would have been weakened by his method even more than I was weakened by mine. He needs to replenish his power."

"If memory serves," Saanji said, "the Dragonkin replenished their power by absorbing the life essence of dragons… but the dragons are gone. Chorlga used Namundvar's Well, but that doesn't work, either."

Krym's snicker returned. "Actually, there's another way."

Rowen remembered how Chorlga had enhanced his abilities to terrifying heights by draining the life force of hundreds of dragon-worshippers. He reached for his sword hilt. "I know what you're talking about, Dragonkin, and I swear there will be none of that while I am alive."

Krym blinked then laughed. "You misunderstand me, Knight. I am not speaking of draining a few magicless Humans. Or Shel'ai, either." He cast a sidelong glance at Zeia. "All the Shel'ai left on Ruun might not be enough to sate Nekiel's hunger once he becomes aware of it. No, Nekiel would need more. *Much* more. He'd need a dragon."

Igrid said, "Good thing your kind hunted them to extinction, what, twenty centuries ago?"

"More like thirty," Krym corrected. "For a time, we kept some in pens, like cattle, and tried to breed them. But even those disappeared long ago. Or so the stories say. But not all stories are correct."

Rowen tried to swallow his impatience. "What are you saying, Dragonkin?"

Krym faced him, unblinking. "I am saying that there is still one dragon left on Ruun. Nekiel captured her himself when the dragons' numbers waned, long before I was even born. Rather than absorb her fantastic power, as he could have done, he hid her. He resisted his urges and decided to save her for a day when he really needed her. He buried her, ensnared but still alive, and cloaked his prize in so many concealment spells that not even Chorlga learned of her existence."

Silence filled the chamber again. Rowen saw by his friends' expressions that they scarcely believed what the Dragonkin had just said. Then another dizzying thought occurred to Rowen. He remembered a fragment of a vision he'd had, in the midst of a telepathic threat from Chorlga, of a massive dragon buried below the ice of the Wintersea. At the time, he'd thought it nothing but a frightening image imparted by Chorlga to scare him.

"Not a threat." Krym faced him. "That was Khyrshar, calling out to you from the ice, begging you for help." His voice quivered as though he were fighting back either tears or laughter. "She used Chorlga's own powers to call out to you, and you didn't even realize."

Rowen fought back dizziness as he remembered how, in the years since the War of the Lotus, he'd had a handful of nightmares about the same mournful dragon trapped below the ice. He wondered if those had been the dragon as well, calling out to him.

Igrid appeared beside Rowen and took his arm. She said to Krym, "You said Nekiel captured this dragon thirty centuries ago. Just how old *is* this bastard?"

"Nekiel?" Krym's expression sobered. "Nobody knows. Some say he was born centuries before the great Namundvar, even. Others say he has *always* existed, even before the gods cast Zet from the heavens. I'd invite you to ask him once we find him. But I suggest you stab him first."

Rowen touched Igrid's arm. He guessed Igrid's question had come less from curiosity than from a desire to distract the Dragonkin while Rowen regained his composure. "You have told us quite a tale."

Krym nodded. "And what frightens you, no doubt, is the knowledge that a good portion of it must be true."

"You still haven't told us what you want in exchange for our help."

"Nor will I," Krym said. "Not just yet. But be assured my price is far lower than what Nekiel would demand. And my price will *not* involve the death of thousands, let alone the millions who died banishing Nekiel in the first place."

Saanji said, "Forgive me if I don't find that terribly reassuring."

"I would not expect you to. After all, I was Nekiel's servant. I fought against Nâya and her Human lover. I used to catch Shel'ai like rabbits and drink down their essence like strong wine." He smacked his lips and glanced at Zeia again.

Zeia's hands of wytchfire smoldered to life an instant before Saanji stopped her from drawing her sword. Still, she said, "You'll not be drinking *my* essence in this life, Dragonkin."

Krym smiled in grudging respect. "People change. Even Dragonkin, sometimes. Nekiel's ambitions are no longer my own. So I will help you find him. In fact, I am the only one who would recognize him, perhaps before he himself even knows what he is. Once he is dead, the giant will go one way while the ants go another, in peace."

Rowen said, "And the dragon? I assume you will take her power, in place of Nekiel?"

"If that is my choice, you should be glad of it. This is... a very old dragon, Human. Even before the Shattering War, Nekiel had already been hoarding her for many centuries. Believe me, she is not as docile as the others we used to hunt. Unleashing her on Ruun would be nearly as disastrous as allowing Nekiel to reign." Krym paused, unblinking. "But we can discuss that later if we must. For now, do we have an agreement?"

Rowen was quiet for a moment then stepped closer to Krym—close enough to offer his hand, though he did not. "The ants will help you, Dragonkin, because they must."

Krym bowed. "The giant thanks you and promises to treat you fairly. Fear not. Time will demonstrate my sincerity." He turned and walked briskly from the temple. He had hardly passed through the doors when his words rang through Rowen's mind: *"Gather a small force, whomever you choose, and meet on the plains at dawn."*

Rowen winced at the ringing power of Krym's telepathy. He glanced around, saw grimaces on his friends' faces, and guessed that Krym had projected his words into their minds as well. For a moment, the four lingered in the temple. No one spoke.

Finally, Rowen faced Igrid. "We'll leave Sariel with Jalist and Maddoc,

49

for now. She's probably safer with them, anyway. And I'll send word to… everyone." He rubbed his eyes, running down the list of everyone who would have to be told what had happened. *Aeko, Hráthbam, the king of Lyos, Briel in the Wytchforest. And Jalist, of course. But what about Ivairia? Gods know who's even in charge there!*

Igrid said, "Who will command Cadavash while you're gone?"

Rowen caught her meaning. The last time he'd left, he'd placed Igrid in charge—partly because he trusted no one more and partly so that, in case he and everyone with him were killed, she could still care for Thessa and Sariel. He knew he should do so again. "Sir Jontin," he said instead. "If I leave you here, you'll just abandon your post and come after me like last time."

Igrid nodded, her cockeyed smile forming a moment before it vanished. "I'm glad we finally understand each other."

Rowen turned to Saanji and Zeia. "If you want to return to Dhargoth, I'll understand." He fixed his gaze on Saanji. "You're not a prince anymore. With your father gone—"

"I'm in no rush to become emperor," Saanji said, smiling weakly. "*Prince* will suffice for now, and General Laanti can keep things in order for a while."

Rowen hesitated, remembering the legendary Dhargothi reputation for cold-hearted ambition. "With your father gone and you here, this general is basically the ruler of a new empire. Do you trust him?"

Saanji snickered. "For the moment. Even among the Earless, you don't get to be a general without developing certain… disquieting qualities. But my men have no interest in seeing him made emperor. As hard as it may be to believe, they insist on passing that putrid duty on to me. Besides, Krym didn't exactly hide himself. When we left Dhargoth, everyone was still too scared to leave their beds."

Rowen turned to Zeia for confirmation.

"Laanti's always been loyal," she said after a moment's hesitation, "but Saanji's right. We're building a new kind of Dhargoth, and that takes time. I've never sensed any disloyalty from him, but—"

Rowen shook his head. "You should go back. We can't risk another fanatical emperor taking over, not after all that's happened."

"I might be inclined to agree," Saanji said, "but it's not my decision.

Or yours. Krym *wants* us along, and he's already made it clear what will happen if we try to slip away."

"Some alliance," Igrid muttered before Rowen could stop her.

"We'll have to worry about Dhargoth later," Zeia said. "Nekiel is the bigger threat. Besides, you'll need us."

Saanji added, "Or, failing that, our graves will make loyal company."

Rowen fought back a grin. "I don't have time to raise an army, and with the Ivairians being surly, I don't want to drag an entire army up to the Wintersea, anyway. We need to move quickly—and *quietly*. Just bring that dour bodyguard of yours if he's willing. I'll choose a few—"

"Keswen should be one of them," Igrid said.

Rowen nodded. "If she'll agree. And Sir Issa." He paused. "And Breaksteel if you think he's ready."

"He is," Igrid said. "Not sure about the rest of us, though."

Nor am I. "We'll do what we must." Rowen turned toward the door. He feared again that Krym might be listening, reading his thoughts—and giving voice to his feelings would not help matters.

CHAPTER FIVE

ROWEN TRACED HIS FINGERTIPS ALONG the cold stone rim of Namundvar's Well and listened as Zeia recounted all that had befallen Saanji during his first meeting with Krym. When she finished, he was speechless for a moment. He looked about the chamber, trying to remember what it had been like before Chorlga's excessive magic had all but destroyed it. He remembered lush murals covering the ground and a strange, alternate type of luminstone on the walls, but all that was gone.

Finally, unable to think of anything else to say, he answered with, "You have no idea how much it took to convince Igrid not to come down here, too. I trust it was the same with Saanji."

Zeia said, "Actually, it was Saanji's idea that everyone else stay behind, to avoid making the Dragonkin suspicious." She stood in the shadows, all but invisible save for the frightful illumination from her burning hands.

"Something tells me we've achieved that anyway." Rowen sighed. "All right, let's get straight to it. I reread the scroll that Silwren gave me. It says nothing else about Krym, aside from naming him as one of Nekiel's trusted men. That still means he's powerful, though. I don't think we can kill him... at least, not without most everyone dying in the attempt. And if he's telling the truth about Nekiel—"

"Why does Krym need us?" Zeia cut in.

Rowen blinked, unsure how to answer her question. Instead, he looked down into the impenetrable darkness of Namundvar's Well. "I don't know," he said finally, "but I know what you're about to say—we should go get Knightswrath. But even if we could get inside Shigella's Tomb, we don't dare risk bringing down the Dragonward."

"Unless Krym was lying about how many Dragonkin are waiting outside Ruun."

"He might be, but we can't take that chance. We have to deal with what's in front of us as best we can."

"But we already know Krym's a liar," Zeia said. "When he met Saanji, he implied that he slipped through the Dragonward while it was still down. Now, he says he teleported through after it went back up."

"A strange thing to lie about," Rowen said.

"Unless you're someone who lies without a second thought, for whatever pleasure it brings in the moment. And that's someone I don't care to trust." Zeia's flaming hands brightened a moment.

Rowen wondered whether it was disgust or fear that caused the flames to intensify. "Agreed. But again, we can't risk—"

"If Krym is so determined to betray his master, why doesn't he just hunt him down by himself?"

"He didn't teleport here," Rowen said. "He could have grabbed Saanji and gone straight from U'dan to Cadavash in the blink of an eye. He didn't. Maybe he's weaker than we thought."

"But he'll get stronger," Zeia said. "I tried reading his mind. He walled himself against me, of course, but I sensed his power before he did that. It's... not as great as Chorlga's, not yet, but still three or four times greater than mine. And he'll only get more powerful over time."

Rowen sighed. "I hear you. I do. But gods strike me down if I know what you expect me to do about it."

Zeia hesitated. "All right, maybe Krym needs us. But do *we* need *him*? Remember, he said Nekiel doesn't even know what he is. If we're quick, if Keswen and Vaari fill him full of arrows—"

"We might not even be able to recognize him."

"I don't think we're likely to find an overabundance of innocent travelers on the Wintersea."

"Maybe not," Rowen conceded, "but if Nekiel has regained even half his power, steel and arrows won't be enough. The only other weapons besides Knightswrath that seem to work against Dragonkin are the freyd." Rowen shuddered at the mention of those cursed daggers, made by the Dragonkin long before and supposedly given to their assassins to kill political rivals.

Zeia nodded. "I know. Father Matua showed me the stories, but there might not be any left. I've been through the Scrollhouse a dozen times and never seen one. The only one I've ever even heard of was the one Chorlga had."

Rowen winced, remembering how that freyd had been used against Silwren. "I doubt we're likely to stumble upon one before we reach the Wintersea. All the more reason why we might need Krym before this is over."

"But you know what he wants," Zeia insisted. "His price. He doesn't have to tell us what it is. It's obvious. He wants the dragon!"

Rowen hesitated. "We can't let him have her."

"Exactly. So now we're talking about fighting *two* Dragonkin, not just one."

Rowen gave her a warning glance. Though he doubted Krym was eavesdropping on their conversation, that late and so far down in the chasm, he did not want to risk speaking more openly than they already were.

Zeia was quiet for a time. "We barely defeated Chorlga. So many died. And now—"

"I know," Rowen said. *Maybe Nekiel and Krym will kill each other. "And if they don't?"*

Rowen winced. If Zeia could read his thoughts that easily—

"Imagine veils around your mind," Zeia said. "Or brick walls. Straw. Wood. Doesn't matter. Just surround your mind with layer after layer—"

"You've told me." Rowen sighed. "Enough. We only have a few hours before dawn, and honestly, I don't want to spend them down here."

"I don't either, but understand what's coming. This will be even worse than what we've faced before. We're not all going to survive." Her hands vanished, plunging the chamber into darkness. "You'd better be prepared for that, Knight."

"I am." He wondered if she knew he was lying. A moment later, he heard the sound of footsteps as Zeia walked away.

Rowen started to follow, suddenly fearing being left in the dark, then stopped. He traced his fingertips along the rim of Namundvar's

Well again. He thought of the first time he'd seen it, years before, when Silwren and El'rash'lin were still alive. To give him courage for what lay ahead, the latter had shown him the Well as it was intended: radiating power and serenity, a conduit into the Light itself.

Rowen peered into the darkness of Namundvar's Well again, noting that it matched the thick, unforgiving darkness around him. He shuddered then walked away.

Miriam paused, breathless, and glanced back into the dark forest behind her. Gruff shouts and laughter reached her ears. A moment later, the flicker of a distant torch shone through the trees. Miriam started running again.

At first, she'd thought Jem and Will had come to punish her and drag her back to the Dead Shores, but there were too many voices, and they were laughing. Jem and Will never laughed when they were angry.

Maybe they aren't actually chasing after me.

Then an unfriendly voice split the night behind her: "Run all you like, child! We prefer you tired out, anyway!" Cold laughter accompanied the statement, echoing through the trees.

Despite her exhaustion, Miriam ran even harder. Her mother had warned her that bad things could happen, to girls in particular, if they weren't careful. At the time, she'd protested that if someone hurt her, that was the fault of whoever did the hurting. Besides, she had her brothers to protect her. They might not be nice all the time, maybe they even disliked her a little bit, but surely they'd protect her from *that*.

But Jem and Will aren't here, she told herself.

A tree root caught her foot, and she fell. Miriam put up her hands to catch herself, and one bent the wrong way. A terrible sound accompanied a wave of pain so hot that, for a moment, the darkness turned white. Too late, Miriam heard herself screaming. By the time she stopped, the boys were shouting in her direction, drawing closer and closer.

Miriam rolled over. Hugging her wrist against her body, she forced herself to stand. For a moment, she reeled, unsure where to go. She waited until the boys were shouting again, then she took off in the opposite direction.

The moon was a faint blurry sliver, and clouds blocked the stars. She knew that if she kept running, she would only trip again, but she dared not stop or slow down, either. Swallowing a lump of panic in her throat, Miriam hesitated then changed directions. She moved to the left instead, pressing her back to one tree after another. She hoped the boys would think she'd kept running straight ahead. *Even with a torch, it's too dark to see my footsteps.*

A fresh chorus of shouts told her the boys were even closer—almost close enough to touch. Miriam froze. Orange-yellow light flickered through the trees. She peeked out from behind a tree and saw the boys had not just one torch but three. She could not tell how many boys there were, but she guessed at least six. All looked tall and strong, like giants. Some held clubs. Others had knives that gleamed in the torchlight, with patches of rust that looked like bloodstains.

Miriam thought of her own knife. She touched it with her good hand but did not draw it. Instead, she held her breath and kept her back pressed to the trees. She moved and moved, slowly circling around the tree as the boys passed by. She wanted to run, but she forced herself to wait until they were far away. She closed her eyes for a moment and prayed the gods would protect her.

When she opened her eyes, the blond boy from the sea was standing right in front of her, staring at her. Miriam screamed.

The boy winced. "You should not have done that." He paused, unblinking. "They heard you. We have to run."

"They're after me," Miriam said. "I hurt my hand. I can't run—"

"They aren't after you. They're after me." The boy took her good hand.

She noticed his rich clothes were torn, his limbs and nose crusted in dried blood. She wondered if the other boys had done that or if he'd simply fallen as she had.

The nameless boy led her away from the approaching shouts and angry torch glare. "You have to keep running," the boy said. "If you can't run, I'll have to leave you behind. Do you understand?"

Miriam bit her lip, and her eyes swelled with tears. She nodded even though the boy had his back to her, and tried her best to keep up.

Somehow, the nameless boy did not seem to tire. He moved easily through the forest, as though he could see perfectly well in the dark. In fact, his feet moved faster and faster. Miriam wept harder, crying with desperation as she tried in vain to keep up. Finally, she stumbled.

Instead of catching her, the nameless boy let go of her hand, and she fell. Miriam managed to turn sideways and catch herself with her good hand, but when she rolled over, she saw the glare of torchlight only a few yards away. Strong, laughing bodies tumbled out of the darkness. They stopped and formed a rough circle around her. They looked surprised then pleased.

The nameless boy was gone.

Miriam drew her knife and waved it in the air. "Stay back," she said. She avoided using her maimed wrist by bracing her elbow against the ground and pushing up until she was on her knees. Then she stood. "I won't let you hurt him."

The dark figures exchanged glances.

"Forget about him," one said. "He's good as gone anyway."

"Agreed," said another.

A third boy said something she could not understand, though his tone made her blood run cold.

The boys advanced. Miriam screamed and slashed with her knife. One of the boys cried out. Someone grabbed her arm. Miriam could not break free. In desperation, she switched her knife to her injured hand. It hurt when she gripped it, but the cold feeling that came whenever she held the knife numbed some of the pain.

She slashed again, that time at the boy holding her. He swore and let go. She twisted away, intending to run. A big, dark shape blocked her, and Miriam thrust her knife at the shape. Instead of screaming, that boy yelped. The sound reminded her of a stray dog she'd seen once—she had tried to make friends with it, but Jem had crept up, smiling, and hit it with his axe.

The dark shape fell away, and Miriam was free. She started to run. Another boy dove to catch her, calling her names and swinging his torch. Miriam recoiled. The torch scalded the side of her face and filled her nostrils with the smell of burnt hair, but she kept moving.

Miriam ran and ran until the blood pounded in her ears and drowned out the sound of her pursuers. Finally, when she could run no farther, she pressed her back to a tree and held her knife out in front of her. Her arm shook with fear and exhaustion, but she prepared to slash the face of the first boy who came at her.

Instead, she saw nothing but trees, faintly illuminated by a golden slant of sunrise. Miriam blinked as she looked around—no boys, no torches. She relaxed. Then she winced.

For the first time, she realized that her face hurt even more than her wrist. She touched it with her good hand as gently as she could. Pain swept through her. Fresh tears formed in her eyes, but she shook her head, refusing to shed them.

"I got away. The boy's safe. I'm safe. I just have to rest. Then my brothers can find me, and I can go home."

Miriam rested another moment, resisting the impulse to lie down, then pushed herself away from the tree and kept going. Ahead of her, the ground gradually sloped down. She remembered her father saying that was usually a sign that water was close by. Suddenly realizing how thirsty she was, she moved as quickly as she could.

When she spotted a tiny stream, she cried out with glee and managed to run the rest of the way toward it. She knelt heavily, wincing when the motion hurt her injured wrist. Then, leaning forward on her elbows, she used her good hand to splash water on her face.

The water was cold and good against her burn. She splashed more and more water against her face until the pain subsided. Then she stopped to drink. The water soothed her throat and erased her thirst, but as soon as she stopped splashing the burn on her face, the pain returned. Miriam decided to ignore it for the moment and inspect her wrist.

She feared that she would see bones jutting from the skin—white, sharp, and bloody, like what had happened to her father's leg when he fell off the roof—but all she saw was a massive, ugly bruise that wrapped all the way around her wrist, like a bracelet she did not want.

She held it in the stream for a while. Then she splashed her face one last time and lay down. After a moment, she drew the knife from her belt and held it in her bad hand. She did that not just for protection but so the strange coldness emanating from the knife would numb the pain a little. After a moment, she had an idea and lay on her side, moving her arm so the flat sides of the knife pressed against both her wrist and her burned face.

Finally, she went to sleep.

When she woke, her hand and wrist still hurt, though not as badly. In their place, a sharp pain twisted inside her stomach. Miriam realized she still had not eaten anything. The pain grew and grew, so much that she lay on her side and raised her knees toward her chest, praying it would stop. Eventually, the pain subsided, but something told her it would return soon. Miriam straightened her legs and sat up.

Then she saw the nameless boy sitting on a rock, staring at her. Sunlight shone through his blond hair.

Miriam smiled. Then her eyes swelled with tears again. "You left me..."

"I told you I would." The boy stood up and approached her. All the blood had vanished from his face and arms.

He offered her something. Miriam realized it was a piece of fruit, bright and unfamiliar. She took it. When she bit into it, a sour taste filled her mouth, and warm juice ran down her chin. She hated the taste but kept eating.

The boy watched her, blinking evenly. When she was done, he offered her another. She took that one, too, though she wiped her chin and did not eat it right away.

"Stop staring at me," she said.

The boy stared at her a moment longer then said, "Sorry," and turned away. He stared at the stream, unblinking, as though lost in thought.

"Did you remember your name yet?" Miriam asked.

The boy did not answer. Instead, he turned back to the trees. "People are following us." He frowned. "Not those boys from last night, though. I think it's your brothers. They're close."

Miriam was so delighted that she ignored the boy's sudden, strange accent. "How do you know?"

The boy turned back to the stream. "I have to keep going north."

"Why?"

The boy looked at her. "I'm sorry I left you. I was... scared. Not just of the boys, though." He frowned as though confused by his own words. Then he bent down and placed another piece of fruit at Miriam's feet—even though Miriam was sure his hands had been empty a moment before. "I'm sorry," he said again. Then he turned and started walking.

"Wait," Miriam cried. "Don't leave me here."

When the boy kept walking, Miriam pulled the gold medallion from her pocket and threw it at him. The boy turned, caught it, and stared at it. He gave her an incomprehensible look then slipped the medallion over his head and left.

Miriam watched him as she picked up the last piece of fruit. She bit into the one she had already been holding and chewed as she faced the trees. She wondered if she should save some of the fruit for her brothers. Maybe that would make them less angry at her. She still could not hear them, but she believed the boy when he told her they were close.

They'll beat me when they find me... especially if I tell them how I gave him back the medallion!

She looked down at her wrist then knelt by the stream and tried to see her reflection in the water. The shimmer kept breaking the image, making it hard to see herself, but it looked as though some of her hair was gone and part of her face was red and blistered.

"Jem will say I'm ugly, but maybe they'll feel sorry for me." She straightened.

It occurred to her that she could just say she'd been kidnapped, that the nameless boy had taken her and she'd only just managed to get free. She didn't even have to mention the medallion if she didn't want to. Instead of beating her, her brothers might swear revenge on the boy.

"But I don't want them to hurt *him,* either."

She looked down at the fruit in her hands. After a moment's hesitation, she took another bite out of the piece she had already started. By then, she was getting used to the taste. She didn't even hate it anymore. She started to walk away then stopped. She placed the second piece of fruit on the ground behind her. She knew her brothers had to be hungry and hoped they would find it.

CHAPTER SIX

AFTER A SLEEPLESS NIGHT, ROWEN rose to find Igrid already awake, standing naked in front of a washbasin, grimacing into handfuls of cold water. Sunlight streamed through the window, highlighting her pale freckled skin and damp red hair.

Igrid caught him staring and smirked. "Stop looking at me like I'm beautiful."

"You are."

"I know." Igrid winked. "But that look makes me want to come back to bed, and we're supposed to go off and get ourselves killed today."

"Maybe not today." Rowen slowly rose from bed, stretched, and rubbed his eyes. "Might happen tomorrow."

Igrid pointed at a table beside the door. "The servants brought food. Some kind of sweet roll and that damn strong tea you like. There was wine, too, but I drank that while you were snoring."

Rowen turned. On a gleaming metal tray lay the foodstuffs Igrid had mentioned, along with bowls of chopped fruit, a platter of spiced and blackened fish, and toast slathered in jam.

Rowen smiled. "We should take the servants on the road with us. All this good food has probably spoiled our taste for rotten fruit and moldy bread."

"Agreed." Igrid dried herself with a towel then started dressing. "Just load the kitchen and the larder on a wagon, and tell the servants we're going to Phaegos to swim in Artisan Bay. The world can save itself this time." She sat down and started buckling on her armor.

Rowen had little appetite, but he forced himself to eat then filled a small ceramic cup with strong tea. He drank that cup then poured another. "We'll have to say goodbye to Thessa, convince her to stop hating us somehow—"

"She was sleeping outside the door in the hallway," Igrid said. "She was afraid we'd leave without telling her goodbye."

"Gods…" Rowen drank the rest of his tea in one gulp and winced when it burned him. "How does anyone survive being a parent—or a child, for that matter?"

"Now she's in the practice yard, pouting." Igrid buckled on a pair of shortswords then carefully concealed a breast knife in her cleavage. "She's still mad that we're leaving. When I woke her, she cried and hugged me then tried to claw my eyes out."

"Sounds like she's taking after you." Rowen stood, hugged her, and dressed. When he finished donning his armor, he slipped on a tabard of azure silk, sewn with the nine-pointed lotus blossom of his Order. "I miss the balancing crane," he muttered, remembering the sigil of the lowest rank, which he'd used to wear.

"As well you should," Igrid laughed. "That damn flower looks like a target, right on your chest."

"How nice."

Rowen considered a fashionable blue cloak, richly sewn with all the symbols of the Knighthood, then remembered they were heading for the Wintersea and selected a drab but heavy gray cloak instead. He touched Igrid's shoulder as she laced up her vambraces. She hugged his hand by tipping her head and pressing it to her shoulder.

Rowen found Thessa sitting on a stone bench beside the practice yard, cupping a luminstone in her hands. The soft blue light spilled through her fingers. Thessa hardly seemed to notice, but the boy, Galem, stood in front of her, entranced. He still looked filthy and was idly waving a wooden sword within inches of Thessa's head as he told a convoluted story about dragons, to which Thessa was paying no attention.

Gods, I should get the Knights to confine him to a washtub for a while. Tightening his gloves, he ruffled Galem's greasy hair. "Go check on my horse, will you? Make sure it's ready."

Galem's eyes widened at the charge, and he rushed off, swinging his wooden sword at empty air. Rowen sat down beside Thessa. She scooted away from him, still cupping the luminstone.

She said, "I don't like you today."

Rowen said, "That's fair," and looked at the luminstone Thessa was holding, noticing that when her fingers closed over it, the light still shone through, turning her fingers red and highlighting the slim bones underneath. "I wish we could take you with us, but you know we can't."

"You just left a couple months ago, and you almost died. *Both* of you!"

Rowen considered downplaying all that had happened, insisting the dangers he and Igrid had faced had been exaggerated by minstrels. "You're right," he said instead, "but what kept us alive wasn't just knowing how to fight. Or luck. It was having something to come back to, as well." Rowen blushed as he spoke.

Thessa looked up at him. "I have things to fight for, too," she said in a small voice.

"I know." Rowen put his arm around her and left it there, despite how awkward it made him feel. "The best fighters always do." He wasn't sure if that was true, but the statement made Thessa smile.

"When will you be back?"

"I don't know. As soon as we can, though."

Thessa crossed her arms. "I'll be alone until you are. Sariel isn't even coming back!"

"Not for a while," he admitted, "but you have your friends. And Galem, the Dirty Swordsman." He nudged her. "Don't tell him I said that, but once we're gone, tell Jontin I said to give him a bath."

Thessa kept her arms crossed and tried her best not to smile again. "Galem won't like that."

"Tell him it's a sign of a true warrior. My brother did that with me, and it worked for years."

Rowen's stomach tightened at the mention of his brother then looked up in time to see Krym strolling out of the temple in plain traveling clothes. He smiled and waved at Rowen, as though they were old friends. Rowen forced himself to wave back, glad when Krym walked directly to the stables, where the others had already gathered.

Sir Issa broke away from the group and strode toward Rowen. The young Knight was clad in kingsteel armor and an azure tunic sewn with the sigil of a crane balancing on one foot. Unlike Rowen, the young Knight had chosen a thin but eye-catching cloak of blue, sewn all over with a detailed depiction of Knights riding into battle.

Though such a garment was fine for the midlands, Rowen considered ordering the young Knight to go find something more appropriate for their destination. Then he noticed how Thessa straightened at Sir Issa's approach, arching her back and cupping her hands completely around the luminstone so that it faded and went out.

Gods, she is *getting older!* Rowen suppressed a groan and stood to greet Issa.

The latter offered a slight, Knightly bow and said, "We are ready, Sword Marshal. If you like, the rest of us can proceed outside the fortress and wait for you." He glanced at Thessa.

Realizing the young Knight was giving Rowen and Igrid a moment longer to say goodbye to Thessa, he nodded. "Thank you, Issa. We'll join you as soon as we can." He glanced east and noticed the first tendrils of sunrise rising over the battlements, which divided them into red-gold slats that spilled across the courtyard like bloody lances.

Issa added, "I believe Sir Jontin wanted to have a word with you, as well." He smiled at Thessa then returned to the stables.

Thessa relaxed her shoulders, opened her fingers, and let her luminstone glow again. Rowen sat back down, unsure what to say, and waited for Igrid. She emerged from the manse a few minutes later, cloaked and armored, her red hair gathered behind her in a tight braid. At her approach, Thessa looked down, but Igrid grabbed Thessa's wrists and pulled her to her feet. Before the girl could protest, Igrid hugged her.

"I'm going to miss you, sewer rat. Remember everything I said. Keep practicing. We'll be back as soon as we can." She hesitated then kissed Thessa's forehead. "For what it's worth, we love you."

Thessa blinked, her eyes filling with tears. Before she could answer, though, Sir Jontin joined them. The white-haired Knight was scowling more than usual. He gave Igrid and Thessa a quick glance then faced Rowen.

"Sword Marshal, again, I must protest. I'd still feel better if you'd let me send a full squad to—"

"Attract attention? No, thank you." Rowen smiled to soften his words. "Did you send all the messages I wrote?"

Sir Jontin nodded. "I dispatched them this morning. We're nearly out of wytch-ravens, by the way. As much as I mistrust those things, I suggest we ask General Briel for more."

"I'll keep that in mind," Rowen said. "I'm trusting you with Cadavash while we're gone. You're a good Knight, but remember what I told you. Keep the Knights, squires, and Shel'ai all working together, whether they like it or not. Mind the orphans. And give Galem a bath." He winked at Thessa, who wept softly and clutched Igrid's hand.

Sir Jontin cleared his throat. "As you say, m'lord."

Rowen turned toward the barracks used by the Knights and squires. Though Rowen had specifically forbidden a formal send-off, a few emerged anyway, formed a line in the distance, and bowed in unison. Rowen bowed back. A moment later, the doors to the barracks used by the Shel'ai opened as well, and all the Shel'ai—young and old alike—emerged. They silently formed a line, like the Knights and squires, and bowed as well.

Igrid whispered, "Wytchfriend, indeed," and squeezed Rowen's hand.

Fighting back sudden tears, Rowen bowed a second time, to Islemen and Shel'ai alike, then turned, gave Thessa a final hug, and started toward the gates.

Rowen reined in his horse just outside the gates and looked eastward again. He winced from the glare of sunlight off Sir Issa's armor and turned to Igrid. "I don't like this."

"Neither do I," Igrid whispered back, adjusting the matching curved shortswords at her belt. "But Thessa's life will be better if both of us come back alive, and that's more likely if I'm with you."

"Agreed." Rowen said even though he had not been speaking just about Thessa. He studied the others, who were waiting restlessly just down the road. All had horses except for Breaksteel. The quiet Olg was too heavy for any but the strongest destrier. Besides that, an Olg could keep pace with anything but the fastest gallop, anyway. Though no one spoke, Breaksteel seemed the least somber of the group. He wore the leather armor of a squire but held his new weapon with special reverence.

When Sir Jontin had pointed out that tradition prevented squires from wielding adamunes, Rowen was tempted to remind Jontin that Rowen himself had carried Knightswrath for months before being knighted by Aeko. He considered rearming Breaksteel with his old mace—a gigantic, clunky thing that was nevertheless devastating in battle. Jontin suggested a more elegant tashi, like the pair Igrid was carrying, lest the Olg forget his training. But the traditional shortsword used by squires looked laughably absurd in Breaksteel's grasp—one hand was bigger than the shortsword's entire hilt. Finally, Rowen decided on a kashpa—an obscure type of polearm that was tall as a man, with a handle nearly as long as its wide, curving blade.

Almost no Knights used them because of their weight, but Rowen found one in the armory, dust coating its kingsteel blade and long handle of leather-wrapped oak. Breaksteel's eyes lit up when Rowen offered it to him. The Olg bowed and had appeared in a kind of awe ever since.

I wish I shared the sentiment. Rowen turned his gaze to Krym. The Dragonkin sat on his horse far ahead of the others, staring northward so stoically that he might as well have been carved from stone. The air around him seemed to shimmer. Rowen remembered Zeia's warning about how powerful Krym already was—and how powerful he would likely become. He reminded himself to keep his mind clear since the Dragonkin had already demonstrated a penchant for reading people's minds.

He turned to Igrid. "I'm glad Jontin sent the letters, at least. Sariel will be safer in Stillhammer."

Igrid said, "Jalist will still want to come help you. Aeko and Hráthbam will, too. And that new queen of the Wytchforest will probably send somebody."

Rowen nodded. Though part of him was desperate for aid, he feared what would happen if any of his friends sought them out. He doubted Krym would approve and feared that the Dragonkin might use force to dismiss them... or worse. "These lands can't survive another war," he said quickly, just to help himself clear his thoughts. "We'll ride north. If we're quick—and lucky, for once—we'll end this long before their help is even needed."

"That is my hope, as well," Krym's voice said. His harsh tone grated inside Rowen's mind, filling him with a sense of violation. He turned his horse and moved slowly to join the others.

Everyone exchanged uneasy glances at Krym's approach, except for Keswen, who eyed the Dragonkin with the same chilly indifference she used to study her straw dummies in the practice yard.

Krym glanced at the huntress then turned his gaze to Zeia. He lowered his eyes, as though momentarily mesmerized by the hands of wytchfire she used to hold the reins. Then he lifted his head abruptly and faced Sir Issa. "Young Knight, please ride back to the stables and fetch us another horse. A small one. Gentle. Give it a saddle and reins and bring it to me at once."

Rowen frowned, wondering if that was another of the Dragonkin's jokes.

Meanwhile, Sir Issa paled under the Dragonkin's attention then cleared his throat. "Apologies, m'lord. If you dislike the mount you have been provided, I would be happy to—"

"I did not say I was dissatisfied." Krym smiled as his eyes narrowed. "I asked you to bring me another horse. Now."

Sir Issa glanced at Rowen, who nodded. As Issa turned and rode back to Cadavash, Rowen said, "May I ask about this delay? We have mounts and supplies enough for—"

"All will be clear in a moment." Krym continued smiling but did not blink. "Now, shall we proceed?"

Rowen glanced back at the walls of Cadavash. He spotted Thessa on the battlements, watching them, as immobile as Krym had been a moment before. "But Sir Issa—"

"The young Knight can catch up. Besides, this is all part of what the good prince would call a demonstration." Krym looked at Saanji and chuckled.

The Dhargothi prince gave Rowen a warning glance.

Rowen touched his sword hilt, biting back his rage. "Very well."

The company rode out, Krym in the lead and Breaksteel bringing up the rear on foot. Keswen rode just behind the Dragonkin. She looked back, catching Rowen's eye, and touched an arrow in her quiver. Rowen caught her meaning. Before he could tell her no, Keswen winced. The huntress's whole body convulsed, as though she'd been stabbed, and she dropped her bow. She reeled for a moment, almost falling from the saddle, then leaned forward and hugged her horse's neck.

Krym did not turn around, but Rowen heard the Dragonkin chuckle.

"Keep moving," Rowen said sternly, resisting the impulse to ride ahead and see if Keswen was all right. Breaksteel retrieved Keswen's bow off the road and carried it to her. She accepted it, hugged it to her chest, and straightened.

They rode in silence until Sir Issa galloped up to join them, leading a rouncey behind him. He offered the reins to Krym, but the latter ignored him. Rowen took the reins instead. Shrugging, Sir Issa took his place in line. Keswen drooped in the saddle, visibly pained, but voiced no complaint.

They rode an hour in silence before Zeia's voice whispered in Rowen's mind: *"A mind-stab. He could have killed her—"*

"But I didn't," Krym interjected. The Dragonkin reined in so abruptly that the closest riders, Keswen and Vaari, nearly ran into him. He turned his horse, addressing Rowen. "The time has come for our little demonstration, I think." He held out his hand. "The other horse, please."

Rowen let go of the reins. Instead of falling, they hovered in the air. Then, an invisible hand tugged them forward. The palfrey cried out but obeyed. When the reins settled in Krym's hand, the Dragonkin turned to regard the empty saddle then looked back at Rowen. "I have acted in good faith. So far, though, all of you have entertained thoughts of mistrust and even murder. Thus, in addition to serving as a demonstration of my power, I hope this will also serve as a suitable but unnecessary warning." He closed his eyes just as an aura of violet light formed around his body. The glow brightened until everyone was forced to look away. Then it shifted.

Wincing, Rowen made himself look. The light moved off Krym's body and coalesced over the saddle of the extra horse. The light swirled and gradually took shape. Too late, Rowen realized what was happening.

"Krym, damn you, stop this!" He drew his sword.

Krym idly stretched out one hand, and a jolt of pain swept through Rowen's arm. A moment later, Rowen lost control of his own limb and watched, horrified, as he stretched out his arm and held the edge of his sword against Igrid's throat.

Keswen and Vaari reached for arrows, but they had hardly fit them to their bowstrings when, strangely, they swiveled in the saddle and aimed not at Krym, but at each other. Surprise showed on their faces, which tightened a moment later in expressions of pain. Zeia and Saanji sat, unmoving. Breaksteel growled like a bear and started forward, light gleaming off the gigantic kingsteel blade of his kashpa, but Sir Issa angled his horse and blocked him.

"Enough," Rowen said. "You've made your point."

"Not just yet." Krym stretched out one hand, reaching for the light that still hovered over the saddle of the palfrey. By then, the light had formed a roughly Human shape. When he touched it, the light took on substance. A moment later, Thessa appeared in the saddle, wide eyed and shaking. Equally surprised by the sudden weight on its back, the palfrey reared up, almost spilling Thessa from the saddle, then pawed the ground.

"Leave her alone," Igrid growled, despite the sword pressed against her throat.

Krym's voice became hard as iron. "If you permit me to leave her alone, I will."

Thessa's eyes met Rowen's then fixed on the drawn sword pressed to Igrid's neck. Then Krym's control faded, and Rowen was able to sheathe his sword.

"It's all right," he called. "I'm sorry, Thessa. Don't be afraid."

"Yes," Krym echoed. "Don't be afraid." He offered Thessa the reins.

The girl blinked and accepted them.

Krym smiled at her then turned north. "Shall we?" He gently flicked the reins and started forward again.

CHAPTER SEVEN

R OWEN MARVELED AT THESSA'S COURAGE. Though the girl had understandably been equal parts terrified and confused, she had sensed the need not to ask questions for the time being. Thus, as the company continued to ride north across the Simurgh Plains, she straightened in the saddle and defiantly ignored all of Krym's various attempts at small talk. Once, though, the Dragonkin reached out and brushed a lock of hair from her eyes. Thessa recoiled, and it took all of Rowen's restraint to keep from drawing his sword again.

Beside him, Igrid tensed, seething, but made no move. Rowen guessed she recognized that they were being baited, just as he did. He remembered what Zeia had told him about the sardonic jest Krym had played on Saanji at their first meeting—having already visited U'dan and killed Saanji's father.

He's not just threatening us, like he said. He's toying with us. Rowen reminded himself of the necessity of keeping his thoughts clear. He tried imagining a wall around his mind, built brick by brick, though he wondered how good he was at such a thing.

They rode on and on in nearly unendurable silence then stopped at midday. Igrid dismounted and went straight to Thessa. Helping the girl down from the saddle, Igrid drew her away and embraced her. When they parted, Igrid whispered something that Rowen could not hear. Meanwhile, Krym watched, expressionless.

He could tell what they're saying if he wanted to. Rowen considered calling out to distract the Dragonkin, but Saanji acted first. The prince urged his horse forward, blocking Krym's view of Igrid and Thessa. To Rowen's surprise, the prince managed to fix the Dragonkin in a cold, unflinching look. Rowen dismounted, but instead of rushing to Thessa as he wanted to, he studied Krym.

With aggravating nonchalance, Krym dismounted next. He stretched then withdrew a canteen from his saddlebag. Despite Krym's demeanor, Rowen saw deep lines of weariness in the Dragonkin's face. Before Rowen could stop himself, he wondered if teleporting Thessa out of Cadavash had wearied Krym more than he was letting on. When Krym did not answer the thought with a sharp retort, Rowen guessed the Dragonkin was not currently reading his mind, either.

He's weaker now. We could attack…

He glanced at Zeia who, like Igrid, was wearing matching shortswords. Zeia gripped each sword hilt with a flaming hand. Her eyes met Rowen's, and Rowen guessed they were thinking the same thing. He looked past her and saw that Keswen and Vaari had drawn back a little, their nearly identical Queshi bows in hand. Something about their easy posture told him that a nod from him and they would fly into action, fitting arrows and firing in a blur of motion. Rowen hesitated. Then he shook his head.

Not yet.

Sir Issa approached and whispered, "Sword Marshal, surely the child need not be a part of this." He nodded toward Thessa, whom Igrid had drawn behind a line of trees for privacy. "This was not part of our deal. Even if all goes well, we're on a hard road. I cannot guarantee—"

"I'm not asking you to guarantee her safety, Issa. I can't guarantee it, either." *Or anyone's.* "Just… keep close to her. You and Breaksteel." The Olg had drawn up behind Issa, close enough to hear, and nodded his shaggy head. Rowen remembered the rodent skulls the Olg had once worn, woven through his braids, and wished Breaksteel had replaced them. If nothing else, they had been a disconcerting sight, and right then, Rowen wanted every advantage he could get. He lowered his voice further. "Krym will expect me and Igrid to—"

"No need for concern, Knight," Krym's voice echoed, making everyone wince. *"None of you can guarantee the child's safety, or your own, for that matter, but I can."*

Rowen felt his temper fray. "If Nekiel is that easily thwarted, I guess you don't need us after all. With your permission, we'll all go home."

Krym patted his horse's neck. "I never said I didn't need you, Knight. I sought out your help, did I not? I could have been content with the Dhargothi prince and his army. Instead, I requested someone with your experience, your honor." A faint tone of mockery showed in Krym's voice.

When Saanji shook his head in warning, Rowen realized he'd half drawn his sword and let it go. "Since you're so fond of altering bargains, Dragonkin, let me propose a change of my own. Let the others go. I'll stay with you." He hesitated. "I'll even submit to a Blood Thrall if that's what it takes."

Igrid flashed him a murderous look, but Krym smiled, impressed. "A tempting offer. I've seen your mind, Knight. I know your brother died from such a thing. And it's true, such agreements must be entered into voluntarily. I should know. We've trained countless assassins that way. Still, personally, I've never cared for Blood Thralls. Blind obedience robs fighters of their passion, and I'd prefer you keep your passions, Knight."

Before Rowen could formulate a proper response, Krym straightened in the saddle, taking on a formal air. "Besides, without Knightswrath, you are no more formidable an ally than any of your friends. The girl stays. *All* of you stay. And since I am already growing weary of this conversation, I insist you not make me suffer it again." Krym mounted his horse and started forward without looking back.

Rowen resisted the impulse either to tell Keswen and Vaari to fire or to order Zeia to strike the Dragonkin with a mind-stab. Instead, he squeezed Thessa's hand. "Gods, child, I'm so sorry," he whispered. "Listen, we're here. Igrid and I are right here. Just—"

"Ride next to me, child," Krym called sweetly.

Thessa winced then stiffened. Forcing a brave smile, she mounted her horse and rode after Krym. Rowen cursed and followed suit, as did the others.

They rode on in silence again. Krym did not signal another halt until sundown. The Dragonkin's eyelids were heavy, and he slumped in the saddle, despite his faint, smug smile. He dismounted, tossed the reins to Breaksteel, and moved toward a copse of trees. "I would like to rest now," he declared. "Carry on as you like, but should I wake and find that any of you have left, I will be irritated."

Rowen considered what Krym had done when amused and shuddered to think what the Dragonkin would do if he were truly angry.

Meanwhile, Krym lay down on the hard ground, still fully dressed, and closed his eyes. A moment later, he opened them and sat up. "One final precaution—though I trust it will not be necessary."

Krym held out one hand, and wytchfire sparked from his fingertips. Rowen braced for an attack. Instead, Krym slowly traced his hand in the dirt around the spot where he had chosen to sleep. The fire lingered faintly in the dirt. When he had completely outlined his body, he lay down, smiling, and shut his eyes.

Rowen saw the others breathe a sigh of relief and wished he could share the sentiment. He moved first to Thessa and embraced her. "Are you all right?"

Thessa nodded. "Don't say you're sorry again. It's all right. I wanted to come anyway." She took her luminstone out of her pocket, cupped it in her open hands, and made it glow. After staring at it a moment, she just as quickly extinguished it and shoved it back into her pocket.

She moved away and sat by the circle of twigs and lumber that Sir Issa and Breaksteel had gathered. Zeia touched the wood with one of her burning hands and ignited it.

"I remember when Maddoc did that," Rowen said. "Scared Sir Berric half to death!" He smiled sadly at the memory of the dead Knight then glanced down at the adamune he was wearing: a newly reforged blade with chrysanthemums etched on the hilt. *Sang Wei's sword... That's two Knights I've lost already.* He thought of Zeia's warning again and glanced around, wondering who would be next.

"Do we act?" Igrid asked. She nodded toward Krym, who slept with his arms crossed, like a carefully composed corpse.

Rowen looked at Zeia, and the Shel'ai approached. She faced Krym for a moment, closed her eyes, and stretched out one flaming hand. Then she opened her eyes and whispered, "He's asleep. He's not listening. I'm sure of it."

"That's all I need to hear," Keswen said, drawing an arrow from her quiver. "Whether or not he can help us against Nekiel, personally, I'd rather face one Dragonkin instead of two."

"Don't be a fool," Zeia said. "I know he hurt you, but you're not going to get revenge with a pointed stick and a string made out of catgut. That fire he conjured isn't the only thing warding him. He has a second invisible wall surrounding him on all sides, I think. Unless he drops his guard, I don't think anything but Knightswrath or another Dragonkin could—"

"Never hurts to try," Keswen said with a shrug.

"Actually," Zeia said, "in this case, it will."

Keswen met Zeia's fierce gaze, unflinching. "Don't glare at *me*, wytch. And don't presume that I'd trust a Shel'ai to—"

"Enough." Rowen stepped between them, then between the huntress and the sleeping Dragonkin. He pushed Keswen's bow down. "Not yet."

"Bastard's toying with us," Vaari grumbled, scratching a sore on his face. "I feel like we're all the doe-eyed virgins and he's the god who came down for a bit of—"

Saanji cleared his throat, cutting off the rest. "I propose we change the subject from suicide to something more helpful. I don't know if anyone's noticed, but the way Krym is taking us, we'll miss Lyos, but we'll pass through Cassica in a few days."

Rowen remembered Saanji had once been a part of the Dhargothi host occupying the city during the war. "Will that be a problem?"

Saanji shrugged. "The Cassicans liked me better than my brothers. Some even followed me and Royce to Hesod. But a few didn't care for me." He touched his ear, part of which was missing. "Mainly, I'm worried about what *he* will do." He nodded toward Krym.

"Agreed," Igrid grumbled. "He doesn't appear to behave in crowds."

Rowen rubbed his eyes. "We'll deal with that later. If we must."

Everyone returned to the fire, where Breaksteel sat cross-legged, his massive kashpa resting across his knees. Thessa held her luminstone for a moment then shyly offered it to Sir Issa, showing him how to cup his hands to summon and dismiss the glow.

"It's happening," Igrid whispered.

"Don't remind me," Rowen growled.

Sir Issa handed the luminstone back to Thessa, smiled, then faced Rowen and cleared his throat. "One thing puzzles me, Sword Marshal."

"Only one?"

"This Krym has been Nekiel's servant for thousands of years. I cannot even fathom that… let alone betraying someone after all that time."

"That's because you're not a Dragonkin." Rowen faced Thessa again and saw a faint spark of excitement in her eyes, a childlike thrill at being part of something big and dangerous. *Gods, what do I tell her?*

As they sat by the fire, Breaksteel put down his kashpa and prepared dinner: a bland vegetable mash, hydrated with water from a canteen and reheated in a copper pot held over the fire. As it simmered, Rowen stood, returned to his horse, and fetched a second sword. It was an old but sturdy shortsword, waisted in the style of Ivairian blades. The sword had been given to him by his brother, stolen, and only recently retrieved.

Rowen looked at Igrid, who read his intent, hesitated, and nodded. For some reason, tears shone in her eyes. Rowen returned to Thessa. He started to prepare a speech, but a lump rose in his throat, so he simply offered her the shortsword, hilt first. She blinked at it.

"For you," he said finally.

Thessa's eyes moistened, and she wobbled as she rose to her feet. Then she accepted the shortsword and slowly drew it. The clean, sharp blade rasped out of its plain leather scabbard, flashing in the setting sun.

"Does it have a name?"

"I never gave it one," Rowen said. "If you want to, that's your business." He remembered Kayden saying that naming weapons or horses was foolish since both tended not to last, but he kept that to himself.

Igrid joined them, gently but insistently took the shortsword and scabbard from Thessa's hands, and sheathed it. Unwinding the sword belt wrapped around the scabbard, she slowly, carefully girded the sword around Thessa's waist. "Listen, sewer rat. This isn't a toy, and we aren't in Cadavash anymore. Out here, your enemies won't be made of shadows or straw. They'll be flesh and blood—same as the people counting on you to protect them. Understand?"

Thessa nodded, speechless.

"Good girl," Igrid said. "Congratulations. You're standing the first watch."

Keswen kept an arrow on her bowstring, holding it in place with the same hand that held the bow, and squeezed Thessa's shoulder. "I'll sit with you," she offered. "There's a rock over there with moss on it. If we're lucky, it won't give us welts."

The two walked off, Keswen warily eyeing Krym, Thessa still speechless and beaming. Igrid slid her arm through Rowen's. Everyone else sat by the fire—save Vaari, who rose, stretched, and stepped away. The Dhargothi bodyguard shifted from one foot to the other, idly twirling his bow between his fingers. Then he spun on his heel, drew an arrow from his quiver, and fired.

The arrow sped through the darkening air, perfectly aimed at Krym's sleeping face. When it met the space above the flaming line Krym had traced in the dirt, though, a sheet of violet fire roared to life. The flames leapt up, slapping the arrow higher into the air, and it arced over Krym's body, burning to ashes in midair.

Krym continued to sleep, unperturbed.

Rowen wheeled to face Vaari, who shrugged and twirled his bow again. "Don't scowl at *me*, Knight. It was worth a try." Vaari returned to the fire and sat back down, too far away for Rowen to strike him.

Aeko Shingawa sat in her study, scowling into her steaming cup of tea and waiting for her friend to finish with the scrap of paper she had handed him. She guessed that, by then, Father Matua must have read the message a dozen times. However, when she looked up, the one-armed cleric still clutched the message and stared at it, his brow knit with consternation.

"Staring at it won't change what it says," Aeko said. "I know. I've tried."

Father Matua finally looked up, returning the parchment with a trembling hand. As he did so, lamplight illuminated the half of his face that had been ravaged by fire, where the skin still retained the appearance of wrinkled cloth. "And... you're sure this isn't a trick of some kind?"

Aeko glanced down at the message again even though, like Matua, she had read it so many times by then that she could have committed it to memory. "It's Rowen's signature, it arrived by wytch-raven, and it's bad news. I'm not sure we need any more proof than that."

Father Matua sat back in his chair, steam from his own untouched teacup rising in the air before him. "More Dragonkin..."

"Most of them corpses, at least. I'll send a message of my own to Briel. He's the closest to the Dead Shores. Locke probably already did the same, but I'll make sure Briel sends men to see if those bodies are there, like Krym says."

For the first time, Father Matua grasped his teacup. He stared into it but did not drink. "I have a bad feeling they will be."

"Which means the rest of what Krym said might be true as well," Aeko finished. "Nekiel..." She could not finish, thinking of all those who had died—first in fighting Fadarah, then the Dhargots, then Chorlga. Most recently, still more had died trying to keep Crovis Ammerhel and Algol from bringing down the Dragonward, but the thought of Nekiel loose in Ruun was even more horrific.

"Do you think this is a coincidence?" Father Matua set his cup down, sloshing it slightly, so that some of the dark tea ran down the side onto the table. "You only just agreed to Lord Jalist's request and sent Gaulgodd to stand trial in Stillhammer."

"Gods, I hadn't thought of that." Aeko rubbed her eyes. "It *could* be a coincidence, I suppose. Rowen didn't even know about that yet. I don't see how this Krym could have known, either, or what good that knowledge would do him."

"Could be they'll miss each other entirely," Matua offered. "If the Knights take the most direct route, they'll follow the coast, straight down to Stillhammer. If Krym is taking Rowen and the others to the Wintersea, he'll likely go straight north, across the Simurgh Plains. Depending on which they prefer to avoid, they'll either pass Cassica or Ivairia, neither of which would be glad to see them."

Aeko smiled sourly. "Except that I told the prisoner escorts to *avoid* the most obvious route, in case there are still any Sons of Maelmohr left hiding in the Red Steppes." She traced one fingertip on the table, imagining it was a map. "As it is, all of this lines up a bit too perfectly."

"But Gaulgodd's nothing to Krym," Matua said. "Besides, given Gaulgodd's hatred for all things associated with magic, wouldn't a Dragonkin regard him as an enemy, albeit a puny one?"

"Yes," Aeko conceded, "but I've given up on expecting our enemies to behave the way we'd expect them to." She drained her teacup despite the heat of the liquid. Swallowing it made her eyes water, but the pain helped her focus.

For a long time, neither spoke. A squire quietly entered the study, refilled their teacups, gave Aeko a worried look when she declined an offer of food, and left.

Finally, Matua said, "You think Gaulgodd and Krym are working together?"

"Unlikely," Aeko said. "Then again, I always thought it was a bit too convenient that Gaulgodd formed an alliance with Crovis, of all people, just in time to help him bring down the Dragonward."

"I trust your interrogators asked him that."

"I asked him myself," Aeko said. "He never answered, no matter how much I threatened him. Not one solitary word. Part of me wanted to enlist the aid of a couple Dhargothi torturers, but the way Gaulgodd smirked through his cell bars, something told me he'd enjoy that." Aeko shrugged. "I miss the days when my enemies simply appeared on the battlefield, as plain as daylight."

"Oh, really, Grand Marshal? And when were those days?"

"Never," Aeko conceded. She lifted her tea and took a small sip. "But it would make a better dream than the ones I'm likely to have tonight."

Matua lifted his own cup. "To better dreams."

"Perhaps in the next life." Aeko stared at the table, imagining a map again.

"Do you want to send a warning to Rowen?" Matua interrupted.

Aeko was already considering that very thing. She traced the tabletop, imagining the various cities and towns of the Simurgh Plains, as well as the hills and small rivers that might affect the trajectory of travelers. "No," she said finally. "Locke needs an army, not a messenger. If past events are any indication, though, he'll go from throat-deep in trouble to drowning in it, long before any help arrives."

"And... what help will you be sending?"

Aeko considered that. If Rowen had tentatively agreed to help Krym hunt down Nekiel, the sudden arrival of hundreds of anxious, angry Knights might complicate matters. On the other hand, even if Nekiel was slain, they would still have Krym to deal with. Finally, Aeko said, "I'll ride west and find them myself."

Matua's brow furrowed with disapproval. "Are you sure? You're the Grand Marshal now. Your place—"

"If you can name one duty more important than protecting Ruun from Dragonkin, I'll gladly stay behind."

Matua shifted uneasily. "And how many Knights will you take with you?"

"That depends. How many swords does it take to kill a god?"

"The Dragonkin aren't gods."

"They might as well be." Aeko sighed. "I'll take a hundred Knights. Any more than that, and we'll get there too late to be of use."

Matua's scarred face tensed with disapproval. "Are you sure a hundred is enough?"

"I'm not sure a thousand is enough," Aeko said, "but that's more than I have." She lifted.

her teacup. "To the end of the world."

"To the end of the world," Matua answered weakly and drank.

CHAPTER EIGHT

MIRIAM STARED AT THE TOWN before her, its windows lit by lanterns as twilight darkened the countryside. She had seen small fishing villages before but never anything like that. Instead of straw huts, the buildings were built from adobe or even wood. Though she guessed the town was nothing compared to the big cities farther east, the tavern had real glass in the windows. A fat well sat in the middle of town, where people of all sorts gathered freely, laughing in the waning light.

She leaned against a barn and listened to the strangers speaking in friendly voices to each other. She could not make out the words, but they seemed to be talking about battles to the north, battles to the east—everywhere, someone fighting. *But not here.*

She studied the townspeople. Though they were not as finely dressed as the boy from the sea, they still wore clean and untattered clothes. She even saw pretty young women walking alone, smiling, with no men mistreating them. Then the smell of stew, emanating from the tavern, reached her nostrils. Her stomach growled. Before Miriam realized what she was doing, she took a step from the shadows, toward the tavern. She quickly caught herself and stepped back, but not before a man saw her.

He wiped his hands on an apron girded around his thick belly. Despite his white hair and wrinkled face, his arms were thick and well muscled, streaked with soot that made her think he must be a blacksmith. "Gods, *another* orphan?"

A passing woman paused at the blacksmith's statement, eyeing

Miriam with suspicion, as did the little girl she was leading by the hand. Both the woman and the girl had hair that hung to their waists, the color of a raven's wing. Miriam blushed, withdrawing farther into the shadows, wishing she could disappear.

Then a young man joined them, the light from his lantern flashing off armor comprised of overlapping scales of black and brown leather. "Easy, girl. You don't have to run. Old Farl didn't mean to scare you. If you're hungry, we'll feed you. But don't steal unless you want Farl to flatten your hands with his hammer." The armored man winked.

"That's right," the blacksmith growled. "Fact is, I like smashing little girls almost as much as I like feeding them and sending them on their way." He pulled a thick iron hammer from his apron and brandished it.

The woman with the little girl rolled her eyes. "Enough, Farl." She held out her hand. "Come, girl. Don't be afraid. They're just teasing you. Farl would sooner smash his own hands than harm a fly."

"Fine, Lorna. Tell the hungry little orphans *all* my secrets!" The blacksmith laughed and walked away.

Miriam hesitated then moved slowly out of the shadows and took Lorna's hand.

The woman's eyes widened. "Your face, child! Gods, you're hurt."

The armored man frowned. He stepped closer, raising his lantern. "Did someone hurt you, child? Are they still close by?"

"What about your family?" Lorna pressed. "Do you have one?"

Just my brothers, Miriam wanted to say. Instead, she thought once again of her farmhouse burning, burning with the bodies of her parents inside it, and her eyes welled with tears. She opened her mouth, but no words came out. Instead, she fell forward, sobbing.

Lorna caught her. "It's all right, child." She stroked Miriam's hair.

Miriam felt a smaller hand touching her shoulder, too, and realized it was Lorna's daughter's.

Then Lorna's tone changed, taking on an edge. "I'll tend to her, Glem, but gather some strong lads and arm them, in case whoever did this is still close by."

Miriam saw the armored man, Glem, standing behind Lorna. He smiled at Miriam, then his expression hardened. With a gruff nod, he turned and moved through the town, calling for volunteers.

Miriam could not tell what was happening. She tried to stop crying, but that only made her cry harder. Finally, Lorna half led, half carried her toward a nearby cottage. As they passed Glem and a growing crowd of young men, they sounded as though they were getting ready to go hunt something.

Rowen had the last watch before dawn. Krym woke first, though instead of rising, the Dragonkin simply sat cross-legged in the same place where he had slept and closed his eyes. The earth around him continued to glimmer with a faint sputter of wytchfire, and Rowen had no doubt that the Dragonkin's magical barriers still protected him, though he could not guess what Krym was doing.

"Divination," Zeia whispered, joining him a moment later.

Rowen frowned. "Why? We know the direction we're going, and we must still be too far to look for Nekiel."

Zeia shrugged and went to help Breaksteel, Vaari, and Keswen ready the horses. Meanwhile, Igrid and Thessa stood off in the distance, the former showing the latter how to hold and swing her new shortsword, the heft and balance of which were far different than the wooden practice sword she was used to. Saanji and Issa approached Rowen a moment later.

Issa said, "Do we ride north, Sword Marshal?"

Rowen glanced at Krym, who still sat statue-like in his meditative pose. "Not yet, it seems. But I'd appreciate it if you two would scout around a little. I don't recall any villages in these parts, but if any have sprung up or if there's a merchant caravan passing by, I'd like to know about it." Though he doubted Krym was eavesdropping, he lowered his voice. "The less attention we draw, the better."

Saanji nodded. "That's such a good reason, I won't even blame you for making me get back on a horse." The Dhargothi prince attempted to rub a sore spot in his back as he moved toward the horses.

Zeia intercepted him, ignited one flaming hand, and pressed the spot exactly.

Saanji jerked then smiled. "Gods, woman…" He turned and embraced the Shel'ai for a moment then kissed her. To Rowen's surprise, Zeia returned his affection then noticed Rowen's scrutiny and scowled.

These days are full of surprises. Rowen smiled to himself as he moved to join Igrid and Thessa. He offered some additional instruction, but mostly he just watched, heartened just to be near them.

An hour passed, then two. The companions broke their fast on bland but hot porridge, then Saanji and Issa rode ahead to scout. They returned while the others were still resting and said they'd found neither a village nor a traveler for miles in any direction.

Saanji glanced at Krym, who remained unmoved. "Perhaps he's lost in prayer," he muttered.

We should be so lucky. Though Rowen hoped Krym was still too distracted with his divination to eavesdrop on them, he knew that could change any moment. "Keep your thoughts as clear as you can," he told everyone.

They nodded, though Thessa's eyes darted back and forth until Igrid leaned and whispered something in her ear that made Thessa laugh.

More time passed. Though the horses stood saddled and ready, Krym still had not stirred. Rowen considered addressing him then decided the others could use a little time away from the Dragonkin to adjust to their new and frightful situation. He began a rotating schedule, sending them out in pairs to scout the surrounding countryside while he remained near Krym to explain, in case the Dragonkin came to and wondered where some of them had gone.

Though the exercise seemed to raise spirits, Rowen was surprised when midday came and Krym still had not moved. Finally, all at once, Krym opened his eyes and stood. Without a hint of weariness or sore muscles, the Dragonkin stood and strode so purposefully toward Rowen that the latter tensed.

"We will not move from this place until midday tomorrow." He turned and started back toward the spot where he'd been before.

Rowen followed. "Wait, m'lord. Can you tell us why—"

"All will be made clear tomorrow." Krym knelt and traced wytchfire around his body again. "All my previous warnings remain in place. Continue to scout the area, or play with your swords, or make love if it suits you. But do not run away." Despite the levity in his tone, a spark of malice shone in Krym's eyes.

"Are we waiting for someone?" Rowen pressed.

"Yes," Krym answered, "though it isn't Nekiel. My former master remains hidden from me for the time being." The Dragonkin closed his eyes.

Rowen was tempted to drop the matter, but his irritation grew. "Lord Krym, I am responsible for my friends' lives. If we're waiting for someone, I need to know who it is."

Krym smiled but did not open his eyes. "Your objection is noted, Knight. Now, please be quiet. I suggest you not disturb me again, let alone touch me—unless you want your hand to burn up like that Dhargot's arrow did."

Rowen blinked then stepped back. He cast a withering glance at Vaari, who watched from a distance then moved toward the horses. He decided that he might as well do a little scouting himself before his temper got the best of him. Igrid started to follow then appeared to think better of it and moved closer to Thessa. Meanwhile, Thessa was busy swinging her gleaming shortsword at thin air. Igrid chided the girl for overcommitting to her swings then for spacing her feet too widely apart.

May you never have to swing at anything more solid than air. Rowen flicked his reins.

Miriam woke on a straw bed with no knowledge of how she'd gotten there. She looked down and saw that in place of her torn and filthy clothing, she was wearing a dress of plain wool. Though it was too big for her, the cloth felt soft against her skin. She turned her head and saw Lorna standing nearby over a cooking fire, singing softly to herself as she stirred a pot with a wooden spoon. The smoke from the fire rose and floated out a hole in the roof.

The little girl Miriam had seen earlier was sitting in a washtub, talking to her doll. She looked up and saw Miriam was awake. She grinned, called to her mother, and pointed. Miriam blushed.

Lorna smiled. "Are you hungry, child? You slept so long I was about to fetch a priest!"

Miriam did not know whether to say yes or apologize for sleeping too long. "My name is Miriam," she said instead.

"Glad to meet you, Miriam. My name is Lorna. That's Roslind."

She nodded to the little girl, who waved happily, splashing water onto the floor. Lorna dropped a towel and mopped up the water with her foot then pivoted and handed Miriam a bowl of vegetables floating in steaming broth. "It's not much, I'm afraid. Bad harvest this year."

Miriam seized the wooden spoon and raised the broth to her lips. The smell of pepper filled her nostrils and made her stomach growl. She started on the bowl and did not stop until it was gone.

Lorna laughed and refilled it then wrapped Roslind in a towel and lifted her from the washtub. "Do you have any family nearby, little one?"

Miriam stopped eating. "My brothers. But I don't know where they are."

"Are they the ones who hurt you?" When Miriam did not answer, Lorna finished drying Roslind's hair then hung the wet towel from a thick wire suspended from the ceiling, near the cooking fire. "I'm sorry to press, child, but if there are bad men nearby, Glem and Farl need to know. We have to be careful if we're going to protect this town from robbers."

"I'm not a robber," Miriam said.

"I know. But others are. And some are worse than that."

While Roslind stood over the cooking pot and stirred it, still nude, Lorna nodded toward a table by the bed. For the first time, Miriam saw her black glass knife lying there. Lorna came closer and sat on the edge of the bed. "That knife had some blood on it. That's good, child. That means you defended yourself. Nobody's angry. But we need to know if there are other bad men out there."

Miriam shuddered, remembering the boys that had chased her. "I don't think so. I think they're far away." She paused. "They tried to hurt my friend, too."

Lorna raised one eyebrow. "Your friend. Where is she now?"

"*He,*" Miriam corrected. "I don't know his name, but I met him by the Dead Shores. They were chasing him, too. But he got away and left me." She looked down and stirred her broth with the wooden spoon.

"And your brothers. Do you think they're looking for you?"

Miriam shrugged. "Maybe. They were. But they'll be mad. I ran away from them to help my friend."

Lorna took the bowl then set it on the table. "Lie down, child. Rest some more. We'll talk more after—"

A harsh knock on the door made Miriam jump. The door opened before Lorna could answer, and the blacksmith walked in. He hardly glanced at Miriam but smiled warmly at Roslind, who waved from the cooking fire. Then he looked at Lorna. His expression darkened.

"We found... something." The blacksmith scowled at Miriam. "Bodies. A whole heap of them."

Miriam reached for her knife and held it. Numbness crept up her arm from where she was gripping the handle, but she held it anyway. "That wasn't me! I cut one boy when he tried to grab me and another when he—"

"That couldn't have been her," Lorna echoed, rising to her feet.

"I know." The blacksmith glanced at Miriam's knife. "All these boys were"—he glanced at Roslind and lowered his voice—"*burned*. Charred black as firewood. Their mouths were open, and it looked like they died screaming."

Lorna gave the blacksmith a look of disapproval. "Gods, Farl."

"We found one boy alive, though," Farl continued. "Scared half to death, running so fast Glem had to throw the butt of his spear to knock him down. The boy said he and his friends had been chasing two children, but they got away. Then one came back, only he wasn't the same as before."

Lorna said, "Not the same—how?"

Farl leaned toward Lorna and whispered something in her ear. Lorna's eyes widened. Farl straightened and crossed his arms. "The boy said the man wanted revenge. He told the boys he was doing this to get even for a girl they'd tried to hurt." Farl fixed his gaze on Miriam. "Anything else you want to tell us, child?"

Miriam stared, uncomprehending.

Lorna said, "Child, you said you had a friend—"

"A boy," Miriam said. "My age. I pulled him from the sea."

Farl took a menacing step closer. "Did he have purple eyes?"

Miriam blinked. "No. Blue. *Weird* blue, kind of like ice."

Lorna touched Farl's arm. "She's telling the truth. Besides, this boy sounds too young to be who you're talking about."

Farl scowled. "None of this makes any damn sense." He took a step back. "Put that knife down, girl. I won't hurt you, but I'll not have you waving that thing around my wife and daughter."

Miriam lowered the knife.

Farl grunted his approval, walked over to the cooking fire, and tasted the contents of the pot. Then he scooped up Roslind, tossed her toward the ceiling, and caught her as she tumbled back down. Farl, Lorna, and Roslind all laughed in unison.

Miriam touched her knife and stared, speechless.

CHAPTER NINE

ROWEN GLARED AT THE SUNRISE, irritated that the new day had found them camped exactly where they had been before. Krym slept, woke, and meditated, all without moving from his spot. He neither ate nor spoke, and everyone else kept their distance. Rowen sent Keswen, Issa, and Breaksteel to scout the area, though Keswen looked none too pleased at being forced to travel in the Olg's company.

When they returned, Issa reported they'd seen a company of clerics traveling in the distance. Luckily, the mere sight of Breaksteel had driven them away. *All the better for them.* Rowen eyed Krym. Then he sent the three out again. They returned at midday. That time, they'd spotted a caravan of merchants.

"They're heading northwest, right for us. Noshans and Queshi, looks like," Issa said. "Maybe twenty guards. They look peaceful enough, though."

"It's not them I'm afraid of." Rowen glanced at Krym again, who remained unstirred. Rowen was tempted to ride out and meet the caravan himself, but he did not want to leave Krym's side. "Breaksteel, stay here this time. Issa, ride out and meet them. Tell them you've seen bandits in the area. Warn them to veer north. Make up whatever story you have to."

Issa blushed. "The Codex Lotius says that lying is—"

"I'll do the lying," Saanji offered. "If they're heading northwest, they're probably hoping to trade with us, anyway."

Igrid said, "I didn't know Noshans and Queshi thought much of Dhargots."

Saanji chuckled. "I've been working hard to change that. At any rate, in the interest of avoiding awkward questions, I might avoid telling them who I am." He turned to Zeia. "You stay here, for the same reason."

Issa blushed further. "Forgive me, but I cannot lie—"

"You won't have to," Saanji said. "Just sit there quietly and scowl. I'll take care of the rest. In fact, it'll be my pleasure. It's been too long since I told a good lie. Vaari, let's go."

Rowen turned to find Saanji's bodyguard eyeing Igrid a bit too closely. "Good idea," he said dourly.

Saanji, Vaari, and Issa mounted their horses and rode southeast, and Rowen watched them go.

Zeia joined Rowen a moment later. "Not to start trouble, Locke, but did you catch how Saanji's man was looking at Igrid?"

"I was just thinking of how I'd like to drown him in boiling tar, if that answers your question."

"That wasn't the first time," Zeia said, "and back at Cadavash, I saw him eyeing that dark-skinned squire like it was all he could do to—"

"Saanji vouched for him," Rowen interrupted. "I figured you would, too."

Zeia shook her head. "He keeps his mind walled, even when he's asleep. I've never known anybody who wasn't a Shel'ai who could do that. Might just be that he's clever. But no, I don't exactly trust him. Neither does Saanji." She paused. "It's not that he's done anything particularly loathsome. It's more like a feeling that if Saanji told him to cut a child's throat or drown a sack full of kittens, he would do it without batting an eyelash."

"Some would call that loyalty," Rowen offered with a cold smile.

"True," Zeia said, "but you aren't one of them. Neither is Saanji. And the world is better for it."

"What else do you know about him?"

"Vaari?" Zeia shrugged. "Almost nothing. We found him in a cell after we liberated a city held by the Red Emperor. He said he was jailed for killing some general's son in a bar fight. The Red Emperor's men had done... all manner of things to him. He said he wanted revenge. Some of the generals advised us to just kill him, but Saanji wouldn't listen." She hesitated. "Truth is, he's probably saved Saanji's life just as many times as I have, but he has a taste for killing that reminds me of Shade."

Rowen felt his stomach tighten at the mention of the late Shel'ai who had so terribly tormented Rowen's brother, Kayden. "If Vaari killed somebody's favorite Dhargot, they'd impale him, not imprison him. Could be he's lying."

"I can't imagine why," Zeia countered. "Like I said, Locke, I don't trust him. But he's had plenty of opportunities to cut Saanji's throat when I'm not around and hasn't taken them. Besides, when we found him, he was cut half to pieces and was supposed to be impaled the next morning. I'm surprised he lived at all."

"What are you asking me to do here, Zeia?"

"Same thing I'm doing," Zeia said. "Keep your damn eyes open."

Rowen rubbed his eyes, fighting back a sudden headache. "Fine. I'll watch him. Anything else?"

"Yes."

Zeia touched Rowen's temple, erasing his headache with a warm jolt of magic, then nodded toward Breaksteel. The Olg was standing at the far edge of the camp, practicing with his kashpa, the great blade hissing as it swept through the air.

That time, Rowen smiled at Zeia's complaint. "Aren't you the one who saved his life after that battle with the Sons of Maelmohr?"

Zeia shrugged. "That was Igrid's order. Besides, not wanting him dead is one thing. Arming a gigantic Olg with a massive horse-cleaver and asking him to stand guard while we sleep is quite another."

"I see your point, but he's a squire—and a good one. Sir Jontin and Sir Issa didn't trust him either, at first. Now—"

"What about Keswen?"

Rowen looked toward where the huntress sat, facing away from the campfire, meticulously inspecting each of her arrows. "Well, she's stopped threatening to kill him. That's a start." Rowen glanced at Krym again. "Listen, you don't need to convince me that we're a godsdamned mess, but that's nothing new. We just need to hold this together until—"

"Until we face the deadliest Dragonkin who ever lived." Zeia sighed. "Perfect." She walked away.

Rowen approached Igrid and Thessa next.

Igrid caught the look on Rowen's face and told Thessa to practice her fighting steps while she drew away to talk to him in private. "What is it?"

"Vaari was staring at you." Rowen felt ridiculous as soon as he said it.

Igrid laughed. "Two thirds of your Knights stare at me, including a few I think prefer the bed company of men. What does it matter?"

"Maybe it doesn't," Rowen said, "but you saw how he fired that arrow at Krym—"

"Which I would have done, too, if I'd had a bow handy." Igrid flashed a cockeyed grin and prodded his arm. "Relax, Sword Marshal. You look like an oaf when you're tense." She went back to instructing Thessa.

Rowen restlessly paced the camp. When Breaksteel took notice, the Olg stopped swinging his kashpa, picked up a wooden bowl, and waved it at Rowen. For a moment, Rowen thought the squire was asking to be fed. Then he realized he had it backward.

"I'm fine." He reminded himself of the Olg's famous appetite, which was all the more difficult to sate since Breaksteel ate no meat. "But start on the midday meal if you like."

Breaksteel smiled, flashing teeth that Rowen was glad to see were in better shape than they'd been when the Olg first came to Cadavash. He sighed and paced the camp some more, stopped to tend the horses, then drew closer to Krym, minding the Dragonkin's warning not to get too close. Instead, he sat on a boulder a few yards from where the Dragonkin continued to mediate. Rowen drew his sword—slowly, to keep the blade from rasping too loudly—and used his fingertip to trace the chrysanthemums etched into the kingsteel.

I wish Sang Wei were here. We could use someone with faith.

The sound of galloping horses brought him to his feet. He turned to see Saanji, Vaari, and Issa rushing back to the camp. All three wore scowls on their faces. Issa had his adamune drawn, blood trickling down the blade. Blood streaked Vaari's face as well.

"What happened?"

"What happened is my bodyguard nearly got us killed," Saanji snapped. He dismounted and stalked off without saying more.

Vaari rolled his eyes, dismounted, and started toward the fire.

Rowen grabbed his arm. "What a coincidence. We were just talking about you."

"How lovely for you." Vaari twisted his arm in a peculiar circle, breaking free of Rowen's grip.

Rowen concealed his surprise behind a scowl. "Why don't *you* tell me what happened?"

"What happened is that the prince was talking, spinning a fine yarn of golden dung, and one of the merchants' guards loosed a crossbow bolt. It barely missed us. *My* arrow didn't."

"And the blood on your face?"

Issa spoke next. "After Vaari felled the guard, three more rushed us. The merchants were shouting for them to stop. They wouldn't." His expression brimmed with regret as he drew out a cloth, wiped his blade, and returned it to its scabbard.

Vaari said, "The young Knight and I killed those three, quick as lightning, and the rest slumped off—which is what I'm going to do unless you insist otherwise." The bodyguard touched the hilt of his sword, unmistakable threat in his eyes.

Rowen let him back away. When Vaari was gone, he faced Issa again. "Is that how it happened?"

Issa hesitated. "The merchants were shouting at the guards the whole time. They didn't want a fight. Most of the guards didn't, either... which was lucky for us since they outnumbered us seven to one. It was just those three who wouldn't quit. I cut two—not fatal, but enough to stop them. Vaari did worse with the last one. If the man hasn't returned to the Light by now, I'd guess he will by sundown."

Rowen swore and scanned the eastern horizon. "Well, they aren't charging us."

"Nor will they, I think. The merchants took responsibility. They swore they wouldn't take revenge. But the guard who fired his crossbow, the one who started all this, I don't think it was deliberate. He just had his crossbow spanned, and he was holding the damn thing up, trying to look tough, and—"

Rowen waved off the rest. *Two men dead.* "I'm surprised I didn't hear anything."

"It was quick." Issa hesitated again. "Vaari moved faster than anything I've ever seen. He had that arrow fitted and fired before the crossbow bolt had even hit the ground. Even Saanji looked surprised, and he's known Vaari for a year. I'd… I'd be careful with him, m'lord." Issa headed toward the fire, still shaking his head.

Rowen stood for a moment, unsure how to proceed. He cursed again, pressing his knuckles against the hard surface of the boulder on which he had been sitting. Then he looked up and noticed that even though Krym's eyes were still closed, the Dragonkin smiled faintly.

Miriam winced as Lorna dragged a comb of bone through her wet, tangled hair. "Ouch!"

"Sorry, child," Lorna said.

Instead of answering, Miriam picked up a ball made of wadded-up rags and tossed it back to Roslind. The little girl dove for it, missed, laughed, then chased after it like a puppy. Miriam wanted to go outside, but Lorna had forbidden her from leaving the cottage. However, given the suspicious way Farl kept looking at her, Miriam half expected the residents of the town would drive her away at any moment, back into the wild. As scared as she still was of Farl, after two days of meals and rest, Miriam was even more scared of being on her own again.

Miriam eyed the cooking fire by which Farl sat, scowling at the head of a spear. The shaft of the spear rested on the wooden floor while Farl turned and turned the spearhead on his lap, sometimes scraping part of it with a sharpening stone, other times wiping it with an oiled rag.

Miriam said, "Are you going to make me leave soon?"

"Not if you don't want to," Lorna answered. "This town isn't some clerics' orphanage, though. If you want to stay here, at least until your brothers find you, you'll have to work. We have gardens, farms, roofs that need mending—"

"And I could always use an apprentice," Farl snarled, "provided those straw arms of yours have more muscle than they appear to!"

"I can work," Miriam snapped. "When Ma was alive, I helped her wash clothes. And I helped Da take care of the goats and fish and stack wood… until the winter sickness killed them both."

Farl raised one eyebrow then returned his attention to his spear. Lorna's comb paused then resumed its motion through Miriam's hair.

Miriam felt tiny droplets of water shooting off her hair, peppering her bare shoulders.

Lorna said, "No winter sickness here. And no robbers or plague, either, so long as we all stick together. Everybody in this town helps each other. We have to, with the world the way it is."

"I understand."

Lorna squeezed Miriam's shoulder and kept combing. "I know you do, child."

"Tell her what the town's called," Farl said. Though his voice sounded gruff, there was a touch of pride in it.

Lorna said, "This town is called Strongwall, child. Can you guess why?"

Miriam shook her head. "I didn't see any walls around the town."

"That's because here, the walls aren't made of wood and iron. They're made of men and women who are sworn to protect each other."

Miriam thought her brothers would have laughed if they'd heard that, but Miriam smiled. "I like that. What about my friend? If he comes back, can he stay in Strongwall, too?"

Farl lifted his gaze and scowled at her but said nothing. Lorna was quiet for so long that Miriam thought the woman had not heard her.

When she finally spoke, her voice sounded softer. "Are you sure he's your friend, child? Whatever he is, it sounds more like he's—"

Someone pounded on the door. Farl leapt up, spear in hand. Miriam reached reflexively for her knife then remembered that Farl had taken it—cursing at how cold it felt—and placed it on the top shelf in the pantry. Lorna gathered Roslind and carried her to the back of the tiny cottage while Farl answered the door.

Glem, the town guard, stood in the doorway. He looked out of breath. "Greatwolf," he said.

Farl swore. "Where?"

"A ways east of here. Gnawed up a couple of Lem's sheep. His son went after it, but—"

"Alone?" Farl swore again. "Didn't Lem try and stop him?"

"He tried, but the greatwolf had already taken a chunk out of *his* leg, too. His girls ran all the way to Strongwall to tell us."

Farl hefted his spear and turned to Lorna, who was already approaching, Roslind in her arms. "Back in a while, my little ravens."

Farl kissed Roslind's forehead then his wife's lips, and he followed Glem out the door.

"I should go, too," Miriam said. "Give me back my knife, and I'll help."

Lorna set Roslind down and stared out the window. Miriam repeated her request. When Lorna still did not answer, Miriam started to say it a third time.

"Enough," Lorna snapped. "I've seen broomsticks more threatening than you, child. Just keep quiet and let me worry." She moved toward the cooking fire.

Miriam followed. "But Farl doesn't trust me."

"So? He doesn't know you yet, child. It takes time to earn trust."

"But *you* trust me."

"That's different."

"How?"

"Gods know. It just is!" Lorna rubbed her eyes, as though she'd gotten something in both of them at once. Finally, she grabbed a towel and used it to shield her fingers as she lifted a cooking pot away from the fire. When Roslind moved toward the cooking pot, Lorna said, "Not yet, little one. It's not ready yet." She straightened and faced Miriam. "I'm going out to go talk to the other mothers. Stay with Roslind. Keep her inside. Can you do that?"

Miriam nodded. She was about to speak, but Lorna was already heading for the door. Miriam watched her go. She looked at Roslind—who stared up at her, smiling, raising her arms to show she wanted to be held—then at the cooking fire, then Farl's empty chair.

"If they trusted me, I bet they'd let my friend stay here, too. Maybe even my brothers, if they promise to be nice."

Realizing she was talking to herself again, Miriam stopped. She slipped on a pair of shoes Lorna had given her then grasped Farl's chair and dragged it toward the pantry.

CHAPTER TEN

G ENERAL BRIEL MUTTERED A STREAM of curses as he briskly
ascended the massive walkway through the city of Shaffrilon,
higher and higher up the World Tree, toward the palace. Sun
spilled through the trees and warmed his face, making him perspire in his
armor as he hastened along. He had been stationed on the World Gate
when the messenger arrived. The tiny scrap of parchment, sent from
Cadavash by Rowen Locke, had arrived in the forest by wytch-raven.
Such birds were supposed to know the way blindfolded, but somehow,
this one had gone to the garrison at Ish'kana, instead of Shaffrilon, the
capital. Though the delay had been relatively minor, Briel knew that
seconds might as well be hours, as far as Dragonkin were concerned.

Too late. It's probably already too damn late.

Shaking his head, Briel quickened his pace, ducking around carts
and ignoring the salutes of guards, hurrying higher and higher up the
walkway. By the time he passed the Hall of Questions, his legs ached, but
he kept going. Glancing over the side of the walkway, he saw the sheer
drop hundreds of feet down to the forest floor. Someone called his name.

Briel whirled, one hand on his sword. Kilisti was rushing to catch up
with him. Like Briel, she was dressed in black fighting leathers. Her face
was badly scarred, and the tip of her nose and part of one ear were missing.

She slowed and frowned. "I wondered if you were ever going to
hear me!"

Briel noted that, once again, Kilisti had not bothered referring to him by his title. He had all but given up chiding her for that, though. "Apologies. Now, if you'll stop shouting, I have to—"

"No threats or insults? Gods, it must be even worse news than I thought."

Before Briel could stop her, Kilisti snatched the parchment from his hand then turned sideways before he could snatch it back. Briel glared at her. Kilisti's eyes widened when she read the message.

She passed it back. "Is this real?"

Briel spun around and continued toward the palace. Kilisti fell in beside him, the pace of her shadow matching his own. "I'll send some men to look for the bodies," she offered.

Briel nodded gruffly. "Do that." He half hoped she would see to the duty immediately. Instead, she continued to match his pace toward the palace, which was finally visible in the distance: a tall, narrow structure topped in dizzying white spires, draped in green banners, and surrounded by statues of the gods, all of it built at the very edge of the walkway. Smartly armored guards stood outside. They tensed at the sight of Briel and Kilisti's rapid approach but saluted when they recognized them.

"We need to see the queen." Briel's tone brokered no argument.

The guards had barely stepped aside before Briel pushed the door open and strode into the palace, Kilisti a step behind. Inside the palace, servants and more guards turned, startled by their abrupt entrance.

Briel grabbed a passing servant. "Garden or tomb?"

The servant's eyes widened. "General?"

Briel shook the man.

Kilisti touched Briel's arm and asked, "Is the queen in the garden or not?"

The servant shook his head. "She broke her fast in the garden, but that was two hours ago. By now, I don't know—"

"Is she meeting with anyone?" Briel demanded.

"I don't think so, General."

Briel released the man's tunic. "Tomb," he said to Kilisti and moved briskly to a nearby stairwell.

Despite the weariness in his legs and the sweat beading on his forehead, he rushed up the stairs, nearly colliding with servants as he strode down one corridor and up another. He climbed a staircase that was so narrow he had to turn sideways. Finally, he stopped. Before him lay a blank wall. Briel hesitated. He hated the next part.

"Allow me," Kilisti said. "It's probably my turn, anyway."

She reached past him and touched the wall. She winced as magic jarred her. A moment later, though, the wall shimmered and vanished, revealing a long, dark corridor.

Briel led the way, pressing one hand to each wall to feel his way along. Stone gave way to wood. The corridor narrowed then widened. Briel remembered what had happened the first time he'd visited the tomb of Fâyu Jinn. Memories of Silwren's death mingled with that of the simpering Sylvan prince, Quivalen, the latter burned alive. He remembered, too, how the ghost of Fâyu Jinn himself had appeared. Briel almost wished the darkness would continue awhile longer, delaying the inevitable, but a flash of soft blue light meant they were almost to the tomb.

The corridor came to a dead end next to a pedestal on which sat a glowing luminstone. A black silk cloth lay beside it, meaning someone had passed by recently and moved the cloth so the luminstone would be lit when they returned. Briel hesitated. He eyed the mural covering the dead-end wall. Centuries old, it depicted a host of Dragonkin and Jolym battling a small, defiant alliance of Sylvs, Isle Knights, and Shel'ai.

"The Shattering War," Briel muttered.

"I never would have believed it." Kilisti started to reach past him, as though to touch the painting.

However, Briel touched it first. A strange jolt passed through his body, rattling his senses, followed by a tingling sensation that lingered—even as that wall, too, shimmered and disappeared.

Beyond lay the tomb of Fâyu Jinn: a small, plain chamber containing nothing but an ornate stone sarcophagus and a plain wooden chair. A lit luminstone sat on the sarcophagus. Ahmashura, the queen of Sylvos, sat in the chair, reading a book, one elbow propped on the sarcophagus. She looked up, her eyes watery with age.

"General, you have no idea how frustrating it is to be interrupted in my favorite hiding place."

Briel sank to one knee. Kilisti followed suit.

Briel said, "Forgive the interruption, my queen, but—"

"Who's making trouble this time: Olgrym, Shel'ai, or renegade Sylvs? Or all three?"

Briel rose to his feet, a second behind Kilisti. He glanced at the sarcophagus and remembered how, years before, he'd opened it, expecting to find Jinn's bones but finding only a hollow suit of armor instead. He stepped forward and handed over the parchment to the queen.

The old queen frowned at it. "Young man, I am flattered by your faith in my eyesight, but in case you have forgotten, I am three hundred years older than you are and two hundred years older than that mad nephew of mine." She paused. "I mention the latter so that you'll remember how much you owe me for letting you stick a crown on my head."

Briel noted that, as usual, the queen was not wearing her crown. "You need never remind me, my queen." He took back the slip of parchment. As he did so, he glanced down at the open book on the queen's lap and saw that its contents—ancient Sylvan poetry—had been written in extra-large print. He read the message to her.

Queen Ahmashura hardly reacted at all. For a moment, she stared at Fâyu Jinn's sarcophagus, tracing its ornate carvings with her wrinkled fingers. Then, bracing herself against the sarcophagus, she pushed herself back onto her feet. "One war ends, and another begins," she muttered. "Is that all the Light has in mind for us, I wonder?"

Briel looked down and saw a scorched patch of stonework where, years before, Silwren had turned Prince Quivalen into a screaming, living candlewick. "I'm not sure there's ever been anything else."

Kilisti cleared her throat. "Might not be a war yet, my queen. Only two Dragonkin—"

"Chorlga was *one* Dragonkin," Queen Ahmashura cut in, "and he nearly ruined the entire continent." She turned and picked up the luminstone. Blue light spilled from between her fingers. Briel shifted to let her by, but she stayed where she was. "I trust you will verify Krym's story by seeing if those Dragonkin's corpses are still moldering on the coast. In the meantime, send word to the Wyldkin and all our outposts." She faced Kilisti. "How many Shal'tiar could you muster if you had to?"

"We're still training to replenish the ranks. I can get you fifty right away—a hundred if you don't mind them a little wet behind the ears."

"We can raise another four hundred regular army," Briel added. "With conscriptions, we might raise as many as—"

"No conscriptions," the queen said. "Not unless you want a revolt on your hands."

Briel and Kilisti exchanged glances.

Briel said, "If there's a war coming, we'll need every—"

"We lost too many souls fighting the Olgrym and Shel'ai," the queen snapped. "You should know that since you were the one leading the fight. The people won't stand for another war. You might talk them into picking up a longbow and standing a post in the trees, in case Sylvos is invaded, but they won't march to war."

"They might not have a choice," Kilisti said. "Sylvos is the Dragonkin's ancient homeland. Even if they don't come here right away, sooner or later, they will. They'll want to take back Shaffrilon and the World Tree for themselves. Better we fight them out in the wild, where we still have allies."

"What allies?" the queen asked. "The Isle Knights, the Dwarrs, and the Free Cities are still trying to recover. The Queshi won't let foreigners in their realm, and they seem just as reticent to leave. And according to stories, the Ivairians are starting to turn as fey as those Sons of Maelmohr." She shook her head. "All the realms are in tatters."

"True," Briel said, "but Locke can sew them back together."

Ahmashura raised one white eyebrow. "You have that much faith in him?"

Briel hesitated. "As much as I hate to admit it... yes, I do."

"Well, I'm sure he'll be flattered. That is, if he hasn't already been turned to cinders," the queen said. "We need more allies, and the truth is, there aren't any."

Briel hesitated. "There are always the Tongueless."

The queen's expression darkened. "And how would the people respond if I parleyed an alliance with Olgrym, I wonder?"

"Technically, the Tongueless are renegades," Briel reminded her. "They didn't take part in the war."

"Good luck explaining that to the peace-loving souls who watched Olgrym rampaging through the forests and the city streets not four years ago." Ahmashura shook her head. "No, not the Tongueless. Not yet. But put together a token force—whatever you can—and send it east. If you can get some of the Iron Sisters from Hesod to join you, all the better. Then, take whomever you can muster north, toward the Wintersea. Since I'm an old woman who knows as much about warfare as a fish knows about climbing mountains, I'll let the two of you plan the rest. Decide who's leading the host."

Briel and Kilisti exchanged glances again. The duty sounded neither easy nor glorious.

Kilisti said, "I'll do it. The general's needed here."

Briel shook his head. "No, Captain. I'll go. I'd rather you stay here and protect the queen."

Kilisti frowned. "And why is that?"

"Because you look scarier than I do."

Kilisti's frown broke into a rare, faint smile. "Look in a mirror sometime, General."

"He *does* have an affecting scowl," the queen agreed. "All right, both of you go. I may be old, but I don't need a nursemaid. Besides, if Locke fails, my safety won't make much difference."

Briel considered arguing then reminded himself that Kilisti was the most experienced soldier he had left, and an expert tracker besides. Whatever chance he had to help Rowen, slim though it might be, would be greater if he had her along. He turned to face her. "We'll assign two more men to guard the queen. Rhos'ari and Faeli, I think." After Kilisti nodded her approval of his choices, Briel continued, "In the meantime, while I'm mustering the host, take a fast horse and a handful of men to the Dead Shores. Find those bodies. Then meet me at Que'ahl."

"Don't be late," Kilisti said.

The queen fixed both of them in a fierce stare. "Give my regards to Sir Locke, and more importantly, see to it that you two come back in one piece. I prefer to surround myself with people who detest politics as much as I do, you know." She turned and glanced down at her book, tracing her weathered fingertips across the page. "Good for you that my nephew ran away, I suppose. If he hadn't, no Sylvs would be riding to Locke's aid, and I'm sure the Humans would be facing this threat alone." She added, "To be honest, I don't altogether oppose such a course of action, but the days when we Sylvs could ignore the outside world are as dead and gone as the practice of stabbing infants who are born with purple eyes. I hope so, anyway."

The queen picked up the luminstone and headed for the open doorway, taking the glowing illumination with her. Shadows quietly reclaimed the tomb in her wake. Briel glanced once more at the scorched spot on the floor where Prince Quivalen had died. Then he directed his attention back to the sarcophagus. He noted that the queen had left her book behind, resting open on the stone lid. He considered carrying the book for her then left the book where it was. He hoped that one day she would return to finish it.

Jalist Hewn stared into the roaring fire at the center of the great hall of Tarator. Its heat made the air shimmer. Though a hole carved into the arches of the massive stone ceiling allowed smoke to escape, his eyes watered anyway. He remembered feasting there when he was still a Housecarl in the service of King Fedwyr, making eyes at the king's son—who had been Jalist's lover until they were caught and Jalist was beaten within an inch of his life. He'd been banished, driven beyond the borders of Stillhammer, condemned to wander the wild for the rest of his life.

And now, here I am… the governor of the same damn kingdom that swore I'd burn in Maelmohr's own hell!

He did not know whether to laugh or cry at the irony. Turning from the fire, he looked around at the great hall's only other occupants: a tall, lean man and a little girl. Both of them had violet eyes and tapered ears that accented their angular features and quick limbs as they ran about the hall. The man was pretending to try to escape the little girl, who laughed constantly and tried to hit the man with a sword of purple flames that she'd conjured out of thin air and swung wildly with both hands.

Jalist had seen plenty of Shel'ai, including Maddoc, who could cast wytchfire from their fingers. But he had never seen one who could shape it into a sword and swing it. The ability reminded him of Zeia. Somehow, though, Sariel's ability was even more disconcerting. After all, she was not yet five years old.

Maddoc turned suddenly, pretended to lose his footing, and allowed

Sariel to strike him across the back with her sword of wytchfire. The flaming sword scattered into hundreds of tiny cinders. Maddoc stood, unharmed. Sariel laughed.

A month ago, she wouldn't have been able to control the heat. She might have killed him, doing that. Jalist shook his head. Maddoc trusted the little girl far more than he did. Still, the progress she'd made since she'd left Cadavash was astounding—as was her lingering temper.

Jalist glanced across the great hall at an empty suit of armor, a decorative piece that had so frightened Sariel that she'd unleashed wytchfire on it, melting it into the stone wall. Jalist had been about to order it removed, but Maddoc insisted that it be left in place to remind Sariel of the need to develop self-control. There was also the matter of three servants that Sariel had burned—one so badly that Maddoc's own magic was barely enough to save his life. To everyone's surprise, though, the Dwarrs had not sought retribution.

Jalist shook his head and stood up. Sometimes, he could scarcely believe that this was the same kingdom that first had driven him away for loving another man then had undertaken a campaign to eradicate all the magic from the realms. Of course, it didn't hurt that Father Gaulgodd had been resoundingly vilified since then, and Jalist—who had also negotiated a trade agreement with Lyos, which made Stillhammer richer than ever—had been the hero of the battle.

Some hero I am. Jalist sloshed some of his ale as he made his way toward Maddoc and Sariel. The two had changed games. Now, they were gently tossing a sphere of wytchfire back and forth, the object being not only to catch it but to preserve its shape without burning oneself or the other player. Maddoc winced, his palms already red as cherries, but there too, Sariel was improving.

The child turned, saw Jalist's approach, and grinned. "Fire catch!" she cried and threw the flaming sphere at Jalist.

Jalist's eyes widened as he leapt sideways, but Maddoc stretched out his hand and closed his fingers, and the sphere dissipated before it reached him.

"Fire catch with *me*," Maddoc scolded. "No one else. Not ever. Remember?"

Sariel blushed. Her lip quivered, and Jalist feared she was about to throw another of her infamously destructive tantrums. Instead, she nodded. "I'm sorry," she told Jalist.

"No harm done," Jalist mumbled, inspecting the fresh ale stain on his doublet. "Throw one back at Uncle Maddoc, as hard as you can!"

Maddoc gave Jalist a scathing look. Sariel giggled and held both hands in front of her. Little tendrils of wytchfire spilled out of her fingertips, knitting together. When she had a sphere the size of her fist, she threw it. Maddoc caught it but winced.

Sariel started to form another flaming sphere, but Jalist said, "Enough," and kissed Sariel's tangled hair. "Let's get you in a bathtub before you burn down half the kingdom."

Sariel's face reddened. Jalist backed up, but Maddoc scowled at her. Sariel held firm for a moment, then her anger withered, and she sprinted away. Maddoc sighed and approached Jalist.

Jalist squeezed his hand. "She's getting better."

"True," Maddoc said, "but it might not last once she gets back to Cadavash. She needs a Shel'ai to look after her, and none of the ones there want the job."

"That surprises me," Jalist said. "Locke and Igrid basically took her as their daughter, same as Thessa. You'd think they'd want to curry favor."

"With a Human?" Maddoc laughed. "They might call him Wytchfriend, but that's a far cry from being eager to help him raise a child whose powers are greater than theirs."

Jalist frowned. "You're sure, then?"

Maddoc's expression sobered. "You've seen the flaming sword. She summons that easy as breathing. I've spent hours trying, and I still can't do it. And she hasn't had a tenth as much training as I have."

Jalist scratched his beard. "Zeia says that magic is like a muscle. The more you work it—"

"I know. That's how Zeia conjures her hands, and how Algol made his eyes. Still, there are supposed to be limits to what a Shel'ai can do. I'm sure Sariel has them, but I haven't seen them yet." Maddoc hesitated. "She's no Dragonkin, but right now, I'd say she's already more powerful than Fadarah or Shade ever were. And she's *five*. That worries me."

"Not me," Jalist lied. "Just think of how easy life will be, never having to bother with flint and tinder. Maybe she could even be a cook in a tavern somewhere."

Maddoc did not laugh. "When I take her back to Cadavash, I think I should stay with her for a while." He hesitated. "I know you don't want me to, but—"

"No, you're right," Jalist said. "In fact, I'll come with you."

Maddoc blinked. "No, you won't. You *can't*, and you know it. You're needed here."

"You're right about that, too, I suppose. Still, it was a fun idea." Jalist turned back to the fire at the center of the great hall. It had died down, the flames leaping only half as high as before. "Maybe we should just keep her here. You said she's better with you, anyway. And truth be told, Locke and Igrid might miss her less than they enjoy stamping out fires every time she has a nightmare."

Maddoc hesitated. "I would *like* to keep her here. I would. But I don't think—"

The door to the great hall flew open, and a Dwarrish steward rushed in. Jalist groaned. The steward was a young man who had previously fought alongside the Sons of Maelmohr. After their defeat and Gaulgodd's capture, Jalist had offered blanket amnesty to all who wanted it. Falder had been among the first to accept. The steward had served faithfully ever since, but Jalist could read the constant disapproval in the man's expression.

At least I can't read his mind. Poor Maddoc. "What is it, Falder?"

The young man cast an uncomfortable look at Maddoc then told Jalist, "A message just arrived from Cadavash."

Jalist noted Falder's scowl and wondered if the message had arrived by wytch-raven, birds that had been bred in ages past with the use of magic. Jalist imagined the steward wincing as he was forced to touch the bird in order to remove the message. Jalist smiled and held out his hand. Falder handed him the message.

"That'll be all," Jalist said and watched Falder hurry from the great hall.

"I still think you should let me have a talk with that man," Maddoc said in a low voice.

"Would this talk involve burning off parts of his body?"

"Not necessarily," Maddoc said. "I could put some of my memories into his mind, memories of mobs, let him see how I've had to live because of—"

"Wouldn't help. He'd just think it was a trick and hate you even more for tainting him with your devilry." Jalist rolled his eyes and started to open the message. A child's laughter startled him before he could read it, though. He and Maddoc turned.

Sariel stood in an open doorway at the opposite end of the great hall. As soon as she had their attention, wytchfire blazed up all around her, blackening the doorway. Sariel laughed as her clothes turned to cinders.

"Not again," Maddoc groaned and ran to stop her.

Jalist started to follow then returned his attention to the message instead. He expected it to be nothing more than well-wishes from Rowen, perhaps a statement that he planned on riding out and meeting Jalist halfway. When Jalist read what had been written, though, his eyes widened.

"Gods…"

Jalist turned, just in time to see Maddoc hustling Sariel through the doorway, presumably toward the washtub in the next room. Jalist took a step after them. Then he looked down at the message again.

"Guess I'll be leaving Stillhammer after all." He returned to his place by the fire, sat down, and refilled his cup of ale. He eyed the kingsteel long axe that Rowen had given him, hanging on a distant wall. Jalist had taken to calling the axe Freija, after the Dwarrish word for *friend* carved into the blade. He rose, walked over the axe, and took it down, admiring its heft. Then he returned to the table, leaned the axe against his seat, and reread the message. As he did so, he sipped his ale, savoring it, knowing it might be his last drink for a while.

CHAPTER ELEVEN

S UNDOWN FOUND ROWEN SITTING BY the campfire with the others—all save Vaari, Igrid, and Issa, who had ridden out to scout the area again. Issa had volunteered for the duty and drafted Vaari to accompany him, probably sensing that getting him away from Rowen and Saanji would be a good idea. The bodyguard had refused until Igrid announced that she would go as well. The presence of the fetching swordswoman was enough to change Vaari's mind.

"I can handle this," she'd whispered to Rowen, and the three had ridden off.

Thessa sat, staring at the luminstone glowing in her cupped hands. Then she put it away in favor of the vegetable stew Rowen handed her. She devoured her stew but recoiled when Breaksteel reached out with the steaming ladle to refill her bowl. Rowen was about to chide her, but the Olg seemed to sense his intentions and shook his head.

Rowen fixed his concerns on Igrid instead. They had already been gone too long for his liking. He scanned the horizon, hoping to catch a sign of her red curls in the distance.

"The caravan's already moved on, Knight," Keswen whispered, leaning toward him. "Stop worrying."

Easier said than done, Rowen thought but nodded his agreement.

Saanji filled a bowl and looked at Rowen. "Should I..." He hooked his thumb at Krym.

"No," Rowen said. "To be honest, I don't know if Dragonkin even eat."

"Oh, they eat," Zeia muttered. "They just don't eat stew and bread."

Rowen shuddered, remembering the hundreds of dead, frozen bodies he'd found outside Cadavash, their eyes blackened. He glanced at Thessa, glad she had not understood, then told Saanji, "Besides, if you reach past that line he drew in the ground, you'll..."

Rowen trailed off as Krym slowly rose to his feet, turned, and approached them from the other end of the camp. Rowen stood, too. The others saw his expression and did likewise.

"We will have visitors soon," Krym announced. He fixed his unblinking gaze on Rowen. "Isle Knights. You will meet them then order them away."

"All right. But—"

"They have a prisoner with them. The Knights must leave, but the prisoner remains. Is that understood?" Without waiting for an answer, Krym turned and strode back to the edge of the camp, facing eastward.

Rowen followed. "Spread out," he told the others. "Thessa, stay by the fire." He hesitated. "Breaksteel, stay with her."

Breaksteel nodded, his dark locks clacking. Thessa opened her mouth to protest, but Rowen was already walking away.

"Keswen, go disappear into the shadows," Rowen said, "and don't start loosing arrows unless—"

"I know my job, Knight," Keswen said, sidestepping behind a tree, a single arrow poised on her bowstring.

Rowen went to stand beside Krym. "If you want me to do this, I need to know who this prisoner—"

"You will know everything soon enough."

A prisoner, being escorted east by Isle Knights. That has to be Gaulgodd. "Listen, Dragonkin, I already know who the prisoner is. I just don't understand why—"

"I have told you what you must do," Krym interrupted. "Must we argue, or will you simply act as my ally without complaint for once?"

Rowen was about to lecture the Dragonkin on the difference between slaves and allies but decided otherwise. "When they get here, this will go better if they don't see you."

"You would have me hide? Human, I have not done that for ten times longer than you have been alive. Besides, Sir Locke, are these not *your* Knights?"

"They're men sworn to a task. That task happens to be escorting a prisoner—one I intend to take from them, likely without any explanation. If you want to talk about alliances, why don't you do what *I* ask, for a change?"

Krym smiled and bowed. "Very well. But remember what I said." He stepped back as Rowen strode ahead, farther from the campfire, into darkness.

Rowen waited. Moments later, the sound of hoofbeats preceded the return of his scouts.

Igrid dismounted first and ran to him. "You aren't going to believe—"

"Isle Knights," Rowen said.

Igrid blinked and glanced over Rowen's shoulder, presumably in Krym's direction. "All right, but did he tell you what they're doing?"

"They're escorting a prisoner. And yes, I can guess who it is. Krym wants him. Don't ask me why."

"He can have what's left of him," Igrid said, "after I cut his throat for—"

"No." Rowen thought of Fen-Shea and all the people from Lyos, as well as all the Isle Knights, who had died because of Gaulgodd. "I want him dead, too. But for now..."

Issa joined them, a spyglass still in hand. The young Knight's expression was that of a man holding back a stream of curses.

Before he could speak, though, Igrid shouted over Rowen's shoulder, toward Krym. "Oh, great one, would you kindly explain how the leader of the Sons of Maelmohr just happens to be riding by exactly where we're camped?"

Rowen winced. He resisted the impulse to turn around, waiting for Krym to respond. When the Dragonkin did not answer, Rowen strode even farther from the camp. The others fell in behind him. A moment later, the thundering of horses preceded a gleaming wall of kingsteel shimmering on the horizon, illuminated by the starlight of Armahg's Eye.

Rowen asked, "How many Knights?"

"At least fifty," Igrid said. "I didn't recognize the commander."

"Let's hope he recognizes me." Rowen strode toward the approaching riders.

Issa left then reappeared with Rowen's horse. Rowen mounted, hoping the young Knight was right in his assumption that it would make him appear more official, and rode out.

The Isle Knights slowed and fanned out, forming a massive, steely row in the darkness. Though none drew a sword, many held polearms whose blades gleamed nakedly in the night. Others held bows or openly rested their hands on their swords, frowning at Rowen.

Their commander rode forward. A middle-aged Knight of the Stag with olive skin and hair the color of sackcloth, he eyed the emblem of a white lotus on Rowen's azure tabard. "Greetings, Brother. I did not think to find a Knight of the Lotus so far from..." His eyes widened. "Forgive me, Sword Marshal!" He bowed from the saddle.

Word quickly spread, and the Knights behind him relaxed though Rowen could sense their confusion.

"The apology is mine, Brother, for I cannot remember your name."

"Nor would I expect you to." The Knight of the Stag bowed again. "Sir Lamrey, Sword Marshal. I fought with you at Saikaido, in the sea battle."

"Of course. Sir Lamrey. Many Knights died in that fight... most of them Crovis's, thanks to the courage and honor of men like you." Rowen shifted uncomfortably, unaccustomed to such formal speech. He urged his horse a little closer to Sir Lamrey. "You are escorting a prisoner, I understand... a certain cleric of Maelmohr who once called himself the Scion."

"And would still call himself that, I'd wager, if he weren't refusing to talk," Sir Lamrey said. "Lady Aeko ordered us to take the bastard to Stillhammer and deliver him directly to Governor Jalist"—he raised his voice—"where I'm told the governor will personally lop off the bastard's head."

Rowen looked over Sir Lamrey's shoulder and finally spotted Gaulgodd at the center of the Knights' line. His blood boiled at the sight of the man. The Dwarr still wore the robes of a cleric, and he looked as though he had not been ill-treated by his captors though his strong arms were shackled and two Knights held polearms to this throat. Unnervingly, the Dwarrish cleric had a faint smile on his face. His dark eyes met Rowen's as though they were sharing some private joke.

Gods, Krym, what do you want with this man? "There has been a change in orders, Sir Lamrey. My comrades and I will take possession of the prisoner and escort him to Stillhammer ourselves."

Sir Lamrey frowned. "Begging your pardon, Sword Marshal, but I see only one Knight with you, along with what I take to be Ladies Igrid and Zeia, and a few others. The Grand Marshal gave me fifty-seven Knights, just in case any remaining Sons of Maelmohr attempted to rescue their foul leader and restore him to power. Perhaps we should combine our forces and—"

"That will not be necessary." Rowen thought up a lie. "I have a second force waiting half a day south of here—a hundred Knights. They have thoroughly secured the road and will see us safely to Stillhammer."

Sir Lamrey nodded. "Very good, Sword Marshal. We can provide you with safe escort back to your force. If you'd like to rest for the night, we would be honored to welcome you to our camp. Then we can ride out in the morning."

Rowen tensed but forced a smile. "Again, Sir Lamrey, I appreciate your generosity, but that will not be necessary. I will take possession of the prisoner. This is all in accord with the Grand Marshal's wishes, with whom I have a secret arrangement. The best thing you can do now is make haste back to Saikaido and inform her that everything has proceeded as planned."

Sir Lamrey did not answer. For a moment, Rowen could not make out the Knight's expression, as a cloud blocked the light of Armahg's Eye. When the cloud passed, he saw the Knight looked pained.

"Forgive me, Sword Marshal," Sir Lamrey said finally, "but the Grand Marshal's orders were specific. I was not to surrender this prisoner to anyone, save Governor Jalist." He added quickly, "I trust your word and will bend those orders if I must, but only if I am certain this prisoner is adequately guarded." He bowed. "Forgive me, Sword Marshal. I mean no disrespect, especially to such a venerated Knight as—"

Sir Lamrey jerked. His eyes widened as though he'd been struck by an arrow. Then he doubled over in the saddle a moment before he tumbled to the ground. Acting on instinct, Rowen drew his sword, scanning the darkness for an attacker. The air echoed with the sound of steel scraping against leather as Sir Lamrey's Knights did likewise. Then, one by one, all of them tensed. A few screamed. Weapons fell from shaking hands.

Horses reared up, neighing in sudden panic. Rider after rider fell onto the plains. Horses jerked about, some galloping away.

Rowen stared, aghast. Within seconds, the orderly host of well-disciplined fighters had utterly withered. Every last Knight lay on the plains, writhing in pain—all save Gaulgodd, who continued to sit in his saddle, shackled but smirking.

"Krym." Rowen spat the word out. He turned in time to see the Dragonkin striding forward.

"Have no fear," the Dragonkin said without turning. "I have incapacitated them. Nothing more. None of your brave Knights will die at my hands." Krym had hardly finished speaking when a distant Knight forced herself onto her knees, her face taut with agony, and lifted her bow. Somehow, she managed to fit an arrow and fire.

Krym waved one hand and the arrow burst into flames, vanishing long before it reached him. He waved again and the woman crumpled, screaming. Krym kept walking. He arrived at Gaulgodd's horse and reached out. The horse started to shy away, but Krym touched the side of its head. The beast tensed then lowered its head in surrender as its legs folded. Gaulgodd slid off, stepped forward, and knelt.

"Thank you, Master."

"The thanks are mine, for fulfilling your charge so admirably." Krym seized Gaulgodd by the shoulders and helped him rise. Then he touched the Dwarr's manacles. They shattered like glass. Krym strode back toward the camp. Gaulgodd followed, leading his horse behind him.

Rowen cast a final look of worry at Sir Lamrey, who was still grimacing in agony, then moved his horse to block them. "Release the Knights."

"I will," Krym said, "but not until we are gone from here. To do otherwise would endanger *your* lives more than it would mine."

As Igrid shook her head, Rowen said nothing. Instead, he dismounted and knelt beside Sir Lamrey. "I'm sorry, Brother," he whispered. "Tell Aeko what happened. She'll explain." He squeezed the Knight's shoulder.

Sir Lamrey whimpered, his eyes wide and distant, streaming tears.

Damn you, Krym. Rowen mounted his horse and followed the Dragonkin, waving for the others to do likewise.

By nightfall, Miriam knew she'd made a mistake. Still, it had been easy enough to slip out of Strongwall unseen and easier still to follow the hunting party as they made their way east. She stuck to the shadows, often pressing herself against the trees whenever one of the men with torches turned in her direction, reminding her of the boys that had chased her. All the courage she'd felt earlier had dried up. She was close enough to hear what the men were saying, too, and to her dismay, none of them were boasting over a fresh kill.

"Fight together," she heard Farl advise.

"Farl's right," Glem said.

Miriam peeked out from behind a tree and saw the guard at the head of company.

"Remember, this is a greatwolf, not a common wolf or a robber. I've seen just one of these things rip three grown men to pieces faster than you can pray the gods'll save you."

Miriam tightened her grip around her knife. *I shouldn't be here. I'm too small to fight something like that.* She considered sneaking back to Strongwall, but Lorna must have returned and discovered her missing. She'd be angry. Maybe she'd even tell the other townspeople that it was time to drive her away.

Tears swelled in Miriam's eyes. "They have real glass in the windows," she whispered to herself. She watched the men's torches moving farther and farther away, flickering in the night. She realized that the only way they would let her stay is if she proved to them that she was worth something. To do that, she would have to help them find and kill the greatwolf.

Besides, if it kills me, I'll just go back to the Light, where Ma and Da are... won't I?

She glanced up at the night sky, faced the starry swirl that was Armahg's Eye, and said a quick prayer. Then she hurried through the trees, doing her best to keep quiet. However, someone in the hunting party heard her and called out to the others. Everyone stopped and listened. Glem even headed in her direction, torch in one hand, a shortsword in the other. Miriam pressed her back to a tree and slid slowly to the ground. Cold dampness soaked through her woolen dress as she held her breath. Glem got so close that she saw the rust flecking his shortsword, but then he gave up and rejoined the company, and they pressed eastward again.

Miriam followed more slowly, letting some distance form between her and the men even though she feared doing so might make her a ripe target for the greatwolf. Then she heard the men shouting. She froze. The shouting grew louder, punctuated by curses and what even sounded like a grown man wailing and sobbing. She forced herself to move, drawing closer and closer to get a better look.

In a clearing, she saw all the men gathered in a somber circle, looking down. Miriam wondered if they were praying. Then a few of them moved, revealing a boy lying on the ground. She thought for a moment that he'd spilled red wine all over himself and gotten so drunk, like her brothers, that he'd fallen asleep. Then she saw a man kneeling beside the boy, crying. He held the boy's hand, shaking it. The boy did not stir or answer even though his eyes were wide open.

Miriam's stomach tightened. Then the men moved, blocking her view again.

Farl said, "We have to keep going."

Glem called a few men's names and told them to build a fire and stay with the boy's body. Then the rest set out. Miriam thought about giving up again. She did not want to go all the way back to Strongwall by herself, but if she stayed and helped guard and comfort the man whose son had died, the townspeople might still be grateful to her.

But that will be enough to make them trust me? Will Lorna still be mad that I left her daughter alone? Will they let me stay in Strongwall or make me leave?

She listened to the father's sobbing, which had not slackened, and shuddered. Finally, she made her choice. Facing the darkness, she followed after the hunting party, holding her knife in front of her. Because of the color of the knife, she could not see it in the darkness, but she felt the chill creep up her arm.

CHAPTER TWELVE

R OWEN SWORE AND SWORE BETWEEN his teeth as they galloped
through the night air. When he looked back, he saw they were
moving so quickly that Breaksteel was having trouble keeping
up. The Olg had been running for the better part of an hour, but when
he and Rowen locked gazes, Breaksteel did not give the hand-sign for
rest—one of the few that Rowen knew.

That doesn't mean he doesn't need it, though.

Sir Issa veered his horse until it was galloping beside Rowen's. "We
should stop," he called. "The Olg will run until his heart bursts, but—"

"Let him," Keswen called over her shoulder. The huntress rode just
ahead of them, an arrow resting on her bowstring. "He's slowing us down.
Better he slow down the Knights instead."

Would she say that if it were anyone else? "No." Rowen pointed to a
distant forest, toward which the Dragonkin was leading them. "The
Knights will have a hard time tracking us once we get there. We'll
rest then."

Zeia answered him telepathically, riding in front of him, immediately
behind Gaulgodd. *"That's if the Knights are even following us."*

Rowen considered that. *They are,* he thought though he wondered if
the Knights believed he was Krym's captive or now regarded Rowen as
a traitor.

Zeia answered telepathically, *"Whatever harm was done can be remedied
later. For now, best we focus on what to do about Gaulgodd."* Zeia gripped

the reins with her hands of flame and left a faint smell of smoke in the air.

The Shel'ai's tension brought Rowen's attention back to the Dwarrish cleric, who was riding at the head of the company beside Krym, his head thrown back, his crimson robes trailing in the wind. Rowen thought of all the suffering that Gaulgodd had wrought and considered how much he would enjoy driving his sword right through the Dwarr's back.

"*None of that, Knight,*" Krym said. "*This one is mine.*"

Rowen wondered for a moment if Krym was claiming Gaulgodd as his pet or his next victim. The Dragonkin offered no clarification. The company rode on until they reached the forest, then they slowed. Krym led them a little farther then dismounted and tossed the reins to Gaulgodd.

Rowen hesitated then signaled for the others to dismount. Breaksteel joined them a moment later. Sweat soaked through his clothes, and his breath came in heavy gasps. Thessa drew away from him, but Igrid handed him a canteen. Breaksteel thrust his kashpa into the ground and accepted it with a nod of thanks. Sir Issa offered him his shoulder and helped him toward a fallen tree trunk, wincing when the Olg leaned a measure of his great weight on him.

Meanwhile, Gaulgodd was kneeling in front of Krym again.

The Dragonkin touched the Dwarr's dark hair. "Are you ready to be as you were?"

Gaulgodd's lip lifted in a sneer. "Yes, Master."

"Then I return your power, in recognition of your service. Let this serve as a sign of the rewards to come."

Krym reached into his cloak and removed a golden medallion. He pressed it to Gaulgodd's head, and violet light flared from the medallion. Gaulgodd gasped then screamed with pain. He crumpled. Krym looked down at him, unmoved.

Out of the corner of his eye, Rowen saw Vaari and Keswen raising their bows. Saanji moved to stop the former, and Zeia blocked the latter. Rowen drew his sword and approached Krym just as the latter was tucking away the golden medallion.

"Did you kill him?"

"Hardly."

As though in answer, Gaulgodd groaned. Slowly, the Dwarr pushed himself to his knees—only he was not a Dwarr anymore. He was leaner, and his skin had changed from ash gray to a faint, icy blue. Right before Rowen's eyes, his dark hair turned white. Then the creature rose to his feet, nearly as tall as Breaksteel. His eyes had become wider and wholly white. Worst of all was the mouth, though, which turned into a kind of maw that hung open just enough to reveal excessive rows of daggerlike teeth.

"A Maalbolg," Krym said. "They are… a rather malleable race, I suppose you could say, fashioned by the Dragonkin several centuries ago to serve as an alternative to our Jolym."

"Are they as mindless as Jolym?" Zeia asked.

Krym did not look at her. "Think of them as living clay, ever ready to be shaped by the hands of a Dragonkin. In truth, I wish we'd had them during the Shattering War. Things might have gone differently." He smiled at Rowen. "Naturally, their skills and senses are greatly heightened, to suit our needs. Sometimes, in recognition of loyal service, we allow them a measure of freedom. I doubt anyone on Ruun has ever knowingly laid eyes on one of their kind, though. I would introduce you, but I fear you would find his true name unpronounceable."

What had once been a fanatical Dwarrish priest named Gaulgodd answered Krym's statement with a cold, mirthless smile.

Rowen turned from Maalbolg to Dragonkin and back again. "A Dwarrish priest, a fanatical cleric of Maelmohr, infamous for calling magic an abomination and inciting his people to revolt… and you're saying he was actually an agent of the Dragonkin?"

Krym chuckled. "Did you really think Algol was Nekiel's only disciple? No, Human. Our agents are as numerous as the stars, though I must confess the heavens are not as bright as they once were." He unbuckled his Dhargothi shortsword and offered it to the Maalbolg.

The Maalbolg accepted the weapon, drew it, and began whirling the sword about. The blade blurred faster and faster then hummed, moving more quickly than anything Rowen had ever seen. Then the Maalbolg stopped, sheathed the sword, and took a step forward. The creature clicked his tongue strangely, as though that were his native speech.

Krym said, "The one you knew as Gaulgodd will be invaluable when we face Nekiel. You need not trust him. You need only trust *my* promises and judgment."

Sir Issa stalked forward, sword drawn. Rowen barely managed to catch his arm and stop him before he swung.

Still, Issa faced Krym and spat, "Trust *you?* You just struck down a whole company of our kind for no reason!"

"An interesting interpretation." Krym stared unblinking at Issa's sword, hovering an inch from his face. "The fact that I incapacitated your Knights without killing them should demonstrate my good will."

Rowen pulled Issa back a step. The young Knight of the Crane caught his meaning and sheathed his adamune, stalking to the rear of the camp.

Rowen said, "You could have told me."

Krym nodded. "I could have. You will have to forgive me for that. I am not accustomed to treating your kind as equals." He bowed. "No offense."

Rowen directed his gaze toward the Maalbolg, realizing that Krym's new bodyguard still had not blinked. He forced himself to sheathe his sword. "Any other surprises, m'lord?"

"No surprises, but news you might find interesting." Krym nodded toward Saanji. "The prince need not fear. We will not be passing through Cassica. As the wytch surmised, I have passed the last two days in divination. In part, I was tracking the Maalbolg's captors, of course, but I was also looking for Nekiel. And I have found him."

All Rowen's anger turned to dread. He fought the impulse to turn and check on Igrid and Thessa. "Where is he?"

"West of here, only a few days from the Dead Shores. He has not traveled as far or as fast as I would have expected. We can easily reach the Wintersea before he does." He added, "Of course, if you allowed me to feast on two or three of your companions, I'd have power enough to teleport the rest of you straight to the Wintersea without further waste of time."

Is this another of his jokes? Rowen had the awful feeling that Krym's offer might be sincere. "None of that, Dragonkin. I told you—"

"Of course." Krym's smile broadened. "Stop worrying, Knight. If I wished to drain the innocent, I could have done so countless times before this. Strange that I must keep reminding you of my own trustworthiness."

"Indeed." Rowen faced Krym for a moment then turned toward the

Maalbolg again. "Stranger still that you're willing to betray Nekiel, who's been your master a hundred times longer than I've been alive. Tell me, why would this Maalbolg help *you* instead of Nekiel?"

"Nekiel has his agents, and I have mine."

Saanji stepped forward. "Agent or disciple? You've already described this creature as both."

The Maalbolg turned his icy stare from Rowen to Saanji and answered with a chorus of awful, derisive clicks.

Krym said, "So I did. Have no fear, Prince. I have not undertaken this course of action lightly. There are only two creatures in the world that I trust with my life, and this Maalbolg is one of them."

Vaari stepped forward, an arrow on his bowstring. "And the other?"

Krym's eyes narrowed, and he regarded the man as though facing the dung of an animal. "Pray you never meet him, Dhargot." Krym turned back to Rowen. "Enough of this. If you have rested enough, I suggest we continue. Nekiel is three days west of here, and I am as anxious to finish this as you are."

Krym and the Maalbolg mounted their horses and started forward into the night. Rowen reached out, snatched the arrow off Vaari's bowstring, and snapped it. The Dhargot scowled but offered no reply.

Saanji moved closer. "This is getting worse by the minute."

Zeia added, "And there are a lot of minutes left."

Rowen was about to answer, but Thessa rushed up and threw her arms around him.

"Don't worry, little one," he whispered. "You're strong. Just keep that sword close, remember what we taught you, and nothing can possibly hurt you. I promise." He looked over Thessa's shoulder at Igrid and saw by her pained expression that she was as uncomfortable with the lie as he was.

Miriam tried to keep pace with the hunting party, but Glem shouted, Farl followed suit, and all the men were soon running too quickly for her to catch up. Panic surged inside her when the distance of their torches and a thickening of clouds plunged her into darkness. She remembered running from the boys who wanted to hurt her and tripping. She slowed down.

They saw the greatwolf. They're chasing it. That means it's far away. I don't have any reason to be scared. She caught her breath and tried to decide what to do next.

If the men from Strongwall killed the greatwolf before she arrived to help, she would face the same problem as before. She could not go back to the town. She would have to continue on her own and maybe find the strange boy from the sea and convince him to be her friend. However, all she had was the soft dress and new shoes that Lorna had given her, along with her knife—no coins, no food.

Still, that's more than I had before. She remembered her torn clothes and the worn, too-small shoes that had left her toes bloody. She remembered the boy saying he was going north. She had never seen a map, but her father had told her once that the far north was an endless field of snow and ice, all year long. She could not imagine why the boy wanted to go there, but if she could catch up with him, maybe she could talk him out of it. Maybe together, they could even find a way to convince the people of Strongwall to let them both stay there.

Miriam turned toward what she hoped was north. She had hardly taken a step when she heard a wolf howl. Then she heard men shouting. Both sounded far away. A moment later, though, the shouting grew closer.

Miriam broke into a run. A branch snagged her clothes. She pulled away to the sound of cloth tearing. A moment later, a second branch scraped against her cheek. She bit back a scream at the stinging pain. Holding her arms in front of her, she kept running as blood ran warm down her cheek. Her hands deflected another branch. Then the clouds eased off Armahg's Eye in time for the swirl of starlight to prevent her from running straight into a gnarled, ancient oak.

Miriam got around the oak, but her feet caught on one of its dark roots, and she fell. That time, she covered her face, rolled, leapt up, and kept running almost without pause, but a chorus of distant shouts, made all the more terrifying by the sound of snarling that rose over the din, told her the greatwolf was gaining.

Miriam screamed and ran even more quickly, shoving blindly at the branches that scratched and tore at her arms. She had seen wolves before but never a greatwolf. She'd heard they were something like a cross between a wolf and a bear, as big as horses, red-furred, and so ferocious

120

that bringing them down took ten men—or twenty, depending on whom you asked.

Somehow, Miriam ran even faster. She hoped the greatwolf was so busy fleeing the hunters that it would pass her by, but she changed direction again and again, and each time, the distant snarling seemed to get closer, accompanied by what sounded like an army crashing through the underbrush. Her legs ached from running. Miriam drew her knife and wished the numbness creeping up her arm could be transferred to her legs, where it might do some good.

I don't have to kill it, she realized. *The hunters are close. I just have to fend it off for a few seconds.*

Miriam stopped, pressed her back to a tree, and turned to face the darkness. She scanned the shadows, her heart in her throat. She saw nothing but the vague outline of trees, which loomed over her like burly men with their arms outstretched. She thought maybe the greatwolf was not following her after all. Maybe she had imagined the whole thing. Then she saw yellow eyes.

Dagger thin, the eyes slid toward her, so close to the ground that they might have been those of a snake. Red fur covered bulging muscles. Miriam forgot her back was already against a tree and tried to retreat even farther. When she could not, she uttered a small yelp of fright.

The thin yellow eyes widened a little. The thing had already seen her, she knew, but it sensed she was afraid. Miriam waved her little knife in front of her. Sharp as it was, the knife seemed small and pitiful compared to what came closer each time she drew a ragged breath. Miriam had the wild thought that maybe the greatwolf's approach was tied to her breathing. She held her breath. The greatwolf drew closer anyway.

More shouting reached her ears. Miriam remembered the hunting party and thought for sure they were running to help her. Then, to her horror, she realized the shouts were growing fainter. The hunters were going in the wrong direction.

Miriam opened her mouth, about to cry out for help, but the greatwolf straightened. It rose on its hind legs, like a bear, so tall that it loomed over her like some kind of malevolent tree. Startled into silence, Miriam watched the greatwolf take a few steps before it returned to all fours. By then, it filled her field of view. Its crimson snout exhaled right into her face. Miriam remembered her knife. She slashed, drawing a ribbon of blood from the greatwolf's snout.

The yellow eyes widened. The great jaws flew open, revealing white teeth that snapped at her. Miriam screamed and dove out of the way. She landed in a pile of branches and dry leaves. Still screaming, she rolled over and slashed again, cutting nothing but empty air. She thought maybe the greatwolf had retreated. Then she felt its jaws close on her ankle.

Miriam found herself unable to scream. Tears filled her eyes, blurring the darkened world. She sat up and stared, entranced, at the great mouth closed around her leg. Where the greatwolf's body met hers, her pants were changing color, turning red that looked almost black in the darkness. Miriam had the odd thought that her clothes matched the color of the greatwolf's fur, as if it was absorbing her. Then she remembered her knife. She leaned forward and sliced off the tip of the greatwolf's ear.

The jaws released as the greatwolf yelped and retreated a bit. Miriam tried to pull her leg toward her chest, but the moment the greatwolf let go, the pain grew, instead of fading. Wiping her eyes with the back of her hand, she waved her knife with the other.

"Stay back," she cried, her voice breaking. "Stay back," she repeated, more sternly.

The greatwolf thrashed about for a moment then turned to face her once more. It crouched low, even as its hindquarters rose. Miriam sensed it was about to pounce. She held out her knife, imagining that she might impale it when it leapt, though the greatwolf's weight would surely crush her.

"You should run," she said. "The hunters are coming."

By then, however, she could barely even hear the men from Strongwall. She wondered if they had just gone home. Using one elbow, she tried to push herself away. Her mangled leg dragged behind her, throbbing with pain. The greatwolf followed, maintaining the same distance between them. When Miriam could drag herself no farther, the greatwolf growled and tensed to spring.

Someone stepped in front of her.

The greatwolf drew back, as startled as Miriam, then growled at the newcomer. The boy was taller than she remembered, though his pretty golden hair was the same, as were his gold-and-purple clothes—even dirty and torn. He said nothing but stood in front of Miriam and crossed his arms, looking down at the greatwolf.

"Take my knife," Miriam whispered.

The boy ignored her and kept staring down at the greatwolf. A moment later, the beast relaxed. Its tongue lolled. Padding forward, it nuzzled the boy's feet. The boy crouched down, as though petting a beloved dog. He whispered something Miriam could not hear. Then he grasped the greatwolf's mangled ear.

The greatwolf yelped then growled and tried to jerk away, but the boy held on. The greatwolf's growl became a whimper. It went slack again, lying on the forest floor. Still, the boy held on, squeezing. Miriam watched, unsure what was happening. Waves of heat rolled off the boy's body, as though he were on fire. He seemed unhurt, though.

When the boy finally let go of the greatwolf and straightened, the greatwolf nuzzled him then turned and bounded off into the darkness. Miriam saw it only for an instant, but it looked as though the ear she'd severed had been completely restored. The boy turned to face her. He regarded her a moment, unblinking, then held out his hand.

Miriam did not take it. "My leg…"

The boy looked down and frowned at her leg then at her, as though she had done something wrong. "You should not have hurt the wolf. It was just hungry. It's terrible, you know, to be hungry." He knelt and pressed a hand to her leg.

He did it gently at first, and Miriam thought he was only trying to stop the bleeding, but he pressed harder and harder until it felt as though he was standing on her wound. Her eyes watered, and she covered her mouth to muffle her screams.

Still, the pressure increased. Miriam had the feeling that so much weight was piling onto her wounded ankle that her leg was being driven into the ground, that she was being buried alive. Her vision darkened then turned white with pain. The weight became cold then hot. Miriam then felt she was being burned one inch at a time, starting with her toes. The heat stretched all the way to her eyes, which burned then turned cold.

Then, all at once, the burning stopped, and her vision returned. The boy was standing over her again, blank faced, holding out his hand. The pain had gone. Miriam stuck her knife in her belt then stretched out a hand and placed it in his.

CHAPTER THIRTEEN

G ENERAL BRIEL'S HORSE THUNDERED ACROSS the Ash'bana
Plains as quickly as it could go, hooves tearing at the grassy
earth. Briel looked over his shoulder and saw his bodyguards
struggling to keep up. He considered slowing down, not just so they
could catch up but to prevent his mount's heart from bursting, then
decided against it.

Sorry, he thought, patting the horse's sweat-streaked neck. He braced
himself, preparing to leap free of the saddle if the horse fell, and flicked
the reins again. The grasslands rushed by. Finally, a haze of blue appeared
on the western horizon. Briel slowed his horse, but only to more safely
navigate between the patches of rocky earth that began to appear before
him, intermingled with the grasslands. *Could be worse,* he thought,
grateful they'd avoided the thorns and razor-sharp obsidian of Godsfall,
where most of the Olgrym lived, though the dark smear to the northeast
was still too close for his liking.

The land before him continued to be overtaken by gray. Briel's
bodyguards caught up, looking no less exhausted than his horse. Briel
dismounted, tossed them the reins, and told them to stay behind. Then
he hurried down the rocky slope, toward the sea.

Kilisti was waiting for him, surrounded by a handful of Wyldkin.
All milled about, speaking in hushed whispers, arrows resting on their
bowstrings. Snowdark, a piebald palfrey she'd half stolen from Rowen
Locke, restlessly pawed the sand. The men moved aside at Briel's
approach. Briel came to stand before Kilisti, who did not bother saluting.

Briel said, "You were supposed to meet me at Que'ahl."

"Sorry, General," Kilisti said, "but you needed to see this." She pointed north along the beach.

Briel turned, and a flash of color caught his eyes. He squinted and discerned a row of dark shapes lying on the sand, a few hundred yards away. "You found them..." He cleared his throat. "Krym was telling the truth. So be it. You could have told me that in person."

"You... need to see them more closely, General." For the first time, Briel thought he saw an ember of fear in Kilisti's expression. That chilled him even more than the sight of the dead Dragonkin. A heavy dread built inside him as he hurried toward the unmoving figures.

As he drew closer, he saw that they all lay in a row, face up. A foul smell filled his nostrils. Whatever clothing they had been wearing was burned away, revealing bodies that were stiff and blackened to a crisp. Moreover, patches of sand around them had a jagged glint, as though the Dragonkin had burned so intensely that they had turned the sand beneath them to glass.

"Your message said this was urgent. If you wanted me to see the bodies so badly, you should have piled them into a wagon and brought them to Que'ahl."

"I tried," Kilisti said. "Even tried tying one of them to Snowdark and dragging him. We simply can't move them. Each one weighs as much as a hundred oxen... or a dragon."

Briel winced. "So? Why am I—"

Kilisti stepped forward so fiercely that Briel tensed, thinking she was about to strike him. "Listen, General. Locke's message said nine Dragonkin tried to pass through the Dragonward. Seven died in the attempt. That leaves two: Nekiel and Krym. There should be seven bodies here." She pointed at the bodies. "Count."

Briel did so then paled. "Six..."

Kilisti drew closer to the bodies and examined the dark, glassy sand. "We found some footprints, but nothing got dragged away. Besides, like I said, they're too heavy to move. These six are all there are."

Briel turned and stared farther down the beach. "Maybe Krym miscounted."

"Either that, or he lied."

"He said they started off with nine. Why would he lie about that?"

Kilisti shook her head. "Maybe he didn't. It sounds like this one likes to play games. Maybe he only lied about the number that survived."

Briel faced the sea. "By the Light... *three* Dragonkin?"

"Maybe," Kilisti said. "If so, though, where's the third? And more important, is its mind rattled like Nekiel's, or is it whole but just a little weakened like Krym?"

Briel looked down at the blackened figures again. "We have to warn Locke."

"Do we?" Kilisti drew closer. "Locke is traveling *with* Krym. Assuming we find them, how will you warn Locke without Krym knowing? Besides, what would you tell him—that Krym's a liar? Locke may be Human, but he's smart enough to figure that out for himself."

Briel faced the sea again. "What are you suggesting, Captain?"

"That we go back to Sylvos with whatever force we can muster. Whatever's happening, it's bigger than we thought. Maybe we *should* let the other realms deal with it. They can fight it out, and we'll defend ourselves against whatever's left."

Briel smiled faintly. "King Loslandril might have agreed to that. Maybe the other generals would have, too. But the king has vanished, and all his generals are dead."

Kilisti's face hardened. "Your point?"

"That isolating ourselves hasn't done much good in the past. Maybe we should try believing in Locke's alliance for a while."

Kilisti raised one eyebrow. "Didn't you try to kill Locke not that many years ago?"

"We all make mistakes." Briel backed away from the blackened corpses and headed for his horse. "Enough. Leave them. Let's get out of here." Even though it had not been long, he hoped his horse was rested, given the hard ride that lay ahead.

Miriam said, "Your face looks different."

The boy sat beside a stream, running one hand through the ruddy fur of the greatwolf lying at his feet. In truth, the boy no longer looked like a boy, though. He was taller than Jem, broad shouldered like Will, and his once-oversized clothing barely fit him. Miriam might have thought he was an entirely different person but for the medallion around his neck and the look in his eyes—inquisitive but somehow detached.

"What's your name? I can't keep calling you *boy*."

Ice-blue eyes met hers. "What was your father's name?"

Miriam blinked away sudden tears. "Emrael."

"Call me Emrael, then."

"No." Miriam crossed her arms. "That's not your name."

"One name is as good as another." His voice still sounded similar to the boy's but deeper, giving way sometimes to an odd accent that reminded her of two seashells clacking together. "Don't you agree?"

Miriam shrugged. "Do you remember *my* name?"

"Miriam," Emrael said. "Your brothers are Jem and Will. You lived in a farmhouse half a day east of the Dead Shores. Your parents died from—"

"I never told you my brothers' names!"

Emrael's faint smile returned. "Yes, you did. On the Dead Shores… after you pulled me out of the sea."

Miriam tried to remember. "Did I?" She shook her head. "Maybe, but I know I didn't tell you how my parents died."

Emrael's expression grew more distant. He stopped petting the greatwolf, which sat up and licked his face. He gently pushed it away. "No, but you showed me."

"Showed you how?" Miriam felt like crying though she could not say why. "That's far away from here. The farm, I mean. There's nothing left. I never showed you—"

"I saw it when I looked at you." Emrael cocked his head. "I see it now. A little field for turnips and cabbage. A pond, more mud than water. A clothesline running between two yew trees, which your mother weaved out of—"

"Stop it!" Miriam shuddered and looked at her feet. She wept, half expecting the boy to come closer and comfort her.

Instead, the greatwolf padded over, licked her face, then went back to the boy.

Finally, Miriam said, "We could have stayed in Strongwall. That town. The people seemed nice there." She got an idea. "Maybe we could go back! The wolf can't come, but if we go back, maybe they'll let us stay there if we agree to work."

Emrael frowned, as though he had not understood a single word she'd said. "I have to go north. I told you that." He caressed the greatwolf's ear—the one he had restored somehow—and the greatwolf jerked away, growling. Emrael ignored the sound and stroked the ear again. That time, the greatwolf whimpered and put its head on his knee.

"Why? What's north?"

"It's a direction."

Miriam frowned. "You know what I mean."

"I do, but I don't know how to answer your question. Not yet." Emrael paused. "Tell me about your brothers."

The question caught Miriam off guard. "Why?"

"Because I asked."

"But... you don't really want to know."

"Maybe I do."

Miriam bit her lip and gave in. "They both have bad tempers, like Da. Sometimes, they're not very nice, but they keep me safe, like they promised they would, and they can be nice sometimes, too. Like when we found those bodies on the beach and Will said not to look and Jem tried to cover my eyes."

Emrael frowned. "What bodies?"

Miriam shrugged. "Just people. They looked... burnt. You couldn't hardly make out what they looked like. They were just lying in the sand, all in a row. Jem said they must have been on a boat that caught on fire. We didn't see any burnt wood, though, and the only boat I saw was yours. That was days later, though."

Emrael stopped petting the greatwolf but left his hand on the beast's head. It whimpered, as though Emrael's hand were too heavy. Miriam thought she smelled burning fur.

"How many bodies?" he asked.

"Six," Miriam said. "I remember because that's half a dozen, and once, Da traded half a dozen eggs for a rag doll. Only my brothers made me leave that in the fire, with Ma's dresses." She stopped, unsure whether her answer had pleased or angered Emrael. "Why, did you know them? The people, I mean—"

"I think so." Emrael removed his hand from the greatwolf's head and rubbed his eyes. "Nine. There were nine of us at first."

Miriam wondered if others had drowned on the ship. She'd seen only the boy, but others could have been sleeping or injured down below. She shuddered, afraid she'd accidentally left them behind, left them to drown. "I promise, I didn't see anyone else on your ship. Anyway, I told you, we found those bodies a few days before—"

"That means two are still alive. But where are they?" Emrael stared at the ground for a moment then looked up sharply. "The two strongest, the ones who would have made it through… they're special, somehow. I know them. I *care* for them, like they're… mine."

Miriam touched her knife as something in Emrael's tone frightened her. "Like, slaves?" When Emrael did not answer, she asked, "If you know them, what are their names?"

Emrael's shook his head. "I don't remember, but I trusted them." He grimaced. "Or maybe I hated them. Maybe both." He rubbed his eyes again.

Miriam said, "I don't understand."

"I don't either. I just know that I have to go north." Emrael stood up so suddenly that the greatwolf jerked away, startled. "You cannot come with me. I don't know what will happen if you do."

Miriam noticed Emrael did not seem to blink anymore. She looked down at her feet again. "I don't want to go back with my brothers. If they're still chasing me after all this time, they'll beat me."

"I could see to it that they don't."

Emrael spoke with such nonchalance that it took Miriam a moment to realize what he meant. "You'd kill them?"

"If you wanted me to."

"Why?"

"You pulled me out of the sea. You saved my life."

"That's not a very good reason to kill someone."

"I have killed for less, I think." Emrael paused. "Is your answer no?"

"No, they're my brothers. Besides, they're tough. You couldn't hurt them."

Emrael smirked. "Where will you go?"

Miriam tried to recall the names of one of the cities her father and mother used to talk about, long after her brothers had gone to sleep and the house was so quiet that she could lie in her bed and hear them. However, she could not remember even one of them. "I don't know. Maybe I want to go north, too."

"There is nothing there for you."

"What about you?"

"That's different."

"How?"

"I don't know." Emrael held out his hand.

The greatwolf hesitated then padded over. It sat so tall that its head reached Emrael's breastbone.

"I will not stop you from following me. If I can, I'll protect you, but understand this will probably end with your death."

Miriam blinked and reached for her knife. "What are you talking about?"

Emrael eyed the knife at her belt. "I don't know."

"Is there anything you *do* know?"

Emrael was quiet for a moment. Then he removed the medallion from around his neck and tossed it to her. Miriam caught it then almost dropped it when it felt strangely cold—numbing, like her knife. Her anger melted into curiosity. She looked at the dragon carving, tracing her fingertip over the wings. Then she smiled and slipped the medallion over her neck. When she looked up, Emrael was already walking away, following the stream. The greatwolf followed, its rust-red muzzle dragging in the grass.

Rowen sat on a fallen tree, resting. He took a drink of water from a canteen, held the cool water in his mouth before swallowing, and passed the canteen back to Igrid. He wished it was wine. He glanced at a nearby ridge, on which Krym was kneeling, lost in divination. The Maalbolg hovered protectively nearby, casting derisive glances at the others. Gaulgodd's wholly white eyes alternately narrowed and widened but never blinked. From time to time, the strange creature's maw widened in a kind of clicking, antagonistic smile.

Igrid leaned close and whispered, "Something tells me, before this is over, one of us is going to have to kill that toothy bastard."

Rowen thought back to what Krym had said about how the Shattering War might have gone differently had the armies of the Dragonkin been filled with Maalbolgs instead of Jolym. "We could try, but did you see how fast it moves? Unless we can guess where it's going to be before it even gets there, we'd have better luck cutting down the wind."

Igrid's expression soured. "Then I suggest we start practicing."

Rowen turned to look for Thessa. The girl was standing at the far edge of the camp, near Sir Issa and Breaksteel. Though the girl seemed to be doing her best to avoid the latter, she had leapt at the chance to spar with Issa. The young Knight of the Crane was going easier on her than Igrid had. As a consequence, Thessa had a wild grin on her face as she charged, Rowen's shortsword flailing. Sir Issa let her get closer to striking him than he should have, speaking encouraging words as he narrowly blocked a wild swing with his vambraces.

"He isn't doing her any favors," Igrid said. "Look how far apart her feet are! Gods, she's already forgotten how to—"

"She's scared," Rowen said. "Issa knows that. He's just trying to build her up."

"If she were a squire, he would have beaten her black and blue by now."

"But she's *not* a squire. She's a child."

"You're the one who gave her the sword. If the Dragonkin won't let us send her home, she'd best learn how to defend herself."

Rowen shook his head. "Krym won't expect her to fight. If and when we face Nekiel, I mean to lock her as far away as possible. Or would you prefer her on the front lines?"

Igrid scowled. "Of course not. But a lot can happen between here and the Wintersea. We could meet another caravan, to say nothing of thieves, wolves, even a squad of Lancers who don't think kindly of a Dragonkin passing through their kingdom."

Rowen tensed, realizing he had hardly considered the latter. Krym had avoided the city of Cassica, to everyone's relief, but that had taken them closer to Ivairia. Rowen remembered the stories of the Dragonjol utterly devastating the countryside and incinerating the Ivairian king. Soon after, the mighty Arnil Royce fell in battle against the Bloody

Prince, as well. Ever since, the Ivairians had been mired in civil war. They did not ally with the Sons of Maelmohr, but the king's heirs still warred over the crown, which had changed hands at least three times in the past few years.

"I should have taken Maddoc and the others to Ivairia. I should have used their magic to heal the sick and injured, like we did at New Atheion. If I had—"

"This may come as a shock to you, Sir Locke, but you are not responsible for safeguarding all the lives on Ruun." Igrid removed the breast-knife from her bodice and used it to trim her fingernails. "I just meant that I want Thessa to be ready in case we encounter trouble."

"Which we always do." Rowen stood. "But you're not wrong."

"I'm usually not." Igrid returned the breast knife to its hiding place and stood.

She moved toward Saanji and Zeia while Rowen headed toward Thessa. Keswen met him halfway, and Rowen noted the scowl on the huntress's face.

"Vaari," she said, nodding toward where the Dhargot sat at the far edge of the camp, inspecting each of his arrows. "He's been eyeing that girl a bit too closely for my liking."

Rowen frowned. He saw a faint snicker on the Dhargot's scarred face though Vaari currently seemed most interested in an arrowhead he was holding up to the sunlight. Rowen turned to look at Thessa. For the first time, he noticed that, in place of britches, Thessa was wearing a fighting skirt made of thin leather strips that twirled when she moved, revealing the strong pale thighs underneath. Presumably, she'd borrowed the fighting skirt from Igrid, though Igrid had not mentioned it.

Rowen blushed. Igrid often wore revealing attire to distract her enemies, with great success, but it was quite another thing to notice such clothing on Thessa. "Tell me, Keswen. Do you think you could put an arrow through Vaari's eye from here?"

"Easily," Keswen said, "though I had another target in mind." She paused. "The girl's not doing anything wrong. Gods know she shouldn't even be here, but—"

"I know." Rowen sighed. "This isn't the time for a fight. If it happens again, I'll tell Saanji to throttle him. In the meantime, take him on patrol with you. Don't kill him, but if he aggravates you, feel free to bloody his lip a bit."

A rare, faint smile touched the Sylvan huntress's lips. "Gladly, Sword Marshal."

"And take Breaksteel with you."

Keswen's smile vanished. "I don't want the Olg with me."

"I didn't think you did, but take him anyway."

Rowen went to join Thessa and Sir Issa before Keswen could argue. Breaksteel was on one knee, sharpening his kashpa, but he stood and bowed at Rowen's approach then went to follow Keswen when she furiously waved at him. Rowen faced Sir Issa and tried to stop the duel, but Thessa laughed and kept swinging. Rowen saw Issa wince as the shortsword landed a jarring blow on one of the young Knight's spaulders. Thessa pulled back her sword, intending to jab the Knight's shoulder a second time. Rowen drew his adamune and disarmed Thessa with one quick swing.

Thessa frowned. "That's not fair. I didn't see you—"

"Look at your sword," Rowen said, forcing himself to sound stern.

Thessa blinked. Then she stooped and recovered her shortsword. She backed up, holding her blade at the ready, but Rowen did not attack. Instead, he sheathed his adamune and waited. Finally, Thessa lifted her shortsword to her face, studying the blade.

Her eyes widened, and she cried out in dismay. "The edges are all chipped!"

"Of course they are," Rowen said. "Half the time, you're blocking Issa's blade with your own. The other half, you're swinging at solid armor. His gear is made of kingsteel. Yours isn't. That means yours will chip like glass if you mistreat it." Rowen glanced at Sir Issa and saw the young Knight blush, catching the rebuke.

"Then what am I supposed to do?" Thessa said.

"Don't block if you don't have to. Get out of the way. Swing for the soft parts of the body. This is fighting, not fencing." Rowen drew his sword and jabbed for Thessa's throat.

Though he moved only half as fast as he could have, the girl's eyes widened. She started to parry the blow, remembered his advice, and sidestepped.

"Better," Rowen said, "but too slow." He lunged twice more, faster each time.

Thessa dodged the first blow but tried to spin away from the second—an overcomplicated move that required Rowen to stop short before he ran her through.

"Less flourish. Keep it simple," Rowen advised. "There's looking good in front of the lords and ladies, and there's staying alive. Your goal is the latter." He moved in more quickly. That time, he parried Thessa's sword and pressed the unsharpened edge of his adamune to her throat. Despite a rush of guilt, he gave her a stern look as he pushed her back.

Thessa glanced worriedly at the edge of her shortsword. "But you said—"

"*My* sword is kingsteel. Yours isn't. Don't expect your enemy to accommodate you." Rowen feigned a lunge then stopped. "Do you know where that sword came from?" When Thessa shook her head, he said, "My brother gave me that, years and years ago."

"Kayden." Thessa gasped. "Igrid told me about him."

Thessa looked as though she wanted to say more, but Rowen resumed his attack, forcing her to dodge and sidestep, faster and faster, her eyes wide, her fighting skirt flying.

"Did she tell you I killed him?"

Thessa bit her lip and nodded. "She said you had to. He was possessed. The Shel'ai named Shade made him—"

Rowen knocked the shortsword from Thessa's grasp then kicked it back toward her. "Kayden was a good fighter. At least at the time, he was better than me. I'm sure of it. But he *wanted* me to beat him. So he fought against the magic as best he could, even as he fought me, until I finally killed him." Rowen paused. "When I pulled my sword out, I felt the blade scraping against the bones of his ribcage."

Thessa paled, speechless.

Rowen continued. "Other times, I've stabbed men in the lungs and seen them drown in their own blood or lopped off their limbs and watched them cry as they bled to death." He paused. "Why do you think I'm telling you this?"

Thessa started to speak, had to clear her throat, and started again. "You want me to know... what it's like to kill someone."

Rowen nodded. "The Codex Lotius says—"

"I know what it says," Thessa interrupted. "I've read it. Twice."

"But have you understood it?" Rowen stepped forward and held out his adamune, letting the sunlight flash off the chrysanthemums etched into the blade. "This belonged to Sang Wei. Remember how brave and fast he was? He was a better swordsman than I am, and a great and honorable Knight besides, and he still died."

Thessa stared at the adamune with reverence. She started to touch it but stopped herself. "I know. Crovis killed him. But you killed Crovis. That means you're better than both of them!"

Rowen shook his head and sheathed the adamune. "I beat Crovis because I had Knightswrath. I defeated Fadarah and Chorlga the same way. I cut them down with a burning sword they could not possibly block or avoid. It was not honorable or glorious. But it was necessary." He paused again. "Why am I telling you this?"

That time, Thessa had no guess.

Rowen squeezed her shoulder. "You don't have to be a fighter, child, but if that's the life you choose, know what you're getting into." He saw tears forming in her eyes but forced himself to turn and walk away. As he did so, he nearly collided with Igrid.

"That was a damn foolish thing to do," she whispered hotly.

"You said you wanted her prepared—"

"All that talk will do is make her hesitate if and when the time comes." Igrid shook her head. "Let her think that killing is all pleasure and glory if it'll keep her alive. She'll learn the truth soon enough."

Before Rowen could argue, Krym rose from his knees and descended from the ridge, the Maalbolg at his elbow. He came to stand before Rowen but raised his voice so all could hear. "Nekiel's power grows as his memory returns, but for now, he remains weak. While that makes him less dangerous at the moment, that also makes him far more difficult to locate. I have only a vague impression of where he might be."

Rowen bit back his anger. "You said yesterday that you'd found him!"

Krym smiled faintly. "I did. Unfortunately, he chose not to turn himself into a statue and simply wait for us to come and kill him."

Saanji edged closer. "A vague impression might be more than we

135

need. These lands are sparsely inhabited. There can't be more than one or two villages between here and the Wintersea."

Zeia said, "Agreed. If we watch the roads, we could set up an ambush—"

"No," Krym said. "He is weakened, but he is by no means powerless. If he were to bypass us and reach the Wintersea before we can find Khyrshar, he would be unstoppable. Our safest course of action is to reach the dragon first then lie in wait." The Dragonkin strode toward the horses.

The Maalbolg backed away from the others, holding his sword hilt as his maw clacked derisively.

Krym called back, "I see that three are missing. We have no time to waste. They will have to catch up."

Rowen was about to insist on riding out himself, finding Keswen and the others, and bringing them back.

Zeia moved closer. "Don't," she whispered. "The huntress can track us. If he wants to leave so damn badly, we should go."

Without waiting for a reply, Zeia headed for her horse. Rowen did likewise. As he mounted, he glanced back at Thessa and saw the fright in the girl's expression. She held her shortsword with a trembling hand and fumbled as she sheathed it. Remembering Igrid's rebuke, Rowen cursed himself and wished he had not told the girl a thing.

CHAPTER FOURTEEN

THE KING WOKE IN MUD. He looked around. The late afternoon sun felt hot against his sunburnt face and limbs. Then he noticed a cracked clay jar lying next to him. A little wine remained at the bottom. The king drank it then spat out a jagged bit of clay. He tried to stand, but a jolt of pain raced from brain to foot. He shut his eyes for a moment.

Gods, where am I? Slowly, he opened his eyes. He stared at the muddy earth, the stark and naked grasslands beneath a blue, cruelly open sky. *The wildlands. I'm in the wildlands… outside my kingdom.* The king laughed. "Not my kingdom anymore." Noting the sword at his side, he drew it. Mud crusted the elaborate brass wire of the pommel. Dirt flecked the blade, though he could not remember how it had gotten there.

Using his sword as a crutch, the king pushed himself to his feet. His head roiled again, but he shut his eyes until the pain passed. Then he took stock of his possessions. Aside from his attire—fine leather boots, silken britches and a tunic, both torn and stained—he had a coin pouch at his belt. He opened it. Empty. Still, his right hand wore three solid gold rings, one of them crusted with sapphires, while a platinum ring adorned his left thumb.

I could sell those for a horse and supplies. Maybe even hire a few bodyguards. They could take me back to Sylvos, back to the trees—

"No." The king sheathed his unclean sword. "Sylvos is ashes now. Like my son." He turned in a slow circle, surveying the strange land before him. He could not remember how long he had been here, but he figured it had to be weeks, perhaps months. He vaguely remembered riding from Shaffrilon in the dead of night, on horseback, screaming at everyone who tried to stop him, but it seemed impossible that he could have gotten away, that his subjects would simply let him go.

Why should they try and stop me? Because of me, our ancient homeland was destroyed. Even as he had the thought, the king dimly remembered someone—Captain Briel, maybe—yelling at him, insisting that the war was over and the Olgrym had been driven back, along with their Shel'ai allies. The king knew the truth, though. He had seen his own son reduced to a blackened husk. He had heard the screams of his people. He had witnessed the awful power of Chorlga. Surely, all these months of suffering were all just a trick designed to torment him… or some terrible limbo inflicted by the gods as punishment.

The king considered drawing his sword and falling on the blade. It occurred to him that he must have considered that many times over the past few months, but that was the coward's way. "I am no coward," The king told the mud. "I will atone for my crimes. I will find those who wrecked my kingdom and kill them. I will kill them all or die trying."

As he spoke, the king gripped his sword hilt. A memory came back to him: a ragged band of Humans stopping him on the road, perhaps only a day or two before. The king had intended to ignore them, aggravated by their grating Human speech, but then they'd tried to rob him, perhaps taking note of his rich attire. He could not remember for sure what had happened, but the fact that he was still alive probably meant that he'd proven less feeble than the robbers expected.

The Sylvan king half drew his sword, noting that what he had taken at first for dirt looked more like dried blood. A cold smile formed on his lips. "I am old. I am broken. But I am not dead yet. I will see my enemies slain. I will see Quivalen avenged. I will—"

As though to mock his resolve, one of his legs shuddered and gave way beneath him, and the king fell hard. Nausea twisted his guts, making him retch up the bit of wine he'd swallowed then continue dry heaving until his eyes watered. He wondered how much time had passed since he'd eaten. He could not remember but knew it must have been a great while, given how his tattered clothes hung off his body.

For the moment, though, thirst was his greatest adversary. His throat ached, unleashing tendrils of pain that spread throughout his skull and dissipated down into the rest of his body. The king wondered how far he was from water. *Could be miles.* He considered closing his eyes and simply letting sleep or death close over him.

Instead, he chose a direction and started crawling.

Keswen shifted her glare from Vaari to Breaksteel and wondered which man she hated more. Finally settling on the latter, she looked down at where the Olg walked, just a few yards from her horse. "I wonder if you've killed more Sylvs than I've killed Olgrym."

Breaksteel looked at her, unflinching, and made a quick hand-sign.

Keswen laughed. "None? I find that hard to believe." She turned to Vaari. "What about you, Dhargot? Spilled any Olgish blood in this lifetime? Or Sylvan blood, maybe? Your kind took mine captive for a while, if memory serves. Sold them as slaves. Probably raped some to death."

Vaari used one finger to squash a mosquito that was crawling on his armor and flicked it in her direction.

"That's not the detailed answer I was hoping for."

Vaari said, "Keep your venom to yourself, Sylv. I serve the Tomato Prince, not you."

"Yet you mock him."

Vaari scoffed. "Half the Earless call him that, and both halves would die for him if it came to it." After a moment, he added, "Besides, *Earless* was originally meant as an insult, too. Now, we embrace it."

"True," Keswen said, "but something tells me you tied plenty of dead men's ears around your neck before Saanji made you stop."

Vaari yawned. "Sylv, what part of *keep your venom to yourself* did you not understand?"

Keswen drew an arrow from her quiver and fit it to her bowstring, holding it in place with one finger. "To be honest, the last Dhargot I killed was General Brahasti. And he—"

"I heard," Vaari said. "He drugged a whole pit full of pretty Sylvan girls and tried to fill up their bellies with Shel'ai bastards. Only yours was born dead." He scratched at a deep scar on his cheek. "I assume that's the source of your ire even though it's been, what, five years almost?"

"Four." Keswen glanced at Vaari then Breaksteel. "You'll have to pardon my temper, Dhargot. I don't often find myself wedged between two former enemies."

"Yeah, I suppose it's been a while since that happened." Vaari chuckled. "Look on the bright side, Sylv. At least we're better company than the Dragonkin."

That's debatable. Keswen edged her horse closer to Vaari's, which instinctively responded by moving farther away. Then she did the same to Breaksteel. Keswen's temper eased with more breathing room on either side, though it still irked her that she'd been sent on patrol with those two men. She suspected that had been deliberate on Locke's part and wondered if the Sword Marshal knew his attempt to teach her a lesson would likely have the opposite effect.

She tried to concentrate on her surroundings. Telling herself that the Olg and the Dhargot might be reprehensible but did not pose an actual threat to her—at least at the moment—she studied the hills and grasslands before her, scanning them for hidden enemies. However, those lands were so sparsely inhabited that she doubted they would encounter any travelers or villagers. The trees had thinned, and a chill in the air told her approximately where they were without having to consult a map. She missed the warmth of the Ash'bana Plains, with the familiar heights of the forest in the distance, even though she doubted more than ever that she would ever go back and rejoin the Wyldkin.

That's not my home anymore. Then again, maybe Cadavash isn't, either.

Vaari whistled and pointed. Keswen turned southeast in time to see a line of riders in the distance. Irked that the Dhargot had spotted them before her, she reached for her Soroccan spyglass.

She peered through the lens and frowned. "Lancers." After a moment's hesitation, she offered the spyglass to Vaari, who shook his head.

"No need. I can already smell their perfume and smugness."

Keswen considered offering the spyglass to Breaksteel and decided she did not want to risk the Olg's gigantic hands crushing it. She raised it to her own eye again. "A few score plus half again as many squires." She swore. "They've spotted us."

"So do we ride back to Locke and let him handle this or talk to them ourselves?"

Breaksteel made a hand gesture opting for the former, but Keswen did not bother translating his vote to Vaari.

She made her choice and said, "I'll talk to them. Keep those arrows in the quiver, Dhargot. And both of you, stay here." She glared at Breaksteel in particular, imagining how puzzled the Lancers would be by an Olg in the garb of a squire from the Lotus Isles.

Keswen forced herself to take the arrow off her bowstring and return it to her quiver. Then she rode straight at the Lancers. She rode quickly at first, eager to put some distance between herself and her scouting companions, then she slowed and held up her hand. "Well met, Lancers. My name is Keswen. I serve Rowen Locke, Sword Marshal of—"

"Who are those two you're traveling with?" one of the Lancers demanded, riding ahead of the others. He was a balding man with a scar on his face, which ran through the corner of his mouth. Like the front half of the column, he wore full, heavy armor decorated with a bright, multicolored tabard depicting a crowned horse.

Keswen bristled at the man's rude tone. "Both serve Sir Locke, who rides nearby. He pursues a company of brigands that raided a village a few days ago." She paused, wondering how eager the Lancers might be to join in the hunt. She eyed the column again, noting that those in the rear appeared to be humble squires, donned in leather and solemnly carrying their betters' lances and provisions. "If you wish to aid us in their capture, you could continue northeast and watch the roads for—"

"You're a Sylv." The Lancer frowned. "One of your friends back there looks like an Olg. You really expect me to believe you're serving Rowen Locke, the famous Isle Knight?"

"If you need to verify my words with Sir Locke, that's your business. I can take you to him. I just thought I'd greet you and save you the trouble of—"

"Cadavash is days and days south of here." The Lancer's scowl deepened. "And your other friend looks like he's wearing Dhargothi armor."

Keswen considered lying then thought better of it. "He serves Prince Saanji, who was a close friend and ally to Sir Arnil Royce."

The Lancer glanced back at the armored men behind him, all of whom eyed Keswen with distrust. "Sir Royce is dead. He died at Hesod, fighting the Bloody Prince."

"I never said otherwise." Keswen resisted the sudden urge to nock an arrow. "In fact, I am also acquainted with Prince Saanji, who was the one who avenged Sir Royce's death."

"And I suppose you're going to tell me that Prince Saanji is traveling with you, too? Quite the distinguished band of friends you have!" A few Lancers laughed.

Keswen gave the commanding Lancer a hard look. "What is your name, Sir?"

"Tell me *your* name first."

I already did. "Keswen of Cadavash." Remembering the diplomatic title given to her by General Briel, which she never used, she added, "I serve Sir Locke as the emissary of Sylvos, what you'd call the Wytchforest. Yes, we are far from home, but we're hunting—"

"Village-burning brigands. So you said." The Lancer looked her over, urging his armored horse a little closer. "You're a pretty one, Keswen of Cadavash, but a little savage for my liking. I've never met a woman with feathers in her hair. Then again, I've never seen a Sylv before, either. Tell me, are they all pretty liars?"

Keswen measured the distance between her and the Lancer, rehearsing the motion needed to put an arrow through the man's eye. "You have asked a number of questions, Lancer. I have asked only one. I'd appreciate an answer."

The Lancer snickered. "I am Sir Ferinald of Houster. It's my job to safeguard our borders from… foreign elements. And if I seem discourteous, perhaps it has something to do with reports of Isle Knights traveling south of our borders, accompanied by a hundred Dwarrs… and a godsdamned Shel'ai."

Keswen frowned. She thought at first that the Isle Knights must belong to the party of Sir Lamrey, which had been escorting Gaulgodd, but then she wondered if they had been joined by Jalist and Maddoc. *Maybe the Isle Knights even sent a second force to help Locke, after his message.* She cleared her throat, choosing her words carefully. "Much has happened, Sir Ferinald. Your wariness is understandable. Sir Locke can answer your questions more fully than I can." *And decide if he wants to tell you the truth about the Dragonkin.* "With your leave, I'll guide you to him."

Sir Ferinald urged his horse so close to Keswen's that her mount shied away. The Lancer leaned toward her, resting one hand on the hilt of a bastard sword. Since he was too close for an arrow, Keswen considered drawing a knife and putting it through his eye but tried her best to look demure instead.

"Here's the problem, Sylv," Sir Ferinald said finally. "In addition to the strange reports from the south, we found someone on the road yesterday... a woman with pointed ears, only her eyes were purple instead of blue. Maybe you know her?"

"I'm sure I don't."

"What about what she's doing here? Can you tell me that?"

"If I can't answer one question, how am I supposed to answer the other?" Keswen shook her head. "Apologies, Sir Ferinald, but I don't know every Shel'ai in the world. I doubt Sir Locke does, either."

"I might believe that," Sir Ferinald said, "but *this* wytch happened to be stumbling around in a daze, speaking Rowen Locke's name. She hasn't stopped repeating it since we found her." The Lancer paused. "Do you have an explanation for that?"

Keswen met the Lancer's hard gaze for a moment then risked looking back over her shoulder. Vaari and Breaksteel were where she had left them, still watching. They were distant enough that they would have no trouble getting away from the Lancers, though she could only guess what would happen after that.

She turned back to Sir Ferinald. "I do not."

"I didn't think so." Sir Ferinald drew his sword.

Keswen drew her own, prepared to block. Instead of swinging at her, though, the Lancer swung at her horse's neck. The great beast's body opened in a shower of blood. Keswen instinctively leapt from the saddle a moment before her horse crashed to the earth. She managed to roll clear, still holding her sword in one hand and her bow in the other. Dropping her sword, she drew an arrow instead.

Keswen had the pleasure of seeing Sir Ferinald's smug expression melt into wide-eyed panic. She loosed an arrow at the Lancer's throat.

Somehow, the Lancer lifted his head in time, and the arrow rebounded off his heavy steel gorget.

Keswen fit another arrow with lightning speed, but the other Lancers were already moving. Hooves thundered, and muscles surged as the riders encircled her. Swords blurred from their scabbards.

Keswen kept her eyes on Sir Ferinald. "Careful, Lancer. This next one goes through your eye unless your men back off."

But one Lancer moved to block her shot with a wide metal shield. Cursing, Keswen ducked beneath one mailed hand after another as she tried to slip free of the circle. She had almost made it when a Lancer's backhand brought the flat of a blade slapping across her face. Keswen fell. She considered slashing off the foot of the Lancer who had struck her or cutting open the underbelly of his horse but restrained herself.

"Mistake," she said, spitting blood. "Not an enemy. I told you, I serve—"

A heavy weight struck the back of her neck, scattering the rest of her words.

CHAPTER FIFTEEN

MADDOC TRIED TO IGNORE THE armed men moving all around them as he bathed Sariel in the creek. Still, the flash of azure tabards and kingsteel armor contrasted with the dark ring mail of the Dwarrs and the scarlet uniforms of the Red Watch. Strangely, the knowledge that he was surrounded by allies increased his anxiety rather than heartening him. Sariel, on the other hand, seemed fascinated by the activity, laughing with joy and pointing each time a mounted Isle Knight rode by. As Maddoc stood knee-deep in cold water, with his britches folded up to his thighs, palming water over Sariel's pale curls, he eyed the war tent in the distance.

Jalist had been in that tent for hours, arguing with Aeko Shingawa and some other Isle Knight, whose name Maddoc could not remember. Apparently, the latter had encountered Rowen Locke on the road a few days before, traveling in the company of a less-than-cordial Dragonkin. The Knight whose name Maddoc could not remember insisted that Rowen was in league with the Dragonkin, had stolen the prisoner, Gaulgodd, and should therefore be considered a traitor. He had even tried to convene a kind of trial, though Aeko arrived with a hundred more Knights in time to stop him.

Since then, though, nobody could agree on anything. Aeko insisted their combined force of Knights and Dwarrs should keep its distance, assisting Rowen only if and when it was absolutely necessary. Jalist, on the other hand, was all in favor of racing north and hurtling every sword, axe, and arrow at any Dragonkin they found.

"Locke's gone and made himself a prisoner again," Jalist insisted, "and as thickheaded as he may be, he still deserves a rescue."

Maddoc was inclined to agree with Aeko but kept that to himself. After all, he had little room to argue, since Jalist had been reluctant to let Maddoc come along and had roundly refused to let Sariel join them—that was, until Maddoc reminded Jalist what would probably happen to the mead halls of Tarator if they left Sariel alone. Nor had circumstances allowed them the time it would take to return her to Cadavash and entrust her to whatever Shel'ai remained there.

Gods, we're going to war with a five-year-old...

As though in answer, Sariel twisted around, water flying off her body, and conjured a flaming sword out of thin air. Caught off guard, Maddoc had no time to counter the spell. Instead, he threw himself backward, into the cold water, just as the flaming sword passed right through the air where his face had been.

Sariel laughed.

Maddoc swore so fiercely that Sariel's expression changed instantly, and the flaming sword vanished. She started to back away, but Maddoc leapt up, thoroughly drenched, and hugged her.

"Easy, child. There are a hundred anxious men with swords watching. No tantrums, please." He tickled her.

Sariel responded with laughter then turned and let Maddoc continue washing her hair. Unable to free his hands long enough to wring out his clothes, Maddoc allowed a little wytchfire to rise from his skin as he continued bathing the child. The flames made steam rise from his clothes without singeing the fabric.

"Enough, little one. Time to dry off." Maddoc allowed the fire to spread gently over Sariel's body. Sariel answered with more laughter a moment before she summoned wytchfire of her own. Hers burned unchecked, though, and Maddoc stepped back an instant before the child became a violet fireball. Stream water boiled around her, bubbling like a cauldron.

"Enough." Maddoc dismissed Sariel's wytchfire, scooped up the child with his cloak, and carried her toward the shore. He pretended not to notice the scowls of all the Isle Knights and Dwarrs who lingered by the stream, watching.

146

A Dwarrish servant reluctantly approached, handed him a towel, and backed away.

Maddoc dried and dressed the child, pressing her hair in the towel one long pale tendril at a time. He had just finished when someone nearby cleared his throat. Maddoc turned and saw Falder. In place of a steward's clothing, the young Dwarr wore ring mail and a matching pair of blackened steel maces.

"Lord Maddoc, we have visitors." The steward cast a mistrustful eye at Sariel then turned and glanced at the war tent. "Governor Jalist is still occupied, so I thought—"

"Who and how many?"

"Fifty. All women, all armored. They're wearing a sigil I've never seen before—a madwoman with her breasts out, spearing a dragon."

Maddoc smothered a grin. "Iron Sisters. Does Captain Haesha lead them?"

"She didn't give a name, m'lord. But it's a black-skinned woman with blue eyes—long hair, all tied up. She didn't seem fond of conversation."

"Take me to her." Maddoc considered sending Sariel back to his tent or entrusting her with one of the servants, but he had already tried that twice since leaving Stillhammer, and the results had been less than pleasant. He held out a hand, and Sariel took it. "Come, my little tempest. Let's go meet our new friends."

Falder led the way, striding well ahead of them. Maddoc followed, leading Sariel through a chaotic mass of tents and mounts, guiding her around the impressive mess left by a passing horse. At the edge of the camp, a dozen armored women on horseback waited in tense silence with an equal number of Dwarrish footmen and scowling Isle Knights, plus a handful of Red Watch.

Maddoc found the leader, a beautiful woman with the dark skin of a Soroccan, and bowed. "Well met. I am Maddoc, Governor Jalist's aide-de-camp. The Isle Knights are led by—"

"Aeko Shingawa, the Grand Marshal herself," the Iron Sister interrupted with a smirk. "I've heard. Where is she?"

"She and Governor Jalist are in the middle of a council. I can take you to them." Maddoc hesitated. "This is Sariel, the adopted daughter of—"

"Wytchfriend." The Iron Sister laughed. She bowed at Sariel from the saddle. "Hello, little one. You have eyes like lilacs."

Sariel grinned, speechless.

Maddoc said, "Did Captain Haesha send you?"

The Iron Sister nodded. "She got Sir Locke's message. Once she decided it wasn't a ruse, she sent us—all she could spare, I'm afraid. Just so you know, General Briel of the Wytchforest is a few days behind us with a few hundred Sylvs. We considered waiting, but this business seemed urgent." She looked around. "I don't see any charred bodies or hear any wailing. Was the message a ruse after all?"

Maddoc gave her a sour look. "Sadly, no. Locke is a day or three north with the Dragonkin called Krym. Beyond that, we know no more than you do." He paused. "Your name, please?"

"Apologies. I am Captain Tansil. My older sister was Ailynn, who trained and commanded Locke's wife, Igrid."

Maddoc saw no need to correct Tansil by informing her that Rowen and Igrid were not actually married. "Greetings, Captain. I am sorry for your sister."

"Don't be. She died in battle. Better that than the cage they had her in before." Tansil dismounted, cracked her neck, and passed the reins to the woman next to her.

Maddoc noted that the Iron Sister's armor seemed to cover less than it left exposed. Falder eyed the Iron Sister with a mixture of interest and disdain. Maddoc also noted the long, deep scars on her thighs as she readjusted her sword belt and stepped forward.

"Now, sorcerer, suppose you take me to your commanders so we can figure out how to save the world?" She stepped forward and held out her hand to Sariel. "If I hold your hand, Lilac, you won't burn it off, will you?"

Sariel shook her head, wide-eyed and solemn, and took Captain Tansil's hand in her own.

Rowen heard Vaari shouting a continuous stream of curses long before the Dhargot rode into view. Breaksteel followed. Vaari nearly leapt from the saddle and stomped toward Rowen, his face purple with rage. "A damn fine chase you led us on! What part of—"

Breaksteel grabbed Vaari by the tunic and hauled him backward. Vaari wheeled, his mismatched eyes wide with rage as he drew his sword. Breaksteel took a step back and readied his kashpa. The Olg glanced past Vaari's shoulder at Rowen and asked through hand-speech for permission to cut Vaari in half.

Rowen shook his head. "Sheathe your sword and turn around," he said to Vaari. "And while you're at it, calm down. Where's Keswen?"

Breaksteel started to answer in hand-speech, but Vaari stepped sideways, blocking Rowen's view.

The Dhargot swung his sword at empty air then sheathed it. "Dead," he snapped. "Probably." He faced Breaksteel again. "Want to tell me what you just said? I don't know your hand-signs, but I know a threat when—"

Saanji joined them and placed a restraining hand on Vaari's arm. "Enough bluster. Just tell us what happened."

"Attacked." Vaari spat on the ground and recounted his tale. Breaksteel confirmed it all with a curt nod of his dark, shaggy locks.

Rowen stood still for a moment, unsure what to do next. The horses were grazing in the distance. Thessa and Issa were sparring nearby. The young Knight of the Crane had noted the way Vaari and Breaksteel rushed into the camp and appeared to be trying to keep Thessa distracted. Krym was eyeing Rowen from the far end of the camp, where he was presumably in telepathic conversation with the Maalbolg, both of them smiling indifferently. Rowen had the feeling that if he asked the Dragonkin to go and retrieve Keswen from the Lancers, he would happily do so.

But what happens afterward? How many would he kill? Rowen started toward his horse. "Everyone, wait here until I return. I'm going alone." He waved a fly from his face.

Igrid grabbed his arm. "And I've got gods' spit for blood."

Saanji joined them. "No sense giving them another prisoner. If you want to free her, Zeia can slip in, quick and quiet, and cut her free."

Zeia answered with a slight nod.

"No," Rowen said. "They'll have too many guards, and they'll be expecting something like that. We can't shed blood over this. This isn't just about rescuing Keswen. The Lancers won't start a war unless I give them a reason."

Vaari spat on the ground. "Seems *they* started the war when they cuffed your huntress across the back of the neck."

Rowen said, "He'll pay for that. But we'll be the ones who pay if we start cutting down his men, so I'll go in and tell them to give me Keswen back, and they will."

Saanji frowned. "Are you sure about that?"

Krym approached them with smug slowness. "Allow me to tend to this matter, Sir Locke. You and your companions should stay here and rest. The Maalbolg and I can easily recover your friend."

The Maalbolg clicked in answer, the ends of his lips twisting in a gruesome, toothy smile. Then the creature held one claw in the air. Rowen wondered what he was doing until the fly that had pestered him earlier landed—as though summoned—on the very tip of the Maalbolg's claw. The creature made a clicking sound, like a demon cooing at a baby. Then the hand twisted, obscenely fast, pinching the fly between two claws.

I wonder if he could kill Lancers just as easily. Rowen had a feeling that he already knew the answer. He shifted his gaze to Krym, recalling what the Dragonkin had done to Sir Lamrey and his Isle Knights. "No. This must be done without bloodshed. It might not bother *you* to see Ruun subjected to another war but—"

"There will be no bloodshed," Krym insisted. "I swear it on the soul of Namundvar. I can pluck the Sylv from their clutches without a single drop of blood being spilled."

"But they will know it was done with magic," Rowen countered. "If they were bold enough to take Keswen in the first place, they're looking for an excuse to fight."

Igrid said, "All the more reason for you to stay away from them!"

Rowen shook his head. "I've known men like their commander. This is a game to him. That's why he let Vaari and Breaksteel go. It's a test. If I answer with the right amount of force, he'll let Keswen go. Any more than that, and—"

"Could be she's already dead," Vaari said, scraping under one fingernail with a knife. "Looked like they hit her pretty good. Probably stripped her bare and had some fun afterwards. If she wouldn't play along with that, they might have—"

"They wouldn't do that," Rowen said. *Not yet, anyway.* He looked at Saanji. "Any chance these are the same Lancers you fought beside at Hesod?"

"I doubt it," Saanji said. "Royce's men weren't the type to club women across the back of the neck. Besides that, I spent most of the campaign blind drunk. But I'll go with you, just in case."

Rowen nodded his thanks. "The Lancers don't need to know what we're doing here"—he glanced at Krym—"and I'd like to avoid telling them if possible. Keswen probably already told them a story about chasing down highwaymen or trying to recover some sacred relic, so—"

"You forget yourself," Krym said. "*All* of you forget yourselves." The air shimmered around the Dragonkin's body. Rowen beheld Krym's shadow stretching across the ground, becoming massive and winged as a wave of heat made everyone but the Maalbolg step back. "We have more pressing concerns than the fate of one scout. If you'll not let me resolve this quickly, we cannot waste the time you are proposing."

Rowen forced himself to meet Krym's unblinking gaze despite the Dragonkin's threatening tone. "I have done everything you asked, Dragonkin, but Keswen is my friend. I will not leave her behind."

"You will if you agree that an entire continent matters more than one lone Sylv whom you might very well be able to retrieve later, once Nekiel has been killed."

"You said yourself Nekiel is still weak. We can reach the Wintersea well ahead of him. I'll save Keswen now, so that she can help us, if it's all the same to you."

Krym's smile contrasted with his narrow, unblinking gaze. "I'm afraid it isn't."

Rowen steeled himself. "I wasn't asking permission, Dragonkin. Torture or kill me if you like, but so long as I am able, I will see this done. Either accept that or consider our alliance finished."

Krym smirked as though he were being rebuked by an unruly child. His shadow shifted, becoming that of a man again. "Very well, Sir Locke. You are a credit to your Order. Go, then, with my blessing. But your woman and the child stay here." Without waiting for a reply, Krym turned, walked back to the edge of the camp, and knelt in meditation.

The Maalbolg hovered over him, pacing back and forth, his eyes never leaving Rowen and the others. A moment later, a sparrow alighted on the branch of a nearby tree. The Maalbolg turned, cocked his head, and regarded the sparrow a dozen yards away. Then he leapt—an awful blue-white blur, claws flashing. The Maalbolg's mouth made an awful crunching sound a moment before it sauntered back to Krym's side, its maw splattered in blood.

Igrid slid her hand down Rowen's arm, squeezed his sword hand, and moved it away from his blade. "We'll be all right. Take Sir Issa with you. The more kingsteel they see, the better."

Rowen shook his head. "I'm not leaving the two of you with *them*."

"You are if you want to get Keswen back." Igrid kissed his cheek. "They won't hurt us. Whatever's going to happen, it won't happen until we meet Nekiel." She smirked. "Strange to say that name out loud. I half expect to see Fâyu Jinn and Nâya springing up any moment, along with whatever other fairy tales I can remember."

Rowen sensed the unease behind her joke. "I'll leave someone. Maybe Breaksteel or Zeia—"

"Your two scariest fighters? No. You'll need them." Igrid gave him a gentle shove. "Go. I'll explain things to Thessa."

Rowen hesitated then nodded. He waved to Sir Issa, who was busy trying to appear hard pressed by Thessa's assault, and hoped he was not making a mistake.

Keswen woke. Dried blood had crusted in her eyes and around her nose. As she brushed it away, she marveled that the Lancers had not bothered to bind her hands. She looked around. Waning sunlight streaming through the white fabric of a war tent told her the Lancers had made camp. The tent was empty, save for another prisoner.

At first, Keswen thought the prisoner—a woman—was dead. The prisoner was turned away, and unlike Keswen, her hands and feet were bound. Her silk clothing was immodestly torn and so mud stained that Keswen could not discern its original color. Bruises and welts covered the exposed flesh. An ugly, blood-crusted cut ran between the woman's shoulder blades.

Rather than calling out to her, Keswen crawled over and lifted the prisoner's matted dark curls, revealing long, tapered ears. Though Sir

Ferinald had mentioned finding a Shel'ai in the wild, Keswen had only ever known one other Shel'ai who had dark hair, and that was Zeia. Keswen felt for a pulse and considered shaking the woman awake. Instead, she gently rolled the prisoner onto her back to get a better look at her face.

Keswen gasped. Though the young woman was unconscious, her violet eyes were wide and staring. The woman's eyes appeared a darker shade of purple than any Shel'ai that Keswen had ever seen, though—almost black but flecked in places with gold.

Could be from her injuries. Keswen had seen men's eyes go wide and dark as inkwells after sustaining a head wound. The woman's nose and mouth were crusted in dried blood, and as filthy as she was, Keswen could not tell whether the woman had received a blow to the head as well. Keswen considered trying to shake her awake. Before she could make up her mind, the rattle of armor told her someone was approaching the tent.

Keswen lay down and closed her eyes, pretending to sleep. She heard the shift of armor and the stomp of boots as men—she counted three—strode into the tent. One barked at her to sit up. Keswen did not move. Someone kicked her, and pain swept through her ribcage, radiating throughout her entire body. Keswen had anticipated being struck, but the blow jarred her. Instinctively rolling away, she pressed her arms to her sides.

"A word of advice," she said after a moment. "If you want me to talk, don't kick my ribs into my lungs."

A fourth Lancer strode into the tent. He was plain faced and looked nearly indistinguishable from the others, save for the startling greenness of his eyes. He looked down at her and frowned. "Which of you struck her?" When no one answered, he said, "Get out."

The others hesitated then obeyed.

The fourth Lancer stared down at Keswen for a moment, crossing his arms. Finally, he said, "I am Sir Hale. I am sorry you were mistreated. In a moment, I'll bring you water and a towel—food, later. But first, I have to ask you some questions."

Keswen sat up. She nodded toward the other prisoner. "You might want to do the same for her... if she's still alive, that is." She hoped the

Lancer would be alarmed enough to check the prisoner's pulse, giving Keswen a chance to strike from behind.

Instead, he took a step back. "I'm not particularly concerned with wytches. But Sylvs are not wytches, in spite of the pointed ears. Most Lancers don't realize that. Then again, few have ever seen—"

"Where is Sir Ferinald?"

"Elsewhere."

"So I figured." Keswen touched the back of her head and made an exaggerated wince, still hoping to lure the Lancer into dropping his guard. "I'm afraid I don't know much about Lancers. Tell me, why—"

"Sir Ferinald should not have attacked you." Sir Hale's voice sounded believably contrite though he so lowered his voice that she could barely hear him. "Things are... tense, lately. As I'm sure you know, our true king died in the war—burned alive, burned in his castle along with most of his family. Two of his surviving nephews are fighting over the crown. We have no one left like Sir Royce to lead us. Add to that, strange reports of foreigners massing on our borders, and..." Sir Hale cleared his throat. "Sometimes, men overreact."

"Tell that to my horse."

"At any rate, I might be able to convince Sir Ferinald to let you go. First, though, I need to know what Sir Locke is doing in Ivairia." He paused. "The *real* reason."

"Then ask him yourself," Keswen said. "I offered to take you to him. I still will if—"

"Are we being invaded?"

Keswen caught the hint of panic in the young Lancer's voice. Despite her injuries, she found herself pitying the man. "No. We have business in the north. We're only passing through your lands. Had our luck been better, you never would have even known we were here."

"And the hundreds of warriors gathering to the south?"

"Allies of Sir Locke's. He didn't request them, didn't want them, but I'm guessing they came anyway."

"All that, just to hunt down a company of brigands?"

Keswen hesitated. "If you want to know what Locke's doing here, ask Locke. I'm sure you'll be seeing him soon." She pointed at the unconscious prisoner. "Now, I have some questions of my own."

Sir Hale drew a bastard sword with startling quickness and held the tip of the blade between Keswen's throat and bosom. "I'm not done yet."

Keswen looked down at the sword. She considered grasping it, letting it cut her hand so she could immobilize it while she kicked Sir Hale's legs out from under him.

Taking her silence as acquiescence, Sir Hale continued. "After the war, there were reports of Shel'ai passing back and forth through our lands. Since then, our crops have failed. A plague sprang up in Houster. Then, we heard about the fighting on the Lotus Isles, disturbing rumors of the previous Grand Marshal working with a Shel'ai to try and bring down the Dragonward."

"That was Crovis's doing," Keswen said, "and it's been dealt with. Locke cut the bastard in half. And Algol, the Shel'ai who was helping him, is a pile of ashes."

"And the other dark deeds I mentioned?"

Keswen shrugged. "Crops fail. Plagues spring out of thin air. If you wanted help, you should have asked Locke. He has a whole cadre of Shel'ai who might have aided you. He did the same thing in New Atheion after—"

"We're not interested in magical assistance."

Keswen snickered. "Unless said assistance means bringing down the Dragonjol or defeating Chorlga. You're welcome for that, by the way."

Sir Hale's expression hardened. "Did Sir Locke send Shel'ai to infiltrate our realm and weaken us from within?" He quickly added, "If you speak the truth, I swear on my honor we will grant you mercy."

Keswen held up her hand, showing the Lancer the dried blood covering it. "I've bled over some damn foolish things, Lancer, but never for turnips and potatoes. No, we aren't trying to conquer Ivairia. I'll grant you, there's been no shortage of insanity these past few years, but that doesn't mean—"

"I have a duty to protect my homeland." Sir Hale's voice sounded strained. "We've faced threats from the Shel'ai, the Dhargots, even each other. I must know what other mad threats are out there if I am to face them. And *you* will tell me."

Keswen touched her abdomen, remembering the life that had once grown there. Her eyes moistened. "I know something of madness, Lancer.

My people fought the Shel'ai for centuries. Sometimes, we had cause. Sometimes, we did not. But I've come to believe that—"

Sir Hale flicked his blade across Keswen's cheek. Keswen pressed one hand to the cut, stunned by the man's quickness. She aimed a kick at the Lancer's kneecap but stopped herself from delivering it, knowing his armor would protect him.

Meanwhile, Sir Hale blushed as though the cut had been an accident. "Understand this, Sylv. I do not enjoy inflicting pain, but I am sworn to defend my homeland, and we have had quite enough of magic." He stepped back and gestured with his sword at the unconscious woman. "We found this one in the wild, wide-eyed and ranting. She asked us where Shigella's Tomb was. When we wouldn't answer, she begged us to take her to Rowen Locke. To call all this alarming would be an understatement."

Keswen kept her hand pressed to her cheek. "That's quite a tale. At what point did she beat herself and slash her own back open?"

Sir Hale cleared his throat. "I was not there, but I'm told she attacked several of Sir Ferinald's men. She's lucky they did not kill her, but I've seen to it that she is not molested, and I've insisted that—"

"How very honorable of you." Keswen started to remove her hand from her cheek, felt blood welling from the cut again, and continued pressing on it. Though the Lancer's sword had not cut all the way through, she could still taste blood on her lips. She waited until the bleeding slowed, during which time Sir Hale continued to glare at her. Finally, she said, "I've never seen this woman before. To my knowledge, Locke hasn't either."

Before Sir Hale could reply, one of the Lancers he'd dismissed earlier rushed back into the tent and whispered something in Sir Hale's ear. Sir Hale paled. He sheathed his sword and hurried from the tent, the other Lancer in tow.

A few minutes later, to Keswen's surprise, a squire came into the tent, escorted by two Lancers. The squire scowled as he handed Keswen a wooden tray containing a bowl of water, a rag, a needle, and a spool of thread. Keswen waited until the squire and his escorts were gone then set to cleaning her injuries and stitching her cheek. She had sewn her own wounds countless times, but doing so without the numbing influence of wine or Sylvan herbs made her wince. She did not even have a mirror.

Still, she did her best, gingerly touching the damp stitches when she was finished.

Another scar, she thought with a smirk. She wondered if Zeia or Maddoc would be able to heal it. She hoped so though she loathed asking. Just then, a whimper caught her attention. She turned in time to see the Shel'ai prisoner sit up. The woman jerked then turned and faced Keswen with eyes wide as wounds. Then the prisoner lifted her hands. Her bonds burned away. She reached out before Keswen could recoil, grabbed Keswen's arm, and jerked her close. The woman said something Keswen did not understand. Keswen tried to twist free, but the woman's grip felt like iron.

"Let me go, damn you. I'm a prisoner, like you. What—"

Violet flames leaked from the woman's grasp.

Keswen cursed. Fighting through the pain, she pivoted and kicked the woman in the chest as hard as she could, but the woman did not let go. Tears blurred Keswen's vision. She aimed a second kick at the woman's face, right into her jaw, but that felt as if she was kicking a statue.

The woman spoke again, unfazed, but all Keswen could perceive was pain—blazing hot at first, then icy cold. She thought back to the cold grip of the Jolym, how years before, the metallic creatures had quietly and methodically dragged her out of the pits so that she could be brutalized by Brahasti and his men.

Fresh panic heightened Keswen's strength. She twisted and kicked again. That time, she broke free. Crawling away from the woman, Keswen looked down at the finger-shaped blisters burned into her forearm. Her arm throbbed as though she was suffering from burns and frostbite at the same time.

"Gods, I hate Shel'ai." Simultaneously amazed and angered that the commotion had not lured in the guards, she returned her gaze to the other woman.

The prisoner made no move to follow her. Instead, she stared blankly at the earth, rocking herself. All the while, she continued talking to herself in a foreign language. Keswen listened through the pain. Finally, she realized that amidst what otherwise sounded like gibberish, the woman was repeating Rowen Locke's name.

CHAPTER SIXTEEN

ROWEN TRIED TO CONCEAL HIS fear as he sat on his horse and surveyed the bustling camp before him. He guessed well over a hundred Lancers and squires all braced for combat at his approach. The Lancers had already mounted horses and were currently in the process of arraying themselves in steely, armored rows in front of the tents. Their squires followed, half of them mounting horses of their own but lingering at the rear while the rest grabbed crossbows and took up positions on foot.

Saanji asked, "Didn't your father used to be a Lancer?"

"A squire," Rowen said, surprised by the question. "He died when I was young, though. I barely—"

"He died here, up in Ivairia?"

Rowen glanced at the Dhargothi prince with irritation. "No, a little village east of Lyos. He took us out of Ivairia because he got tired of..." Rowen shook his head. "Jinn's name, what does it matter?"

"Sorry, Locke. Just trying to make conversation," Saanji said. "I get nervous whenever men point spears and crossbows at me. What can I say? I've never been my father's son."

Rowen noted how the prince was white-knuckling the reins of his horse, and his anger slacked. "Don't worry. We're out of range of their bolts, and their riders will be heavy and slow. We can get away in plenty of time if we have to."

"Provided I don't fall off my horse. This might surprise you, but I'm not the world's most accomplished rider."

Rowen glanced left and right, at the others. Zeia, Breaksteel, Sir Issa, and Vaari had taken up position a few yards behind them. Rowen had instructed Zeia not to conjure her flaming hands—the less the Lancers saw of magic, the better—but to be prepared to unleash a flurry of mind-stabs to cover their retreat if necessary.

Rowen wondered if he'd made the wrong choice. The Lancers vastly outnumbered them, and given the protection afforded by their heavy armor, Zeia was likely the only one capable of hurting them. Besides that, if Rowen had to retreat, the Lancers would be too guarded afterward. Even Zeia would not be able to rescue Keswen, meaning Rowen would have no choice but to trust the matter to Krym and his unsavory bodyguard.

Unless I leave Keswen behind. Rowen dismissed the thought, ashamed for having it in the first place. He shifted in the saddle, impatiently awaiting the arrival of the Ivairian commander. Though no words had been exchanged yet, he had no doubt the man would either appear soon or stay back and order his men to charge.

When two Lancers finally appeared and rode out ahead of the rest, Saanji groaned. "Not *this* bastard!" He lowered his voice. "I don't know the younger one, but the older one with the scarred lip was at Hesod. Royce never trusted him. Once, he described him as what happens when a jackal beds down with—"

The Lancers were so close by then that Rowen rode ahead to meet him, cutting off the rest of Saanji's statement. Rowen studied the lead Lancer's scarred, unsmiling face and waited for the man to speak.

When he did not, Rowen said, "I am Rowen Locke, Sword Marshal and Knight of the Lotus. You are holding one of my warriors without cause. I want her released."

"I am Sir Ferinald, protector of Houster and guardian of the realm." The Lancer looked him over again. "I thought you'd be taller."

"And I thought you'd be smarter," Rowen countered sharply. "Honorable men do not start wars for no reason."

The younger Lancer's eyes widened at the insult, but Sir Ferinald snickered. "Then I must thank you for giving me one. A reason, that is. Most generous of you."

"I have done no such thing."

"Then we have differing opinions on how to feel when foreign powers infiltrate our homelands and armed men mass on our borders."

"This is no invasion." Rowen gestured to Saanji. "This man is Prince Saanji, ally to Sir Arnil Royce. He can vouch for my words."

Saanji rode forward and cleared his throat. "Consider Locke's words thoroughly and wholeheartedly vouched for." He grinned. "Hello, Sir Ferinald. Good to see you again."

Sir Ferinald scowled. "I'm not sure what surprises me more, Dhargot—that you're still alive or that you're sober."

"Drunkenness has more layers than an onion. Do not presume to know which one is mine."

Neither Sir Ferinald nor the younger Lancer laughed.

"This is Sir Hale, my cousin," Sir Ferinald said, almost as an afterthought.

Saanji asked, "What of Sir Hector? Or Sir Bowen, or Sir Bors? Perhaps we—"

"All dead," Sir Ferinald said. His eyes narrowed. "I don't like staring into the sunset. Either finish your speech or ride away."

"This is no speech," Rowen said. "I've come for the Sylv. Bring her. Now."

Sir Ferinald scoffed. Without a word, he started to turn his horse back toward his camp. Rowen tried to think of something to say, a plea or threat that would give the Lancer pause, but could not think of anything. He turned to Saanji.

"My turn?" Saanji sighed. "Sir Ferinald, a moment, if you please." He urged his horse forward, alongside Sir Ferinald's. Saanji smiled, blinked several times, then leaned forward and slapped Sir Ferinald across the face.

Rowen drew his sword, biting back a curse. Sir Hale drew his sword, as well. Saanji continued to smile at Sir Ferinald. The latter's face had turned red, but he had yet to draw his own weapon. Rowen looked past the men and saw the massive body of Lancers bristling in the distance, some of them shouting oaths and threats.

Sir Ferinald held up his hand, though, and they did not charge. He touched his lip and looked at the smear of blood on the tip of his glove. "Bold move, Tomato Prince. I did not think you had it in you."

Saanji said nothing but continued to smile as he edged his horse backward, rejoining Rowen.

Rowen hesitated then sheathed his sword. "Sir Ferinald, I don't know why you've done this, but I'll be kind and assume you aren't dumb enough to want a war any more than I do. So return my friend. I assure you, my presence here is no prelude to invasion."

"Then kindly tell me why you are here."

Rowen mentally rehearsed the lie he had concocted on the way there, which he hoped would more or less match the one Keswen must have delivered. Instead, he said, "We are escorting a Dragonkin to the Wintersea."

Saanji groaned. Sir Ferinald's eyes widened. Rowen rested one hand on his sword hilt, expecting that he'd be forced to draw it again at any moment.

Finally, Sir Ferinald laughed. "I feared you were a cunning strategist. Now, I see you're nothing but a madman."

"It's not as mad as it sounds," Rowen said. "You have heard of a Dragonkin named Nekiel?"

Sir Ferinald nodded. "My nursemaid probably told me much the same stories that yours told you."

I never had a nursemaid, you jackass. "Nekiel is real. He's still alive. And he has returned to Ruun." Rowen paused, allowing a moment for the impact of his words to settle in. "Don't ask me to explain *how*. The *why* is what's important. Suffice to say, Nekiel must be stopped. Another Dragonkin, one named Krym, has arrived as well. The two are enemies. With reluctance, we are helping one fight the other."

When neither Lancer spoke, Rowen continued. "As I said, we are bound for the Wintersea. That's where the fight will take place."

Sir Ferinald said, "I thought you a liar. I hope you still are, because if I remember my nursemaid's stories, the Dragonkin had the power to—"

"Nekiel is still weak. That's why we must hurry. If we act quickly, this can be ended without thousands dying."

Sir Ferinald turned to look at Sir Hale. Neither Lancer spoke.

Finally, Sir Ferinald turned back to Rowen and said, "We have more than enough fighting in our own lands. What new troubles have you

161

brought down on us? All we want is to defend our homeland, and now, you threaten—"

"Not a threat. If you return the Sylv and let us pass unharmed, we can deal with Nekiel. He'll be vanquished and all of Ruun saved, and it won't cost you a single Lancer's life."

Saanji added, "A preferable alternative to a second War of the Lotus, is it not? You could even claim the credit if you like."

Sir Ferinald ignored Saanji and looked past Rowen, visibly studying their companions. "Is the Dragonkin with you now?"

Rowen shook his head. "We've sought to keep him separated from everyone else, for reasons that should be obvious. That's why Keswen was scouting, hoping to intercept and dissuade any travelers in the area."

"And why she lied," Sir Hale said.

"The fault is mine," Rowen said. "I'm told you injured her and struck down her horse. We've both acted foolishly. Provided no other harm has been done to her, let our sins balance, and we'll part ways in peace."

Both Lancers flushed though Rowen sensed they had different reasons.

Sir Ferinald said, "I am trying to defend my kingdom against magic, yet you come here *with* magic." He pointed. "I see a wytch skulking back there. If that's the Dragonkin you spoke of, it's at least a Shel'ai. You've brought magic into my kingdom, and now, you freely admit to bringing more."

"I do," Rowen said. "I could have lied. I didn't. I could have rescued Keswen from your camp, killing a dozen Lancers in the process. I didn't do that, either. A smart man would see that for what it is."

"The actions of an honorable man trying to avert a war," Sir Ferinald said slowly. "That's what you want me to think, is it not? But all men are liars. I doubt your pretty blue tabard and bright swirly armor make you an exception."

Rowen felt his patience wearing thin. "The Sylv is my friend. She has done nothing wrong. Release her, or—"

Sir Ferinald drew his sword and swung at the neck of Rowen's horse.

Rowen drew his own sword and narrowly parried the blow. "Stop!" he cried, but Sir Ferinald lunged, forcing Rowen to parry again.

Sir Hale drew his sword and pressed forward just as a massive roar signaled the advance of the entire host beyond. Rowen prepared to fend off two attackers at once.

Then Saanji drew a knife and threw it.

Sir Ferinald's horse reared up, mortally struck, dumping its rider to the ground. Sir Hale recoiled, eyeing his fallen commander. Taking advantage of the delay, Rowen swung fast and hard, landing a jarring blow on Sir Hale's pauldron. A second blow knocked the Lancer clean off his horse. Rowen grabbed the reins of Sir Hale's mount and wheeled around. Saanji followed.

The others were already rushing to join them, but Rowen tossed the reins of Sir Hale's horse to Breaksteel. Rowen faced scores of charging Lancers, surging toward them in a thundering wall of muscle and iron.

His face flushed with shame. *I'm sorry, Keswen.* "Run," he said finally, sheathing his sword.

Keswen woke to the feel of sunlight on her face. She looked about, surprised to find she was lying in a clearing instead of an Ivairian tent. A patch of lilacs grew near the spot where her face lay, their scent filling her nostrils. Keswen took a deep breath then rubbed her throat. She felt parched. Almost as soon as she had the feeling, though, she noticed a wooden bowl lying in the grass. She peered inside and found it full of clear water. Somehow, not a single insect or spot of grass floated on the surface.

Puzzled, Keswen nevertheless sat up, raised the wooden bowl to her lips, and drank. The water was cool, and she drank it all then examined the bowl. It bore no carvings, no maker's mark to indicate where it had come from. She was about to set it down when it shimmered and faded from her grasp.

"Gods..."

Keswen looked around and, for the first time, spotted the dark-haired Shel'ai nearby though Keswen could not understand how she had failed to see her earlier. The woman knelt on the grass, pale but conscious, staring at her, her eyes shimmering with tears. Her clothes still hung from her in filthy tatters, but no injuries showed on her body.

"I am sorry I burned you. I was not myself. But I healed your wounds while you slept. Forgive me if you can."

Keswen winced. The woman's voice sounded strange, as though coming half from the woman herself and half from another voice, identical but faraway.

The woman continued. "While I was healing you, I saw... your memories. I know about Krym. That you are Rowen Locke's friend." She paused. "And I saw... what Chorlga and those Humans did to you." She looked at Keswen's belly. "Though I had no part in that, it grieves me."

Keswen looked around for a weapon. She grabbed a fist-sized stone but did not throw it. "Where are we?"

The woman blinked her violet, gold-flecked eyes. "Far from the Human camp. East, beyond what you know as Ivairia, near the coast."

Keswen stood. Aside from dizziness, she seemed uninjured. She touched her cheek, where Sir Hale had cut her, but the wound and the stitches were gone as well. "My friends will be looking for me. So will the Lancers, I'm sure. So I'll ask one more time. Where are we?"

The sorceress sighed. "Those who seek lies often find what they seek, no matter where and how they look." She pointed. "Look beyond the trees if you do not believe me."

Keswen considered tackling the sorceress and beating the truth out of her but decided that a Shel'ai who could heal such serious wounds was not one to be trifled with. Keswen backed away, still holding her stone at the ready. She edged around a line of trees, turned, and strode the final few yards through a thinning forest. On the other side, she stopped at the edge of a cliff and stared, speechless, at an ocean.

The dark-haired sorceress moved quietly through the trees and stood beside her. As before, she seemed unconcerned with her immodestly tattered clothing. "You see? I did not lie. As it happens, that is something I do not do."

Keswen squinted down at a bay of merchant ships, all sailing in and out of a great harbor joined to a bustling white city. "Gods, I passed by here a few months ago, after the fighting on the Isles. That looks like Artisan Bay." She shook her head. "But that city *can't* be Phaegos! How long was I asleep?"

"You slept from yesterday's sunset to today's midafternoon."

164

Keswen clenched her stone. "Even if you got me out of the camp somehow, you couldn't have carried me through Ivairia, all the way to Phaegos, in less than a day."

"I did not carry you."

"But you couldn't have teleported me, either. Shel'ai don't have that kind of power. Dragonkin do, but Krym was far away. For the last time, tell me..." Keswen struggled to finish.

The woman stared at Keswen and said no more, waiting for her to figure it out herself. When Keswen finally did, she took a step backward, away from the woman—so close to the cliff edge that she lost her balance. For one dizzying moment, the world reeled. Keswen dropped her stone and reached. Instead of grasping Keswen's flailing arms, the woman waved one hand, and an invisible force yanked Keswen back.

"I am not a Shel'ai," the woman said simply. "But I was... *am*... Krym's sister. I am also Nekiel's daughter." She winced as she spoke, pained by the words. "Perhaps you have heard of me. My name is Nâya."

CHAPTER SEVENTEEN

ROWEN PEERED THROUGH THE TREES as a squad of Lancers thundered by. He counted ten Lancers followed by a dozen squires carrying bows and armloads of spears. He waited until they were gone then went back to rejoin his companions. "Another damn patrol. They followed Issa's trail."

Saanji offered Rowen a wineskin. "Good thing Lancers can't track worth a damn."

Despite his thirst, Rowen waved off the wineskin. "Their heavier armor slows them down so Issa can easily outrun them." *I hope.* "But keeping them away from Igrid and Thessa still means keeping them closer to us."

Saanji took a sip of wine. "Which isn't exactly helping our rescue efforts."

"What efforts?" Vaari muttered. "All we've done so far is run for our lives."

He's right, Rowen thought even as he fought another impulse to answer an observation from the Dhargot with a backhand across the face. "We'll wait until nightfall—then you're all riding north. Everyone but Zeia. Sorry, but I need you to help get me into the camp."

The Shel'ai nodded, unsurprised. "I can do that. But I'd still have better luck sneaking in by myself."

Rowen said, "There's no way you can free Keswen without killing."

"No offense, Locke, but neither can you," Zeia countered. "Let me do this, Knight. The Wyldkin and your woman saved me once, when the Sons of Maelmohr made me their prisoner. She may be surly as a greatwolf, but I owe her."

"We *all* owe her, probably." Saanji smiled at Zeia. "Or maybe I just don't want you going alone."

Vaari rolled his eyes. "Dying for a Sylv isn't my idea of a good time. Don't we have more important things to worry about?"

Saanji muttered something to Vaari that Rowen could not hear, but the bodyguard drew back a step.

Ignoring Vaari's words, Zeia moved closer to Saanji. "No way *you're* coming with me. This calls for quiet, and you're about as good at being an assassin as you'd be a cleric." She conjured one flaming hand and snatched the wineskin from his grasp.

Saanji said, "Then what about Breaksteel? He might not be quiet, but the mere sight of him would scare the piss out of—"

"No," Zeia said. "It takes an entire forest to hide him." She turned to the Olg. "No offense."

Breaksteel said something in hand-speech. Though Rowen did not know it as well as Keswen or Sir Issa, he could still guess the Olg was volunteering to come along.

Rowen shook his head. "I want Igrid to know what's happened, and gods know I don't want her alone with Krym and his creature! Zeia and I will go. No one else. If we can free Keswen without—"

"You won't free her without killing," Saanji said. "Sorry, Knight, but if that didn't work yesterday, it sure as hells won't work tonight or tomorrow, either."

He's right. "You're wrong," Rowen said. "Half the Lancers are out chasing us. She'll be guarded, yes, but—"

"Only a Dragonkin could get her out of that camp without someone seeing," Zeia said. She handed the wineskin, faintly smoldering, back to Saanji. "I understand why you don't want to ask for Krym's help, but make no mistake, Knight—without it, this *will* end in blood. Let me go alone, though, and maybe only two or three guards will die."

Rowen shook his head. "If you're caught, you'll need me. Besides, if it comes to it, I can challenge Ferinald to single combat. Might be that not all the Lancers agree with him. If I can kill him—"

"Oh, you could take him in a duel, all right," Saanji interrupted, "but

Lancers aren't Isle Knights. The others would probably kill you as soon as Ferinald hit the ground." He hiccupped.

He's drunk, Rowen realized. He considered chiding the Dhargothi prince then decided not to. He thought of Igrid and wondered how she was faring. He wondered if Thessa was terrified or merely afraid. *I have to get back to them, but I can't leave Keswen behind.*

He faced Zeia. "A compromise. You'll go into the camp alone, but I'll wait for you just beyond, in case you're chased—which we both know you will be." He turned to Vaari. A spark of dark enjoyment kindled inside him. "And I won't be alone."

Vaari scowled. "Sorry, Knight. I serve Prince Saanji—not you."

"Fine. Then I'll stay, too." Saanji hiccupped again.

He was about to say more, but Zeia ignited one flaming hand and touched his lips.

"No, Prince," Rowen said, "We'll need Breaksteel's horse for Keswen. That means you have to help him get back to Igrid." He faced Vaari. "And unless Saanji says otherwise, Dhargot, you *will* do what I say, or my first duel will be against you."

Vaari's hand went for his sword, but Saanji grabbed his arm first and whispered in his ear again.

Vaari looked livid for a moment then nodded. "So be it, Knight, but you better not get me killed."

Saanji said, "What about Sir Issa?"

Rowen glanced through the line of trees, at the empty plains across which horses had thundered just moments before. "Issa can find his own way back—either that or ride back to Cadavash."

Saanji snickered. "You *know* he isn't about to leave his Sword Marshal. You'd better hope he gets through."

Is he saying I was wrong to send him? "He will," Rowen said, hoping he was right.

Issa tried his best not to enjoy himself as he led the Lancers on a wild chase. He could tell they were growing frustrated in the waning daylight. At that point, they must have guessed their prey had split up, but Issa's trail was all they had.

Smiling faintly, the Isle Knight reined in and listened for the approach of horses. While he waited, he took a long drink from his canteen. Then he poured the last of the water over his horse's neck, rubbing it in to cool her off. He waited until he heard the Lancers' approach then tossed the canteen onto the ground—where he hoped they would see it—and started off again. Moments later, they nearly had him.

Issa was having no trouble keeping ahead of the first force, but he was so preoccupied that he did not see a second squad of Lancers flanking him until it was almost too late. Squinting in the sunset, he veered away from the flash of armor and spearheads. He winced as arrows hissed through the air, so close that they blurred by his face. Though he knew his kingsteel armor could protect him, his horse had no such protection.

As he rode, steering his horse with his knees, he retrieved the kingsteel helmet and facemask from his saddlebag and put them on. Shaped like a grinning fox, the mask was too warm for his liking, but if his horse was shot out from under him, he would need all the protection he could get.

Issa steered his horse down one hill and around another then guided her through a thin copse of trees. By then, twilight had spread its blue-black shawl over the countryside. He heard his pursuers shouting and cursing in the distance. They sounded far away.

Smiling again, Issa patted his horse's neck. "They lost our trail again. Seems we're too good at this."

He wondered what to do next. His orders had been to draw the Lancers away—not just from Sir Locke himself, so he could rescue Keswen, but from the Dragonkin's camp. Issa remembered how Krym had effortlessly struck down the company of Isle Knights escorting Gaulgodd. He shuddered, as much from fear as revulsion. Issa had no love for the Lancers, especially after how they had attacked Keswen, but he understood Sir Locke's position as well. The Ivairians were apparently starting down the same fanatical path that the Dwarrs had followed when they formed the Sons of Maelmohr. If a Dragonkin glibly tormented—or even annihilated—a great many of them, that would do little to dissuade them.

Issa patted his horse's neck again. "What shall we do next, girl? Head north, back to that Dragonkin bastard, or find those poor Lancers and—"

A shrill scream scattered his thoughts. Issa reached for his sword, confused. The scream sounded like that of a young woman—Thessa, perhaps—but it came from the south. The Isle Knight hesitated. His instincts told him that what he'd just heard was the sound of some traveler being assailed by highwaymen, probably a common occurrence in those parts. He had no wish to stand by while some poor girl was robbed—or worse—but he already had orders. If he was not going to aid in Keswen's rescue, he should hurry north and do what he could to safeguard Igrid and Thessa.

Issa glanced down at the sigil of a balancing crane on his tabard. "The Codex Lotius might not agree with that assessment. Neither would Sir Locke." Still, it was not until the girl screamed a second time that Issa spurred his horse southward, drawing his sword as he rode.

Miriam said, "I'm thirsty."

"There's a stream just ahead." Emrael pointed.

Miriam could not see anything through the trees but did not doubt him. Nor did she bother asking how her new friend could have known such a thing since, so far, he had been right about practically everything. Earlier, when she'd been hungry, he found the lone fruit tree in an otherwise withered and burnt forest. And he'd been right when he insisted the greatwolf would not harm her. She reached down and scratched the wolf behind the ears. It responded by rubbing its massive head against her, nearly knocking her off her feet. Miriam laughed, starting to like how the wolf's fur looked in the ruddy glow of sunset.

"Is it a boy or a girl?"

Emrael looked back at her and frowned. "The stream?"

Miriam laughed. "No, the wolf!"

"Ah. Female."

"Then what should we call her?"

Emrael's expression said he could not care less. "Whatever you like."

"No, it's your turn. I already named you. Well, sort of."

As Emrael walked, he reached out to move a branch away from his face, though it really seemed to move on its own, right before he would have touched it. He said, "I can't think of anything."

"Well, name her after someone you know. Who's a woman you care about? Your mother, maybe." When Emrael did not speak, she asked, "What's your mother's name?"

Emrael held out his hand so that the greatwolf moved away from Miriam and walked beside him instead. "I don't know."

"You mean you can't even remember your own mother's name?"

"I'm not sure I ever had one."

"You had to," Miriam said. "Otherwise, you wouldn't be here."

"Perhaps," Emrael said. Though he was only petting the greatwolf's head, as Miriam had, the beast whimpered.

"Then we'll call her Challa, after *my* mother." When Emrael did not acknowledge the statement, she added, "Is that all right?"

"If you wish."

They walked in silence for a moment. Then Miriam asked, "And you still don't remember what you're looking for in the north?"

"No," Emrael answered in a low voice, "I remember now."

Miriam stopped walking. "Well, what is it?"

Emrael continued forward without answering. Finally, exasperated, Miriam ran to catch up. They walked awhile longer. Then, all at once, Emrael stopped. The greatwolf growled. Miriam nearly ran into them, then her eyes widened.

Before them, down at the bottom of a hill, lay a stream. A few trees lined the stream, but like the forest they had passed through earlier, they were blackened and dead. A moss-covered boulder, as big as Challa, rose from the center of the stream. A man lay sprawled upon the boulder, facedown.

Miriam touched her knife. "Is he dead?"

"No." Emrael started toward the stream.

Miriam followed.

The man was tall but gaunt, dressed in silken clothes that might once have been as exotic and expensive as Emrael's. They hung from the man in muddy tatters, though. She saw what looked like slashes on his arms and legs, crusted with dried blood. Then she noticed a sword hanging from his waist. A moment after that, she noticed tapered ears protruding from his white, matted hair.

Fearful, she moved closer to Challa. "Is he a Shel'ai?"

"No, just a Sylv." Emrael reached the edge of the bank, as though he meant to wade into the water and help the man, but stopped short of entering the stream.

Miriam said, "He's hurt. What should we do?" Despite her trepidation, she joined Emrael at the edge of the stream. She had never seen a Sylv, though her father had told her stories of how he'd traded with the Wyldkin once, long before.

"Nothing," Emrael said finally. "Leave him to die."

Miriam drew away, surprised by the callousness in Emrael's voice. "Why? If we can help him—"

"Leave him to die," Emrael repeated. "That's already better than he deserves."

"How do you know?"

Emrael turned and gave her so fierce a look that Miriam drew back even farther. Then his expression softened. "I just know," he answered softly and turned to leave.

Miriam started to follow but turned back and looked at the man. He stirred, slightly lifting his head, and dropped it back down.

"No," she said. Without waiting for a reply, she waded into the stream. She hissed through her teeth as the cold water shocked her, but she kept going. By the time she reached the boulder, the water was past her thighs, almost to her waist. She stopped to look at the man, and since she was closer, she saw that, despite his thinness, he was even taller than her father. She turned back to Emrael. "I can't do this by myself. You have to help me."

Emrael stared at her from the shore, unblinking. Challa looked at Miriam, then at Emrael, and whimpered. The greatwolf pulled away from Emrael and lay down, covering its face with its gigantic paws. Emrael stared at Miriam a moment longer. Then he waved.

Miriam did not understand the gesture. Before she could ask what he was doing, though, something blocked the sun, darkening the water around her. Instinctively, Miriam ducked. Something floated overhead. Then, stunned, she realized it was the Sylv. His body floated through the air like something out of a dream, dripping water, then settled on the grass.

That was magic. Emrael did that.

Emrael looked down at the Sylv with contempt then stepped back.

172

He crossed his arms. "There," he said. "Now, he won't drown, but that's as much as I will do for him."

Miriam crossed the stream and returned to the shore. Shivering, she stepped out of the water. "But we can't just leave him here. Somebody might come along and—"

"He killed your brothers."

Miriam blinked. "What?"

"You heard me. Their bodies are over there, behind the reeds. That's where he hid them."

Miriam thought she saw a large, dark shape in the distance, in the water, a few yards away from the boulder. She quickly looked away. "You're lying."

Emrael stepped around the Sylv and strode toward her. Something in his expression frightened her. She tried to back away, but Emrael quickened his pace. He loomed over her, seemingly taller than he'd been before, a faintly menacing look on his face.

"Would you like to see?" Before Miriam could answer, Emrael stretched out his hand and touched Miriam's forehead, making her skin tingle. Then the tingling became searing pain.

Miriam tried to pull away but found she could not move. Emrael moved even closer. His other hand touched the back of her head, holding her steady.

"I'll show you," he whispered.

Miriam's vision dimmed then darkened. She feared for a moment that she'd been struck blind, but then she saw the Sylv kneeling beside the stream, palming water to his lips. His whole body was shaking, though she could not tell the reason.

Then, her brothers appeared. They approached the stream slowly, frowning. Jem was holding a knife. Will had a club. They called out to the Sylv, asking first if he was all right, then if he'd seen a girl wandering through those parts. Miriam cried out to her brothers, held out her arms, and tried to run to them, but she passed through them as though they were made of vapor.

Her brothers did not see her, but a moment later, the Sylv leapt to his feet and turned around. With a wild cry, the old Sylv drew his sword and attacked. Miriam screamed a warning, but the cry died in her throat as Jem fell, his knife splashing into the water. Miriam drew her own knife and tried to stab the Sylv in the back. Like her brothers, the Sylv's body turned to vapor where she touched it then solidified the instant she withdrew her blade.

Helpless, Miriam screamed for Will to run. Whether he heard her or not, he answered by swinging his club at the Sylv's head, but the Sylv's sword flashed through the air, cutting the club in half. Will's eyes widened, and he turned to flee. The Sylv followed—half laughing, half screaming—and the sword flashed a second time.

Miriam screamed, too. Then, just as quickly as it had begun, the vision disappeared. Miriam found herself standing before Emrael again. She recoiled.

Tears filled her eyes, blurring everything in front of her. "Why... why did you do that?"

Emrael blinked. Challa lifted her head and whimpered then hid her face behind her paws again.

Emrael looked confused for a moment, then all the malice drained from his expression. "I'm sorry..." He reached for her.

Miriam recoiled even farther. She lost her balance and fell backward into the stream. The shock of cold water made her cry out again. Rather than stand and return to the shore, though, she crawled blindly through the water, toward the far side. She thought she heard Emrael call out to her, but she kept going. Her head struck the boulder. Miriam opened her mouth to scream, but cold water rushed in.

Choking, Miriam tried to stand, but her foot slipped, and she tumbled back into the water. Everything darkened and blurred. Panic swelled, matching the agony in her lungs. She tried feebly to rise, but the water seemed to sweep her along, like a thousand tiny hands all shoving her at once, all holding her down.

Then, a hand grabbed her arm and pulled her up. Powerful arms lifted her in the air, holding her like a baby, carrying her to the shore. Her rescuer's body felt strange—cold and smooth. Miriam coughed and blinked away the water. By the time her rescuer lowered her gently onto the grass, she could tell it was not Emrael.

"Easy, child." The voice spoke from behind a facemask of orange-and-brown-painted steel, shaped like a fox. Her rescuer removed his helmet then the facemask, showing a handsome smiling face. He straightened, revealing gleaming armor and a beautiful blue tunic. He turned, then his expression hardened. "Keep back," he said in a stern, commanding voice. The helmet and facemask slipped from his grasp and fell onto the grass.

Miriam pushed herself up on her elbows in time to see Emrael wading across the stream toward them, expressionless. Challa remained on the other side of the stream, whimpering and pacing back and forth.

The armored man stepped in front of Miriam, as though to shield her. "Keep back," he repeated. That time, he drew his sword and pointed it at Emrael.

Emrael continued wading through the water until he reached the shore. He stepped onto the grass but came no closer. "I won't hurt her."

The armored man gave Emrael a suspicious look then looked down at Miriam. "Are you all right, child? I heard you scream."

"I didn't hurt her," Emrael insisted. "It was the Sylvan king. He killed her brothers."

The armored man frowned. He looked past Emrael, to the far side of the stream, where the Sylv still lay unmoving on the grass. Then the armored man turned his head toward the reeds, noting the bodies lying in the water. Miriam followed his gaze before she could stop herself, then she cried out and covered her eyes.

Her rescuer said, "Jinn's name, I don't know what's going on here, but I'm going to ask a question or two. If you answer—"

"You have a horse," Emrael interrupted. "I need it. I'm going to take it. I am sorry."

Miriam tightened her eyes so hard that splotches of white interrupted the darkness. She tried to cover her ears, too, but she still heard her rescuer laugh. His armor jingled as he took a step away from her, toward Emrael. She heard him warn Emrael once again to stay away. Then, she felt a wave of scalding heat a moment before her rescuer screamed.

The sour smell of burning flesh filled her nostrils. Miriam recognized that smell. Remembering her parents, she screamed and screamed and kept her eyes shut until it was over.

CHAPTER EIGHTEEN

ROWEN SAID, "STAY WITH THE horses," and walked away before
Vaari had a chance to complain. He followed Zeia toward the
Lancers' camp, trying without success to match the effortless,
deathly quiet manner in which she crept through the darkness. He
wrapped his cloak around his armor to keep the moon from glinting off
the metal. He cursed himself for not having left his armor behind. *Then
again, if Zeia runs into trouble, I may need it.*

Zeia moved in a low crouch, cloaked and hooded, two shortswords
buckled to her waist. She had not yet summoned her flaming hands,
and both sleeves hung low, concealing her scarred wrist stumps. Quick
and catlike, she moved so far ahead of him that Rowen wondered if she
were deliberately trying to leave him behind. But when she reached a
thin copse of trees just beyond the camp, she pressed low to the ground
and waited.

Rowen joined her, cursing inwardly as the act of kneeling made his
knees crack. He thought he saw Zeia snicker but fixed his gaze on the
camp instead. The Ivairians had already built campfires. A line of sentries
paced just beyond a massive body of tents. Unlike other camps he'd seen,
which tended to be rowdy places filled with drinking and laughter, that
camp seemed well disciplined and tensely silent despite the number of
armored men moving about.

Rowen whispered, "Is it my imagination, or are there more of them
than before?"

"A second company must have joined them," Zeia answered so softly that Rowen barely heard her. She pointed.

Rowen followed the gesture and saw a series of banners placed in the ground at the edge of the camp. Each showed a different insignia or color, but all were some variation on the crowned horse of Ivairia. Rowen studied the banners.

"We might need the Dragonkin's help after all."

"Now, don't you go discounting me just yet, Knight." Zeia crawled backward and knelt behind a tree. "I can use divination to search the camp. That'll help me find out where they've hidden Keswen, but there's a catch. I can't be any farther away than this for it to work, and I won't be able to do it again for weeks, perhaps as long as a month, or it might kill me."

Rowen understood her point. If she used divination to locate Keswen, she would be unable to use such magic later in their fight against Nekiel. "So long as we have Krym with us, you shouldn't need to."

"Also, the spell will leave me weakened. When and if this turns into a fight, it'll be largely up to you and the Dhargot to get us away." Zeia waited until Rowen nodded then added, "While I'm in the trance, it'll be up to you to keep some lucky sentry from sticking a spear in me."

Rowen nodded again. He loosened his sword but did not draw it, lest the glint of metal betray their location. Instead, making sure that his cloak still covered his armor, he knelt on the ground in front of Zeia. From time to time, he switched his gaze back to the Ivairian camp, perhaps fifty yards away, to make sure the sentries had not moved farther out in their patrol.

Meanwhile, Zeia crossed her legs and placed both hands on her knees, palms upward. She closed her eyes, and a faint blue glow formed around her body. Luckily, her cloak concealed most of it. Rowen felt tingling power radiating off her body. He looked toward the Ivairian camp again, half expecting to see a Lancer sounding the alarm and rushing toward them.

He studied Zeia's face for a moment, noting how it had turned as blank as stone. From time to time, though, her eyelids twitched or she winced, as though the spell itself were painful for her. Rowen reminded himself that any great use of magic came with an equally great risk, especially for a Shel'ai, but that did little to quell his impatience.

Minutes passed with agonizing slowness. Once, Rowen thought he heard the twang of a bow, but the sound came from behind them, in the direction of Vaari and the horses. He listened but heard no cry of alarm and decided that the Dhargot must simply have been trying to assuage his own boredom by hunting.

Gods, I'm going to throttle that bastard. Though Rowen was sure the sound had been too faint to be heard from the camp, he still kept a close watch on the sentries. One of the men headed away from the camp, in Rowen's direction. Rowen tensed. The man had not cried out yet, which either meant he'd seen or heard something but wanted to investigate first, or he was simply answering the call of nature. Rowen prayed it was the latter.

He tried to take shallow breaths as slowly as possible, mentally rehearsing the quick, precise motion it would take to draw his sword and slice through the Lancer's unprotected neck. At the same time, he moved closer to Zeia, using his cloak to further conceal the faint glow around her body.

The Lancer came closer and closer, his heavy armor jingling with every step. Finally, the Lancer stopped just a few yards away from the tree. He jammed his spear into the ground, loosened his pants, and squatted in the grass. Rowen pinched his nose with one hand and kept the other on his sword hilt. The Lancer looked up at the stars as he finished his business, then he yawned, retrieved his spear, and returned to the camp.

A moment later, as the glow faded from Zeia's body, she opened her eyes. "She's not here."

"Are you sure?" An awful thought occurred to Rowen. "Is she—"

"I searched the whole camp, every inch of it. Twice. No Keswen, no corpse—but I heard the Lancers talking. They're saying Keswen escaped along with another prisoner of theirs, a Shel'ai."

Rowen frowned, wondering who the other Shel'ai could be, but decided that was a mystery they could solve another day. "If she got away, she'll try to make her way back to us. She may already be back with Igrid and the others by now." He rose slowly, still concealing his armor with his cloak, and offered Zeia his hand.

Rather than summoning a bright hand of wytchfire that might have given away their position, she held out her wrist stump. Rowen hesitated, seized it, and pulled her to her feet.

The two made their way back toward Vaari and the horses. When they arrived, they found the Dhargot kneeling over the body of a Lancer, searching him for valuables. A single arrow protruded from the Lancer's visor.

Vaari glanced up. "Unlucky bastard must have been out scouting and heard the horses. He walked right up to me. No choice. Good thing I saw him first." He found a pouch, looked inside, and whistled. "What, no huntress?"

"She's not here." Rowen scowled down at the slain Lancer. He was about to scold the Dhargot, but Zeia touched his arm.

"We have to hurry," she whispered.

"Right." Rowen pointed at the corpse. "Help me put him on the empty horse," he told Vaari. "We'll need to hide the body."

Vaari glowered at him but did not protest, perhaps heartened by his new pouch of coins. Rowen grabbed the Lancer's limp arms while Vaari grabbed his legs. Rowen thought the words of a Shao prayer as he carried the corpse toward one of the horses. Vaari yawned. They draped the dead man over the saddle, then the three mounted their own horses and rode off quietly into the darkness.

They had not ridden far when Zeia gave Rowen a telepathic warning. A moment later, Rowen heard low voices to the west. Guessing it was an Ivairian patrol, he turned his horse southward instead. To his relief, the patrol passed by without hearing them. But Zeia's sharp instincts detected a second patrol, only a few hundred yards beyond the first. Frustrated, Rowen was forced to lead them farther and farther south to avoid detection.

By the time they finally turned northwest, toward Igrid and the others, dawn was breaking.

Vaari yawned again and took a sip from a wineskin. "Some night," he muttered, checking his belt to make sure the stolen coin purse was still there.

"We're still alive," Zeia said.

"Maybe the huntress is, too," Vaari said, though his tone hinted that he cared very little one way or the other. "Truth be told, I'm glad to be away from that Dragonkin for a while. Believe it or not, I don't like him much."

Rowen said, "For the first time, we're in agreement." He pointed. "We'll rest at that stream for a moment then ride the rest of the way. By noon, we should be back at—"

He reined in as the smell of charred flesh filled his nostrils. He turned to Zeia. The Shel'ai had already summoned both her flaming hands. One held the reins of her horse while the other drew a shortsword. Seeing that, Vaari readied his composite bow, holding an arrow on the bowstring as he scowled at the stream.

"What is that?" the Dhargot asked. "Smells like a burned rabbit."

Rowen dismounted and edged toward the stream, one hand on his hilt. A dreadful heaviness filled his stomach. At the edge of the stream, he knelt beside a heap of blackened metal and scorched cloth. The dead man lay facedown. Rowen braced himself and rolled him over. The face was too blackened to be recognizable, but Zeia joined him a moment later and cleared her throat, pointing. In the distance, a familiar helmet and facemask lay on the grass.

A Shao prayer formed on Rowen's lips, but he had hardly begun reciting it when a surge of emotion made him replace the prayer with a cry of rage. He turned away from the body. "Did he die from magic?" When Zeia nodded, Rowen asked, "Shel'ai or Dragonkin?"

Zeia knelt and slowly passed one blazing hand over the charred body. She frowned. "I cannot tell."

Vaari dismounted. The Dhargot returned his arrow to his quiver and left his bow on his horse. Joining them, he frowned at the charred body. "This your man, Knight? Looks like he found himself on the wrong end of—"

Rowen backhanded the Dhargot across the face. Vaari fell. Rowen followed, aiming a savage kick at Vaari's ribs. The Dhargot rolled away, caught Rowen's foot, and pulled him off balance. Vaari was on his feet in an instant, but before he could deliver a kick of his own, Rowen drove his foot into Vaari's kneecap. The Dhargot did not cry out but staggered backward. Rowen leapt back onto his feet and feigned a punch at Vaari's face. When the Dhargot moved to block, Rowen kicked him in the ribs then slammed his vambrace into the side of Vaari's head.

Vaari staggered again but did not fall. Twisting clear, he threw a punch at Rowen's side, winced when his fist struck kingsteel, and followed that up with a hard shove. He drew his shortsword and spat. "Don't make me kill you, Knight."

Before Rowen could answer, Zeia stepped between them. She said nothing but held one blazing hand before each of them. Both men stepped back.

Zeia said, "There are two more bodies in the water. Strange tracks. Whoever did this took Issa's horse. Looks like there were two of them, plus a greatwolf."

Rowen blinked. "You can't tame a greatwolf."

"Maybe a Dragonkin could." Zeia glared at Vaari until he sheathed his shortsword, then she turned back to Rowen. "The tracks lead north."

Rowen turned back to Issa's body, all his anger evaporating. "Whoever did this—"

Zeia said, "Don't worry about Igrid and Thessa. They're probably a lot safer than we are."

I doubt it. "You said the Lancers had a Shel'ai prisoner."

"But it sounds like she's traveling with Keswen. The Wyldkin's already none too fond of magic. I doubt she'd stand by while a Shel'ai did that to Issa." Zeia pointed at two more bodies floating in the stream. "Gods only know who they were."

With a final cold look at Rowen, Vaari turned and waded across the stream. The Dhargot turned the corpses over and searched them for valuables. Finding nothing, he cursed.

Meanwhile, Rowen returned to Issa's corpse. He whispered the prayer he'd started earlier. Finding the Knight's adamune on the grass, he returned it to its scabbard. Then he went back to the horses, seized the corpse of the Lancer, and dragged it off. "We're taking Issa with us."

Vaari waded back across the stream, cursing the cold water. "Why? He's dead, Knight. Say your words and leave him be."

"He's a Knight of the Crane," Rowen snapped. "He deserves a ceremony. We don't have time now, so we'll give him one once we rejoin the others."

Vaari snickered. "Perfect. I'm sure the Dragonkin won't mind waiting. And I'm sure that pretty child of yours won't mind seeing her teacher charred to a crisp, either."

Rowen retrieved Issa's helmet and facemask. As gently as he could, he slid them over the blackened face. Then he used his own cloak to wipe Issa's scorched armor as best he could. Zeia watched, saying nothing.

Finally, Rowen straightened. "Help me get him on the horse," he told Vaari, curling his fingers into fists as he spoke.

Vaari only sighed then helped without further protest.

The three rode north in silence, Rowen leading the horse that held Issa's body. They continued for hours then jerked to a stop when the sound of trumpets flooded the air, drifting over the treetops behind them.

Zeia asked, "Is that coming from the Lancers?"

"Or another host coming to join them," Rowen said darkly. He felt the leather reins with his fingers and tried not to look at Issa's body as he continued on.

Keswen said, "Where in the gods' names are you taking me?"

Nâya stood before her at the front of a small fishing boat they'd found along the shore. The Dragonkin stared calmly at the sea. The little boat sped northeast, seemingly of its own accord, as though two strong men were rowing. Keswen eyed the oars lying unused at her feet. She considered grabbing one and striking Nâya while her back was turned.

Nâya said, "I have no intention of harming you."

"Well, I have every intention of harming you if you don't answer my question."

Keswen picked up one of the oars, but before she could swing it, Nâya turned.

The Dragonkin smiled faintly. "You cannot hurt me with that."

"Well, it's worth a try." Keswen stood, gripping the oar. "Unless you want to answer my question, that is."

"We are going to an island that has no name. But you have been there before. We are going to Shigella's Tomb."

Keswen nodded, unsurprised. "Fair enough. Is there something you can do to stop Nekiel there? Something with the Dragonward?"

"No." Nâya turned and faced the sea again.

It seemed to Keswen that their little boat increased in speed, plowing through the water so quickly that her stomach lurched. She nearly lost her balance. Using the oar as a crutch, she waited until she'd regained her footing. Then she swung the oar at Nâya's head. Before it could make contact, though, it burst into flames. Keswen cried out and dropped it. As soon as the oar hit the boat, it exploded in a shower of cinders. Keswen inspected her hands. Somehow, she had not been burned.

Keswen sat down. She grabbed the other oar but did not swing it. "Either you're helping Nekiel, or you're helping Krym. Which is it?"

"Neither," Nâya answered, her echoing voice both near and hauntingly distant.

"So you're fighting to claim Ruun for yourself, then?" When Keswen received no answer, she shook her head. "Gods, Dragonkin, say something before I go mad!"

Slowly, Nâya turned again. "I do not serve Nekiel. That means I do not serve Krym either... since they are on the same side."

"But Krym is betraying Nekiel. He told us—"

"He told you what he wished, for his own amusement. When Nekiel comes, Rowen Locke will be the prize Krym lays at Nekiel's feet." Nâya paused. "I had hoped that none of the others would make it through the Dragonward. I should have known Krym would survive." A faint, sad smile touched her lips. "I do not have the strength to face both Nekiel *and* Krym. So I must help the Isle Knight in a different way. I must reclaim Knightswrath and take it to him."

Keswen nearly dropped the oar. "But if you take Knightswrath from the tomb—"

"The Dragonward will fall," Nâya finished. "But that does not matter. There are only three Dragonkin left in the world, and they are already on Ruun. The Dragonward is no longer needed." She turned back to the sea.

Keswen hesitated. "Krym spoke of a dragon, trapped under the ice of the Wintersea. Locke says he's seen it in his dreams once or twice. Was that a lie, too?"

Nâya shook her head. "Khyrshar is real. And *old*. You cannot imagine the torment she has endured, penned up so long, like a wounded animal in a slaughterhouse."

Keswen swallowed hard, appalled by the thought. "We thought Krym wanted to drain her power before Nekiel could."

"He cannot. Believe me, throughout the ages, countless Dragonkin have tried in vain to free her—or devour her. But Khyrshar is my father's prize." She paused. "I cannot tell you how many of our allies died during the Shattering War, just to keep Nekiel from reaching her, from absorbing her when he needed it most."

"Can she help us fight him?"

"I do not know. Nor do I know if seeking her help would be... entirely wise." Nâya paused. "But make no mistake. She is the prize that my father has been waiting centuries to savor. His need now is as great as it was during the Shattering War, perhaps greater. He will not hesitate to add her power to his own."

"What happens if he does?"

"If he survives it, he will be too powerful, even for Knightswrath."

"If he survives?"

"A vessel can only hold so much before it shatters. That could be why Nekiel never absorbed her when he had the chance, for fear that so much power would kill him—or drive him mad. But now, he has no choice. And if he survives it, he will practically become a god."

Keswen remembered the stories she'd heard about Fâyu Jinn's final, fateful duel against Nekiel. In the end, the first Isle Knight had only been able to fight the evil Dragonkin to a stalemate. Nekiel had retreated to gather his strength, only to be trapped on the other side when the Dragonward was raised. *Unless that's just a legend.* Keswen eyed Nâya and considered asking her what had really happened.

Before she could speak, though, Nâya said, "Even with Knightswrath, Rowen Locke might not be able to defeat my father. Many have tried." Her voice trembled. "But I will do everything I can to make amends for the sins of my people... in exchange for a promise."

"What promise?"

Nâya did not answer. Finally, exhausted, Keswen laid down her oar and rested her face in her hands. She closed her eyes and tried to sleep, even as the little boat pulsed with magic and raced ahead like a god-thrown spear through the empty blue waves.

CHAPTER NINETEEN

ROWEN SLOWED WHEN HE SPOTTED smoke rising over the distant trees. The horse carrying Issa's body continued forward to lick Rowen's hand, which still held the reins. Rowen turned to Zeia. Though he did not speak, Zeia nodded. Moving her horse around the others, she rode ahead to the camp.

Rowen turned to Vaari. "I'm sorry I struck you." *Though you deserved it.*

The Dhargot grunted and touched the bruise covering his cheek. His mismatched eyes sparked with malice. "Already forgotten," he said icily and moved his horse beside Rowen's.

They continued slowly toward the camp. By the time they arrived, Zeia had obviously already told the others what had happened. Breaksteel moved ahead of the others. Without a word, the Olg gathered Issa's body in his gigantic arms and carried him with silent reverence to the shade of a tree then laid Issa down and covered him with a cloak. Rowen dismounted, so exhausted that his eyelids sagged. Igrid came forward and embraced him. Rowen buried his face in her red curls for a moment.

"I'm all right," Igrid whispered. "So is Thessa. She spent half the time swinging her sword at shadows and the other half staring at that damn luminstone. Krym's creature snarled at us a bit, but he didn't do anything." She repeated, "We're all right."

Rowen looked past her and saw Thessa staring at Issa's body, wide-eyed and crying. He was about to go and comfort her when Krym appeared. The Dragonkin approached slowly, his bodyguard a step behind. While Krym's face was impassive, the Maalbolg's lips broke into a hissing smile. What had been Gaulgodd sniffed the air and looked at Issa. The Maalbolg's smile broadened.

Before he knew what he was doing, Rowen separated from Igrid, drew his adamune in spite of the dampness in his eyes, and strode forward. Krym slowed, unblinking. Rowen aimed his drawn sword at the Maalbolg, the tip just inches from his icy face. The Maalbolg answered with a derisive hiss.

"Send your creature away before I cut its laughing head off."

"If you value your life, you will not attempt such a thing," Krym said but turned.

Though Krym did not speak, the Maalbolg nodded and backed away.

Krym faced Rowen again. "Better?" When Rowen did not answer, Krym turned toward Issa.

Breaksteel still hovered over the Knight's body, joined by Saanji and Zeia. Vaari stood in the distance, half hidden by a tree, answering the call of nature.

"You know," Krym said, "in the ancient days, Dragonkin could revive those loyal servants who had just been slain. That was a long time ago, though, when there were still dragons on which to feed. Apologies." He looked around. "I do not see your Sylvan companion. I trust you were unsuccessful in rescuing her?"

"Could be that she freed herself," Rowen answered heavily. "She wasn't in the camp. We found no sign of her on the road. I was hoping she got away then came back here."

"Then you're in luck, Knight. We *did* receive a rather unexpected visitor, not an hour before you returned. If I could direct your gaze to that sleeping figure over there..." Krym pointed at a cloaked mass at the other end of the camp.

Igrid said something Rowen did not hear and reached for his arm, but Rowen was already racing toward the far end of the meager camp. He called out Keswen's name. As soon as he stood before the prone figure, though, he saw it was not Keswen. He eyed the old man's tapered ears, the matted white hair hanging over his face, and the empty scabbard at his side.

Igrid joined him. "I think he's mad. He was screaming nonsense. He even took a swing at Thessa." She pointed at an extravagant, jeweled sword stuck in the ground a few yards away. "I took that from him and broke his arm."

Rowen smiled then frowned. The sword was unmistakably Sylvan in design, with elegant curves and sapphires crusting the hilt. The unconscious man's tapered ears made Rowen fear for a moment that he was Nekiel. Rowen used the tip of his adamune to lift the man's hair, ready to plunge his sword into the man's throat if necessary. When he saw the face, his eyes widened. He considered stabbing the unconscious man anyway.

"We checked his eyes," Igrid said. "Blue. Krym assures us that's *not* Nekiel."

Saanji moved away from Zeia, toward them. "What is he? He looks like half a beggar, but that sword…"

"Some rich bastard who fled the Wytchforest when the war started?" Igrid suggested. "Or maybe he stole it."

"Looks like he's been cut to ribbons a dozen times," Saanji noted, pointing at the many scars and unhealed cuts covering the man's arms and legs, along with the dried blood on his tattered clothing.

Rowen stared at the unconscious man with contempt. He noticed the arm Igrid must have broken. Someone had made a token effort to straighten it, but the arm still hung, unnaturally limp. Rowen turned to find Krym and saw the Dragonkin smiling at him from a distance, openly enjoying the joke.

You wanted me to think this was Keswen. Rowen hoped the Dragonkin was reading his mind. *Damn you. What purpose did that even serve?*

Krym continued smiling and did not answer.

Damn you, Rowen thought again, then he turned back toward the unconscious Sylv. "Zeia, find out if he knows who killed Issa. Drag it from his mind if you have to."

Zeia hesitated. "I don't suppose I need to remind you that—"

"I don't care what it does to him," Rowen snapped. "He's mad already. Just find out what he knows."

Krym drew closer. "No need for that, my friends. I can read the poor man's thoughts far more easily than the Shel'ai."

Rowen gave the Dragonkin a murderous look. "And?"

"It was as you think," Krym said. "Nekiel slew your Knight. The Sylv saw it all. I can inject the images into your mind if you'd like."

Saanji swore, but Rowen merely nodded. "But he didn't turn Issa to ash. That could mean he's not at full power yet."

Igrid stood in the distance, her arms around a crying Thessa, trying to block the girl's view of Issa's body. "Then we hunt him down," she called. "Now."

"Impossible," Krym countered. "I cannot sense him. While we're chasing him through the forests, he could continue north. Better we continue to the Wintersea and find poor trapped Khyrshar before Nekiel can." Before anyone could argue, the Dragonkin stepped back, the Maalbolg at his elbow, and nodded toward the unconscious Sylv. "I'll leave this one to your mercy, Sir Locke."

Rowen caught the lingering amusement in the Dragonkin's voice. He looked down at the unconscious Sylv again, touched his sword hilt, and wondered if he should kill him. *Gods knew he had nothing better in mind for me.*

Saanji said, "Mercy, for a beggar? If this Sylv didn't kill Issa, why does he need mercy? He might be a madman, but I say cut him loose. We'll keep his sword."

Rowen made a point of stepping between the unconscious Sylv and Zeia since he had no idea how the Shel'ai would react. "This isn't a beggar," he said. "This is Loslandril, the Sylvan king."

Jalist stared at the vast open field that had been empty the day before but was roiling with hundreds of armed and armored men. Banners of every color rippled in the morning breeze. Horses grazed in a massive corral erected beside a vast sea of bright tents. Jalist was just thinking that the bustling sight was rather beautiful when the Lancers spotted him and began to hurl insults. Some even fired crossbows, though the bolts fell far short of Jalist and the other commanders, thudding into the ground.

"I'd call that less than cordial," Tansil said.

Jalist turned in the saddle to face Aeko. "Is it my imagination, or have their numbers doubled yet again?"

Aeko was silent for a moment, then she swore so fiercely that Jalist's horse jerked. She pointed. "That's Cadwallis's banner."

Jalist squinted. "Looks like a tongue of flame getting buggered by a horse."

Tansil laughed. "I think we are meant to think the hooves are stamping out the fire." She turned to Maddoc, who was busy trying to keep Sariel from leaping down from the horse he shared with the child. "Given the fire's color, I presume that's meant for you?"

Maddoc gave the distant banner a token glance. "One of these days, rulers will stop thinking that all magic users think with one mind." He grabbed Sariel before she could wriggle free then chided her when she summoned wytchfire that singed their horse's mane. Sariel giggled.

Jalist reached out, grabbed Sariel by her dress, and hefted her from Maddoc's horse onto his own. He gave the child so fierce a scowl that her eyes widened and she fell silent.

Then Jalist turned to Aeko. "Who's Cadwallis?"

"The Ivairian version of Gaulgodd, more or less." Aeko sighed. "A nephew of the dead king. He was too busy fighting his own kind to join with the Sons of Maelmohr. Besides, I don't think he's interested in erasing magic from the continent so much as eviscerating any shred of it that dares set foot in his lands."

Maddoc snickered. "How kind of him to show such restraint."

Aeko added, "If he's not yet Ivairia's latest king, he soon will be."

"This is a fight we can avoid, Grand Marshal," Tansil said. "They have a point. We *are* on their borders with three hundred souls, plus a few hundred Sylvs still on the way."

"And a dozen Soroccan ships if we can find a use for them," Jalist added. He remembered the note they'd just received from Hráthbam. Though he was just a merchant, Hráthbam's standing among his people was such that, in the wake of the latest threat, he'd once again been made the captain of their naval militia.

Tansil nodded. "If we pull back—"

"If we pull back, we leave Locke to deal with Nekiel alone," Jalist said.

"Not alone," Tansil countered. "His message spoke of—"

"Another Dragonkin who might turn on us any minute," Jalist finished.

189

Aeko said, "I sent a long message to that Lancer, Ferinald, detailing the real reason we're here. Presumably, he passed that on to Lord Cadwallis."

"Or burned it," Jalist muttered. He kissed the back of Sariel's head then hefted her from his saddle and passed her—laughing—back to Maddoc. "I trust you want to have a word with them?"

Aeko answered by spurring her horse forward.

Jalist cursed. "Stay here," he told Maddoc then raced after her. Tansil followed, joined by a dozen other officers from the Lotus Isles, the Red Watch, and Stillhammer. When Jalist saw the potential size of Aeko's escort, he ordered all of them to stay behind. Jalist reached Aeko's side, joined only by Tansil. Jalist was glad he'd thought to wear the emblem of the Lyosi falcon over his Dwarrish armor.

The Isle Knights, The Iron Sisters, the Dwarrs, the Red Watch, and soon enough, the Sylvs—all in one place, all ready to fight on the same side. If that doesn't intimidate these Lancers, nothing will.

Aeko had drawn up at the very edge of crossbow range, so near that bolts thudded into the soil just a few feet from their horses' hooves. The Lancers continued to shout at them, urging them to attack and offering additional less-than-savory suggestions for Aeko and Tansil. The women stared back with chilly indifference.

Finally, an Ivairian officer rode out and silenced the men by holding up his hand. He was a stocky figure with long, flowing hair, dressed in enameled armor and an exotic tunic of different colors. Two other Lancers rode out and joined him, each taking up position on either side. The one Jalist presumed was Sir Ferinald looked so stern and different from the flamboyant Lord Cadwallis that Jalist stifled a laugh. As the three Lancers drew nearer, Jalist noted that Cadwallis also had jewel-crusted barrettes in his hair.

Aeko rode to meet them halfway. She introduced Jalist and Tansil then bowed. "I greet you as a friend, Lord Cadwallis. Much has happened, but I hope that we can still find a way to—"

"Regent," Cadwallis interrupted with shrill curtness.

Aeko bowed again. "Greetings, Regent. As I said in my earlier message—"

"What message?"

Aeko gave Sir Ferinald a cold look. "Three days ago, I delivered a message to Sir Ferinald, clarifying our presence on your border and assuring you that we are not—"

"Lies," Sir Ferinald muttered. "I burned the note, Regent, rather than waste your time with such rambling nonsense."

Cadwallis nodded. "That was well done, Sir Ferinald. As for you, Grand Marshal, is there any truth to these rumors of Shel'ai and Dragonkin in my lands?"

Aeko blinked. "Regent, the message I spoke of addressed that very subject." She continued before the Lancers had a chance to interrupt. "As unlikely as this sounds, we have strong reason to believe that Nekiel has returned. Rowen Locke has already gone ahead to fight him. We are raising an army to—"

"Rowen Locke killed one of my men in the forest," Sir Ferinald snapped. "And he abducted two prisoners who were awaiting trial, injuring several more Lancers in the process."

He's lying. Jalist noted the look of disapproval on the face of the third Lancer, Sir Hale, who shifted uncomfortably but remained silent.

Aeko said, "I assure you, on my honor as the Grand Marshal, that Rowen Locke is not a murderer. If you will just—"

"Crovis Ammerhel was a Grand Marshal," Cadwallis said. "It doesn't seem that he was particularly honorable, given the stories coming from your islands."

Aeko flushed. "True enough, Regent, but what matters now is—"

"How poor and desperate your Order must be," Ferinald said, "that you would seek to conquer us with wild tales instead of simply meeting us on the field, with honor."

Aeko's face flushed even further. Her voice slowed, lowering dangerously. "This is not an invasion. We have come to aid Rowen Locke. We had hoped that you would join us, but you have no reason to fight us. We can proceed to the Wintersea, in pursuit of Locke, without setting foot in Ivairia."

Cadwallis brushed the hair from his eyes and gave Aeko a cold look. "You cannot."

They waited, expecting more, but Cadwallis merely sat astride his horse and glared at them.

Finally, Sir Hale said, "Perhaps the Grand Marshal is unaware that in the past year, the borders of Ivairia have expanded. They now extend from the coast to as far west as Cassica. Therefore, by our reckoning, any march to the Wintersea will require that you pass through our lands."

Sir Ferinald snickered. "Unless you want to march farther west and go around Cassica."

"That will take weeks," Jalist snapped. "Gods, man, have you heard a word we've said? How much time do you think we have?"

Aeko cast Jalist a warning glance. Cadwallis slowly moved his gaze from Aeko to Jalist, regarding the latter with chilly indifference. "Perhaps some of what you say is true. Perhaps not. Either way, I am obligated to protect my own kingdom. And I will do so, regardless of the consequences. To do otherwise would be a dishonor I shall not suffer in this lifetime."

Jalist took a deep breath and let it go. "Listen, my lords. If it would prevent unnecessary bloodshed, I'd carry our whole damn army around Cassica myself, one mule at a time. But Nekiel has a prize waiting for him on the Wintersea. If he claims it before we stop him…"

Sir Ferinald rolled his eyes. "Ah, yes. Your tale of a dragon buried under the ice. How romantic." He laughed.

Cadwallis laughed, too, though Jalist suspected the regent had no idea what they were talking about. Hale shifted in his saddle and offered only a strained smile.

Aeko straightened in her saddle. "Regent, how many of your Lancers fought beside Rowen Locke against Chorlga? How many fought the Dhargots with Arnil Royce?"

Cadwallis blinked. "Royce is dead. The last Ivairian lord who sided with Locke was Lord Hamperling, who was killed by my cousin… who was in turn killed by me." Cadwallis tapped the jewel-crusted hilt of his broadsword. "Ivairia is a new kingdom. We want nothing to do with magic nor those who befriend it." He shifted his gaze back to Jalist. "Or bed down with it."

Jalist gripped the shaft of Freija and imagined how satisfying it would feel to cut off the Ivairian lord's head. The thought made him smile. "Begging your pardon, Regent, but if Nekiel wins, Ivairia will have to contend with magic the likes of which even the Dragonjol could not have prepared you for."

Cadwallis snickered. "What proof do you have of this… for *any* of this… besides woeful tales and thinly veiled threats?" He looked past them. "I see a few hundred swords, some of them wielded by women, the rest from mixed races who probably distrust each other even more than they distrust us." He straightened his shoulders. "I command one thousand Lancers, with a thousand more on the way. All are united behind one purpose. Do not test me."

"We have not come here to test you," Aeko insisted. "If you like, you can escort our host as we march north, to ensure that we do no harm to your lands. All we want—"

"Your presence alone is an act of harm," Cadwallis snapped. "You will go no farther into Ivairian lands. Not now, not ever. If you attempt to ride around my host, I will chase you to the ends of the earth. In truth, I hope you do not heed my warning. It has been too long since I drew blood." He leaned forward. "My sword is thirsty, woman. Will you sate it?"

Before Aeko could reply, Cadwallis wheeled his horse about and rode back to the Lancers' camp. Ferinald looked at Aeko, spat on the ground, and followed. Hale hesitated, as though he wanted to speak, but the Ivairian camp broke into a deafening cheer at Cadwallis's return, and Sir Hale changed his mind.

Aeko shook her head in disgust. "Let's go."

As they rejoined the rest of their officers, Jalist asked, "Should we ride around them anyway?"

Aeko said, "And reach Locke with a thousand Lancers at our heels? Somehow, I doubt that will help matters."

"Do you think he's lying about the other thousand men?"

Tansil said, "No. Did you see the looks on the other two Lancers' faces when he said that? I think it was supposed to be a surprise."

Aeko nodded her agreement. "I don't want to leave Locke on his own, but starting a war isn't going to help him, either. We'll wait a day or two to see if Cadwallis comes to his senses. If he calms down, maybe we can pour some honey in his ears. If not, we'll ride south." She shook her head in disgust again. "The bastard actually said his *sword* is thirsty…"

Jalist said, "Gods, I'm thirsty, too." He slung Freija and rode toward the spot where Maddoc and Sariel were waiting.

CHAPTER TWENTY

ROWEN EYED THE STARK, ROCKY flatlands and tried to ignore the whimpering of the Sylvan king. Even though he believed Loslandril had not been responsible for Issa's death, Rowen wondered if he shouldn't have killed the king anyway. *Gods know he deserves it!*

They had been riding north for three days through an ever-increasing chill that no campfire seemed able to keep at bay, and the Sylvan king had hardly opened his eyes during that time. However, he moaned and whimpered almost constantly, his body convulsing like a dying man's, though Zeia had already confirmed that he had no fever.

The king slept so long and so fitfully that Rowen wondered if the madness were a ruse. Once, though, they'd untied his hands to let him eat as the king drooped against a rock. Immediately, he leapt up—screaming—and attempted to tear out Saanji's jugular with his teeth. Rowen recognized a stream of Sylvan curse words, all of them related to Shel'ai, before Zeia pressed one flaming hand to Loslandril's face. The king's eyes went wide with terror a moment before he fell unconscious. He'd been bound ever since.

"Gods, he must be mad," Saanji had said. "He thought I was a Shel'ai!"

"A true sign of madness," Zeia said. "Your eyes aren't pretty enough for that." She had kicked the fallen king for good measure.

Three days of this, Rowen thought, staring at the king, whom they'd lashed to a horse. He hated most of all how the king's ranting had sullied Issa's funeral, interrupting with his mad rambling a ceremony that already had to contend with the derisive smiling of Krym and his creature in the distance.

Rowen turned and noted the new jeweled sword that Vaari carried. Despite his contempt for the man, he smiled. So far, Vaari was the only one who appeared unfazed by Loslandril's strange arrival. Vaari had not even protested when Rowen tasked him with keeping hold of Loslandril's horse. In fact, the Dhargot frequently drew the expensive sword and turned it against the sunlight, just to look at it.

Facing the mad king again, Rowen wondered how Loslandril had gotten there. He remembered Briel saying that the king had locked himself in his palace and would not come out. Since rule of the Sylvan kingdom had since passed to Ahmashura, the king's ancient but surprisingly wise great-aunt, it seemed unlikely that anyone would bother trying to abduct Loslandril. However, it seemed equally unlikely that he could have left the Wytchforest on his own.

Yet here he is… still ranting about his son.

Rowen remembered how Silwren—after being stabbed by Prince Quivalen and his evil glass knife—had reduced the prince to a charred and lifeless husk. However, pleasure turned to guilt when he reminded himself that, like so many, both Loslandril and Quivalen had really just been victims of Chorlga's schemes.

Just as I might very well end up being a victim of whatever schemes Krym has concocted. Then Rowen cleared his mind and looked toward the head of the column, where Krym rode next to his bodyguard. The air around the Dragonkin shimmered slightly. From time to time, a snowflake fell, struck the shimmering air, and melted instantly. Rowen had no doubt that the Dragonkin was continuously shielding himself, lest Rowen or one of his companions attempt to strike him from behind, but he wondered if that protection extended to the Maalbolg. Then he tried to wipe that thought from his mind as well, despite how much the thought of killing the Maalbolg pleased him.

"We must be close." Igrid eyed the flecks of snow gathering in the boughs of trees. "Too early for winter unless we're far enough north that winter never stops."

"We're close," Rowen confirmed, "but there's no telling where

Nekiel's prize is hidden. And something tells me our guide is in no hurry to tell us."

Igrid nodded. Leaning away from Rowen, she rubbed Thessa's shoulders as the girl shivered under her cloak. "I was hoping *you* knew. A clue from the dream—"

"All I ever saw was a dragon under ice, staring up at me. Blinking. Nothing more. I haven't even had the dream in months, maybe as long as a year."

"Why do you think it stopped?"

Rowen shrugged. "Maybe she got tired of asking for help." Rowen tried to visualize the image as he'd first seen it, in the middle of a telepathic communication from Chorlga, but wondered which elements were real and which were imagined. He remembered six gigantic wings, three spreading out from each side of the body. He remembered the body itself was huge but sleek, with horns, but he could not remember the exact shape of the horns or the color of the scales. Mainly, he just remembered the great dark eye, staring up at him through the ice—blinking.

Rowen shuddered. *If we set you free, will you be an enemy or a friend?* "Even in that scroll Silwren gave me there's no mention of dragons, let alone this one. Either Jinn didn't know, or he left that out."

Igrid said, "All I've ever heard about them came from fairy tales. Some say they're evil, like rabid wolves with wings and breath that melts steel. Others say they're docile as milking cows."

"Something tells me that the only thing *this* dragon has in common with cattle is the fact that she was imprisoned for the day her captor got hungry."

"Any ideas where Nekiel might have hidden such a thing?"

Rowen shook his head.

Saanji joined them, the cold having left his face even more flushed than usual. "I realize that a tavern isn't on our itinerary, but a warm fire would be appreciated."

Rowen said, "You might have to wait awhile. We're almost to the tundra. After that, there won't be much but a few hills and some jagged glaciers. There's a trading post, but it's far to the east, and we're heading the wrong direction." He added, "Besides, the place is usually crawling with cutthroats."

"Fantastic." Saanji looked around. "Gods, there's not even a tree to block the wind!"

"You should have been here four years ago, when we were chasing after Chorlga. We had blizzards every night for a week. Most of the Sylvs had never even seen snow before, and the Queshi weren't much better. It got so bad the Shel'ai had to light fires to keep us from freezing to death."

"Apologies," Saanji said. "I was busy marching to war against my own father, shortly after killing my brother with my dead friend's sword."

Rowen nodded. "Did I mention these were really *big* blizzards?"

Saanji smiled. "I'll ask Zeia if she can set something on fire. Me, perhaps."

"No need," Krym boomed, his voice so loud and jarring that everyone winced. He reined in and looked back over his shoulder. A faint smile touched the Dragonkin's lips. "Despite our history as enemies, you have served me faithfully and with trust," he said more softly. "Allow me to see to your comforts."

Krym held out one hand. Wytchfire sprang from his grasp, darting through the air. Thessa screamed. The horses screamed, too. Acting on instinct, Rowen reached for his sword, but Saanji grabbed his arm.

"Gods," Igrid gasped, drawing Thessa closer to her.

Loslandril's horse reared up suddenly, pulling the reins from Vaari's grasp. The horse would surely have thrown the Sylvan king to the ground, had he not been tied in place. Breaksteel stepped forward, calmed the horse, and handed the reins back to Vaari, who accepted them without comment.

Meanwhile, more and more wytchfire poured out of Krym's fingertips, as though an endless sea of it were rushing to be unleashed. The flames spread out, writhing but absolutely silent, until they formed a wall. Then the wall stretched, floating just above the rocky earth. By the time Krym lowered his arm, a vast wreath of purple flame had encircled the entire company, except for straight ahead, where the flames parted, allowing them to see the stark-white road before them.

Still smiling, Krym faced north again and began riding. The flaming wreath kept pace with him, floating along with the party. Then, Rowen felt the heat. The wreath of wytchfire pulsed like a furnace though it still made no sound.

"Gods, don't anyone fall too far behind," Saanji muttered, glancing at the raging wall of wytchfire behind them. Already, beads of sweat shimmered on the prince's forehead.

Zeia eyed the flames then gave Rowen an uncertain look. Breaksteel did likewise, tightly gripping his kashpa with both of his strong gray hands. Only Thessa laughed, casting back the hood of her cloak and staring at their new surroundings with wild fascination.

Miriam refused to open her eyes.

"I am sorry," Emrael repeated, just as he had for the past day and a half. For all that time, she'd sat within a shallow cave with rough walls and a surprisingly high ceiling interrupted by a lone stalactite that nearly divided the cave in half. She sat behind the stalactite, using it to block out the glare of sunlight pouring in through the cave mouth.

Emrael touched her hand. Miriam pulled away and squeezed her eyes tighter until the world turned white again. Then she opened them. She stared at the pile of half-eaten fruit that Emrael had been bringing her, along with a wooden bowl of water. Then she lifted her gaze to Emrael—who looked so different that only his voice was familiar.

Miriam studied his features, which had shifted somehow, becoming sharper and more angled. His eyes were still ice blue but flecked with gold, like the color of his hair. *What's happening to you?*

"I have to leave you soon," Emrael said. "I've already waited too long, but I couldn't leave you like this."

"You *did* leave," Miriam snapped, remembering how Emrael had abandoned her in the cave, leaving her to sob throughout the night, only to return, shamefaced, the next morning.

"I did," Emrael confessed, "but I came back."

"You came back because the horse died, and I bet the reason it died is—"

"I came back for *you*," Emrael insisted. "But now, I'll have to go again. Do you understand? I'll have to leave you... unless you still want to come with me."

"Why did you do that?" Miriam wondered if Emrael would misunderstand and think she was asking why he'd left before, but she decided not to clarify—after all, Emrael always seemed to know what she was thinking, regardless of what she said.

"I told you, I thought it would help you, knowing they're gone." Emrael did not blink as he spoke, and the flecks of gold in his eyes made Miriam think the sun must be shining in them. She turned around and found the sun veiled by clouds so that only a little of it trickled into the cave mouth.

"You could have just told me. You didn't have to *show* me."

"You are right. I know that now. I am sorry."

Miriam frowned. "You don't *sound* sorry." She wiped her eyes and rubbed her hand through Challa's fur. "You've been telling me that for days, and you *still* don't sound sorry."

"What do I sound like?"

"You sound like a priest."

Emrael's eyes narrowed even as he smiled. "How so?"

"We had a priest who used to travel up and down the Dead Shores. He'd talk to farmers and fishermen, tell them prayers, but you could tell he'd said them so much they didn't mean anything anymore."

Emrael's smile thinned. "I do not think I've spent that much time apologizing." He touched her face. "You look familiar."

Miriam did not know whether to pull away or not. "Of course I do! I've been traveling with you since—"

"That's not what I mean. I mean you remind me of someone. Someone I lost…" Emrael paused, stared at his own hand on her face as though it alarmed him, and withdrew. "You don't have to be afraid of me. Didn't I make the bad dreams go away?"

Miriam hesitated then nodded. After Emrael had taken her into the cave, all she wanted to do was sleep. Still, she cursed him, even threw the golden medallion back at him, refusing to accept it when he tried to return it to her. But every time she closed her eyes, nightmares overtook her—not just nightmares about her slain brothers, but also images of her parents again, shut up inside the burning house.

Somehow, though, Emrael had made the nightmares stop. All he did was touch her forehead after she woke up crying, and she felt a jolt of heat inside her head and wanted to scream, but then the pain passed and, with it, much of her sadness. Miriam could not explain why or how, but she felt as if her brothers had died years before, instead of days—and her parents, years and years before that.

"How old are you?" she asked suddenly.

Emrael seemed puzzled by the question. "I don't know." He added, "That is, I don't remember anymore."

"But older than my brothers."

"Older than anyone you have ever known, times ten, I should think."

"Are you a Shel'ai?"

Emrael shook his head. "I am... something I cannot explain. I still do not remember it all, but I have gone to places you could not possibly fathom, seen wonders that..." He looked down and blinked at his hands.

Miriam gazed out the cave mouth at the stolen horse grazing in the distance. "You shouldn't have killed that man in armor. He wasn't going to hurt you. He just wanted to help me."

"So you have said, many times," Emrael answered patiently. "Do you still want me to hurt the man who killed your brothers?"

Miriam did not answer. She vaguely remembered screaming at Emrael, cursing him for letting her brothers' killer live, and making Emrael swear he would find that man and hurt him. But that, too, felt like it had taken place a long time ago, during another lifetime. Anger still filled her whenever she thought about what Emrael had shown her, how the strange old man had attacked her brothers and cut them with his sword, but she found her anger evaporated the instant she stopped visualizing him.

"I don't care," she said finally. She thought instead that, with her brothers gone, she was finally and completely alone.

"Not alone," Emrael said. He squeezed her hand, which had the odd effect of making Challa whimper. The greatwolf drew away from both of them.

Miriam looked at Emrael again, awed once more by how different he appeared. She edged toward him so that the stalactite stopped blocking the light. Reaching out, she touched his ears, which were no longer rounded but rose to high, tapered points. Emrael smiled.

Miriam said, "These look like the old man's ears. Why—"

Emrael's smile vanished. Miriam screamed. She jerked her hand back and found it red and blistered, as though she'd pressed it to a lit furnace. Tears welled in her eyes. She looked at Emrael again. His eyes were wide, too, and he started to mouth an apology. Then he grabbed her hand.

"Stop. Hold still so I can heal you…"

Miriam screamed again, afraid. She tried to break free, but Emrael would not let go, and all the while, Challa paced the far end of the cave, her red fur darkened by shadows, alternately growling and whimpering at the air.

CHAPTER TWENTY-ONE

ROWEN STARED AT THE BROAD, stark tundra before them. Krym had only just dismissed his swirling wreath of wytchfire, and already the cold was rushing back in, clawing through his cloak and armor. Rowen's throat tightened. The others drew up beside him.

"Is that a frozen lake?" Thessa asked, worried.

"Some of it," Rowen said, "but some is dry land, covered in ice. It's almost impossible to tell where the water ends and the land starts, so people just call all of it the Wintersea." He added, "Don't worry. You won't fall through. Even where the ice is thinnest, you could still cross with a herd of Dhargothi war elephants."

"Agreed," Saanji added, "especially now that our elephants have mated with dragons and sprouted wings."

Thessa scowled at Saanji despite the faintest hint of a smile. Rowen shifted his gaze from the girl to Krym, who had drawn a short distance ahead of the rest, the Maalbolg beside him. Rowen guessed the two were in telepathic communication. The Maalbolg turned once to meet Rowen's gaze and offer him a toothy, clicking snicker.

Igrid whispered, "I wish that bastard would blink once in a while."

Rowen was about to agree when Breaksteel clapped his hands to get their attention. The Olg made a quick hand-sign then pointed behind them. Rowen looked where the Olgish squire indicated and cursed.

A band of men was approaching. Though still a half mile away, they were close enough for Rowen to see that they traveled on foot, dressed in furs. Several of the men were also exceptionally tall and broad shouldered, at least half again as big as those next to them. Most of the men carried spears, the tips glinting in the cold sunlight, though Rowen discerned a few longbows as well.

"Frostreavers." Rowen saw Igrid's questioning look and said, "Bandits, more or less—those killers I mentioned before. There are little mountains here and there on the Wintersea. Some of them contain gold—*lots* of gold, if you don't freeze to death trying to get it. Merchants and miners come up here from time to time, and these bastards try their best to rob them."

Rowen considered mentioning the time he'd helped protect a merchant against frostreavers, in the company of Jalist and Kayden, but the thought of his brother reminded him of a dream in which he'd accidentally killed Kayden on the Wintersea. The memory made his throat tighten even more than the cold had.

Saanji squinted. "Is it my imagination, or are half of them giants?"

"Olgrym," Rowen said. "Sometimes, Olgrym join the frostreavers and live on the Wintersea as part of their training, I think." He glanced at Breaksteel, who answered with a mute and reluctant nod.

Zeia used one flaming hand to block the sun. "I count twenty-three. Looks like six are Olgrym or have enough Olgish blood that they might as well be."

Vaari sheathed his jeweled sword and reached for his bow. "I'm sure I'm not the only one who's noticed that they aren't exactly trying to hide from us."

"They're trying to scare us, make us run," Rowen said. "There's almost nothing for the horses to eat north of here. No place to hide, either. Sooner or later—"

Igrid stopped him with a look. Rubbing Thessa's shoulders, she said, "Don't worry, child. They'll be the unluckiest bastards in Ruun if they try and rob *us*."

"Indeed," Krym's voice boomed in their minds. The Dragonkin joined them, Saanji's horse fearfully edging aside to let him pass. In his normal voice, Krym continued. "I can dispose of these killers quite easily if you like."

Rowen touched his hilt, tempted to say no. The thought of allowing Krym to harm anyone, even frostreavers, revolted him, but he reminded himself that, in addition to being badly outnumbered, he and his companions had Thessa to worry about. "You don't have to kill them. Just cast enough wytchfire to—"

"Scare them off so they can live to slit the throats of the less fortunate?" Krym interrupted, snickering.

Rowen urged his horse so close to Krym that the Maalbolg clicked in disapproval. Rowen lowered his voice, ignoring the shame reddening his face, and said, "Fine. You're right. Kill them all."

Krym nodded. "No need for the child to see this. I suggest you and your friends ride ahead. Just go straight north. My companion and I will rejoin you presently."

Without having to flick the reins he held, the Dragonkin urged his horse southward. The Maalbolg followed, turning in the saddle to look at Rowen. For a moment, the Maalbolg stared at him, expressionless. Then, all at once, the Maalbolg's face melted and changed, becoming the face of Kayden.

The effect lasted only a moment before the Maalbolg's face changed back to the way it had been before, save for the addition of a cold, derisive grin. Then the Maalbolg turned south, and one clawed hand drew the shortsword from its belt.

Rowen led his companions north. Part of him wanted see how Krym would dispose of the frostreavers, but more than that, he wanted Thessa far away before the fighting started. Igrid stayed close to him, sensing his turmoil. She did not speak, though, and forced a smile for Thessa's benefit.

Zeia followed as well. When they had put some distance between themselves and Krym, her voice echoed softly in Rowen's mind. *I saw what the Maalbolg did. That must mean their kind have telepathy, too. He read your brother's face from your thoughts. We should—*

Rowen silenced her with a scowl.

They rode and rode across a stark wasteland of thick frozen water and snow-dusted rock. Rowen had expected Krym to rejoin them quickly, but hours passed without the Dragonkin's appearance. Rowen clung to the faint hope that perhaps, somehow, the frostreavers had killed him.

Saanji quickened his horse until he rode alongside Rowen. "How long are we supposed to keep this up? My nerves—"

Before the Dhargothi prince could finish, Loslandril began screaming, jerking vainly against the ropes that still secured him to his horse. Panicking, the horse reared up. Rowen signaled a halt. Vaari answered by striking the Sylvan king across the back of the head. Loslandril continued screaming as though he had not noticed the blow. Vaari struck him again and was about to strike him a third time when Breaksteel moved between them.

"I must say that's not helping my nerves, either," Saanji muttered.

Igrid joined them. Despite the smile she forced for Thessa's benefit, she leaned toward Rowen and whispered, "Royal or no, I'll pay you fifty cranáfi if you let me cut that bastard's throat."

Rowen answered with a pointed look at Zeia. The Shel'ai nodded, understanding. She moved to Loslandril's side, conjured one flaming hand, and reached for his temple. The Sylvan king saw her, and his eyes went wide, his screams even more frantic than before. However, Zeia touched the side of his head, and a jolt of magic knocked the Sylvan king unconscious.

"I can't keep doing that, you know," Zeia said.

"Yeah." Vaari snorted. "We'd hate to give the poor king a headache." The Dhargothi bodyguard gazed down yet again to appreciate his jeweled sword.

"That's not what I'm talking about," Zeia said. "Sooner or later, it'll kill him. Gods know, that wouldn't trouble me, but if you want to use him for something—"

"I doubt he's of any use," Rowen said. He stared at the slumped, unconscious king, and his revulsion turned to pity. "The Sylvs don't want him. He doesn't know anything that can help us, and if we let him go, he'll just be a danger to those around him."

Breaksteel frowned. The Olgish squire made a hand-gesture, voicing his disagreement, but Rowen ignored it.

Zeia ignored it, too. "Agreed," she told Rowen. "I can make it quick, painless. The Light knows that's more than he deserves." She started to reach for Loslandril's head again.

"Stop." Rowen glanced at Thessa as the girl stared back at him, wide-eyed and confused. He sighed. "We'll take him with us. Zeia, keep him quiet. If it kills him, so be it. But I won't have him executed." *Not yet.*

Zeia's disagreement was evident in her expression, but she nodded nonetheless.

The company continued on. The sun began to set, turning the Wintersea a frightful shade of red.

When they stopped again to rest, Vaari said, "Doesn't look like the Dragonkin's coming back any time soon. Let me ride ahead, Knight. I'll see if I can find us some shelter."

Surprised by the offer, Rowen nodded. The Dhargot rode north, readying an arrow on his bow.

Meanwhile, Rowen turned to Saanji, who was scanning the southern horizon with a spyglass. "Any sign of our friends?"

Saanji shook his head. "My esteemed bodyguard is right. Krym's getting stronger, but it seems he doesn't like to waste his power teleporting. That means he'll have to catch up with us on horseback. Unless he has a change of heart, I wouldn't expect him until dawn, at the earliest."

"Unless he's dead," Igrid offered.

Thessa brightened. "If he's dead… is it over? Can we go home?"

Saanji flashed her a sympathetic smile. "Nearly. There's still Nekiel, child. But don't worry. You'll be home before long. I swear it."

"In the meantime, let's test that sword arm." Igrid dismounted.

Thessa frowned. "You want to spar *now*? But it's cold, and—"

"A fighter rarely gets the chance to choose her battlefield," Igrid pointed out. Her smile vanished. She snapped her fingers, pointed at the ground, and gave Thessa a stern look.

Thessa looked to Rowen for help. When he shook his head, she sighed and dismounted as well.

Rowen waited until the two were gone then turned back to Saanji. Breaksteel quietly joined them, his shadow spreading across the ice to devour theirs.

Rowen said, "I didn't know Krym's pet could change shape on his own. I figured he needed his master's help to do that."

Saanji's expression turned sympathetic. "Makes me wonder if these Maalbolgs are locked into one form by their masters then released as a reward once they've done what they're supposed to do." He paused.

"Granted, the sight of *my* dead brothers might not affect me the same way it affected you."

Rowen scanned the southern horizon. "You killed your brother. I killed mine. Tell me you don't have nightmares about it, and I'll call you a liar."

Saanji blinked then laughed. "All right, let's discuss something more important. The Maalbolg did that to get a rise out of you. If bodyguards are a reflection of whomever they're guarding, that doesn't speak well for Krym."

Rowen smiled faintly. "And what does Vaari say about you, I wonder?"

"Point taken." Saanji returned his spyglass to his pack.

Rowen's gaze fell on the brass hilt of Saanji's kingsteel longsword, which had once belonged to Arnil Royce. Rowen thought of how his own sword had once belonged to Sang Wei.

Two brother-killers, mournfully wearing the swords of dead friends. Maybe this Dhargot and I have more in common than I'd like to admit.

Zeia joined them, quietly leading the horse carrying the slumped body of Loslandril behind her. "If I can direct everyone's attention back to something more important, we're on the Wintersea. That means wherever this dragon of Nekiel's is buried, we're getting close. We have to decide what we're going to do." Though she spoke in reserved, even tones, the reins began to smolder in her flaming hands.

"My deadly little wytch is right," Saanji said, his phrasing drawing a scowl from Zeia. "Provided this dragon really exists, we can't let either Krym or Nekiel have it. Gods know how we're going to stop them, but..."

"It's real," Rowen said. "But you're right. Even if Krym *does* help us kill Nekiel, we'll still have Krym to deal with. And I don't have Knightswrath."

Breaksteel made a series of quick hand-gestures. Rowen tried to follow but quickly became confused. He looked at Zeia.

Zeia rolled her eyes. "He says you might not have the sword, but you *do* have us."

Breaksteel nodded. He tapped the long handle of his kashpa, smiling.

Rowen nodded his thanks. But his thoughts drifted back to Sir Issa—dead—and Keswen, who was still missing. *Gods, all I do is get my friends killed.* Uncertainty rose and rose within him until his stomach lurched. He stepped away from the others, took a deep breath, then went to join Igrid and Thessa.

Igrid interpreted his expression and gave him a loving look—all without succumbing to Thessa's furious swings. Rowen sat down to watch them. When their motions became too much, he lowered his eyes and watched their shadows dancing and spinning across the ice. Then he closed his eyes. He prayed that, no matter what happened to him, the ice would not break.

CHAPTER TWENTY-TWO

K ESWEN CLUTCHED THE OAR—HER ONLY weapon—as the
fishing boat sped through the blue waters of the Burnished Way.
To her amazement, Nâya continued to stand at the front of the
ship, so unmoving that Keswen might have mistaken her for a statue—or
a Jol, were it not for the wind blowing through her dark hair.

Having given up on trying to draw the Dragonkin into conversation,
Keswen trained her eyes on the surrounding water to watch for ships.
She'd seen a handful of galleons floating on the misty water near the
island of Saikaido, in the shadow of the massive temple, but none had
paid them any attention. Keswen was not surprised. Even that far from
shore, a single fishing boat was of little consequence.

Then, hours past the last ship from the Lotus Isles, she spotted a
Soroccan galleon with bright, multicolored sails emblazoned with a
chalice—an alternate symbol for Dyoni. The ship was sailing northeast,
perpendicular to their route, though far enough away that Keswen could
barely make out the dark-limbed sailors on the deck. "Strange to see a
Soroccan ship this far out."

Nâya stirred. "Fâyu could not have won the war without the
Soroccans." Her voice sounded especially distant. "My father captured
their leader and threatened to kill him unless the Soroccans betrayed
us. They refused. It took their leader six days to die. His screams were
such that Nekiel's own Dragonkin urged my father to put him out of
his misery."

"I trust he refused." When Nâya did not answer, Keswen added,

"Locke will be interested in hearing that. He has a scroll that Silwren gave him. It talks about—"

"The Scroll of Founding," Nâya said.

"I don't think he knew it had a name. But he keeps it locked away like it's his mother's ashes. It sounds like Jinn still left plenty out of the story, though. He never said a thing about the dragon, for instance."

Nâya turned her head and looked at the distant Soroccan ship. "They have seen us." She lifted her hand and pointed.

Keswen leapt up and grabbed Nâya's wrist. She tried to push the woman's arm down, but it did not budge. Nâya gave her a questioning look.

"Don't hurt them," Keswen said.

"I did not intend to." Nâya lowered her arm. "You do not trust me."

Keswen stepped back. "Zeia is the closest thing to a Shel'ai that I don't loathe, and I still wouldn't turn my back on her. Compared to her, you have the powers of a god. So no, I don't trust you."

Nâya gave her a pitying look. "Because of what Chorlga had done to you."

Keswen followed the Dragonkin's gaze to her stomach and laughed. "Dragonkin, my feelings toward magic began years before that. But no, Chorlga did not help. Really, it's Brahasti and his men that are to blame for that, though." She paused. "All Chorlga did was make it so I couldn't move, couldn't protest, but I still knew where I was. I could still feel... everything."

"I am sorry."

"You weren't there, Dragonkin. It's not your fault. I know that."

"Still, I know the sins my kind set in motion," Nâya said. "So did Fâyu. Sometimes, I think that half the war was about us trying to atone for the crimes of our kin."

"I didn't know the great Fâyu Jinn had crimes he needed to atone for."

"He did." Nâya's hard look indicated she did not intend to offer any further explanation on that matter.

Keswen sighed. "I killed Brahasti, who was in charge of... what was done to us. All his men are dead, too. And truth be told, I didn't even want the child they filled me with, so cold as it sounds, it's better it was born dead." Keswen winced as she spoke and cursed herself as she had to blink away tears. "You'd think I'd have forgotten by now."

Nâya turned away from the sea again. "I still remember the first man I killed—a serving boy, actually. He'd spilled something at a feast, and my father commanded me to hurt him. I decided to kill him instead, to win my father's approval." She paused. "That was twelve centuries ago, and I still remember the boy's face, his thoughts—his *last* thoughts—as he looked up at me from the floor." She turned back toward the sea.

Keswen could think of no adequate reply. Finally, she said, "Why did you bring me with you? You should have just sent me back to Locke."

"If I had, Krym would have known you'd seen me. That would have forced his hand. Better he thinks I am hurt, hiding, running for my life."

"But Locke needs to know—"

"He will know everything soon enough."

Keswen started to answer, stopped herself, and turned to check on the progress of the Soroccan ship. "They're pulling ahead. You'd better hope they aren't bound for Shigella's Tomb, or else they'll get there far ahead of us."

"They cannot stop me from entering the tomb."

Keswen watched the Soroccan ship's windblown sails as they sped farther and farther ahead, finally vanishing off the broad blue horizon. She could not decide whether to feel bolstered or terrified by Nâya's words. She decided instead to try to forget them as she sat in the back of the boat, gripping the oar with both hands.

The sun was setting by the time the fishing boat reached the island. Keswen shuddered at the sight of it, recalling that the last time she'd been there, months before, she'd been fighting for her life against renegade Isle Knights, allied with Crovis Ammerhel and Algol. This time, though, the island appeared quiet and abandoned. High jungle trees reached toward the heavens. They beached the boat, and Keswen dragged it farther up the shore, onto the sand. She heard no birds, not even the sound of wind through the trees. She looked around.

"I thought Locke left a garrison of Knights here to guard the tomb."

Nâya closed her eyes for a moment. "He did." Opening her eyes, she pointed north. "They're waiting at the tomb. They know we're coming."

Keswen held the oar and wished it were her old Queshi composite bow. "How many?" When Nâya did not answer, Keswen said, "I have no great fondness for Isle Knights, but I don't want to kill them, either. On the other hand, I don't relish the idea of fighting off kingsteel swords with a wooden oar."

"There will be no fight." Nâya started toward the soaring jungle trees, walking so briskly that Keswen had to jog to keep up.

"No fight." Let's hope there's no slaughter, either.

Keswen noted, to her surprise, that the path through the jungle, which had been hacked clear by swords months before, was still passable. Nâya slowed, gazing at her surroundings as though regarding them with dim recollection. When they reached a series of moss-covered statues depicting Fâyu Jinn's epic battle against Nekiel, she stopped.

"That's not how it was..." Nâya's voice sounded small and distant, like that of a child. Then she straightened and pressed on, and Keswen had to rush to keep pace with her again.

"Weren't you dead by the time Jinn and Nekiel fought?"

"Yes," Nâya said, "and no."

"Care to explain that?" When Nâya did not answer, Keswen said, "The tomb was sealed. I thought only Knightswrath could open it, and Knightswrath is inside. How—"

"I made it," Nâya said. "I can open it."

"I thought Shigella died *after* the Shattering War, but you died *during* it. How—"

"Before it was Shigella's Tomb, it was... something else."

Keswen's frown deepened. "I'm glad Locke's not here. Your poor explanations would have driven him mad by now." She slowed, for at her feet, tangled in the undergrowth, was a shattered adamune. The curved blade had broken off about a foot beyond the crossguard but, owing to the properties of kingsteel, had not rusted even after being left out in the elements for months. Keswen retrieved the broken sword, tucked it into her belt, and hurried to catch up with Nâya, using her oar as a walking stick.

As they walked, Keswen continued to listen closely to her surroundings, both anticipating and dreading the snap of a twig that would signal the approach of a potential enemy. She continued to hear nothing, though, which unnerved her as much as the lack of either a breeze or the music of birds. She began to wonder if the island had been abandoned. Then they passed through the trees, into an enormous clearing at the far side of the island, and came face to face with a hundred armed men.

The men stood in silent rows, shoulder to shoulder, in front of a squat structure of white marble that Keswen recognized as Shigella's Tomb. Some of the men were Isle Knights, clad in azure tabards and glistening kingsteel. Polearms and curved swords gleamed in their grasps, and fearsome masks covered their faces, but most of the men were Soroccans, dark-skinned, in sailor garb, armed with hatchets and cutlasses. A few held crossbows already spanned and loaded.

Nâya slowed but did not stop until she stood directly in front of the men, separated by only a few yards. She said nothing. Heart pounding, Keswen forced herself to follow Nâya. She marveled that the men had stayed so quiet. She scanned the sea of suspicious gazes for a familiar face. Then she spotted one.

Hráthbam stepped forward, recognizing her at the same time. He sheathed his enormous scimitar but did not stop frowning. "Lady Keswen, you are far from home." Though the Soroccan spoke to Keswen, his eyes flicked suspiciously over Nâya.

He's already noticed her purple eyes, but he doesn't know yet if she's a Shel'ai or a Dragonkin. "So I am," Keswen said. "I should have known that was your ship. Where is it docked?"

"Behind the tomb. I nearly breached the hull doing it," Hráthbam answered. "I trust Locke isn't with you?"

Keswen shook her head. As she did so, one Isle Knight moved ahead of the rest. He wore the sigil of a white stag on his azure tabard. Coming to stand beside Hráthbam, he glared at them for a moment then removed a bear mask wrought of painted kingsteel. Youthful eyes narrowed on Keswen then Nâya.

"I am Hideo, Knight-Commander of this garrison," he said. "This island is forbidden. Why have you come?"

Keswen glanced at Hráthbam, wondering how the Soroccan had convinced Hideo to let him come ashore with so many sailors. She guessed it was because Hráthbam was widely known as Rowen's friend.

"We haven't come to fight," Keswen said.

Hráthbam eyed the broken sword in Keswen's belt. "Glad to hear it.

213

When I saw that boat heading in this direction, I feared it was another madman like Algol, hoping to tear down the Dragonward." He switched his gaze to Nâya. "Was I wrong?"

Nâya finally spoke. "The Dragonward serves no further purpose. All the Dragonkin left to the world have either set foot on Ruun or died in the attempt. I have come to reclaim Knightswrath. I must take it to Rowen Locke. He will need it if he is going to do battle with Nekiel." Nâya's peculiar voice drew startled looks from Isle Knights and Soroccans alike.

Luckily, the sailors had had the presence of mind to lower their crossbows, else Keswen feared that same surprise might have resulted in the accidental firing of a crossbow bolt.

She caught Hráthbam's eye and said, "I know it sounds mad, but it's the truth. Locke's walking into a trap. He needs the damn sword, or he's a dead man."

Hráthbam opened his mouth to speak, but Hideo answered first. "The tomb is sealed, as you can see. No one may enter." He eyed Nâya with suspicion. "Besides, even if what you say were true, I could not permit anyone but Sir Locke or Grand Marshal Shingawa to remove the sword from its resting place." Hideo paused. "Unfortunately, the Grand Marshal has already left Saikaido for the mainland. However, there are wytch-ravens on Saikaido that can seek her out. If you write a letter, I will see that she gets it. If she could then present me with a writ—"

"We don't have time for that," Keswen snapped. "If you know what's happening on Ruun, you already know that as well as I do."

Hideo gave her a stern look. "I have been entrusted to safeguard this tomb, m'lady. The tomb contains the sword of Fâyu Jinn himself. I know little of magic, but as I understand it, that sword is all that's maintaining the Dragonward. Honor requires that I protect this with my dying breath if needs be. I assure you, every man here will do the same."

Keswen eyed Hráthbam, wondering if the Soroccan sailors shared the sentiment of the Knight of the Stag.

Hráthbam sighed and said, "I see no reason for Locke's friends and Locke's trusted Knights to shed each other's blood. Surely, there are worse men for us to kill, but you must understand, Sylv, that after all that's happened, including all the Knights and Soroccans who died trying to protect the Dragonward, we're not too keen on letting you tear it down."

Keswen said, "As my companion already explained, the Dragonward is no longer needed. Locke is walking into a trap. If you want him to live, he must have the sword. For the last time—"

Nâya stepped forward as wytchfire roiled to life, engulfing her body in such bright, searing heat that Keswen dove to the ground. Men shouted. Isle Knights and Soroccans recoiled. Crossbows shuddered, but the bolts either missed or burned to ash before they could strike their targets. Hideo leapt forward, his adamune flashing—a moment before the blade melted. The Knight of the Stag gasped. Hráthbam grabbed his arm and hauled him back.

Nâya stepped forward, still blazing. Despite the violet hue of her wytchfire, her entire body had turned white-hot, like iron heated in the forge. Armed men staggered backward, still shouting. Some ran. Hideo and Hráthbam shouted at them to hold their ground. Finally, the men rallied, forming ragged lines in front of the tomb.

Nâya had taken only a few steps toward the tomb when she stopped, curiously regarding the men before her with eyes that had become slits of purple flame. As Keswen struggled to her feet, the shadow of gigantic wings spread across the earth behind the Dragonkin.

"*Stand aside,*" Nâya said. The collective wince on a hundred faces told Keswen that Nâya's voice had seared a path through their minds as well. "*I seek not to harm you, but I must have the sword. I cannot wait.*"

Still, to Keswen's surprise, Nâya did not simply press forward toward the tomb, scattering Knights as she went. Keswen remembered how easily Krym had incapacitated the entire company of Knights that had been escorting Gaulgodd and wondered why Nâya had not done the same.

Maybe she can't. Or maybe she's giving us a chance. Keswen pushed herself to her feet. Dropping her oar, she raced toward Hráthbam, who was still busy shouting orders to his men. She grabbed his arm and spun him around. "She's not a Shel'ai. Don't you see? That's—"

Hideo stepped forward and gave Keswen a hard shove. One hand still held what remained of his adamune. He might have struck her with it, but Hráthbam intervened, giving the Knight of the Stag a hard shove of his own. Isle Knights and Soroccans raced to separate their commanders.

Keswen turned and saw Nâya coolly regarding them. A handful of men took advantage of Nâya's turned gaze to fire more crossbow bolts or swing their weapons at her, all without effect.

She wants to see what we'll do, Keswen realized. She rose to her feet again. Drawing the broken sword from her belt, she caught Hideo's eye, then held out the weapon and dropped it onto the grass. She stepped forward with both hands raised. "Listen to me."

Hideo cast down his own broken sword as well, but only so that he could accept a whole adamune from the Knight next to him, and he pressed it to her throat. At the same time, though, he held up his hand and shouted for silence. Hráthbam did the same. After what felt like an eternity, a relative hush fell over the chaotic scene, even as Nâya continued to stand—blazing—at the heart of the clearing.

Gods, what do I say? How do I begin? Keswen glanced at Hráthbam then fixed her gaze on Hideo, though she spoke loud enough for all to hear. "The woman before you is not a Shel'ai. That much should be obvious by now. But she is not just another Dragonkin, either." She paused. "This is Nâya, for whom Knightswrath was named. If Locke's managed to share the contents of that scroll even half as well as he intended, I trust you Knights in particular are familiar with that name."

Looking around, Keswen saw Knights narrow or widen their gazes, mostly in disbelief. "I swear on the Light it's true. She's come back. Don't ask me how because that's a mad tale and the gods know we don't have time to tell it. What matters is that she's here to help us fight Nekiel as she did a thousand years ago. If you're not going to thank her, I suggest you at least get the hell out of the way."

For one dreadful moment, no one spoke. Keswen half feared that Hideo would order a charge after all. Though the Knights' weapons seemed ineffective against Nâya, Keswen had no doubt that they would work just fine against her.

Finally, Hráthbam stepped forward. The Soroccan had his scimitar drawn. He gently but forcefully used it to push Hideo's blade away from Keswen's throat. "Enough. Let her go. Let them take the sword."

Hideo whirled to face Hráthbam. "Are you mad? This could be a trick! Maybe that's Nekiel himself, in disguise." He stabbed his blade toward Nâya, who continued to stand in the distance, quietly staring at them.

"If it is, Knight, there's not a damn thing we can do about it." Hráthbam turned back to Keswen. "But I don't think it is." He sheathed his scimitar. Then he shouted an order in Soroccan. After a moment's hesitation, Hráthbam's sailors lowered their weapons and stepped back.

Hideo faced Hráthbam again. "Do what you want, Soroccan. My Knights will *not* stand down. We are not honorless bastards like Crovis. We will guard this tomb *and* the sword, even if it means our death!"

"I think not," Hráthbam said. Reaching under his tunic, he pulled out a silver medallion and raised it high in the air. Sunlight flashed off the sigil of a lotus flower. "Hear me, Isle Knights. Your own Grand Marshal granted me the title of Knight of the Lotus as a reward for my services during the war. That makes me the most senior commander on this island. By my order, all of you—including *you*, Sir Hideo—will sheathe your blades and stand down."

Isle Knights exchanged uncertain looks. Hideo snarled, "That's an *honorary* title, Soroccan! You have no authority—"

"Actually, friend, I do." Hráthbam's smile broadened. "I know because Locke himself told me. The Codex Viticus doesn't distinguish between real and honorary titles. He even joked that I could take command of almost any garrison I wanted now. Luckily, I have little fondness for stone keeps. So I think, this moment notwithstanding, I'll keep to the open sea."

Keswen heard a few Isle Knights voice their reluctant agreement.

Sir Hideo's face reddened. "Damn you, Soroccan."

Hráthbam stepped forward. He placed his hand over Hideo's and forced the Knight's sword down. "Sheathe your blades, my friends, and let us hope that we can trust Jinn's wife more than I trust mine." The joke drew scattered laughs, mostly from Hráthbam's sailors. One by one, though, the Isle Knights lowered their weapons. Few sheathed them, but gradually, the Knights cleared a path.

Nâya fixed her fiery gaze on Hráthbam then Keswen. The Dragonkin nodded slightly. Then she turned and strode toward Shigella's Tomb. A moment before she would have collided with the solid wall, the wall itself opened like a wound, bleeding darkness. Nâya strode inside.

Hideo spat on the ground. "I hope you didn't just damn us all."

Keswen did not know whether the Knight was speaking to her or Hráthbam. Uneasy silence filled the clearing, punctuated only by the shifting of weapons and armor. A moment later, Nâya emerged. Knightswrath lay naked in the crook of her arm. As she strode forward, the blaze of her body seemed to dim, as though the sword were absorbing it. By the time she reached Keswen, all trace of magic had vanished. Nâya stood naked, her clothes burned away, though she did not seem to notice.

Hráthbam quietly undid the clasp of his cloak and draped it over her shoulders. Seemingly as an afterthought, he removed his lotus medallion as well. He placed it around Nâya's throat.

The Dragonkin looked at it, then at Keswen. "We are nearly out of time." Her voice had lost much of its haunting reverberation and sounded more like that of a weary child. "Despite the risk, I must take us as close to Locke as I can. But if you wish to stay behind..."

Keswen swallowed hard. "Do whatever it is you're going to do, Dragonkin."

Nâya nodded, and a violet glow enveloped Nâya's body, flitting in bright tendrils around Knightswrath's gleaming blade. The glow extended toward Keswen, and she fought the urge to recoil. Dimly, she was aware of Hráthbam snatching an adamune from a nearby Isle Knight and pressing the hilt into her hand. Then the world around her shimmered and faded.

CHAPTER TWENTY-THREE

ROWEN WAS WORRIED THAT SOMETHING had happened to Vaari. Twilight had darkened the Wintersea, yet the Dhargot had still not returned. Rowen wondered if he'd encountered wolves or another band of frostreavers. Rowen was about to go looking for him when the Dhargot galloped back, a wild grin on his face.

"I found something," he said. "Gods know what it is, but I think it might be important." Before anyone could question him, he wheeled his tired horse about and rode north again.

Saanji ordered him to return, but Vaari shook his head and waved his hand, urging them to follow. Rowen cursed and ordered everyone onto their horses. Loslandril was beginning to wake, but with icy nonchalance, Zeia jolted the Sylvan king back into unconsciousness. Breaksteel gathered the reins of Loslandril's horse. Rowen was tempted to tell Igrid and Thessa to stay behind, but Igrid shook her head sternly, as though reading his thoughts. Moments later, the company was following Vaari across the icy plains.

Twice, Rowen tried to catch up with the Dhargot, but each time, Vaari noticed and urged his horse into a gallop, maintaining their distance. Rowen thought of Krym and the Maalbolg. He wondered if the Maalbolg was impersonating Vaari, trying to lure them into some kind of a trap. He glanced at Igrid and sensed she might be thinking the same thing, but Rowen could not conceive of any purpose behind that.

"This isn't like him," Saanji said, gazing skeptically after Vaari.

"Be ready for anything," Rowen warned the others, loosening his adamune in its scabbard.

"Easier said than done," Saanji said, looking about. The flat wasteland was giving rise to rocky, snow-covered hills that jutted out of the ice at troubling, unnatural angles. Shadows glided across the ice.

Rowen had the sense that their own shadows were acting of their own accord but told himself it had to be a trick played by the fading sunlight. His nerves continued to fray, though, and he considered ordering Zeia to hit Vaari with a mind-stab—not enough to kill him but enough to make him heed their orders and hold his position.

Then Vaari reined in and pointed. He dismounted, still grinning like a madman, and waited for them to catch up. Despite his impatience, Rowen slowed as they drew nearer. He continued to scan the icy rocks around them, just in case they concealed would-be attackers.

"There's no one here," Zeia said. "At least, not that I can sense."

Rowen noted the uncertainty in her voice and remembered that, despite the lack of any visible signs in demeanor, the divination she'd used to search the Lancers' camp had left her weakened. He maneuvered his horse so that he rode on one side of Thessa, and Igrid rode on the other.

Fixing his gaze on Vaari, Rowen said, "The next time I order you to wait for us—"

"Apologies," Vaari laughed, "but I thought you'd want to see this. We'll have to go there on foot, but trust me, it's worth it." He pointed again.

Rowen turned and saw what looked like a narrow canyon running between two great hills of jagged rock, so narrow that he might not have noticed it at all. "Where does that lead?"

"You wouldn't believe me if I told you." Vaari drew closer to the canyon and nodded toward the rock. "That's what caught my attention. I stopped to piss, looked up, and there they were!"

For the first time, Rowen saw a series of small runes carved into the face of the rock on both sides of the canyon. Though the runes were faint, for some reason, no snow covered them.

"What do they say?" he asked.

"Beats the hells out of me." Vaari shrugged. "I can't read. But they looked important, so I checked out where the path leads, and..." He trailed off, still grinning.

Rowen turned to Zeia. "Can you read those?"

Zeia dismounted and approached the narrow canyon. She studied the runes, which had been carved at eye level. Igniting one flaming hand, she moved it slowly over them. She stared at them a moment longer then shook her head and turned back to Rowen. "These aren't Dragonkin. They aren't Sylvan, either. They feel... older, but I don't sense any kind of magic emanating from this place."

Vaari laughed. "Remember you said that, wytch." On foot, he started toward the canyon.

Rowen reached to grab his arm, but the Dhargot dodged his grasp and plunged into the canyon, practically running. Saanji ordered him to return, but Vaari simply laughed. Rowen cursed and drew his sword. "Igrid, Thessa, Breaksteel, stay here with the horses." Before Igrid could argue, Rowen hurried after Vaari. Saanji drew his kingsteel longsword and followed, his face red with anger. Zeia brought up the rear, a shortsword held in each flaming hand.

As Vaari had said, the canyon was narrow—so narrow that they had to turn sideways to pass through. It turned one direction after another so that Rowen felt as though they were going in circles. He also had the sense that the canyon seemed to run on for an impossibly long distance, given the size of the hills it ran between. He glanced back at Zeia.

The Shel'ai frowned. "Something's... changed." She looked up at the canyon walls. "I can sense magic now. I don't recognize it, though. It doesn't feel Dragonkin, let alone Shel'ai." She paused. "I can't explain it, but... this place shouldn't exist."

"That's heartening." Saanji squeezed one of her flaming hands. "Well, if this is a godsdamned trap, let's get it over with."

Rowen pushed ahead again, leading the others as the maddening canyon continued to twist and turn. Then, with dizzying abruptness, the canyon opened into a wide mouth, framed between high walls of sheer, icy rock. Vaari stood before them, arms crossed, smiling triumphantly. Behind him, the bone-white face of a temple had been carved right into the ice, with dark windows like eyes and closed, narrow gates of rune-covered brass.

Vaari said, "This must be where the Dragonkin meant to lead us.

Only we got here first. So if you mean to set up some kind of trap, now's the time."

"Are you mad?" Zeia said. "We still need Krym's help to kill Nekiel!"

"Well, maybe there's something inside that can help us kill both of them." Vaari started toward the brass doors.

Rowen gave Saanji an angry look.

Saanji nodded. "Vaari, enough. Haul your ugly sack of bones back here, or I'll have you impaled."

Vaari glanced back and laughed. "You outlawed that. But if you want to go in first, be my guest." He made a sweeping motion toward the brass doors.

Saanji turned back to Rowen. "On the other hand, the idea of using him as a Human shield has some appeal."

"We'll go in together. Provided we can even get the doors open, that is."

"The sun's setting fast," Saanji noted, surveying the darkness filling the area.

"I'll go first." Zeia sheathed her shortswords and raised her arms. Her hands brightened, spilling violet light over the stark rocks and ice.

As she started toward the doors, Saanji and Rowen followed, swords ready. Vaari drew aside, still holding his bow. Rowen noted the wildness in Vaari's mismatched eyes, ready to cleave Vaari's bow the moment it started to rise.

Meanwhile, Zeia examined the door. "I can't read these runes, but I think they're the same language as what we saw outside the canyon." She gave Rowen a questioning look. When he nodded, she pressed both flaming hands to the doors and pushed hard.

They swung open so quickly that Rowen half expected to see Krym standing on the other side, smiling at another of his pranks, but they saw nothing but a deep, unnatural darkness that Zeia's hands did not diminish. Rowen thought back to the darkness within the Tomb of Fâyu Jinn and shuddered. However, while the tomb had filled him with inexplicable sadness, this place filled him with dread.

"We aren't welcome here," Zeia whispered, her face tight.

"I know." Rowen gently pushed Zeia to one side. "I'm going in first. But I need light."

Zeia nodded. "Here's a new trick I taught myself. I was saving it as a surprise. Hold out your sword." When Rowen did so, Zeia grasped the kingsteel blade with one flaming fist. Slowly, she dragged her fist down the blade, from the base to the tip. Tendrils of wytchfire spread across the kingsteel, bright and writhing.

Vaari cursed. Saanji chuckled and said, "I'll try not to be jealous."

Rowen's eyes widened. He thought immediately of Knightswrath though he did not feel the same throbbing power emanating from Zeia's spell, nor did the hilt warm. However, his blade cast dazzling light as he lifted it.

"Don't worry, it won't burn you," Zeia said. "It won't hurt the steel, either."

"How long will this last?"

"An hour, maybe. But you can wish it away whenever you like. I'm guessing it'll obey your thoughts the same way Knightswrath did."

Rowen marveled at what Zeia had done. He remembered her saying that much of being a Shel'ai meant pushing the limits of one's own power since there was no formal training to be had. *Maybe that's why Algol was so strong. He had Nekiel as a teacher!* Rowen stepped ahead of the others. Violet light spilled off his sword, illuminating some kind of antechamber. Like the outer face of the temple, it looked as though it had been completely carved out of ice. The air smelled stale despite the thin windows they'd seen outside.

Though the antechamber looked at first to be no larger than the common room of a small tavern, Rowen looked up and realized the ceiling rose to the full height of the temple, higher than Zeia's wytchfire could illuminate. Rowen saw more runes on the walls but nothing else— no columns, no furniture. Then he spotted another set of doors on the far wall. Though they were as tall as the brass gates they'd just passed through, they appeared to have been wrought of ice, without visible hinges, nearly indistinguishable from the walls around them.

Saanji scowled. "Are those doors or just carvings of doors?" He stepped ahead of Rowen and ran his fingers along the ice. "I feel like a thirsty man trying to pull a cup of wine out of a painting." When Saanji pressed on the doors, nothing happened. "Care to try your hands at this, my love?"

Zeia took his place. She had hardly pressed her hands to the door when they melted. Stranger still, the water turned to steam before it hit the ground. Zeia blinked, alarmed, and stepped back.

"I bet the prince feels the same way when you touch him," Vaari said with a sneer.

Rowen lifted his still-flaming blade and stepped through the doorway. Immediately, a terrible chill swept through his body, so painful that he wondered if he'd been stabbed. He reeled for a moment. Then, the pain faded, replaced by incomprehensible sadness. Tears welled in Rowen's eyes though he had no idea why. Glancing back, he saw consternation on the faces of his companions—except for Vaari, who looked around, observing their surroundings with mild fascination.

Rowen blinked and studied the new chamber. At first, the only difference from the antechamber seemed to be that it was huge and circular, with walls of ice so distant that their wytchfire barely illuminated them. Again, the chamber held no furniture, no columns, no additional doors or stairwells.

Then he spotted a line of Jolym along one distant wall.

All were identical, taller than Olgrym, with spikes protruding from the unmistakable sheen of kingsteel. Their hands ended in long blades. Placid facemasks covered the armored suits, all with dark and hollow eyes. They did not move.

Saanji said, "Are they... still alive, if that's the term for it?"

Zeia closed her eyes for a moment then shook her head. "I don't think so. They could just be souvenirs. Or they could be waiting for Dragonkin magic to awaken them."

"Let's not take that chance," Rowen said in a low voice. "Stab each one through the eyes." *Before they come to life and tear us to pieces!*

"Allow me, Knight." Vaari stepped away from the others and raised his bow. With hardly a moment to aim, he drew back the bowstring and fired. An arrow arched through the air toward the distant figures and landed perfectly in the right eyehole of the first armored figure, quivering.

Rowen stared, speechless. In the time it took him to find his voice, Vaari calmly fit a second arrow to his bowstring and fired. The arrow struck the right eye of the next Jol in line.

"I don't think even Keswen could have made those shots," Rowen said.

"Don't let *her* hear you say that," Zeia remarked though her voice held the same awe.

Vaari said nothing, but a smug grin spread across his face as he effortlessly put an arrow into an eyehole of the third Jol, then the fourth, then the fifth. He glanced back over his shoulder. "And for my final trick…" Reaching for his quiver, he drew out two arrows at once. He fit them to the string and drew it back. He held them a moment then let them go.

"Impossible," Saanji said when both arrows struck their mark. "Gods, I've seen you make some unlikely shots before, but what—"

"Be thankful I'm *your* bodyguard, m'lord," Vaari said smugly. He shouldered his bow and glanced around. "Think there's anything in here worth taking?"

Rowen cast a final, stunned look at the line of Jolym—each one with an arrow protruding from its facemask—then looked around the chamber as well. He saw that more ancient runes had been carved into the walls, but otherwise, at first glance, the room seemed to contain nothing but the Jolym. With the others' help, he searched in vain for a hidden doorway. Then a terrible thought occurred to him.

Rowen moved back to the center of the chamber. He realized he was shaking and took a deep breath, trying in vain to calm himself. Finally, he raised his sword high. Zeia saw what he was doing and followed suit, lifting her arms so that her wytchfire spread throughout the chamber. But instead of studying the chamber walls or looking up at the shadowy temple roof, Rowen looked down.

Instantly, Rowen's blood turned to ice, and he needed all his willpower to keep from running. He tried to speak, but no words would issue from his throat. Finally, after what felt like an eternity, he managed to croak out one word: "Khyrshar…"

The others looked down. Saanji swore. Vaari's eyes widened, and he backpedaled clear to the distant wall, near the Jolym. Zeia swooned. The motion of her hands made shadows shift, advancing and retreating like uncertain armies.

All the while, Rowen stared at the great dragon frozen far beneath the ice yet so huge that it nearly filled the chamber—wings unfurled, many-colored scales glinting in the faint light. He sought out the long neck, following its mottled scales of silver, burnt gold, and burgundy toward the head, which was turned sideways—like in his dreams. He spotted the tips of the horns, each one thrice the length of a horse. Finally, he came to the jawline and then one eye that, while closed and dagger thin, looked as wide as his arm.

The eye opened.

CHAPTER TWENTY-FOUR

J ALIST WOKE TO THE BLARE of war horns. After leaping from the straw-strewn pallet that served as his and Maddoc's bed, he had his boots on and Freija in hand before Maddoc even sat up. The Shel'ai rubbed his eyes then rose and moved quickly to Sariel. Jalist's urgency had startled her awake, and she was crying despite the fearsome tendrils of wytchfire tangling and untangling from her hands.

Maddoc dismissed Sariel's wytchfire with a wave of his hand. He scooped her up and whispered comforting words but winced when Sariel summoned her wytchfire again. Her small hands made his thin silken robe smolder, singeing the pale flesh underneath. Suffering the damage, Maddoc said, "I thought the Lancers were fighting *each other* just a day ago!"

Jalist thought back to the reports they'd received—noises of arguing coming from within the Ivairian camp, followed by sporadic clashes of steel. "Apparently, they worked it out and decided to kill us instead." A motion caught his eyes, and he spun toward the tent flap, long axe raised.

Falder's eyes widened. The young Dwarr was still half outside, a drawn sword in one hand, a torch in the other. Jalist could not decide whether Falder's surprised look was the result of Jalist's raised axe or the fact that, aside from his boots, Jalist was still naked.

"Forgive the interruption, Governor, but Lady Aeko sent me to—"

A fresh chorus of screams interrupted them, punctuated by a clash of steel that sounded frightfully close.

"Cadwallis," Falder finished instead.

"Damn." Jalist jabbed the butt of his long axe into the earth so that it stayed where it was, and he dressed. Ignoring his smallclothes, he tugged on a leather jerkin, followed by a fighting skirt of studded leather strips.

Just as he was reaching for a heavy mail surcoat, Maddoc pried away Sariel's hands, set the child down on the edge of their bed, and rose. "Let me go," he told Jalist.

Jalist shook his head, hastily girding the belt that carried Forgefang, the large Dwarrish sword he'd reluctantly accepted as part of his governorship. "No, keep an eye on Sariel. We don't need her burning down half the camp while I'm cleaving Lancers' skulls." Jalist wrenched Freija from the ground and started toward the tent flap.

"If killing Lancers is your goal, a Shel'ai can do more than a fighter," Maddoc called, but Jalist was already striding away.

Jalist pushed through the tent flap and winced in the glare of uncontrolled fire, the heat marking an odd contrast to the otherwise cold night air. Nearby, two tents were burning. Judging by the screams, one of the tents was still occupied. Two men of the Red Watch were trying to cut the tent open with their swords to free whomever was still trapped inside, but those men were forced to turn when a squad of horsemen thundered down on them.

Jalist counted five Lancers, all in heavy armor. One of the Red Watch managed to dive to one side, but the other fell, his body pierced clean through by two separate lances. The lances splintered and shattered as the armored men rode by. Discarding the handles of their broken weapons, those two Lancers drew bastard swords and whirled about, probably intending to finish the second Red Watch, while the other three Lancers rode on.

Jalist shouted his challenge and ran straight at them. He did not know if Falder was following until he saw the young warrior's shadow beside his own, sliding along the grass next to the burning tent. Before the closest Lancer could turn, Jalist swung his long axe with both hands. The horse screamed, and the Lancer tumbled to the ground, dazed. Jalist stepped closer. He considered swinging his axe a second time, but the Lancer's helmet ran low, protecting the neck. Instead, Jalist bashed the helmet's visor, and the Lancer fell backward like a felled tree. Then Jalist leapt over him to attack the second horseman.

That Lancer found himself trapped, with the second Red Watch on one side and Falder on the other. When Falder thrust his torch into the man's horse's face, the horse reared up, dumping its rider on the ground. The Red Watch finished the fight by thrusting his dagger through the slits in the Lancer's visor, then he turned back to the burning tent.

By then, the screaming inside the tent had stopped.

"Don't bother," Jalist called.

He turned. The three Lancers who had gotten away had not gone far. Six men—all Isle Knights, though it appeared that none of them had had time to don an entire suit of armor—had converged on them, adamunes glinting in the torchlight. Before Jalist had covered half the distance that separated them, all three Lancers had fallen, taking two Isle Knights with them.

Jalist hoped it was over. Then he heard more shouts in the distance. He turned to see an armored wall bearing down on them. He shoved Falder into the nearby Red Watch, pushing both men out of the way, but barely had time to dive before scores of Lancers thundered by. One tried to steer the tip of his lance into Jalist's face but missed. Jalist caught the shaft of the lance and pulled hard, dragging its bearer from the saddle. Jalist was about to step forward and finish him but stopped. Instead, he watched as, in an effort to avoid trampling their companion, one Lancer after another collided with those around him. At least a dozen Lancers fell—men and horses both, their bodies forming a great tangled mass.

Rather than giving a battle cry that would have alerted them to his presence, Jalist quietly stepped forward and swung Freija through one Lancer's neck, then another. Ignoring the blood that splashed into his face, he turned to find a third opponent, but a bastard sword sang through the air, struck the shaft of his axe, and cleaved it in two.

Locke gave me that... Jalist growled as he drew Forgefang. He blocked one swing then another, but the glare of fire blinded him. Something struck his side. Jalist reeled, but his mail surcoat protected him. Still, he heard more shouts and smelled the odd mixture of blood and sweat as unhorsed Lancers closed around him.

Then he saw Falder, hacking his way toward him. The young Dwarr was joined by two half-armored Isle Knights, both of them swinging adamunes, up to their elbows in gore. Jalist lost sight of them in the

229

melee, but he turned again when a fresh chorus of female cries sliced through the cacophony. *Iron Sisters,* he thought a moment before he spotted Tansil herself leading a countercharge.

Despite the glint of her armor, Tansil's dark skin made her appear part of the surrounding night. Her eyes were wide and wild as she danced past one opponent after another, leaving a trail of death in her wake. By the time she reached Jalist, the rest of the Lancers were fleeing. A dozen Iron Sisters followed.

Tansil faced Jalist. "Lots more Lancers are on the other side of the camp. Care to help us cut them down?"

Something in her icy nonchalance made Jalist laugh. "After you."

Tansil led the Iron Sisters at a brisk march. A smattering of Isle Knights, Red Watch, and Dwarrs joined her. Jalist took a moment to catch his breath then accepted the reins of the horse Falder offered him.

Sheathing Forgefang, Jalist mounted the horse, wondering as he did so which slain Lancer it had belonged to. He told Falder, "I suppose now would be a good time to tell me what in the hells is going on."

"A small force attacked the eastern perimeter," Falder said, wiping at the blood running from a cut in his forehead. "They bound their horses' hooves in cloth to make them quiet. Still, the sentries gave us plenty of warning. But then a second small force hit us from the north."

Jalist looked around. He guessed the second force was the one he'd just been fighting. He listened to the distant clash of steel. "Where's the worst of it?"

"Looks like the rest of the Lancers circled around to the west. *Hundreds* of them. Lady Aeko went to meet them, I think. She was on duty when the attack started." Falder paused. "It all happened so fast…"

"So says everyone the first time they're in a battle." Jalist leaned down and clapped Falder on the shoulder. "You did well. Now, let's see if you can do even better."

Falder stiffened, removed his hand from his wound, and nodded.

The Ivairian horse shifted at the unfamiliar weight, but Jalist snapped the reins, driving the destrier forward, through the heart of the camp. He drew his sword and shouted, rallying everybody he could. A moment later, he overtook Tansil and the Iron Sisters, locked in fierce combat with what remained of the second force of Lancers.

Jalist was tempted to ride around them. Judging by the horrible sounds reaching his ears from the western edge of the camp, he guessed an even more furious battle was being waged there. But he saw at once that the second force of Lancers, while outnumbered and surrounded, still had superior organization and discipline.

Reining in, Jalist dismounted and took command. He forbade a charge. Then, while Isle Knights and Iron Sisters kept the Lancers penned in, he organized a squad of Dwarrish crossbowmen and Red Watch archers. They unleashed a steady, withering storm of missiles that quickly felled every unarmored horse and reduced the number of Lancers by one third. When the rest refused to surrender, Jalist tightened the noose.

Isle Knights and Iron Sisters closed around the Lancers' ranks, forcing them into a tighter and tighter formation until the latter had no room to maneuver. While adamunes and Hesodi steel continued to nip at the Lancers' flanks, Jalist had his archers unleash another flurry of bolts and arrows. Then, in a loud voice, he ordered his engineers to bring in catapults—despite the fact that the camp had none. Finally, exhausted, the remaining Lancers threw down their swords.

Jalist paused to catch his breath again. He surveyed the devastation and listened pitiably to the cries of the dying. *I should have known...* He cursed himself. Rather than waiting for reinforcements, Cadwallis had sought to wipe them out in one fell swoop. Jalist was tempted to go back and check on Maddoc. Instead, he looked for Tansil.

"You're in charge here. Take the Lancers prisoner. Don't bother questioning them yet. Just secure the perimeter—"

"Understood," the Iron Sister said. She wiped her sword on her sleeve, leaving it smeared with blood.

Jalist turned to Falder. "Get men with buckets and put out those fires. And—"

"I'll send men to guard the Shel'ai," Falder promised.

Jalist nodded and hurried off. Two score Isle Knights quietly fell into line behind him. Jalist was about to order them to stay behind and guard the camp, but he reasoned that if Aeko was still fighting, she probably needed any reinforcements he could bring. As Jalist hurried westward, moving through a stinging haze of smoke, he tried to wrap his mind around all that had happened. As near as he could tell, Aeko had taken about a hundred Knights with her to meet the main body of Lancers and stop them from overrunning the camp, and those left behind were anxious to know what had befallen their beloved Grand Marshal. Jalist's stomach sank.

Despite inferior numbers, the other two companies of Lancers had managed to cut deep into the camp, burning tents, hacking down the palisades, and mowing down men while they were still half asleep. Jalist paused, momentarily overcome by the lunatic strategy. He realized that the two smaller forces must have been suicide squads. Given the sheer fury of their assault, a lesser camp commander would have redeployed the entire encamped army to stop them—thus leaving the camp wide open to the even greater force of Lancers sent to attack from the west. But Aeko had recognized the strategy and acted quickly to thwart it.

Jalist quickened his horse's pace so that the Isle Knights following him—about half of them still on foot—had to sprint to keep up. Ragged-looking sentries hurried to get out of his way, most of them still frightened and confused. Jalist passed the shattered palisade guarding the western edge of the camp, his eyes scanning the darkness beyond. The occasional clash of steel and whimper of pain still drifted back through the night, but he saw no trace of the epic battlefield he had expected. He questioned the sentries, but none knew more than he did, saying just that Aeko had taken most of her Knights and ridden west as though she was rushing off to battle the Undergod himself.

"Be ready," Jalist called to the Knights following him.

Their grim expressions told him the warning was unnecessary. As Jalist slowed, a few Knights rode ahead with torches, attempting to drive back the darkness. Firelight glinted off wavering weapons. Jalist led the reinforcements over a swath of empty plains, through a thin line of trees, then onto a second stretch of plains before he saw the first body.

The man lay facedown in the darkness, dressed in a bloodied Red Watch uniform. The remains of a shattered lance protruded from his back. A short distance beyond lay two Dwarrish fighters, mowed down by swords. Horses had torn up the earth, and Jalist studied the tracks.

He scanned the darkness and spotted more corpses in the distance. Those wore glinting armor beneath their torn tabards, but the sheen was not that of kingsteel. Guessing they must be Lancers, Jalist turned his horse toward the darkness and snapped the reins. Moments later, he reined in, aghast.

Ahead, beneath the starry light of Armahg's Eye, lay a massive field choked with the dead. Men and horses alike lay everywhere, hacked and still. Most of the men wore the heavy, dull armor and bright tabards of Lancers, but plenty wore azure and kingsteel.

No one spoke. Dismounting, Jalist carefully picked his way through the grim field. Isle Knights followed, equally silent. Then, Jalist spotted a lone willow tree. It rose from a distant hill, eerily illuminated by the rising moonlight. A single Isle Knight stood on the hill, leaning heavily against the tree. Jalist ordered the Isle Knights to spread out and assist any survivors. Then he rushed ahead. The cold air felt ragged in his lungs.

When he reached Aeko, he saw that her armor was so drenched in red that it looked as though she'd been dipped in blood. More blood ran from the adamune held loosely in her hand. Her tabard hung in ribbons. Her helmet and facemask lay on the ground. More blood caked her dark hair, which had come loose from its braid and hung over one shoulder. Still, she looked up at his approach.

"Good evening, Governor."

Jalist stared, speechless. Then he fixed his gaze on a slain Lancer at her feet. The Lancer's tabard was hopelessly stained, and his head had been cleaved in half, making it impossible to identify him. Jalist saw no sign of Cadwallis's golden locks, though.

"Ferinald?"

Aeko nodded. "He stabbed me in the back then killed Sir Lamrey. I went after him—must have chased him halfway around the battlefield. He kept howling challenges, but every time I got close, he fled. Finally, I caught him here."

"What about Cadwallis?"

"Never saw him."

Jalist frowned. "How badly are you hurt?"

Aeko ignored the question and surveyed the grisly field instead. "It seems we underestimated the Lancers' ire."

"Their *madness*, you mean." Jalist moved closer, intending to help Aeko remove her armor so that he could inspect her wounds.

She stopped him with a cold look. Then she nodded toward the hills behind her.

Jalist looked. "Gods…"

For the first time, he saw them: a long line of mounted Lancers, shoulder to shoulder on a nearby hill, statue-like save for the foggy breath emanating from the mouths of horses and the visors of men. Jalist reached for Freija, remembered the long axe had been broken, and drew his sword instead.

Aeko said, "That's Sir Hale in the center if I'm not mistaken."

"Why aren't they attacking?"

"Don't know," Aeko said heavily. "They broke off from Ferinald's force when the fighting started. I thought they were his reserves, but they never charged in. When I cut Ferinald down, I'm pretty sure a few of them cheered."

"Deserters?"

Aeko did not answer.

Jalist waved toward the Isle Knights in the distance, ordering them to join him. "Find Maddoc!" he shouted.

When he turned back to Aeko, she was staring at the ground. Jalist moved toward her. When he touched her shoulder, she jerked back.

She blinked at him. "The first female Grand Marshal in the history of the Isles, and I didn't even make it one whole year. The minstrels had better be kind, or I'll haunt them. Tell them that… and tell Locke I'm sorry."

She fell forward. Jalist caught her. Speechless, he lowered her to the ground just as stunned Isle Knights raced up the hill and formed a grim circle around them.

"No, not sorry," Aeko said. Though she was speaking to Jalist, she seemed to be looking through him. "Proud. Tell him I'm proud of him. Say, 'I'm proud of you, Squire.' He'll understand."

Aeko turned and looked at the tree she'd been leaning against. She tugged off one gauntlet, reached out, and traced her fingertips along the gnarled bark. She smiled. Then she closed her eyes.

Jalist knelt there for a long time. Then he straightened and realized the rest of the Isle Knights had fallen to one knee. A few of them murmured prayers. Jalist's stomach roiled as he stumbled past the Knights, looked down, and saw two more men—a Lancer and an Isle Knight—lying on the ground, both slain, clasping each other in a kind of grim embrace.

Jalist retched. He did so as quietly as he could, tears streaming from his eyes. When he was done, he used the bloodless corner of a dead man's cloak to wipe his mouth. He straightened. Seeing the bridle of a nearby horse, he mounted and rode toward the distant line of Lancers.

Sir Hale rode ahead of the others to meet him. The young Lancer's face was expressionless, but his eyes were damp. He nodded toward Jalist and held up his empty hands. "Good evening, Dwarr."

"Not so good." Jalist surveyed the watchful Lancers arrayed behind Sir Hale, their lances swaying slightly like young trees in a breeze, their breath rising in ghostly plumes. "I see about two hundred men here. That's less than what I've got left. If you want to fight—"

"We aren't here to fight. We're not cowards, but we're not madmen, either. The regent has gone too far." Hale paused. "If you see the Sylvan woman, the one who got away, tell her I'm sorry."

Jalist had no idea what the Lancer was talking about and decided he did not care. "Where's Cadwallis?" When Hale did not answer, Jalist said, "I have no patience tonight, Lancer. I don't care how many men you have behind you. Answer me, or—"

"The regent left the battlefield almost as soon as the fighting started," Sir Hale said. "He said he was going to take command of the second force."

Jalist thought of the small companies of Lancers that had been sent to attack the camp as a diversion. "I don't think so. We killed most of them and captured the rest. The regent wasn't there."

Hale frowned. "You misunderstand me, Dwarr. I'm not referring to—"

Before he could finish, the blare of distant trumpets carved through the darkness.

Jalist stiffened. The sound had not come from the camp. He faced the Lancer again.

Hale regarded him with a touch of pity. "The regent hoped to drive you away before they arrived, to prove his valor. But the Grand Marshal countered his plans." Hale paused. "Understand, Dwarr. My company has no interest in fighting you. We won't help the regent. But we won't

235

draw steel against our fellow Ivairians, either. You're on your own." As he turned his horse around, he added, "I'm sorry."

Jalist watched as Hale rode off into the night, the deserting Lancers falling in behind him. Then he heard the trumpets again. Fighting back an urge to scream with frustration, Jalist whirled his horse about and returned to the battlefield. Almost immediately, he spotted Maddoc. The Shel'ai rode toward him on a borrowed horse, surrounded by a mismatched guard of Red Watch, Dwarrs, and Iron Sisters.

Maddoc smiled. "Three Lancers cut into your tent right after you left, but I burned them down. Sariel's safe. I made her sleep and left two Knights to guard her. The camp's secure." He looked around. "Where's Aeko?"

Jalist glanced up at the lone tree. "Abandon the camp," he said, his voice breaking. "Put the wounded on horses. Leave the dead. We have to run."

Maddoc's smile vanished. "Run from what? I heard horns, but surely—"

"We have to run," Jalist insisted. He grabbed Maddoc's shoulder. Unable to say more, he stared, tears streaming from his eyes. Jalist began to shake.

Maddoc regarded him soberly then squeezed Jalist's hand. He nodded. "All right." Turning, he gestured to one of the Iron Sisters. "Go back and tell Captain Tansil to release the prisoners." Before the Iron Sister could protest, Maddoc grabbed the nearest Dwarr. "You, tell Falder to get the wounded on horseback and ride south. Any man who can't ride will have to be left behind. If there's time, I'll heal them. Otherwise, we'll have to entrust them to the gods."

Maddoc turned toward the nearest Isle Knight, but Jalist stopped listening to the flurry of orders. He sagged against the head of his horse. Then he dried his eyes on his horse's mane and straightened. Drawing Forgefang, he waved it over his head and added his voice to Maddoc's, shouting orders and trying to ignore the chorus of trumpets in the distance.

The shouting continued. Dying men whimpered. The trumpets drew closer.

CHAPTER TWENTY-FIVE

ROWEN EXPECTED THE DRAGON TO speak, but no booming voice cracked the ice, and no telepathic gasp for help wriggled into his mind. He stared at the dragon's great, open eye—which blazed like a tongue of wytchfire over a field of snow—until it closed. He realized he had been holding his breath.

Vaari whistled. "Well, that's something you don't see every day."

Zeia drew closer, her expression one of awe. She opened her mouth, stammered, and continued to simply stare at the ice-trapped dragon. "I... I can feel its power, I think. Even trapped, it's... By the Light—"

Saanji squeezed her arm. "What do we do now?"

"Not just power," Zeia continued. "How it *feels* to be... trapped so long—" She broke off suddenly, covered her mouth, and wept. Saanji embraced her.

With great difficulty, Rowen wrested his gaze from one gigantic eyelid the color of burnt gold. As much as he needed Knightswrath to face Nekiel, he was suddenly glad he did not have it, remembering how the sword gave him the ability to read thoughts and emotions. "We should get back to the others. We shouldn't be here." *Nobody should be.*

"Bad idea," Vaari said. "Igrid and that tower-sized Olg can keep watch on the horses and the little girl. Better we start thinking about whatever trap we're going to set."

"What trap?" Rowen said. "Like it or not, we need Krym's help to beat Nekiel. All we can do is—"

Vaari pointed. "Over there. Is that another door?"

Something in the Dhargot's tone made Rowen draw back a step before he turned to look. Sure enough, Vaari was pointing toward a doorway of ice along the far wall. The doorway was so hard to see that Rowen marveled that Vaari had noticed it.

Zeia wiped her eyes and started toward the door. Rowen considered stopping her but accompanied her instead. Saanji and Vaari fell in behind him. Rowen disliked Vaari being so close to him, but he trusted Saanji to keep an eye on the man.

When they reached the icy doorway, Zeia touched it with her burning hands. As with the previous doorway, the ice melted, the water turning to steam before it reached the ground. Instead of darkness beyond, though, a faint blue light emanated from the new chamber. Rowen traced its source to a single luminstone glowing atop a pedestal placed at the center of a small, circular chamber, only a few yards across. He wondered how long the luminstone had been glowing. Then he noticed the ground was littered with bones.

Rowen stared at them for a moment, trying to discern their age or nation of origin. Nearly all the bones were covered with ice or a sheen of frost. In places, scraps of torn fabric or rusty metal still clung to the bones, but judging by the amount of ash and dust scattered over the icy floor, he guessed most of the dead had rotted long before. Standing outside the doorway, he peered in, intent on making sure he was not about to be ambushed as soon as we walked in to investigate.

Before he could take a step, though, something grabbed the back of his tunic and hauled him backward with such force that his feet lifted off the ground, a moment before he was dropped like a sack of potatoes.

Rowen leapt to his feet and whirled about, only to find the others staring at him with wide eyes. "I trust that wasn't you."

Zeia looked from Rowen to the trapped dragon. "I think... it was her."

"So she can use magic even though she's trapped?"

"Maybe. Not enough to free herself, though." Zeia shrugged. "I just know it wasn't me."

Rowen directed his gaze toward Khyrshar's eye again. As he suspected, it was open. *What do you want? If you're trying to tell me something—*

"Stay out of the room," Zeia snapped, the sternness in her voice making everybody jerk. She pointed at the bones. "There, Locke. See that?"

Rowen looked, but Saanji saw it first. "Gods…"

Rowen's eyes narrowed. Then he saw it, too. One of the piles of bones had fallen so that the skull pressed against the icy wall. Over time, probably the course of centuries, the side of the dead man's face had melted into the wall so that the ear remained intact, shrouded in ice, while the rest of the body withered. The ear was tapered.

"So? Probably just some Sylvan prisoner," Vaari said.

Saanji shook his head. "A prisoner who couldn't escape through a little ice? No, something's wrong here."

"It could have been a Dragonkin or a Shel'ai." Zeia faced Rowen. "I think she's telling us that room is a prison, designed to hold Nekiel's enemies. I think she wants us to trap Nekiel and Krym in there."

Rowen directed his gaze back at the dragon's eye. It blinked, then widened desperately, as though in answer.

Pity filled him. "Maybe," he said, "but I'm not sure how."

"I think the wytch is wrong." Vaari pointed into the chamber. "See that rune on the pedestal? That looks a little like the Dragonkin word for *peace*. Maybe that room is just a chapel of some kind. Could just be that they tossed corpses in here, or people went there to pray in their last hours. We should check the dead for clues." Vaari turned back to the main entrance into the great chamber. Drawing the last arrow from his quiver, he fit it to his bowstring. "You go on ahead. I'll keep watch."

Rowen and the others exchanged glances. Zeia nodded and stepped forward, her eyes narrowing. Rowen imagined the invisible needle of magic forming just in front of her an instant before she cast it at lightning speed into Vaari's brain. Vaari jerked but did not fall.

For a moment, no one spoke. Finally, Vaari sighed. "Damn." He faced Zeia. "Sorry, wytch. Nice try, but your mind-stabs don't work on my kind."

"Fine," Zeia said, "I'll bash you against the ice until your brains leak out your ears." She stretched out her hands.

"Wait," Rowen said. "Vaari, what—"

Before he could finish, Vaari raised his bow and fired. The arrow sped low across the ice. Rowen swung his sword and cleaved the arrow before it could hit Zeia's throat. The pieces skittered to the icy floor.

"Well done, Knight." Vaari snickered. "It was the thing about the rune, wasn't it?"

239

Saanji stepped forward, his kingsteel longsword gleaming. "That and your improbable little archery display a moment ago."

Vaari nodded. "Yeah, I shouldn't have done that. They'll be angry. But I always *did* like to show off. That's my weakness." He tossed away his bow. Then he drew his old shortsword with one hand while his other drew Loslandril's jeweled blade.

Rowen stepped away from the others, moving slowly in an attempt to flank their opponent. He noted that Saanji did likewise on the other side while Zeia held her ground at the center, hands blazing. Rowen lowered his flaming blade to look less threatening. "Where is Krym?"

"South of here, with his pet." Vaari scratched his face with the quillon of his jeweled sword. "Gods, you can't imagine how sick I am of this form."

Rowen said, "Gaulgodd."

Saanji took an angry step forward. "What did you do with the real Vaari?"

"You mean your precious bodyguard?" Vaari bowed. "Behold, he stands before you."

Saanji's jaw dropped. "Impossible..."

"Not really. Out of your entire family, Nekiel decided you were the one they most wanted on the throne. He sent me to protect you. You should feel honored." Vaari whirled his swords in a dazzlingly quick blur. Facing Rowen, he grinned. "Ready for our rematch, Knight? This time, I won't go easy on you."

"If you aren't Gaulgodd—"

"If you have any questions, Knight, ask away." Vaari grinned. "Each second allows my master to draw even closer."

Rowen edged still closer to Vaari as the latter made no move to step back or move into a defensive posture. Rowen asked the first question that occurred to him. "Why did you bring us here?"

"To open the temple, of course!" Vaari pointed at the distant, unmoving Jolym with one of his swords. "Every spell has its weakness. You can't make a Jol unless you give it eyes, a way to kill it. By the same token, you can't seal a temple against Dragonkin without leaving a way for it to be opened." His grin settled on Zeia.

"Shel'ai magic," she said.

Vaari nodded. "A joke, really. Back in Nekiel's time, the Shel'ai were more like pets… or cattle, I suppose. It would be like barring your door when only the family dog can remove the bar. Who would think of such a thing?" He shrugged. "Anyway, Krym figured this was the best way to trick you."

Rowen edged still closer. He reckoned that he only needed to get a few inches closer and the tip of his sword would reach Vaari's shoulder. He risked a quick glance back at Zeia.

Reading his intent, she called out, "And the frostreavers?"

Vaari said, "A happy coincidence."

"Not for the frostreavers," Saanji grumbled. He shook his head. "So all that time you were protecting me, all those assassins and warriors you killed before they could get to me, it wasn't loyalty or friendship. You were just following orders."

Rowen heard the anger and hurt in Saanji's voice but suspected that the prince was also trying to keep Vaari's attention so that Rowen could get closer. Vaari idly whirled his swords again. "Sorry. You're not a bad sort, m'lord, but you'd need a bosom like Locke's wife to make me betray *my* master."

Rowen leapt forward and swung. His blade cut a flaming arc toward Vaari's neck. With frightful ease, though, Vaari blocked the swing with one sword and thrust the other at Rowen's throat. Rowen backpedaled, awed by the speed of the thrust. He narrowly parried Vaari's blade before it would have killed him. He expected Vaari to press the attack.

Instead, Vaari took a step back, still grinning. He idly twirled his swords again. "It would be much easier and less bloody if the three of you would simply step into your cage like good little underlings." He motioned toward the skull fixed in ice. "Believe me, you'll find me a kinder jailor than Nekiel."

Zeia took a step forward. She had sheathed both her swords, though her hands formed blazing fists in front of her. "Nekiel… not Krym?"

Vaari's smile thinned. "Dragonkin have a cruel sense of humor, wytch. Krym was never going to betray his master. He just wanted to earn his father's favor—and a cheap laugh at your expense, I'm sure."

His father… Rowen lifted his sword into a guard position. "Whatever

241

you are, there's no need for you to die here. The Dragonkin are our enemies, not you."

Vaari gave Rowen a derisive look reminiscent of those given him by the Maalbolg. "You're wrong, Knight. Now step forward and give me your best if you've got the nerve. I promise it won't be enough."

But before Rowen could move, Zeia called out, "I have a better idea." She stretched out one arm, opened her burning fingers, and made a quick slapping gesture.

Vaari staggered backward, blood trickling from his lip. He gave Zeia a grudging nod. "Funny. I know Dragonkin who aren't half as good at telekinesis as you. I guess need really *is* the mother of invention. Care to try that again?"

Zeia aimed her fingers at Vaari and made another gesture—only Vaari was no longer there. The Dhargot leapt sideways then forward so that he suddenly stood behind Saanji. Startled, the prince turned—too slow. Vaari toppled Saanji with a kick to the knee. As Saanji fell, the prince managed to swing his kingsteel longsword with both hands. Vaari easily blocked the blow with his old shortsword. With a sharp ring, the shortsword shattered. Without missing a beat, though, Vaari drove the pommel of his broken sword into Saanji's forehead.

Zeia cried out and moved to strike, but Vaari was already gone. He darted this way and that, like a leaping insect, then flung the hilt of his broken sword at Zeia. The Shel'ai waved her hand and sent it flying. Before she could strike again, though, Vaari was hurtling toward Rowen.

Rowen yelled and swung, fueled by panic as well as rage. Vaari blurred sideways then darted behind Rowen and kicked the back of his knee. Rowen ignored the pain, twisted, and swung again. His sword passed through empty air. A moment later, Vaari stabbed Rowen's chest with such force that, in spite of his cuirass, Rowen tumbled backward. Looking up from the icy floor, Rowen saw Vaari standing in the distance, idly whirling his jeweled sword in slow, lazy circles.

"Could be that Krym rubbed off on me. I hope you won't mind if I have a bit of fun at your expense."

Rowen saw Zeia moving up behind Vaari, a drawn shortsword in each hand, her expression steady and murderous. Vaari slipped sideways, as easily as if his body were entirely made of water. His shortsword cut at

Zeia's left shoulder then reversed and cut at her right shoulder instead. Zeia blocked and whirled, only to find that Vaari had already retreated ten feet.

Zeia's cuirass sagged, the straps cut. Cursing, she yanked it off and threw it away. Rowen rose to his feet, noting as he did so that Vaari had taken care not to cut her. Vaari said, "I have a new idea, wytch. I was going to knock you out, like the prince, but maybe I'll cut all your clothes off first. You aren't as pretty as Locke's wife, but you'll do."

"Gods, for the last time, we aren't married yet," a voice called.

Rowen turned to see Igrid striding into the chamber, matching swords drawn. Breaksteel followed, scowling as he unslung his massive kashpa. Thessa stood in the next room, wide-eyed, fearfully peering around the corner. Rowen gestured for Thessa to stay back then moved to block Vaari's path to the door. "Yet?"

Igrid shrugged. "Looks like you've gotten yourself into trouble again."

"A little," Rowen confessed. "Where is the Sylvan king?"

"Tied up with the horses. With any luck, a wolf will eat him." Igrid glanced at Rowen's flaming blade. "Too bad that's not Knightswrath. Looks like we could use it."

"Vaari isn't Human. Another Maalbolg. He's faster than—"

"I saw." Igrid cracked her neck. "Reminds me of Jaanti dancing circles around you in that village outside Atheion. Remember that?"

Rowen winced. "This time, I think I'll gladly accept any help you can offer."

Saanji rose slowly, groaning. Blood streamed from a gash on his forehead. Zeia's look of rage softened, replaced by worry. She started toward him. Rowen called out a warning but it was too late. Vaari barreled toward her. Zeia twisted sideways, nearly as fast as her opponent. Her shortswords came up. For a moment, steel blurred and clashed, too fast for Rowen's eyes to follow. Then Zeia screamed and fell to one knee, her tunic slashed open, a long diagonal cut running from her shoulder to her breast.

Vaari slipped backward, out of reach. Rowen noted that the Dhargot's grin had vanished and fresh slashes reddened his arm and leg. Rowen found himself wondering if Maalbolg blood was always red or only appeared that way in Human form. Then Zeia straightened. Despite her wound, she threw one of her shortswords.

Vaari caught the sword and threw it back.

Zeia managed to wave her hand, magically casting the sword aside, but it carved a divot out of her arm before burying itself hilt-deep in the icy floor. She pressed one flaming hand to each of her wounds. The flames sputtered, vanished, and reappeared. Through clenched teeth, she told Rowen, "Don't worry about me. Just kill the damn thing."

Rowen glanced at Saanji, who was crawling weakly toward Zeia, then at Igrid. "Any bright ideas?"

"Just one," Igrid said. "Let's cut the bastard in half." She started forward.

Rowen hesitated, torn between fighting beside her and making sure Vaari didn't make a run for Thessa. Breaksteel moved closer. As though reading Rowen's mind, he made a quick hand-gesture then hefted his kashpa and stepped back.

Rowen doubted the muscular but slower-moving Olg stood much chance against Vaari, but he could not bear to let Igrid fight alone. He ran after her, the lingering flames on his blade pushing back the shadows. "Slow down, damn you."

Igrid howled her battle cry and threw herself at Vaari. Her matching tashi executed a complex flurry of deft cuts and feints, using guile and trickery to make up for what the swordswoman lacked in speed. Vaari's smug smile disappeared as Igrid's attack slashed his scale armor and actually drove him back.

Desperate to help, Rowen tried to slash at Vaari from behind, but the unnaturally fast warrior turned and turned, always keeping Igrid between them. Then the tip of Vaari's sword gouged Igrid's exposed thigh. Igrid accepted the wound with an angry grunt—no scream—but for the blink of an eye, her swords slowed.

That was all Vaari needed. He cut Igrid's arm, sidestepped, and drove his boot into her bleeding thigh. That time, Igrid screamed. Vaari moved closer. Laughing anew, he thrust both blades at Igrid's face. Rowen threw himself forward, his sword descending.

Vaari shifted out of the way, narrowly avoiding Rowen's blade, and gave Rowen a hard shove. Rowen lost his balance and tumbled to the floor, his face pressed to the ice right above Khyrshar's open eye. Rowen wondered if he saw pity there… or disappointment. The eye closed.

Rowen rolled and leapt back to his feet. Vaari was looming over Igrid, prodding her backside with the tip of his sword. Rowen resisted the urge to answer with another reckless charge. Instead, he approached slowly, sword raised.

Vaari said, "Give up, Knight. I may not be able to change shape until Krym releases me, but my kind are still twice as fast as yours. Be good and get in your cage, and I'm sure Krym will even heal everyone's wounds when he gets here. He should be wandering in behind the Olg any moment now, with my brother."

His brother must be the other Maalbolg.

Rowen eyed his opponent, trying to think of a way to defeat him, but the Maalbolg was too quick. Rowen's only remaining ally who was fit to fight was Breaksteel, but the Olg was busy barring the Maalbolg from going for Thessa.

Rowen hesitated, considering the desperate idea that had just occurred to him. *Gods, forgive me…* He glanced at Thessa's frightened expression. Then, facing Breaksteel, he made a series of quick hand-signs. He did not know for certain if the Olg understood since Rowen had only a rudimentary knowledge of that language, but the Olg nodded.

Facing Vaari, Rowen took care to clear his mind in case his opponent was able to read his thoughts. Then he started forward. "Kill us if you can, but you won't hurt Thessa."

Vaari had not bothered to pick up another weapon. Instead, he held his sword so lightly that he looked as though he was about to drop it. Magical light flashed off its jeweled hilt. "I grow tired of this, Knight. Must we—"

Rowen swung. Vaari shifted, avoided the swing, and rapped his sword against Rowen's armor. Rowen swung a second time then a third. Vaari avoided each swing with maddening ease, despite his wounds. Though he did not take advantage of openings that would have allowed him to end Rowen's life, he did not hesitate to slash at Rowen's tabard or carve bright scratches in his armor.

Rowen allowed his attacks to become more and more unfocused. Finally, swinging wildly, he had the pleasure of slashing the back of

Vaari's thigh, so deep that the quick fighter grunted and nearly fell. Rowen smirked at the trail of blood that Vaari left behind as he slumped away. "I told you. No matter what happens to us, Thessa's walking out of here. I swear it before the gods!"

Vaari's look of rage turned to bemusement. "Is *that* what you're so afraid of? You are an important prisoner, Knight. The child is not."

Vaari surged forward, faster than ever. Rowen managed to block one swing, but the next two rattled off his cuirass. Then Vaari got behind him and shoved him down, surprisingly strong.

"Stay away from her," Rowen growled.

He looked up and saw Vaari striding toward Breaksteel. Thessa watched from the doorway, her shortsword drawn and shaking in her grasp.

Rowen shouted, "Breaksteel, do something useful and cut that bastard in half!"

Vaari laughed. "Yes, Olg. Here I am! Do your best." As he continued to stride toward Breaksteel, he opened his arms wide.

Breaksteel's head drooped hopelessly, thick braids spilling past his shoulders, as though he was already beaten. Then, with a heavy sigh, the Olg grasped his kashpa with both hands and lifted it high, as though preparing to deliver a massive but slow, sweeping cut right in front of him. Vaari approached at a steady pace, paused to regard Breaksteel with a contemptuous grin, then leapt forward. Breaksteel began his swing.

With inhuman grace, Vaari leapt to one side. But as Rowen hoped, the weapon's long reach forced the Maalbolg to attack the Olg from behind. As Vaari kept twisting like a dancer, Breaksteel twisted with him. When Vaari finally stopped, intending to shove his jeweled sword through the back of Breaksteel's neck, he found himself facing the Olg instead. The Maalbolg's eyes widened. He tried to leap back, but Breaksteel's kashpa caught him between shoulder and neck. The massive blade cut clear through scale armor, leather, flesh, and bone, and emerged—just a little bloody—from Vaari's side.

Vaari stood for a moment, blinking in disbelief. His jeweled sword clattered to the floor. The mute Olg stared at him then gave his body a gentle shove. Vaari shuddered then collapsed in two pieces.

Rowen raced over, surprised by how relatively little blood there was.

246

"I told you," he said to the corpse. Facing Breaksteel, he added, "I wasn't sure that would work. Well done." He turned to Thessa.

The girl stared at Rowen and Breaksteel, speechless, then at the dismembered man at their feet. Rowen was about to order her not to look when Vaari's body began to shimmer. The blood darkened. His face paled, his mismatched, wide eyes whitened, and his mouth grew like an opening wound. When the transformation was complete, another Maalbolg lay on the ice.

Seconds after that, the wytchfire enchanting Rowen's adamune flickered and disappeared. He sheathed the sword. "Thessa, it's all right. You're safe now." He held out his hand.

Thessa stepped forward and blinked at his open hand. Then she looked down at the Maalbolg again. Her face hardened. Gripping her shortsword with both hands, she screamed and plunged the blade into the Maalbolg's open mouth. She gave it a brutal twist then yanked it free. She stared at the blood darkening the blade and stooped and awkwardly wiped the blade on the leg of her own trousers. Then she sheathed it.

Thessa paled, and Rowen wondered if she would vomit. Clenching her jaw, she took Rowen's hand instead. He helped her step over the carnage. Once she was past the Maalbolg, she shook off his grasp and ran to check on Igrid. Rowen looked down to find Vaari's blood spreading across the ice and soaking into Rowen boot, cold as ice water. He stepped back.

CHAPTER TWENTY-SIX

EMRAEL STOOD WITH HIS BACK to the cave and stared down at the valley below just as dawn crested the eastern hills. Dead men lay everywhere, their shattered bodies hampering the escape of the few and whimpering wounded. The battle had raged throughout the night, back and forth, from one end of the valley to another. The larger force, consisting of mounted Humans lance-armed in full gleaming armor, kept trying to demolish a small, motley rearguard. The rearguard itself had been left behind to protect a small, battered army limping southward, hauling wagons filled with the wounded.

Emrael had little interest in the battle. Still, he watched out of hope that it would distract him from a strange hunger that had been gnawing at him for days—a maddening but incomprehensible hunger that food did not seem to satisfy. At first, it had seemed the well-armored attackers would make short work of the rearguard, overwhelming them through sheer force of numbers. But in spite of poor organization, exhaustion, and lack of reinforcements, the stubborn rearguard held on. When they failed to halt the attackers' charge, they broke off and nipped at the flanks, burned the attackers' supply train, and took shelter behind hills so they could rain flaming arrows on passing horses.

Emrael watched, filled with equal measures of fascination and disgust. From time to time, the final thoughts of a dying man drifted up and burrowed into his brain: a flash of pain, a wail of panic. At first, that amused him, as though he were watching animals fight. He even began to root first for one side, then the other. Gradually, though, the slaughter sickened him.

Then, just after dawn, new players entered the fray. They came from the west, racing toward the battle at breakneck speed: hundreds upon hundreds of archers and horsemen, light and agile, with fair hair and tapered ears. They moved at once to aid the beleaguered rearguard, fast and disciplined, unleashing a storm of impeccably aimed arrows that caused the well-armored attackers to wither and retreat.

Emrael did not celebrate. Instead, he surveyed a broad field heaped with the dead and the maimed. It occurred to him that he might go down and help. His gentlest touch could restore severed limbs, knit broken bones, perhaps even raise those who had only just died but still held a spark of warmth in their bodies.

But why should I? What are they to me?

When a small group of scouts started up the hill toward him, armed with bows and curved swords, Emrael rendered himself invisible to their eyes. He did not know how he did it or why, but as the scouts massed within a few feet of where he stood, they apparently had no idea he was there. He listened for a while to their conversation. Though the language they spoke was different from Miriam's, he found he understood every word. The sound of it inexplicably irked him.

They spoke of their homeland, of a great and endless tree they hoped they'd live to see again—a homeland they were willing to die to protect. Finally, when Emrael could stand it no longer, he stepped forward into their midst. They leapt, able at last to see him. One shouted questions. Others reached for their weapons. Emrael reached out and pressed his hand to the closest man's face. The man screamed. A moment later, the man fell, mouth agape, his eye sockets blackened.

Emrael stared in amazement at what he had done. He had acted purely on instinct, but the result was a dizzying rush of warmth that sped throughout his body, driving back his weariness, sating a little of his hunger. Emrael turned to face the next warrior, who drew back and fired an arrow at Emrael's face. Emrael made no move to defend himself but stared, unafraid, as the arrow vanished in a wisp of smoke. Stepping forward, he grasped the second warrior by the face. The warrior screamed. That time, Emrael noted strange tongues of violet flame that leapt from the warrior's eyes, soaking into Emrael's hand like water drawn up into a sponge. He let go of the warrior, whose eyes were blackened like the previous victim's.

Only then did Emrael realize he was being stabbed in the back. He felt faint jabs of pain that evaporated into a faint tingle even as he turned and grasped the face of the third warrior, drawing still more ghostly flame into his body. Emrael laughed. A joyful giddiness filled him, but the satisfaction lasted only a moment before he was eyeing the fourth and final scout, as a starving man might a scrap of fresh-cooked meat.

The scout had fired off all his arrows, each one vanishing into a puff of ash before reaching Emrael's body. The scout backpedaled, shouting for help. Emrael waved his hand, and the scout lost the ability to speak. Emrael considered sprinting after him. He also had the impression that, if he wanted, he could have pointed at the man and paralyzed his body. Then, he could have taken his time, wandered down the path, and drunk fire from his eyes.

Instead, Emrael watched.

Two new figures were moving up the hill, behind the final scout. Emrael saw at once that they were not coming to help. One—a tall, pale, lanky figure with strange eyes and sharp teeth—had a grin on his face that turned Emrael's grin into a frown. Though the pale figure wore a sword, he had not bothered to draw it. The other figure, cloaked and hooded, moved more slowly, his head bowed toward the trail.

The pale figure stood right behind the scout and made a strange clicking sound akin to laughter. The scout whirled as his eyes widened, and he staggered away, drawing his sword. The scout swung his sword at the pale figure. With impossible quickness, the latter ducked beneath the blade, grasped the scout's arm, and broke it.

The scout gasped, unable to scream. The pale figure clicked with laughter again. Then, even quicker, he spun the scout around, grasped him by the head, and snapped his neck. As the scout slumped to the earth, the pale man made a faintly mournful sound, like a cat who had gotten carried away and killed a mouse too soon.

Then the pale figure changed. His body blurred then shifted like clay being reshaped by gigantic invisible hands. A moment later, he looked identical to the dead scout at his feet. The living copy of the dead scout turned to the hooded man, grinning. He tried to speak, choked, and tried again.

"Does this form please you, Master?"

"No," the hooded man answered, reaching out and grasping his comrade by one of his newly pointed ears.

The latter howled with pain. His face shimmered, then his body, until he had resumed his former appearance. The ghastly figure clicked in dismay. The hooded man kicked him, and the pale figure scampered away. The hooded man lifted his face to look at Emrael. Beneath purple eyes, the cloaked man's lips broke into a smile.

For the first time, Emrael noticed that his own hands were on fire. The realization prompted only mild surprise. He watched tendrils of purple flame dance between his fingers, cavorting off his knuckles.

He clenched his hands into fists, and the fire disappeared. "Do not come any closer," Emrael warned. "You are strong. I can tell. But I am stronger."

The cloaked man's smile thinned. "Of course, Great One. Father. I am your servant." He bowed.

Father? Emrael stepped back. "I know you... but I do *not* know you." He felt the answer inside his mind, like a key hidden within a dark room. He had the sense, too, that the life he'd drained from the scouts was inside him now, ready to point the way, ready to drive back any shadows that lingered in his mind after Miriam had pulled him from the water.

Miriam... Emrael looked back at the cave mouth, afraid he would see the girl, but Challa crouched in the doorway. The greatwolf growled—first at the cloaked man then at the pale figure. The latter stretched out one hand and began to move up the path, toward the cave, clicking soothingly.

Challa bared her teeth and did not retreat. When the pale figure was close enough, she leapt forward, jaws snapping. Somehow, the pale figure twisted out of the way, drew his sword, and cut the greatwolf's throat. The soothing click did not stop.

"You should not have done that." Emrael lifted a hand and pointed it at the greatwolf's killer.

The pale figure cocked his head to one side. He looked at the cloaked man, who said nothing, then back at Emrael. Bone-white eyes narrowed then widened. A plaintive stream of clicks and hisses sputtered from the killer's throat—a moment before Emrael gestured and the pale figure's body turned inside out.

Emrael stared, appalled at what he had done. Then he heard the cloaked man laughing. Emrael drew back, averting his eyes from the grisly sight. "I should not have done that…"

"You may do whatever you like, Father," the cloaked man said. He bowed again. "My name is Krym. I am your son. I have gathered all your prizes. They await you, not far from here." He straightened, regarded Emrael for a moment, then frowned. "You do not remember me? Strange. By now, I would have thought…" He reached toward Emrael's face.

Emrael drew away. "Whatever you are, stay back."

Krym's frown deepened as he held up his empty hands. "Let me help you, Father." He backed away from Emrael and moved toward the grisly remains of the pale toothy figure, which lay like a stain on the road. Krym knelt. Without hesitation, he plunged his bare hands into the ravaged mess. His eyes closed, and violet flames spilled from his hands, first in small wisps then in great leaping tongues.

Emrael watched the flames completely obscure the mangled body and hoped they would burn it to ash. Seconds passed, then minutes. Finally, the flames died down, recoiling back into Krym's hands. In their place, the pale figure lay on the stony ground, naked but whole. His eyes opened. Staring up at Krym, the strange figure made a cry that sounded like gratitude.

Krym stared down at his servant for a moment, expressionless, then straightened and stepped back. He gestured. Invisible hands seemed to wrench the pale figure to his feet, thrusting him toward Emrael then driving him back onto his knees. The pale figure's strange eyes widened with terror. Clawed hands pressed together in a supplicating gesture.

Emrael looked past the kneeling figure, at Krym. He noticed the cloaked man suddenly looked haggard and weary, his violet eyes rimmed in red. Still, Krym smiled. He nodded toward the kneeling, struggling figure. "Maalbolgs are a strong vintage. Drink, Father, and be restored."

Emrael hesitated only a moment then stepped forward and pressed both hands against the loathsome figure's face, one covering each of those big pale eyes. The creature howled. Emrael was not sure he knew what to do, but his hands did. Delicious heat leapt from the kneeling Maalbolg's

252

skull, soaking into his palms, sweeter than what he'd felt from the scouts. The heat filled him with power—and answers. He wept and laughed at the same time. When he finally let go, the kneeling figure's head had been blackened down to the skull. The body sagged to the ground, dead once more. Emrael turned to face Krym.

Krym fell to one knee. "The next meal you taste will be the life essence of a dragon."

"Khyrshar..." Emrael's mind reeled with the image of a dragon bigger than any other that had ever lived, bigger even than Godsbane, its many wings blotting out the sun, its many-colored scales barely containing the awesome power that roiled within. He shut his eyes, steadied himself, then faced Krym again. "What about Nâya?"

Krym's expression darkened. "She survived her passage through the Dragonward, as I suspected she would, but then she escaped me. I searched for days, but it seems she has fled."

Emrael considered that. "I think not. But she cannot harm us. I saw to that." He turned back to the cave mouth. He considered the witless, helpless girl still asleep inside. The spell he'd cast on her would keep her unconscious for another hour, perhaps two. By the time she woke, everything would be finished.

Emrael sighed. He marveled at himself, why he had not simply killed her—especially given the weapon she carried. He remembered her face again, her hair dripping water, the urgent concern in her eyes as she pulled him from the sea.

So like Nâya... He stiffened, reminding himself that Nâya lived only so that she might be adequately punished for her sins. Then his gaze fell on Challa. The dead greatwolf lay in a great heap, her ruddy fur matching the pool of blood beneath her. *I could resurrect her. But would she still be kind to Miriam after I'm gone?* "We must go. But first, burn the dead. Leave no trace. Especially the wolf."

Krym looked confused but did not object. He moved from corpse to corpse, unleashing great scalding baths of wytchfire in spite of the weariness in his expression. Emrael waited until Krym's back was turned. Then he removed the golden medallion from his neck, held it up in the air, and floated it quietly into the cave mouth, where he hoped Miriam would see it.

Jalist examined the dent in his helmet. He could not remember putting it on any more than he could remember the last time he'd slept—even though his senses were telling him that could not have been very long before—but apparently, the helmet had saved his life. He touched the dent with his fingertips.

Someone whispered his name. Jalist looked up as Maddoc drew him toward a campfire.

"Not cold," Jalist mumbled. "Tired. Sweating. Need to get this damn armor off..." Dimly, Jalist realized Maddoc was still grasping his arm, turning him to face two other figures who stood by the fire, a man and a woman, both with scarred faces, who looked vaguely familiar. Jalist could not be sure, though, because their faces—like their armor—were speckled in blood.

"Sylvs," Jalist said. "Where in the gods' names did you come from?"

The two Sylvs looked at each other.

Jalist got the impression that he'd said the wrong thing. "Sorry," he mumbled. He looked at Maddoc. "What have I done wrong now?"

Maddoc's hand moved from Jalist's arm to his forehead. A strange purple light clouded Jalist's vision. For the first time Jalist noticed a dull ache in his head. Then the ache faded—replaced by stabbing pain.

Jalist tried to jerk away. With surprising strength, Maddoc kept hold of Jalist, his grip squeezing. Then he let go. The violet fog faded from Jalist's eyes, taking the pain with it. He blinked.

"How close was I—"

"To dying?" Maddoc finished. "We'll discuss that when you're an old man."

Jalist closed his eyes for a moment then opened them. He saw the Sylvs again. "Briel and Kilisti. If I'm not mistaken, one of you took Locke's horse. But you just saved our asses so we'll call it even." Jalist looked around and realized he was standing in a sea of misery. Dead and wounded lay everywhere. Sylvan warriors rushed to and fro, tending the injured as best they could. Jalist's nostrils filled with the scent of blood and waste. Thinking of Aeko, he blinked tears from his eyes.

"Sariel?"

"Falder's guarding her. I made her sleep," Maddoc said. "I should add that the next time we go to war, I might not want to bring a child along."

"Fair point," Jalist said. "Go help the wounded. I'll be fine." He turned back to Briel and Kilisti. "How many have you brought with you?"

Briel said, "Enough to keep the Lancers at bay, but probably not enough to kill them."

Kilisti tried to wipe a smear of blood from her face, but the action only pressed the blood into one of her scars. "Want to tell us what's going on?"

Jalist wiped his eyes. "What's going on is that a lot of good people are dead, Locke needs our help, and there's no way he's going to get it. What's going on is that some fey Ivairian bastard named Cadwallis is out there right now, unaware that I'm going to haul out his guts with my bare hands." Jalist half expected a condemnation from Maddoc before remembering he'd sent the Shel'ai away.

Briel and Kilisti exchanged looks again.

Briel said, "We can send messages, ask for more help. Queshi riders, Earless, Red Watch... maybe even the Tongueless, gods help us."

"And whatever Shel'ai are in Cadavash," Kilisti added. Jalist followed her gaze to a wounded Dwarr in the distance. The Dwarr was shaking, trying not to scream as Maddoc used wytchfire to knit his guts back together.

"They won't get here in time," Jalist said. "Besides, the Lancers are the least of our worries. Judging by your expressions, the two of you know that as well as I do."

Kilisti glared at them. "Then what do you suggest, Dwarr? We didn't ride hundreds of miles just to—"

"The true threat is Nekiel. We have to help Locke put him down as quickly as possible, no matter the cost."

"Agreed," Kilisti said, "but the Lancers are in the way."

"We might get a small force through," Briel said. "Sylvan Shal'tiar, especially. If we wait until nightfall—"

"A few men won't make a difference," Jalist said. "I'm not even sure a whole army will, but at least it's a start."

A scout on horseback thundered toward them, shouting, and Briel ran to meet him halfway. The Sylvan general stood unflinching in the horse's path, and Jalist feared he would be trampled, but the general shifted sideways and grasped the bridle, jerking the horse to a stop so quickly that the scout nearly tumbled from the saddle. The two spoke in Sylvan, which Jalist could not understand, save for a single word, which the scout spoke with open fear and contempt: *Shel'ai.*

The scout was pointing at a distant line of hills. Jalist thought he saw a flash of purple on the horizon. He sighed, one hand touching the hilt of Forgefang, the traditional sword of Dwarrish kings, whose weight he was gradually becoming accustomed to.

Shel'ai... or something much worse.

Despite his weariness, Jalist looked around, digging his fingernails into his palms. He tried to block out the whimpers and screams as he surveyed his surroundings and wondered how much of his army was still fit to fight. Then he spotted Captain Tansil, seated nearby on the body of a dead horse, stoically wrapping bandages around a cut in her forearm. Jalist hurried toward her. The swordswoman looked up at his approach.

Blood and dirt still covered the Iron Sister's face and armor. Jalist had not expected to find her alive, given that throughout the battle he'd often spied her at the thick of the fighting. Then he noticed the slain Lancer pinned beneath the dead horse she was sitting on. Jalist had been about to ask her how many Iron Sisters she had left, but the grisly sight reminded him of another matter.

"Glad you're still alive, Captain." Before she had a chance to answer, he added, "Wytchfire in the distance. Gods know why. I doubt Nekiel's about to sweep down on us, but just in case, we may have to run again. Disarm any Ivairian prisoners and tie them up. We'll leave them behind, same as before."

The Iron Sister finished wrapping her forearm and tied the bandage in place. "Apologies, Governor, but I didn't leave anyone behind before."

The Iron Sister spoke so nonchalantly that, for a moment, Jalist did not understand. "Maddoc told you—"

"No disrespect," Tansil said, "but your lover told me to release a few dozen men back to our enemies so they could help them chase us down. Disarming a man doesn't do much good when there are swords littering the ground for miles."

Jalist felt the blood drain from his face. "What did you do?"

"What had to be done." The Iron Sister slowly moved her bandaged arm, testing it. She nodded to herself. "Truth be told, I'm surprised you didn't hear all the Isle Knights shouting and cursing." She shrugged. "War is war. You won't catch me bragging about what I did, but we both know there's probably a few of your men still alive because of it." Tansil rose to her feet. "If that's a problem, I'll take the rest of my Sisters back to Hesod. We don't run from a fight, but—"

Jalist touched his hilt. "Go," he said, seething.

Tansil's eyes narrowed, then she bowed. "So be it. Good fighting with you, Dwarr. Give my best to Sir Locke when you see him. And tell Lilac I said goodbye." She walked away, calling for her Iron Sisters to join her. Fierce as lionesses, they mounted their horses, scowled in Jalist's direction, and rode away.

Watching them go, Jalist wondered if he'd just made a terrible mistake.

CHAPTER TWENTY-SEVEN

KESWEN PLUNGED INTO DARK WATER. Instinctively, she closed her mouth, but the darkness leaked under her eyelids, poured into her ears, and clawed its way up into her nostrils. She felt it closing around the rest of her body, thick as oil, weighing her down. She struggled against it as her lungs burned. Finally, against her will, her mouth open. Darkness flooded her lungs, seeped through her organs, filled her body.

Then a woman's voice called to her. A hand grasped the darkness—white, blazing—and hauled it away. Even though Keswen's eyes were closed, she saw its radiance as though her eyelids were veil thin. The hand dragged the darkness from her lungs, wrenching it out of her body until she was free.

Finally, Keswen could breathe again. Fighting back waves of pain, she opened her eyes and found herself staring up at a distant, domed ceiling of ice. Shadows nipped at the corners of her vision, driven back by a blazing column of white light. With great effort, Keswen sat up. She spotted an adamune lying beside her and remembered Hráthbam giving her the weapon a moment before the world unraveled.

Rowen Locke stood before her, but his gaze was fixed on the column of light. Igrid leaned heavily on his arm, her thigh wrapped in blood-soaked bandages. Keswen spotted the others a moment later. Zeia and Saanji helped each other rise. Though both were pale and blood splattered, their half-healed wounds indicated that Zeia had probably already treated the worst of the damage. Keswen even saw the Olg,

Breaksteel, in the distance, hovering protectively over Thessa. One great, gray hand rested on the girl's shoulder. For her own part, Thessa seemed too dazed to object to the Olg's presence. Though Keswen could not find Issa and Vaari, she saw blood on the floor and, in the distance, what looked like a body covered by a cloak.

Keswen realized the floor itself was made of ice. A great shadow loomed just under the ice. Then Keswen took a closer look and gasped. Saanji and Zeia turned, alerted by the sound.

Saanji offered her a weak smile. "Glad you're still alive, Sylv."

Keswen rose unsteadily to her feet and made her way toward Rowen. The Isle Knight's tabard hung from his body in shreds. His armor was splattered with blood, but his eyes widened when he saw Keswen.

Igrid spoke first, flashing her a crooked grin. "Well met, Sister. You have a knack for unexpected entrances."

"Second only to *that*." Rowen pointed at the pillar of light.

Keswen was about to explain when she realized she did not have the words. The light dimmed. It faded to a faint glow, emanating from Nâya's body, but did not vanish altogether. Keswen directed her gaze at Rowen's expression. She saw at once that the Isle Knight recognized Nâya, though she wondered how.

Another damn vision, maybe.

Rowen started to bow but stopped himself. "How..."

Nâya stepped forward. One bare arm rose from the cloak Hráthbam had given her. In her hand, she held Knightswrath. The rest of Rowen's question died in his throat as the Dragonkin bowed her head and extended the unsheathed blade, offering it to him.

Igrid's face darkened. Letting go of Rowen's arm, she stepped back. Meanwhile, Zeia managed to rise and limped forward, an expression of awe on her face. Rowen hesitated a moment longer then grasped Knightswrath by the dragonbone pommel. He held the sword against his chest and looked at Nâya, who stepped so close that Igrid took another step back.

Rowen reached out and touched the lotus medallion hanging around Nâya's neck. He smiled faintly. "Hráthbam..." He glanced at Keswen. "Something tells me you have quite a story to tell."

"I do." Keswen looked around. "I don't see Krym or his snarling little pet with you. I gather much has happened here, too." She noted the sadness that passed over Rowen's face and guessed what must have become of Sir Issa and Vaari.

"There is no time for grief," Nâya said. Her voice had changed, no longer reverberating. Instead, despite the light still emanating from her body, spilling from her cloak, she sounded tired and frail.

Rowen nodded. He lifted Knightswrath a little. "Since you've brought this, I trust Krym lied. The Dragonward—"

"Is no longer necessary," Nâya finished. "All the Dragonkin left in the world are gathered here, now, on Ruun." She paused. "The sun rises. Before it sets, if the Light is merciful, all three of us will be dead."

"Easier said than done," Igrid muttered. "Nekiel *and* Krym will be here any moment. Since I'm guessing Vaari's betrayal means they're actually working together, I suggest we either come up with a brilliant plan or run for our lives."

Nâya stepped away from them. She walked along the ice, following the outline of Khyrshar's body. When she reached the eye, she knelt. The eye opened. Nâya touched the ice, her head bowed for a moment. She whispered something that Keswen could not hear, then she stood. When she turned back to face the others, the Dragonkin was weeping. When she spoke, though, her voice echoed with new purpose.

"Isle Knight, it was not Khyrshar who kept you from entering that room. It was me." She pointed at a small, open doorway on the far end of the great chamber. Pale light emanated from the room. "Khyrshar warned me. I was still far away, traveling roads you cannot conceive, but I did what I could." She looked at Keswen, and her voice became apologetic. "There were... consequences." She turned back to Rowen. "My father crafted that room as a prison. Whoever steps within may never leave. He crafted it as a cage in which to keep those prisoners he wished to gloat over." She paused. "He crafted it for *me*. But I gave myself to Knightswrath before he had a chance to use it."

"How... how can you be here?" Rowen managed.

Nâya sighed. "When Silwren gave herself to Knightswrath, she took my place. After centuries of voluntary imprisonment, I was free. I *died*."

A wild, almost giddy smile touched Nâya's lips. "I returned to the Light. I was reunited with Jinn. I was at peace. But from across the sea, Nekiel sensed this. So he drained many of his servants to heighten his power—just as Chorlga did. Hundreds, thousands. He even drained fellow Dragonkin, which is a crime almost unheard of."

Rowen said, "But you were his enemy. Why would he bring you back?"

"His own lust for revenge, perhaps. Or maybe it was loneliness. I doubt even my father could tell you." Nâya smiled for a moment before the smile withered like a burning flower. "But the pain... Gods, Knight, you cannot imagine it. How it feels, being back inside the Light, then ripped away..." Nâya trailed off, her eyes damp and gleaming.

Keswen recalled the torment that El'rash'lin had recounted to Shade, years before, after the former had been inadvertently brought back to life by the same magic Chorlga used to resurrect the Nightmare. Moved by pity, Keswen took a step toward Nâya, but when Nâya spoke again, the fierceness in her voice made everyone recoil.

"When I helped Jinn's allies forge Knightswrath, I knew what I was doing. At least, I thought I did. I thought I understood the price. I paid it because I knew our kind had to be stopped."

Zeia spoke with reverence and certainty. "They *will* be stopped. We have Knightswrath. We have you. That's enough."

Keswen considered the caliber of magic she'd seen Nâya wield so far. *If Nekiel is even stronger, with Krym to help him...* "Maybe we can set up some kind of trap."

Saanji nodded. "Some way to force one or both of those bastards into that room, maybe."

"There are no tricks that will fool my father." Nâya faced the distant room and lifted her hands. Violet flame spilled from her fingertips, expanding as it passed through the air. Everyone leapt back. Nâya's flame poured in through the open doorway like a battering ram. Keswen heard an ominous crack, then the flames spilled back out of the doorway, clawing up the walls.

The purple flames reached the domed ceiling. Then they spread, covering all the walls. Waves of heat buffeted Keswen's face, accompanied by a harsh, glaring light. She closed her eyes. Moments later, she heard rushing water. Dampness soaked her feet through her boots. When she opened her eyes, she blinked in amazement.

The temple was gone.

The group stood, speechless, on an icy lake surrounded on all sides by rocky hills glazed with snow. Water flowed up to their ankles then drained away. As the waters receded, Keswen saw smaller rocks and chunks of ice scattered on the ground, as though Nâya's magic had demolished not only the temple but a small mountain of rock and ice that had been surrounding it.

In the distance stood a line of unmoving armored figures, all of them pierced through the eyes by arrows. Beyond stood horses, tied to a lone evergreen tree. Strangely, one of the horses bore a ragged-looking man who had been bound hand and foot to the horse. The man was too distant to distinguish, but he whimpered and struggled weakly against his restraints. A single path carved through the rocks in the distance. The sky was pale and naked. A cold wind whistled over the rocks, like air drawn through a cavity. Keswen shivered.

Rowen gently pried himself free of Thessa, who was clinging fearfully to him, and faced Nâya. Knightswrath kindled in the crook of his arm, violet flames racing along the length of the blade. "Why—"

"To prevent it from being used against us," Nâya answered calmly.

Saanji said, "The dragon's still here," and pointed at the massive shape beneath the ice.

Keswen noted that all her companions took care to avoid stepping on the ice directly over the gigantic unmoving form.

For the first time, Thessa spoke. "Can she help us?" The girl knelt, tentatively touching the ice that encased the dragon's open, staring eye.

Igrid stroked Thessa's dirty brown hair. "Not sure an angry dragon that's been imprisoned for thousands of years is the best ally, child." Halfway through speaking, Igrid lowered her voice, as though she feared the dragon might hear.

Nâya smiled faintly. "On that, we agree, but I am no longer of this world. It will not be for me to decide." Her gaze sought out Rowen. "There is more. You should know that I cannot fight Nekiel and Krym myself. Nekiel did it when he brought me back to life. It is a condition similar to what you call the Blood Thrall, preventing me from dealing direct harm to a fellow Dragonkin. Still… there is a way." She lowered her gaze to Knightswrath.

Keswen did not know what the Dragonkin meant, but Rowen's expression said that he did.

Aghast, he stepped back. "No. I can't do that again."

Nâya said, "Silwren understood what needed to be done. So do I. But you must promise me something…" When she did not speak further, Keswen got the feeling that something was passing between them unsaid.

Finally, wearily, Rowen said, "I promise." He turned to Igrid. "Take Thessa out of here."

Igrid's look of disapproval grew. "Take her *where?*"

"I'm not afraid," Thessa insisted, shaking as she held her shortsword.

Rowen said, "That trading post. It's far to the east. Frostreavers aren't welcome. Still, it's a rough place."

Igrid crossed her arms. "If you think I'm leaving you on the eve of the greatest battle of your life—"

Rowen pulled Igrid close and whispered in her ear. Igrid looked annoyed then defiant. Still, she returned Rowen's embrace. Finally, pushing away, Igrid wiped her eyes, grabbed Thessa's hand, and pulled the child toward the horses. The girl protested, but Igrid did not slow.

Rowen watched them go then turned to Breaksteel. "Go with them. Keep them safe." His voice broke, half pleading.

Breaksteel hesitated then bowed and strode after the others.

Rowen faced Saanji next. "You, too."

Saanji frowned. "Don't get me wrong, Knight. I'm not looking forward to this. I've been hearing bad stories about Nekiel ever since I was old enough to get the piss beat out of me by my brothers. Still, if you think I'm going to leave—"

"You're the future Emperor of Dhargoth," Rowen said, "not to mention the first sane one it will have had in centuries. Whatever happens here, you have more important things to do."

"It'll be hard to reign over Dhargoth if the whole realm is in cinders," Saanji countered.

Zeia touched Saanji's arm with one flaming hand. "He's right, dunce. We didn't spend years fighting so you could get yourself killed and unravel the whole mess." She stepped closer and kissed Saanji's nose. Then she cupped her hands around his face to warm it.

Keswen turned away, unexpected tears in her eyes. Forcing her voice to sound gruff, she said to Rowen, "Are you going to send *me* away next?"

"No. I need that famous aim of yours, but if you want to go—"

Before Rowen could finish, Keswen picked up Vaari's bow off the ice. She strode over to the armored figures, which she guessed had once been Jolym, and wrenched the arrows from their eye sockets. When she was done, she scouted a place on the rocks where she could hide. By the time she found one, shivering from cold, she turned to see Igrid, Thessa, and Saanji on horseback, solemnly riding away and leading the horse carrying the prisoner. Breaksteel strode well ahead of them, on foot, his kashpa damp and gleaming in a faint snowfall.

Keswen turned back toward Rowen. He stood on the ice with Nâya and Zeia. Though the three spoke, Keswen could not hear the words. Violet flames continued to race along Knightswrath's blade, dripping off and steaming on the ground. Keswen switched her gaze off her companions, watching for Nekiel's and Krym's inevitable approach. She fit an arrow on her bowstring.

Will arrows even work against Dragonkin?

She remembered Vaari firing one at Krym while he slept, only to have the arrow vanish in a puff of smoke. She had questions about the Dhargot's fate—questions she feared she might not live to ask—but she pushed such thoughts from her mind.

Maybe I don't have to kill them. I just have to distract them. The others can use magic to do the rest.

Melting snowflakes ran down her forehead. Keswen blinked away the water. Despite her chattering teeth, she smiled, finding it strange that once again, she was about to place her trust in magic even after all the harm it had wrought on her life. She looked south again, saw the horizon stark and empty, and turned back to her companions—just in time to see Zeia draw a few steps apart from Rowen and Nâya and turn away. She appeared to be crying.

Keswen wondered what was going on. Then Nâya undid her cloak and let it fall to the ice. The Dragonkin stood in front of Rowen, naked but unshivering. The Isle Knight quietly faced her, Knightswrath burning in his grasp. The flames brightened. For a long time, Rowen did not move. Then he shook his head. Nâya said something Keswen could not hear.

Rowen hesitated, an awful sternness building in his expression. Nâya tipped her head back and opened her arms. Her body brightened, awash in white light.

Then Rowen stepped forward and shoved Knightswrath between her breasts.

Keswen leapt up. She drew her arrow but stopped herself, unsure where to fire. Nâya's body vanished in a pillar of violet flame. Rowen gave a bitter cry of anguish, withdrew the blade, and collapsed on the ice. Zeia moved toward him, as though to comfort him, then stopped and drew farther away instead.

Meanwhile, Nâya continued to burn. She did not fall but stood upright as the flames intensified. A scream echoed from the center of the pillar: agonized, bestial, triumphant. The flames rose out of Nâya's body and poured into Knightswrath. Rowen recoiled but did not drop the blade.

When it was over, Nâya was gone. Rowen knelt on the ice, head bowed, shoulders slumped. Knightswrath drooped in his grasp, the blade throbbing with fire, pulsing like a heartbeat. Rowen shuddered, though Keswen could not tell whether that was from anguish or pain. She remembered stories from the War of the Lotus: Rowen reeling from Knightswrath's power, struggling to control it, always fearing it would consume him.

Gods, that better not happen this time. Keswen chided herself, awash in unexpected pity for the Dragonkin who had saved her from the Lancers then given her life—again—to try to save the world. Keswen wondered if the sacrifice would be enough. Then she turned southward and saw two figures slowly crossing the ice. Though they were men, the shadows they left in the waning light were huge—huge and winged.

Nekiel saw Krym stop in his tracks. A chilly smile formed on Krym's face a moment before he said, "They have seen us." He closed his eyes and smelled the air. "They're terrified. Can you sense it?"

Nekiel fought the sudden urge to reach out and burn his son to ashes. "Yes, but I don't sense... my daughter. I thought I did for a moment, but she's gone now. Perhaps she fled."

"Then we will chase her." Krym's smile vanished. "Strange to hear you call her your daughter."

"That's what she is. My child. As are you." Nekiel stomach turned as he said it, but he forced the words out anyway.

Krym frowned. "What has happened to you, Father? Was it the Dragonward? You sound…" He shook his head. "I did not think to hear such… softness from you. Especially now."

Nekiel stretched his mind into his son's and felt Krym's disapproval, tinged with revulsion. Nekiel stepped forward and stretched out his hand. Krym tensed, lifting his hands as well. Nekiel sensed the powerful magic that Krym was summoning to protect himself—a moment before it crumbled. Seconds later, Krym slumped to the ice, wytchfire roiling all around him, clawing at his flesh.

Nekiel said, "You forget yourself… my child."

Krym gritted his teeth. He closed his eyes, but tears leaked out. "Forgive—"

Nekiel smiled, awash in cold satisfaction, followed by an unexpected flutter of guilt. Waving his hand, Nekiel dismissed the tormenting flames and stepped closer. He touched Krym's cheek where crisped skin was already beginning to heal itself. Nekiel struggled against the unexpected impulse to beg forgiveness. *Gods, he's right. What has happened to me?* Nekiel stepped back. "You have served me admirably on many occasions. This is not one of them. You should not have waited so long to find me."

"I thought—" Krym choked, forced himself to stand, and began again. "I thought to bring you those others as a token of my—"

"Then why did you not simply take them captive and bring them to me? Your games endangered everything."

"I did not think my ruses would so offend you. If I had—" Krym withered midsentence, falling onto the ice. Wytchfire roiled all around him, burning him again.

Nekiel stared a moment, uncomprehending, then realized he was the cause. *Gods, what am I doing? Why am I hurting him?* He dismissed the fire, watching as Krym healed himself, albeit more slowly. "Gods, we are wretched things."

He saw at once that Krym had misunderstood, thinking the rebuke was aimed solely at him. Nekiel was tempted to correct him. Instead, he waited for Krym to regain his composure then pointed. Krym bowed then resumed his original course. Nekiel followed.

What has happened to me?

An unfamiliar hollowness filled him, accompanied by guilt and self-loathing he had not experienced in so many centuries that he hardly recognized the sensations. Then he fixed his gaze on the ice and snow before him.

"Nâya," he whispered. *My daughter will explain this. She will help me. I must find her.* Nekiel quickened his pace.

CHAPTER TWENTY-EIGHT

ROWEN STAGGERED, TRIED TO RISE, and fell to the ice. Guilt twisted inside him, regardless of the desperation and absolution he'd seen in Nâya's gold-flecked eyes. The Dragonkin had vanished entirely, leaving no trace on the ice where she'd stood. In her absence, raw power coursed through him, heightening all his senses. The air felt like a million tiny daggers stabbing him through his armor. Then, he realized the daggers had mouths, and they were hungry.

He jerked away, trying to block out the world. Instead, he realized that the night had a smell, that he could taste the ice through his boots—that beyond the darkening clouds above him, he could feel the meticulous balance of the stars in the sky.

Both exhilarated and revolted, he fought the impulse to cast Knightswrath away from him. Every second he continued to hold onto it brought with it the sense that the sword was melting into him—or the other way around. With a rush of panic, he remembered the first time he'd experienced the sword's true power—in the Sylvan capital, in the tomb of Fâyu Jinn—right after Silwren had deliberately thrown herself onto the blade. This, however, was worse.

I'm going to lose myself again…

He sensed Zeia and Keswen nearby. He even sensed with encroaching dread the approach of Nekiel—but time seemed to have slowed to a crawl, such that Nekiel might as well have been on the other side of the world. With reeling panic, Rowen thought of the Blood Thrall the Shel'ai had inflicted on his brother, long before, so that any act of disobedience caused never-ending pain.

Gods, did Nâya trick me? Silwren, where are you?

Desperately, he scanned his surroundings for the platinum-haired wytch who had saved him so many times before. He told himself that she must be there somewhere, buried deep in all that power pouring out of Knightswrath. Seconds passed with agonizing slowness. Then, with nauseating suddenness, he found himself in a room.

The room blurred, filled with people and objects that gradually fell into focus. Though small, the room had walls of beaten gold, hung with tapestries of richly embroidered silk. Richly dressed servants—all with the taut pale skin of Maalbolgs—stood nearby, some of them holding carafes of wine. Others held towels.

For the first time, Rowen realized the room smelled of blood. Then more figures shifted into focus, and he found himself standing amidst a host of Dragonkin. His first impulse was to run, but the panic faded almost as quickly as it had begun. None of the Dragonkin appeared to notice him. Hoping that would not change, he studied their faces. One looked like Krym, though younger, not yet a man. Chorlga stood beside him, bald and handsome despite his rotten teeth, yawning as he scratched at his fingernails. Both wore robes of purple and gold. A rush of fear and rage accompanied the sight of Chorlga, but before he could act, something inexplicably drew his gaze elsewhere.

In the center of the room, a naked woman with tapered ears and a round belly lay upon a birthing couch. Her belly shifted. The woman did not scream but stared—blank, immodest—at the onlookers. Her expression reminded Rowen of the drugged Sylvan women forced by Chorlga to bear Shel'ai children. But no, this woman's expression was not one of hopelessness—she was merely bored.

Her round belly convulsed. The woman winced, yawned, then spread her legs. A Jol approached. Wrought of coldly gleaming silver, the Jol had hands instead of weapons. Its face was permanently shaped into a chilling smile. The Jol knelt between the woman's thighs, hollow eyes staring. With frightful gentleness, silver hands eased the newborn—a blue-faced girl—from the woman's body.

A Maalbolg offered the Jol a towel. The Jol silently wiped some of the blood from the infant then stood, holding its tiny body with gigantic hands. The Jol offered the infant to the woman still lying on the birthing couch, but the woman closed her legs, indifferent, and held out one hand. A Maalbolg servant gave her wine.

The Jol turned, offering the baby to Rowen instead. Rowen started to reach out for her, but Krym interceded, roughly snatching the infant from the Jol's grasp. Krym held the girl at arms' length, frowning as she wriggled in midair.

Krym said, "She isn't breathing."

"Strike her." Chorlga yawned again.

A faint, cold smile touched Krym's lips. He brought the child closer, holding her with one arm. He raised his other hand over her face. He held his palm open for a moment then reshaped it into a fist.

Rowen reached out and seized Krym's wrist. Wytchfire sprang from Rowen's hands. Krym screamed and jerked away, dropping the child in the process. Rowen waved his other hand, and the child stopped, hovering just over the floor. Her eyelids pressed shut so tightly that they wrinkled from the strain. Her blue lips buckled, like the mouth of a drowning fish.

Rowen plucked her from the air and held her close. Instead of striking her, he touched her lips. The lips opened, then the eyes. Tiny, violet irises fixed on Rowen's face as the newborn girl drew in her first breath. A small hand reached out and curled around his finger.

Chorlga drew near even as Maalbolgs covered the Dragonkin mother with a silk blanket and refilled her wine glass. He stopped scratching his fingernails long enough to step closer and wave a glowing palm over the infant girl's head.

Chorlga frowned. "This one is flawed, Master. Soft. Like Namundvar. Best kill her." He glanced at Krym, who had straightened but was still clutching his burned hand. "Or give her to the boy."

Krym grinned, his perfect teeth as white as bone.

"No," Rowen heard himself say in a voice that was not his own. He smoothed back the infant's wispy, dark hair. Then he looked at Chorlga and saw surprise on the bald Dragonkin's face. "No," Rowen repeated, erasing the softness from his voice. "Not yet. I might need her."

Chorlga shrugged. "As you say, Master. And Lady Jesriel?" Chorlga nodded toward the Dragonkin woman who was still lying on the couch.

The woman's eyes met his. Rowen saw no love there, no desire—only impatience, tinged with eagerness for a promised reward. He remembered the same look on her face when they'd slept together, pressing in the darkness.

"Kill her," Rowen said.

Jesriel's eyes widened. She sat up, dropping her glass, and wine spilled on the birthing couch. Wytchfire flared at her fingertips, forming a protective shield. "Master, wait. Have I not served you well? You promised—"

Chorlga's wytchfire shattered her defenses and washed over her. Somehow, she did not scream—but the infant did. She was still screaming when Chorlga ceased his attack—grinning—and turned toward Rowen.

"She's still alive. Seems a waste to just kill her... She *is* a Dragonkin, though. As you are so fond of saying, even our kind have rules."

Rowen stared at the blackened, dying woman on the birthing couch, and his contempt faded. He felt no pity for her, either. Turning to Krym, he said, "Drain her as you would a Shel'ai slave. But tell no one."

Krym brightened. He stopped clenching his burned hand and bowed. "Thank you, Father." As he moved toward the birthing couch, Rowen turned away, still holding the infant. She'd fallen silent and closed her eyes as abruptly as she'd begun screaming. Her body twisted as though trying to escape him. Rowen sensed her disapproval, her tiny but profound rage. He was tempted to kill her after all, as Chorlga had suggested. Instead, he returned her to the Jol and turned to go.

"A moment, Master," Chorlga said. "Do you wish to name her?"

Rowen turned back in time to see Krym—his face eager, almost lustful—drawing wytchfire from the dying mother's eye sockets. Rowen fixed his gaze on the infant instead. Upon finding herself in the Jol's cold, metallic grasp, she had begun screaming once more. Rowen fought the desire to retrieve her, to save her.

"Nâya." He walked away.

Krym jerked as Nekiel stopped in his tracks so abruptly that he feared he was about to be punished again. Instead, Nekiel said, "She's awake," and smiled.

Krym shuddered, realizing his father must be referring to Khyrshar. He thought back to a time, many centuries before, when he'd stood on the ice as a child and made faces at the tormented dragon trapped underneath. He'd done it for hours, trying to goad the dragon into opening her eyes and facing him, but she never did.

Then, as he was about to go, she summoned what little power remained to her and injected her mind into Krym's, shattering his defenses. Krym reeled, falling. Though the attack lasted only a moment, in that moment, the dragon had allowed Krym to feel some of the pain, despair, and maddening paralysis that dominated her hellish existence. He guessed later that her goal had been to solicit his sympathy, but he'd felt only rage at her presumption, married to a desire to seek revenge.

Krym tugged at his cloak, mindful of a sudden chill. He remembered his desperate attempts to convince his father to finally drain Khyrshar's essence, only to have Nekiel refuse. Given his father's lust for power—extreme, even by Dragonkin standards—Krym had guessed then why Nekiel restrained himself. Even reduced to her weakest state, barely alive, Khyrshar was still too powerful. To draw her in might heighten Nekiel's power to the point of madness.

But not if he shares her—Krym cursed himself, realizing too late that he'd forgotten to shield his thoughts.

Nekiel turned, frowning. The frown became a withering stare. Nekiel said, "The others who died—the other Dragonkin—you attacked them as they were passing through the Dragonward, didn't you?"

Krym considered lying. "Yes," he said instead. "All save Nâya, who hid from me."

Nekiel shook his head. "Why? There are so few of us left. For centuries, they were your friends. And you killed them."

Krym held back laughter. "I did not know our kind had friends. When in our lives have we ever known anything but hunger?" He fixed his eyes on the ice, expecting pain to wash over him any moment. Instead, he saw Nekiel's great, winged shadow withdraw as though retreating into the darkness of approaching night.

"We must... find another way." Nekiel's voice sounded strange, distant.

Krym straightened. "Had the others survived, all would have insisted you share Khyrshar's power with them. But such a fine meal diminishes when divided into so many portions. It should be saved for the strongest, the most worthy."

A cold wind blew across the ice, but that time, Krym did not shiver. He waited for his father to answer. When he did not, Krym said, "*This* is our way, Father. The gods-given nature of power is simply to desire more power. Anything else is a petty amusement." He paused. "*You* told me that when Nâya was born."

Krym felt water in his eyes and blamed it on the cold. He half expected Nekiel to attack. Instead, Nekiel drew back another step, opened his mouth as though to speak, then turned away. Krym watched his father gazing off into the growing darkness. Krym sensed his father's magical defenses falling away, one after another.

Krym lifted his hands, summoning his full and deadliest strength. Wytchfire roiled to life. It raged at his fingertips, so hot and concentrated that for the first time, Krym's own magic burned him. He held it only a moment then let it go.

Nekiel turned in time to see the approaching firestorm. For one instant, his eyes widened. Krym expected to see those eyes filled with surprise, even fear. Instead, he saw hurt. Then Nekiel lifted his hands, and his palms drank in all of Krym's fire. Nekiel winced, staggered, but did not fall.

Krym prepared a second attack—a wall of raw force designed to strike his father like a battering ram. Before he could unleash it, Nekiel took one step forward and scattered his attack with a wave of the hand. Krym retreated. Desperately, he prepared to teleport away, hoping he had the strength.

"You don't." Nekiel's voice sounded calm, flat. He took another step. Jets of wytchfire exploded from Nekiel's fingers, striking Krym at the knees.

Krym fell onto the ice, biting back a scream. "Forgive me," he managed. "I was not... challenging you. Just... a test..."

Nekiel came still closer and touched Krym's cheek. "Why?"

Krym stared up into Nekiel's eyes and found pity there. Krym's fear turned to revulsion. "You said it yourself. We are wretched creatures. *You,* more than any."

Nekiel blinked, his eyes brimming with tears. "Perhaps... but Nâya isn't." He moved his hand up Krym's face, covering one eye. His other hand pressed over the other eye.

Krym held his breath. He swore he would die quietly, without protest. Still, when the burning started, he screamed.

CHAPTER TWENTY-NINE

Rowen woke from the nightmare and wondered how much of it had been real. He found himself lying on the ice, sweating, Knightswrath still held weakly in his grasp. Faint tendrils of wytchfire raced along the length of the blade, making his arm tingle, but he sensed that its power had receded. Rowen struggled to rise.

Zeia appeared next to him, urgency filling her darkened expression. She helped him with one hand while the other held a drawn sword.

"How long—"

"Barely a minute," Zeia said, "but that's more than we can spare." She nodded toward the distant ridge where Keswen stood, furiously waving at them.

"I was in one of... Nâya's memories, I think. Only I wasn't Nâya. I was Nekiel, somehow. But that shouldn't have been possible. Unless that was the Light, trying to—"

"Unless that memory pertains to the battle we're about to fight, I suggest you save it for another day." Zeia helped him rise.

Rowen glanced at the ice where Nâya had been standing, then down at Knightswrath. Fighting back tears, he lifted the blade. *Maybe it did.* He turned away from the ridge to the face of Khyrshar, who was staring at him through the ice. He took a step toward her then stopped himself. He remembered Nâya's warning before she'd bidden him to kill her: that if freed, Khyrshar might prove as dangerous as Nekiel himself. Furthermore, freeing the dragon would require that he plunge Knightswrath into the ice, expending nearly all its power to break Nekiel's spell—thus leaving him all but powerless, should Khyrshar refuse to help.

Knightswrath flared to life as though of its own accord. Raw power pulsed through Rowen's arm, startling him so much that he nearly dropped the blade. Wytchfire blanketed the steel, dripping off and racing along the ice. The flames stopped above Khyrshar's eyes.

"Free me."

Rowen staggered as though struck in the head. He turned and saw Zeia on her knees, eyes clenched in pain, and realized she'd heard it, too: a telepathic voice like a thousand wild beasts all screaming in unison.

"Free me," the dragon said again, *"and I will help you."*

Rowen closed his eyes, trying to block out the booming voice. At length, he found his own. "And what happens after?" He considered how Godsbane, acting on Chorlga's orders, had ravaged the Ivairian countryside. He thought of Sariel and wondered what would happen to her in a dragon-ravaged world where people feared magic even more than they did currently.

Rowen opened his eyes and waited for Khyrshar to answer. He expected the dragon to point out that Godsbane had been reanimated, a kind of Jol with no will of its own. He expected promises, pleading, even threats. Instead, he heard only silence, interrupted by a mournful wind blowing across the ice, chilling him through his armor.

Zeia stepped close and whispered, "We're out of time."

Rowen turned in time to see a single figure striding toward them across the ice, strangely lit by the starry glow of Armahg's Eye. Clothes, once richly embroidered silk, were tattered and singed. Though handsome and strong-jawed, with a muscular build and long blond hair, something in the man's movements spoke of bone-deep weariness. As he drew closer, Rowen noted that the man's violet eyes were bloodshot.

Knightswrath pulsed in Rowen's grip as though angry—or fearful. Through the sword, Rowen sensed raw power wafting off the man like the reek from a slaughterhouse. He fought the impulse to step back, to close his eyes or turn and run, and lifted Knightswrath before him. Violet flames wrapped the bare blade, flickering in the darkness.

"Nekiel," Rowen managed.

The man cocked his head, regarding Rowen then Zeia. He nodded slightly. "And you must be Fâyu Jinn's successor." He spoke with a hint of mockery then looked around. "I see no army with you. No stoic Knights, no bristling Sylvan archers, no Dwarrs with axes as big as their egos. Where are the galloping Queshi on their red horses? Where are all those Shel'ai you tried so hard to save? I see only one"—Nekiel's eyes lowered to Zeia's hands—"and she appears... incomplete." He looked back at Rowen, smiling faintly. "Did you not have a mighty host at your command when you vanquished Chorlga?"

Rowen had to clear his throat before he could speak. "I see you haven't brought an army, either."

Nekiel did not blink. "I do not need one."

"And Krym? What about his Maalbolg?"

For a moment, a ripple seemed to pass through Nekiel's fearsome focus. Then he said simply, "Gone." Nekiel looked past them at the ice. "Ah, and *there* is the vintage I've been waiting so long to taste. Stand aside, Knight. I am thirsty."

The ice shuddered. Rowen wondered if that was his imagination or Khyrshar's response. Nekiel laughed but did not come any closer. The Dragonkin turned his head slowly, surveying the empty wasteland all around them. "Where is my daughter? She and I have much to discuss."

"She is here." Rowen lifted Knightswrath. He felt the hilt warm, practically burning him.

Nekiel's grin vanished. He stretched out one hand. Rowen braced himself, preparing to absorb wytchfire. Instead of attacking, Nekiel closed his eyes. Magic rippled through the air like a steaming fog. A moment later, Nekiel opened his eyes, and his face turned livid.

"You killed her..."

Rowen braced himself a moment before Nekiel unleashed a torrent of wytchfire that slammed into him like a battering ram. Though Knightswrath absorbed the purple flames, terrible heat swept up his arms, seeping through his armor and nearly driving him off his feet.

Zeia leapt past him. Despite the terror in her wide eyes, she charged, unleashing a furious mind-stab an instant before she swung both swords at Nekiel's throat. But Nekiel suffered the mind-stab without so much as a wince, and Zeia's swords struck an invisible barrier that shattered them like glass. Zeia stumbled backward, her face and arms bleeding from the shards.

Nekiel followed and kicked Zeia's legs out from under her. Still, Zeia fought on. Rolling over, she reached out with one blazing hand, as though to seize Nekiel's clothes and burn him. Nekiel caught her hand instead. He squeezed, and Zeia screamed. Her flaming hands vanished, and she fell onto the ice, convulsing.

On his feet again, Rowen charged. Knightswrath throbbed in his grasp, the blade dripping fire onto the ice. Nekiel turned to face him. Rowen stabbed toward the Dragonkin's eyes, but Knightswrath struck the same invisible wall. The blade shuddered. Though it did not shatter, a wave of pain traveled up Rowen's arms. He resisted it for a moment then fell. Still grasping Knightswrath with one hand, he lifted the blade, pointed it at Nekiel's face, and willed it to strike.

A sea of wytchfire poured out of the blade, spreading as it billowed through the air. Nekiel crossed his arms and waited. The wytchfire passed over him, blocking him from view. As it swirled around the Dragonkin, it seemed to take on new life, leaping away in haphazard jags. Zeia screamed, and Rowen turned to see her burning, trying to crawl to safety.

Gods, no...

The flames faded—save those burning Zeia. Rowen ran to her and tried to smother out the flames with his own body. They would not be quenched. Using Knightswrath, he willed them to disappear. He felt as if his insides were being tugged in different directions, and he had the dim sense that the magic was resisting him. Finally, the wytchfire vanished. Zeia lay facedown, her clothes burnt, her body shaking.

Rowen glanced up at Nekiel. The Dragonkin stood where he had been before, arms crossed, merely watching. Rowen turned back to Zeia. He pressed one hand to her scorched back. Zeia whimpered. As he had done before, Rowen willed Knightswrath's powers to heal. He felt the magic flowing into Zeia's body. When he finally withdrew his hand, though, the burns had only partially healed, leaving ugly blisters in their wake. The smell of scorched flesh filled Rowen's nostrils, almost making him retch.

"The look on your face," Nekiel said. "Fâyu Jinn had that same look when he realized that killing me with magic is like trying to kill a fish with water." He took a step closer.

Using Knightswrath as a crutch, Rowen managed to rise. He fixed his gaze on the great dragon trapped beneath the ice. *No choice.*

Rowen took a deep breath and broke into a run. He expected wytchfire to strike him but resolved that no matter the pain, he would find the strength to finish. He would crawl the rest of the way to Khyrshar, jam Knightswrath into the ice, and will the dragon free.

Instead, the air shimmered, and Nekiel appeared right in front of him. The Dragonkin waved his hand, and Rowen's legs failed him. He fell onto the ice once more but tightened his grip on Knightswrath, determined not to lose it. Nekiel waved again, and invisible hands wrenched the sword from his grasp. It skittered across the ice, sliding well out of reach. Its angry fire dimmed as though suffocated by the surrounding night.

Nekiel crossed his arms again and stared down at Rowen. "Is that all? Is this what my daughter died for?"

For the first time, Rowen noticed the arrows arcing through the night, one after another, each one impeccably aimed for Nekiel's throat—only to burn away in midair. Nekiel ignored all the arrows except the last, which he swatted away like an irksome mosquito. Then Nekiel stepped forward, his hands forming fists that leaked purple flames onto the ice.

Silwren, help me... Rowen straightened. He reached for Sang Wei's sword, still sheathed at his belt. He had only half drawn it when Nekiel leapt forward, impossibly fast—faster even than Vaari—and drove his fist into Rowen's breastplate.

Rowen's world turned white with pain. He blinked. Dimly, he realized he was lying on the ground again. He lifted his head and saw smoke rising from his scorched armor and burning tabard. A massive dent pressed the cuirass into his chest. Blood flowed under his armor. He struggled to rise, but all the air had left his lungs. Still, he managed to lift his head in time to see Nekiel striding off into the darkness.

When the Dragonkin returned, he was holding Knightswrath. One hand gripped the hilt. The other wrapped around the blade. Angry flames leapt from the blade, clawing at Nekiel's arms. His clothes burned away. Flesh blackened, healed, and blackened again. Through it all, Nekiel stared down at Rowen, unblinking.

"My own flesh, the blood of gods and dragons, reduced to *this*." Nekiel lifted the blade. "I could leave her like this, trapped forever. Perhaps that would be a fitting repayment for her sins, her betrayal. But... that does not please me." Nekiel straightened. He held Knightswrath before him, gripping it tightly. Blood ran between the fingers where he gripped the blade. His arms flexed.

Knightswrath broke.

Nekiel held the sword in two pieces, smirking. The blade had snapped in half, well above the hilt. Nekiel's arms lowered as flames poured out of the broken halves, falling onto the ice like spilled wine. Nekiel let go of the halves, and both fell with frightful heaviness and speed, the blade shards burying in the ice.

"Do you know how many souls I just freed, Knight? You have no idea what you were holding. You should be thanking me."

Rowen could only stare. The broken halves pulsed with wytchfire. As seconds passed, the flames dimmed.

"Silwren," he said and gasped, "I'm sorry..."

Nekiel stepped forward and waved, and invisible hands jerked Rowen to his feet, holding him a few inches off the ground. Nekiel regarded him curiously. The anger that had filled his eyes earlier was gone, replaced with confusion and melancholy.

"Strange," Nekiel said. "This does not please me, either. I wonder if Krym was right. Perhaps something *did* happen to me when I passed through—"

A Wyldkin scream split the night. Keswen charged out of the darkness, sword in hand. Nekiel faced her, releasing Rowen to fall back onto the ice in the process. Nekiel waited for her sword to shatter against him, then he waved. The huntress flew backward and tumbled across the ice, landing near Zeia.

Nekiel turned back to Rowen. "What's this, I wonder? Yet another woman you have failed to protect?" He turned back to the dark silhouette of Khyrshar. "Enough of this. My thirst—"

"Emrael?" The voice—small, meek—sounded almost like a trick of the wind.

Still, Nekiel tensed. Then he turned. Rowen turned, too.

A Human girl dressed in rags was slowly crossing the ice, hugging her chest, shivering from cold. She looked to be about Thessa's age. Even without the benefit of Knightswrath's magic, Rowen saw a familiar haunted look in the girl's eyes. He remembered rescuing Thessa from the horrors of the Dhargothi occupation of Hesod and wondered what horrors *this* girl had seen.

"Miriam," Nekiel said. His hands lowered, wytchfire fading from his body.

Miriam looked around her, eyeing first Zeia and Keswen, then Rowen. Her eyes widened at the sight of Rowen's armor, as though she recognized the design. They widened again when she turned and saw the dark winged silhouette under the ice.

Finally, the girl turned back to Nekiel. "When I woke, you were gone…" She stumbled toward him. Her footsteps left blood on the ice. "I… I followed you." Shivering, she drew a golden medallion out of her ratty tunic and held it up, as though offering it to Nekiel.

Nekiel recoiled. "I gave you that…"

"I don't want it."

Miriam pulled the golden chain over her neck, stared at the medallion, then cast it onto the ice. The ice cracked.

"I don't want it," Miriam repeated. "I told you. I just… don't want to be alone."

Nekiel stepped back. His hands rose, wytchfire sparking at his fingertips. "Stand back," he snapped. Relaxing his voice, he said, "You have to leave."

"I saw bodies on the ice," the girl said. "They all had their eyes burned out. Did you do that?"

"No," Nekiel said. "I promise."

Gentleness shone in Nekiel's eyes—and something else. *Is that shame?* Rowen forced himself to rise. "What will become of this girl in your new empire, Nekiel? A lowly Human in rags…"

Nekiel's expression hardened. "There is no sense in reigning over an empire of cinders. I can drink my fill of power without harming the innocent."

"What about Jesriel?"

Nekiel blinked. "I do not acknowledge that name."

"She was Nâya's mother," Rowen pressed. He considered drawing

281

Sang Wei's sword. Instead, he edged toward the hilt of Knightswrath, still thrust into the ice.

"How do you—"

"Nâya showed me. After she gave herself to Knightswrath. She showed me her birth. Or maybe it wasn't her who showed me. Maybe it was the Light." Rowen paused. "Only in the vision, I wasn't her. I was *you*. We held Nâya in our arms. We cared for her. We refused to give her to Krym. Then, for no reason, we ordered her mother's death."

Nekiel scoffed. "No reason? She cared *nothing* for that child, Knight! Jesriel only bore her to please me, to advance her standing among the Dragonkin."

Rowen's eyes widened, struck by the revelation that he'd witnessed Krym thoughtlessly imbibing the essence of his own mother. "And how is that different from anything you have done?"

Nekiel raised one eyebrow. "I require no lessons on morality from an insect. I know what I am. And I know the true nature of my kind, which was established thousands of years before you were born. But this child"—he pointed at Miriam—"need not suffer for our sins."

Rowen risked a sidelong glance at the ice. Only a few yards separated him from the broken halves of Knightswrath. "And what will you do instead? Will you give her a royal gown? Will you give her slaves? Is that what you imagine she wants?"

Nekiel looked back at Miriam, whose eyes were wide with confusion. He stared at her a long time. Finally, he sighed. "No. I suppose not." He stepped forward and gathered Miriam into his embrace. The girl appeared startled then returned the gesture. "I am sorry," Nekiel said. "In my empire, you will never be alone. I swear it." He stepped back. Lifting one hand, he brushed the hair from her eyes.

Miriam smiled. "I believe you."

Nekiel pressed his fingers to the side of her head.

Rowen shouted for Nekiel to stop, but Miriam was already slumping, her final expression one of mild surprise. Nekiel caught her, gently lowering her body onto the ice. Rowen ran to Knightswrath, wrenched the hilt-shard from the ice, and sprinted toward Nekiel. No wytchfire flared from the broken blade. No heat emanated from its dragonbone hilt. Still, Rowen gripped the pommel with both hands and thrust it forward.

He expected to feel the jarring impact of an invisible barrier. Instead, the blade sank deep between Nekiel's shoulder blades. Nekiel stiffened and jerked away, taking the broken sword with him. The Dragonkin reeled. He gave Rowen a strange look then closed his eyes. Wytchfire flared around his body. A moment later, the broken half of Knightswrath slid from Nekiel's back and clattered onto the ice.

Rowen started to draw Sang Wei's sword. Then, as though struck, he felt his eyes pulled downward to the body of the poor girl lying at his feet. For the first time, he saw the knife in her belt—a familiar kind of weapon, wrought of black glass.

Rowen drew the knife and charged. Nekiel's eyes opened. The Dragonkin lifted his hands, blasting wytchfire at Rowen's face. Rowen dove. Fire passed over him, searing his neck and scorching his armor, as he drove the glass knife into Nekiel's foot.

Nekiel screamed. Rowen withdrew the knife, straightened, and thrust it under Nekiel's arm, into his chest. He gave the knife a twist, and the glass blade shattered. Pieces fell from Rowen's hands. Rowen stepped back, expecting wytchfire to wash over him. Instead, Nekiel knelt on the ice, head sagging against his breast.

Rowen started to draw Sang Wei's sword but retrieved the broken hilt half of Knightswrath instead. Slowly, he approached Nekiel.

When Rowen was almost upon him, Nekiel looked up. "So many centuries, so many battles, and *this* is how I die." The Dragonkin smiled. "Strange... that she should have found such a weapon. That I didn't kill her. That she followed me here. I wonder, was that the gods? The Light? Did they want me dead?" Blood bubbled from his mouth. "Or was it my own weakness?"

Rowen was about to thrust Knightswrath's broken blade into Nekiel's throat but lowered his arm. "I don't know," he confessed.

Nekiel did not seem to hear him. His violet eyes clouded. "My daughter..."

"She's free," Rowen said. "You freed her yourself."

Nekiel smiled, his face pale in the light of Armahg's Eye. "That's good. One gesture, at last, for which the gods cannot punish me." He slumped, his gaze fixing on the dark, winged silhouette beneath them.

For the first time, Rowen realized the Dragonkin was kneeling beside Khyrshar's head. Nekiel touched the ice, tracing the outline of the dragon's eye. The eye stared back. Rowen could not tell whether pity or sinister appreciation was showing there.

Then Nekiel turned back to Rowen and laughed. "How could I have forgotten?" Nekiel slumped, lying on his side. Blood pooled beneath him, dark and steaming on the ice. "The medallion. I gave it to Miriam. Why did I do that? I could not even have—" He jerked then laughed. "Weakness. Weakness…" He jerked again then released his last breath in a slow, rasping exhalation.

CHAPTER THIRTY

J ALIST STARED AT MADDOC AS the latter stood—arms crossed,
blocking the exit from the tent—and gauged his chances of getting
past him. Jalist was shorter but stronger. Maddoc had magical
abilities that could knock him back or drive him unconscious, but Jalist
doubted Maddoc was actually willing to employ them. Besides, the
Shel'ai's violet eyes were bloodshot from countless hours spent treating
the wounded.

Jalist said, "I'm going." He glanced over his shoulder, where Sariel
was asleep on a makeshift bed consisting of piled-up cloaks. "Don't start
shouting again, or you'll wake her. Or did you forget that she's still mad
at me for sending Captain Tansil away?"

"She sleeps through battles," Maddoc snapped. "She can sleep
through me saving your life. *Again.*"

"I'm not going to die," Jalist insisted. "I'll have Briel and his Shal'tiar
with me. They're quiet as shadows. Besides, the scouts say the regent's
camp is right next to the mountain. The Lancers didn't bother guarding
that side. So we'll circle around, climb down, and—"

"Cut the regent's throat while he sleeps," Maddoc finished. "I know.
You already explained your plan, if that's what you call it. And I'm
saying no."

Jalist suppressed a grin. "Not your decision, my love. The regent's
been reinforced, and Sir Hale still won't help us. We don't have a big
enough force to cut through the Lancers' whole army. But killing their
leader might foul up their resolve."

"Or it might make them fight harder," Maddoc suggested.

"Maybe," Jalist conceded. "Maybe not. But we can't reach Locke with the Lancers in the way, and he needs all the help he can get, as fast as he can get it." *Besides, I have to tell him about Aeko.*

Maddoc said, "Dying won't accomplish that. The regent may be a bloodthirsty jackass, but he's not stupid. He knows we have Sylvs with us now. Even if you get into the camp without being seen, he'll have guards inside his tent. And let's be honest: Stealth isn't your strong suit."

"But it is *my* strong suit," a woman's voice whispered.

Jalist turned and stared, dumbfounded, as Kilisti stepped into the center of the tent. The huntress wore plain leather armor and carried no visible weapons besides the small knife in her hand. The blade looked as though it had been darkened in fire to keep it from gleaming. Glancing past her, Jalist saw the tear she'd cut in the fabric of the tent, somehow slipping in without either him or Maddoc noticing.

"Impressive," he conceded.

Kilisti took another step forward. The glow from a lamp sitting on a nearby desk illuminated her disfigured face. Ice-blue eyes narrowed. Jalist wondered if she was about to attack. He sidestepped, in case Maddoc wanted to blast her with wytchfire.

However, Kilisti only stared at them for a moment then stuck her knife in her belt. "I trust I've made my point."

Jalist said, "Did Briel send you?"

Kilisti nodded. "He had a feeling you were going to insist on leading the attack. I'm supposed to convince you otherwise."

Maddoc gave Jalist a withering look. "Briel doesn't want you to go, either? That's something you failed to mention."

Jalist shrugged. "Hadn't got around to it yet." Facing Kilisti, he said, "The answer is no, Sylv. No disrespect. Locke told me what a gifted killer you are. But—"

"It's personal for you," Kilisti finished. "I get that. I didn't know the Grand Marshal, but I know what it's like to see a friend cut open"—she smiled as Jalist scowled—"and start thinking more about revenge than about winning."

"She's right," Maddoc said.

"You're just saying that because you don't want me to die."

"Another thing—" Kilisti fixed Jalist in an icy gaze. "You were a fool to send the Iron Sisters away. You might not like what they did, but that's no different than what I'm about to do. If you can't handle one, you shouldn't be volunteering for the other."

Jalist wanted to argue with her, but a pang of nausea struck him. He wondered if Kilisti was right. He considered calling off the mission entirely. Then he wondered what Rowen would do in his place—or Aeko, if she were still alive. He could not imagine either of them condoning what Kilisti was about to do.

What would they say if they knew I was ready to cut Cadwallis's throat myself?

Maddoc squeezed Jalist's arm. "We'll talk about the Iron Sisters later. For now, we have to deal with the Lancers."

"And we will," Kilisti said, "one way or another."

Maddoc faced the disfigured assassin with an expression of cold resolve. "I suspect you're quite good at cutting throats, but what you're suggesting is still next to impossible. You're right that Jalist should stay. But if he stays, I'm going with you."

Jalist looked at Maddoc as though his lover had gone insane. "You just got done saying—"

"I'm against this, make no mistake," Maddoc said, "but this will either end with a dead regent or a dead assassin. If I can't talk you out of it, I can at least make sure it's done right."

Jalist shook his head. "If I'm not going, you certainly aren't either."

"You're the governor of Stillhammer and the leader of an army. I'm just one Shel'ai."

"You're *both* staying," Kilisti interceded. "No offense, sorcerer, but this calls for someone who can move without making a sound, not someone who can conjure up an inferno." She backed toward the slice in the tent fabric.

Maddoc blushed. "I might not be an assassin, but I can knock out guards just by touching them. Are you telling me that's—"

"If I have to knock out a guard to complete a mission, I've done something wrong." Kilisti laughed as she ducked out of the tent.

Jalist shuddered in the cold breeze that blew through the opening.

287

"She's right, you know. We're both about as quiet as Dhargothi elephants." He sighed. "Do you think she can do it?"

Maddoc sat down by Sariel and smoothed the sleeping child's pale hair. Jalist wondered what he was thinking, but Maddoc's expression had turned as placid as the Wintersea.

Jalist cursed. "I hate it when you don't answer me," he mumbled and went to the table to pour himself a drink. He downed a glass of red wine, refilled the glass, and raised it to his lips. He had just taken his first sip when Maddoc touched the side of his head.

Jalist dropped the cup and jerked away. "Damn you…" He turned to face Maddoc, but the world blurred and reeled. Already, Jalist felt his body going numb.

"Quiet after all," Maddoc whispered. The Shel'ai caught him and gently lowered him to the floor a moment before the world turned black.

Kilisti moved briskly through the camp. Even though she did not have a Shel'ai's ability to read minds, she'd guessed Maddoc's intentions and wanted to be gone well before the Shel'ai could join her. Rather than returning to her own distant tent to gather the rest of her weapons, she stopped a passing Sylv and took his shortsword, along with the scabbard and sword belt. Though surprised, the warrior did not protest. Girding the sword as she went, Kilisti stopped beside a campfire to darken the blade in the flames, then she resheathed it. Moving even more quickly, she jogged toward the perimeter of the camp, passing dozens of tired and wounded men as she went.

Kilisti sighed. While casualties had been heaviest among the Isle Knights, all forces appeared to have been hit hard. Beside one campfire were three Dwarrs dressed in bloody rags, one of them shivering and feverish. A little ways beyond, a Sylvan hunter was gently winding clean bandages around the head of a friend who had lost an ear to a Lancer's sword.

Kilisti touched her one ear, the tip of which was missing. She guessed that Maddoc had already done everything he could to help the injured, and messages had been dispatched to Cadavash begging for more Shel'ai, but plenty would die before this was over.

Gods, this army is nothing like the one Locke led against Chorlga! Kilisti smiled, remembering the patchwork host of Knights, Sylvs, Queshi, Lancers, Iron Sisters, and even militias from the Free Cities that had chased Chorlga from one end of the continent to the other, all of them aided considerably by a small host of Shel'ai. But in less than four years—hardly the blink of an eye to a Sylv—that alliance had fractured.

How long before all the realms start hating each other again? She passed a man from the Red Watch who was solemnly sewing a friend's corpse into a canvas bag, assisted by an Isle Knight who had the use of only one arm. She considered stopping to help them then quickened her pace.

She met Briel at the northern edge of the camp. The general had insisted on letting his men take guard duty so that the rest of Jalist's host could rest. Sylvs paced the darkness, armed with bows and swords, their sharp eyes keeping watch, but unlike the sentries, who wore white and forest green, Briel stood with a squad of men and women dressed all in black.

Kilisti looked them over. "No," she said finally.

Briel frowned. "Are we going to argue this again?"

"Only if you decide to argue it." Kilisti started to walk past them.

Briel grabbed her arm. "You can't do this alone, Captain. If you don't want their help, you'll at least take mine."

"And what happens to our war effort if the two foremost leaders of the Sylvan army get themselves killed?"

"Then at least one of us had better make it back."

Kilisti half smiled and glanced down at Briel's sword. Though she'd seen him fight and knew him to be an expert swordsman, trained by Essidel himself, he'd spent the last few years in the capital with Queen Ahmashura, helping her rebuild the kingdom. "When was the last time you cut a sleeping man's throat, General? Trust me. I'm better on my own." She added, "If I die, keep Snowdark. I'm sure Locke has plenty of horses now that he's a famous hero."

Briel's expression darkened. Finally, he let go of her arm. "May the Light go with you."

"I hope it doesn't. I work better in the shadows."

Briel started to grin then stopped himself. Fixing a gruff expression, he stepped back and signaled for the Shal'tiar to return to their original posts. As firelight framed his face, Kilisti stared at Briel and found herself suddenly wanting to embrace him. Instead she blushed, turned, and strode off into the night.

CHAPTER THIRTY-ONE

ROWEN KNELT ON THE ICE for a long time, surrounded by darkness. The cold continued to seep through his dented armor. His breath came in rasps, and he tasted blood on his lips. Overhead, the moon was a bone-white sliver, and clouds veiled Armahg's Eye. With no more wytchfire shedding light or heat, he had the sense that the night itself was closing around him, squeezing him, making it harder and harder to breathe.

Touching the scorched dent in his cuirass, Rowen forced himself to take a slow, deep breath. He wanted to remove his armor but did not have the strength to fumble with the straps. Pain ran jagged through his chest, but he tried to ignore it. He continued to stare at Nekiel's corpse, slumped and dark, the eyes wide and staring.

A chilling smile had frozen on the Dragonkin's lips. Rowen was tempted to look away but forced himself to reach out. He remembered his days as a gravedigger, when he'd learned that the eyes of the dead could only be closed if you held them that way until the muscles gave in. Already, the Dragonkin's skin felt cold. Rowen suppressed a shudder and held Nekiel's eyelids closed until the muscles relaxed, then he withdrew his hand. With Nekiel's eyes closed, the Dragonkin looked like just another corpse—a murdered noble, perhaps, left by cutthroats on the frozen waste, left to feed the wolves.

This isn't over. Rowen lifted Knightswrath, tracing his fingers over the carvings in the dragonbone pommel. No wytchfire kissed the shattered blade. Like the hilt, it felt cold. Rowen wondered if Silwren and Nâya were finally free, at peace. He hoped so. *But what will I do without the sword? How will I face what's to come?*

"Gods, you did it..."

Rowen turned to see Zeia limping toward him, blood streaking her face. Her wrists ended in stumps, her hands unsummoned.

Rowen looked past her. "Keswen—"

"Alive, but her bones are broken."

"Which ones?"

"Not her skull, thanks to its thickness." Zeia smiled. "An ankle and a wrist. And a rib, probably." She touched his armor. "I'm guessing you could use a little mending yourself. I can heal you both, but... I need to rest first." The Shel'ai stared at Nekiel's corpse and shook her head. "I hope you're proud, Knight. You did what even Fâyu Jinn couldn't accomplish!"

Rowen squelched an inexplicable rush of anger. "I did nothing. He beat me, but then his guard was down. And the knife... If anything had been different—"

"He's dead," Zeia interrupted. "Nekiel is dead. No matter how it happened, you won." She shook her head again. "Gods, I can't believe it's over..."

"It's not. This is just the beginning. Before she died, Nâya told me..." Rowen trailed off, realizing he could not bear to finish. Not here, not yet. "Igrid," he said instead. "We have to find her, find the others, get out of here." He slumped, momentarily overwhelmed.

Zeia summoned a hand and touched his arm. "We will, Knight. You'll see. Igrid's safe." She paused. "What's wrong? Do you think Krym's still alive?"

"No, the Dragonkin are gone. All of them." Rowen saw confusion in Zeia's eyes, but he did not have the strength yet to explain. Instead, grunting painfully, he stood and looked back at the body of the girl, Miriam, who looked sad and alone, lying on the ice. Tears brimmed in his eyes, but he fought them back. "Gods, who was she?"

"Just some orphan from the wild. Nekiel must have found her on the road. The question is why did he care about her?" Zeia glanced down at the black glassy shards of the freyd's handle lying on the ice. "And how did she get that knife?"

Rowen looked down at the shattered pieces of the freyd. He

remembered standing in the tomb of Fâyu Jinn, forced to watch as King Loslandril and his son used a similar weapon to stab Silwren. Somehow, the shade of Jinn himself had brought her back to life. Rowen could hardly believe it, given how little interest the gods and the Light had appeared to show in stopping Chorlga.

Rowen remembered what Nekiel had said about Miriam and the freyd. *Was that really the gods' way of helping us? Or was it just coincidence?* "We have to bury her."

"Bury her where? We're surrounded by ice and snow! Unless you want to cut a hole, we'll have to carry her back to Cadavash with us. Or burn her."

Rowen jerked, remembering Khyrshar. "The dragon..."

He turned and found that the dragon's massive silhouette had changed. It looked as though she had somehow rolled onto her back so that she stared squarely at the surface of the ice. Her wings had drawn in, the six folding into two. In the faint glow afforded by Zeia's burning hand, Khyrshar's scales gleamed through the ice.

"Something's wrong." Zeia summoned a second burning hand and held her bow with both, as though to swing it like a club. "I feel something, Locke. Power. Anger. I think—"

"Is it Nekiel?" Rowen lifted Knightswrath and studied Nekiel's naked, motionless corpse for signs of life, some indication that he'd feigned his death and was gathering his strength.

Zeia stepped closer. She drew the second sword from Rowen's belt and swung. The blade split Nekiel's head at the neck. More blood spilled across the ice. Zeia stretched out her other flaming hand over the corpse, closing her eyes. She opened them a moment later. "No."

"Then what—"

The ground shook, and an ominous crack echoed through the frozen night. The clouds parted, allowing the light from Armahg's Eye to spill across the ice again. Sliding Knightswrath into his belt, Rowen took his other sword back from Zeia and looked around. He spotted Keswen in the distance, weakly pushing herself up on one elbow. Miriam's body lay still uncovered, unmoving, her eyes damp and wide open.

Then Rowen swore and pointed. "The medallion!"

Nekiel's golden medallion lay in the distance, where Miriam had thrown it. A massive crack had spread beneath it. A thin stream of wytchfire was leaking from the medallion, straight down into the ice, so muted by the thickness of the ice that Rowen had not noticed it before. He raced toward it. Using the tip of his sword, he caught the golden chain and lifted the medallion off the ice.

Something yanked the medallion back down, so forcefully that it pulled Rowen with it. More wytchfire poured out of the medallion—wildly, that time. Rowen closed his eyes against the heat. Zeia grabbed his arm and tried to haul him back. Then the ice cracked again. The ground shook, sank, then rose so sharply that both of them were thrown.

Rowen gasped with pain as he struck the ground. His broken ribs shifted beneath his battered armor, scraping his insides. Fighting back tears of pain, he looked about frantically for the medallion, just in time to see it slip—blazing—through the widening crack in the ice and vanish into the water.

For a moment, the whole world seemed to stop as though frozen. Rowen thought for one wild moment that he was being given a final moment to pray—for not only his own fate, but also the fate of the world—but he could not summon the words. Then the moment passed, and the Wintersea shattered. With a bone-jarring roar, something huge and terrible rose out of the icy water, high into the air, blocking out the starlight.

EPILOGUE

CADWALLIS ROSE FROM HIS CHAIR, waved off his servants, and crossed his tent to a mahogany table crowded with exotic fruits and pitchers of wine. He made sure to take his time refilling his cup, choosing a thick red made from Queshi grapes that offered up a strange, faintly metallic smell. As an afterthought, he carried the pitcher back to his visitor—a burly, copper-skinned man in armor of darkened scales. Though the Dhargot held his cup steady as Cadwallis refilled it, the Dhargot's brow furrowed in disapproval.

"Begging your pardon, Regent, but isn't there a hostile army camped not a few hours' stroll from here?"

Cadwallis scowled, drained his glass, and immediately refilled it. "I drank before I killed my rivals. I drank before my army cut that Isle Knight bitch to pieces. If I'm going to accept a Dhargot as a vassal, I intend to be drunk before I do it."

General Laanti stared at Cadwallis for a moment then slowly poured his own wine onto the ground. "I'm afraid you're mistaken, Regent. I didn't risk my neck riding across the continent to become your godsdamned vassal. We're allies or nothing. And judging by what I saw the other day, you need all the help you can get."

Laanti idly tossed the delicate wine glass toward one of Cadwallis's scowling bodyguards. The bodyguard overreacted and drew his sword, shattering the cup midair. The pieces scattered across the dark ground, some of them landing in the fire at the center of the tent.

Cadwallis laughed then turned back to the Dhargot to size him up.

The general was still sitting down, but he wore matching shortswords, one of which he touched with a mailed hand. Cadwallis wondered if he should have followed his bodyguards' advice and ordered the Dhargot disarmed, but even though Cadwallis had taken off his own armor, he still wore his longsword, and surely the Dhargot was no match for him. Besides, his bodyguards were close by.

Cadwallis glanced at the four men in full armor, each of whom wore a tabard emblazoned with his new sigil: a rearing horse facing a tongue of purple flame, hooves poised to stamp it out. Cadwallis could tell by the men's tense expressions that they disliked having a Dhargot in their midst. Cadwallis could not blame them. It was only a few years earlier that the Dhargots, led by the Bloody Prince, had ravaged the southernmost districts of Ivairia, impaling peasants and nobles alike on stakes, consigning them to a slow and agonizing death.

Now, this one wants an alliance? Cadwallis scoffed, drained his glass, and refilled it yet again. He had to admit that the general had a point: The untimely arrival of the Sylvs had prevented Cadwallis's Lancers from finishing off his enemies. Though outnumbered, his enemies had still forced him to take up a defensive posture in order to safeguard his borders.

"You have guts, Dhargot. I admit that. But I don't see any ears hanging around your neck."

Laanti frowned. "Prince Saanji forbade that practice... as I'm sure you well know. But rest assured, I've killed my share."

"True. But I don't need another killer, General. I need an ally worthy of my time. I need an ally worthy of the Inquisition."

Laanti rose from his chair. Though he moved slowly, the bodyguards stepped forward, hands on their blades, firelight glinting off their armor. Cadwallis noted with grudging approval that Laanti ignored them, fixing his gaze on the regent.

"Prince Saanji abandoned his own kingdom on the eve of its birth so that he could do the bidding of the magic-tainted," the Dhargot said. "He even shares his bed with one of them. Before that, his brothers served Fadarah, then Chorlga, like dogs begging for scraps from a master's table." Laanti spat on the ground. "This is not the true path."

Cadwallis noted that Laanti was not blinking, his painted eyes filled with quiet derision. Cadwallis wondered how long the Dhargot could maintain that fierce expression and was tempted to wait and see. "And you think your so-called Earless will betray your prince, just as you've done, and follow you instead?"

Laanti blinked. "Some will. Many will not. For all his cowardice and questionable loyalties, the Tomato Prince is well loved throughout his host."

Cadwallis snickered. "Not popular enough, it seems."

Laanti tensed. "Careful, Regent. I may be willing to betray him, but I'm not a traitor. Saanji is a good man. Just... not the man Dhargoth needs."

Cadwallis noted that the Dhargot had partially drawn one of his swords, causing the bodyguards to start forward again. Cadwallis waved them back, resisting the impulse to draw his own blade. *I'll have to be careful with this one.* Cadwallis raised his glass and took another sip of wine. "I understand, General. I felt that way about Arnil Royce. Had the Bloody Prince not killed him, I bet I would have had to do it myself."

"I would have liked to see that." Laanti let go of his sword and sat back down. "I'm always pleased to see the impossible."

Cadwallis let go of his cup, drew his longsword, and leveled it at Laanti's throat. He expected the Dhargot to recoil, but Laanti did not move, did not even flinch. Cadwallis turned the tip of his blade, cleaving a few hairs from the Dhargot's goatee. "Perhaps I've had enough of your insults. Perhaps I'll parley with your successor and demonstrate my skills right here and now." The tip of Cadwallis's sword broke the skin, drawing blood from Laanti's neck, though the Dhargot continued to regard him in silence.

Finally, after what felt like an eternity, Laanti said, "Apologies. I only meant that I risked my life abandoning my post and traveling here, alone, to meet with a possible ally. I did *not* come here to listen to you brag. If it's soft words and flattery you want, go make peace with the Isle Knights. If it's killing and honor, I'm your man."

Cadwallis stared at Laanti for a moment then laughed. He removed his blade, tugged a silk handkerchief from his belt, and tossed it to the Dhargot, who quietly pressed it to his wound. "Well said, Dhargot." Whirling his longsword about him, Cadwallis walked back to the wine table, chose another cup, and filled it with a different wine, a lighter vintage he had not tried yet. "Finish your business in the south. I'll give you soldiers, like we agreed. When you're done, go back to your lands, raise an army, and add it to my own. Together, we'll stamp magic out of existence. And the gods will smile." Cadwallis raised his cup and took a sip. He decided the wine was too sweet, poured out the rest on the ground, and selected another bottle.

Laanti said, "We'll need more than armies, Regent. Even if I'm successful, we'll still have the Dragonkin to worry about."

Cadwallis laughed. "Do not concern yourself with demons and dragons, General. We'll let Rowen Locke and his allies deal with the Dragonkin. Then, once Locke and his pets are weakened from battle and celebration, we'll repay them in kind." He tasted the new wine, found it bitter, but drank it anyway, lest Laanti think him too fickle otherwise.

"Perhaps." Laanti stood, dabbed his throat again, and tossed the handkerchief onto the war table, blood having speckled the white silk. "Locke has friends, though. Even if you kill him or Nekiel does it for you, we're going to need more allies."

"And we shall have them," Cadwallis said. "From Stillhammer to the Lotus Isles, from Ivairia to Dhargoth, this continent has had its fill of magic. The Sons of Maelmohr proved that, at least. Once our movement takes root, it will be like a glorious flower rising from—"

Laanti waved off the rest of the speech. "Forgive me, Regent. It is late, and I have many days of hard travel ahead of me." He bowed ever so slightly. "Good evening, Regent." Turning, Laanti strode out of the tent.

Cadwallis scowled. He considered calling his guards and having Laanti beaten for leaving the tent without permission—and after Cadwallis had just agreed to loan him an entire company of Lancers, no less! Then he decided that a little insubordination was a small price to pay, provided the general actually accomplished what he'd promised.

Cadwallis turned and eyed the standard thrust into the ground at the far side of his tent, depicting the same glorious new sigil worn by his men: the sigil of the Inquisition. Cadwallis's scowl became a smile. He was still smiling when he walked over to the war table and picked up the blood-stained handkerchief General Laanti had left behind. Cadwallis looked it over, appreciating the fact that Laanti's blood looked much like the wine Cadwallis had been drinking. Cadwallis inspected the handkerchief a moment longer and decided to keep it as a memento, a humble reminder of the night the Inquisition was born. Then he imagined having to explain to storytellers whose blood that was, which would in turn necessitate more details about Cadwallis's allies.

This is my Inquisition. Not Laanti's. Mine, and nobody else's. "Except for the Light, of course," Cadwallis muttered and tossed the handkerchief into the fire.

MORE BY MICHAEL MEYERHOFER

ABOUT THE AUTHOR

Michael Meyerhofer grew up in Iowa where he learned to cope with the unbridled excitement of the Midwest by reading books and not getting his hopes up. Probably due to his father's influence, he developed a fondness for Star Trek, weight lifting, and collecting medieval weapons. He is also addicted to caffeine and the History Channel.

Michael Meyerhofer's third poetry book, *Damnatio Memoriae*, won the Brick Road Poetry Book Contest. His previous books of poetry are *Blue Collar Eulogies* (Steel Toe Books, finalist for the Grub Street Book Prize) and *Leaving Iowa* (winner of the Liam Rector First Book Award).

He has also published five chapbooks: *Pure Elysium* (winner of the Palettes and Quills Chapbook Contest*)*, *The Clay-Shaper's Husband* (winner of the Codhill Press Chapbook Award), *Real Courage* (winner of the Terminus Magazine and Jeanne Duval Editions Poetry Chapbook Prize), *The Right Madness of Beggars* (winner of the Uccelli Press 3rd Annual Chapbook Competition), *and Cardboard Urn* (winner of the Copperdome Chapbook Contest).

Individual poems won the Marjorie J. Wilson Best Poem Contest, the Laureate Prize for Poetry, the James Wright Poetry Award, and the Annie Finch Prize for Poetry. He is the Poetry Editor of *Atticus Review*. His work has appeared in a number of journals including *Ploughshares, Hayden's Ferry Review, North American Review, River Styx,* and *Asimov's Science Fiction Magazine.*